Y0-AGU-970

RICE IN SILVER BOWLS

was written by Alice Ekert-Rotholz, who lived in Bangkok from 1939 to 1952. First published in 1954, it became an instant bestseller. Alice Ekert-Rotholz has since written fourteen more novels and has become one of Europe's most popular writers. This is the first American paperback publication of *Rice in Silver Bowls.*

Also by Alice Ekert-Rotholz

Checkpoint Orinoco
The Sydney Circle

forthcoming from
POPULAR LIBRARY

RICE IN SILVER BOWLS

Alice Ekert-Rotholz

POPULAR LIBRARY

An Imprint of Warner Books, Inc.

A Warner Communications Company

If it weren't for Joy Davenport, of Shelburne, Massachusetts, and the
Western Massachusetts Canning, Pickling, Preservation, & Book
Society, *Rice in Silver Bowls* would never have seen the light of day in
a mass-market paperback edition. Thanks to all.

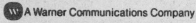

RICE IN SILVER BOWLS

1

The Arrival

By the time Petersen reached the harbor to meet Martha and the children, he was nervous and tired. The sweat was streaming down into the freshly starched collar of his shirt, and a hammer was beating a tattoo at the back of his head as if threatening to crack open his pith helmet.

Bangkok had never seemed hotter; the big city on the banks of the Menam River was seething in the afternoon heat. Petersen would have liked to be in his air-conditioned office with his old Chinese boy serving iced coffee. He stuck to his preference for iced drinks, although his Chinese customers assured him that hot green tea was the best thing to combat the tropical heat. Petersen came from Hamburg, that was why he clung tenaciously to all habits, particularly in unaccustomed surroundings. Whenever the Hamburg summer had dared to indulge in tropical excesses, Petersen had sat on the Alster Pavilion, drinking iced coffee. But the Chinese always thought they knew everything better.

This morning of all mornings he had had to let a Chinese customer annoy him for hours. Naturally he had given no sign of how much the conversation with Mr. Wang irritated him, but had smiled broadly, as if he were enjoying himself immensely. Petersen's smile was famous. He could turn it on and off like a tap. Not long ago it had won him the partnership in Petersen and

Company in Bangkok. Now he could send for Martha and the children to visit him.

Martha had hesitated for a long time because the political news from Siam's neighbors was disturbing, but finally she had decided to come. She was being offered a unique experience, and after the war years she deserved a change. But she had rejected Petersen's suggestion to leave the children with relatives in Hamburg amiably but firmly. Petersen never protested against any of Martha's decisions. She was five years older than he and probably knew best.

In a quarter of an hour the ferry from Paknam was due in Bangkok. Petersen looked at his watch. The ship company was anticipating a delay but Petersen had turned up with German punctuality. He owed it to Martha. Martha...how would she manage in a tropical life style? She had never left Europe. What would she say to the heat, the Asiatic servants, and the easygoing, eternal-vacation life of the white woman in the Far East? Martha had never been idle for a minute in her entire life.

This morning Petersen had laughed aloud when he had seen the flower arrangements on the veranda and the spider webs in every corner of his spacious house. Martha and spider webs! On his orders, Number One Boy, Ah Wong, a grandson of Petersen's Chinese cook, Ah Chang, had swished the toylike feather duster around a bit, smiling but secretly annoyed, and had rearranged the spider webs and swept the dust from one corner to the other, after which he had looked at the results of his work with satisfaction. All year long the master had found things clean enough, but now that Missie was arriving, nothing was right any more. All the Chinese boys who served European bachelors or the men whose wives were not with them said the same thing. The dainty Siamese *amah*, the nursemaid Ah Chang had hired at the last minute to look after Little Missie, was crouching fearfully in the children's room.

Ah Chang had told her in his broken English that the *Mem farang*, the lady foreigner, would be very angry if she found white ants running around in her bureau. Where were they supposed to run? the *amah* asked herself. Since she didn't know what to say, she spat red betel juice onto the white Indian carpet in the children's room. The dark red stain, which no cleaning fluid could erase, didn't bother her, not did it trouble Number One Boy. What the *amah* would have liked was to run home to her rice village, Paklat, but the master had promised her such a lot of money that *khun paw*, or father, would be able to buy a second water buffalo for his plough. Her family had talked about this water buffalo for weeks, and the *amah* knew the animal was much more important to *khun paw* than her insignificant little self.

Petersen, still irritated, looked at the sweet-smelling jasmine garlands the *amah* had braided for the new arrivals, according to the custom of the land—a long one for Martha and two smaller ones for the children. As if for a funeral, Petersen thought, wiping the sweat off his smooth, handsome forehead. His blue eyes had a feverish glow; he hoped he wasn't in for a bout of dengue fever. There wasn't a thing you could do to combat it. It started with chills and ended with a rash that itched; nothing to do but stay in bed and darken the room against the inevitable headache. Petersen couldn't do with either right now.

His uncle, head of Petersen and Company, was sixty-four. Secretly Petersen considered him a tropical old-timer, which meant that like the Siamese, he preferred to allocate work to others, but like every Hamburg businessman could forecast his profits down to the last cent. He always countered Petersen's suggestions for new imports with, "I don't take any risks. I'm not an adventurer!"

Uncle Wilhelm Christian Petersen's taste for adventure was of a strictly private nature. He had married a

Siamese aristocrat and had been living for years in a tropical palace like an Asiatic prince, in overwhelming splendor and disorder. Khunying, or Countess, Siri Kutharamarn—her friends addressed her casually as Nang (Mrs.) Siri—left things, left everything lying around. The head of Petersen and Company had grown accustomed long ago to the luxurious chaos in his house. He had been living in the Far East for forty years, with brief interruptions, and in Bangkok since 1930. He imported machinery and precision instruments, all fated to be broken eventually, and various other things which his Chinese clients ordered regularly and discarded just as regularly after one season. Just the same, Wilhelm C. Petersen nearly always ended up in the black. He combined caution with an insistence on quality. This had made it possible for him, during the years before the Indo-chinese War, to compete with the inferior Japanese merchandise with its phony German trademarks. The Chinese appreciated solid things; they preferred English and German to even American wares, and that was saying something, because the Americans were playing an important and many-faceted role in Siam in 1945.

Petersen wiped his forehead again. His headache was getting worse all the time, and just when Martha was about to arrive! Why had he felt impelled to celebrate the end of his period as a grass widower last night? From now on he would drink lemonade instead of whiskey and talk sense with Martha—thank God!

The heady scent of the jasmine made him feel dizzy. Suddenly he had to think of Karin. One always thought of Karin Holm at inconvenient moments. She had wound a jasmine garland around her shoulders and danced on a tropical veranda in the Bangkok moonlight. Petersen chose not to recall that this had taken place only a week ago, and on his veranda! He had stared wide-eyed at Miss Karin's slanting Asiatic eyes and her blond Swedish hair. His famous smile had been slightly twisted, but he

4

knew what he owed Martha. Miss Karin, as she was called, with disregard of her last name, knew this too. All Eurasians in Bangkok were called by their first names. No one knew why, but a slight denigration went with it.

The news of Martha's pending arrival had cost Miss Karin a lot of tears and Petersen a gold necklace. With his Hamburg business sense he had bought one slightly flawed and dirt cheap from an Indian client, and the man had repaired it so skillfully that the necklace had looked much more expensive than it was. This was the only way he could hope that it would fulfill its purpose because Miss Karin had no appreciation of: it's the loving thought that counts. Nobody in East Asia had any understanding for that sort of thing. All that counted was the material worth of a present. No Far East philosophy could change that.

The Far East was a world in which metaphysics and material values got along well together. Petersen's Chinese clients haggled by day over three *satangs,* or Siamese pennies, in the course of the purchase or sale of a piece of merchandise, and at night they read Tao. Just like the Siamese princes who bought their race horses shrewdly, but for the Buddhist fasting period put on the yellow robe of Buddha. They sold their race horses to naïve Europeans for astonishing profits and three months later wandered through the dawn in Bangkok and surrounding countryside, an unworldly expression on their faces, the beggar's bowl in their fine-boned hands. Martha would be surprised, thought Petersen. She came from a part of the world where contrasts were a matter of principle. He would have a lot to explain to her. He didn't need Miss Karin to be present for that. Miss Karin had asked, sobbing, what the necklace had cost, and without any transition whatsoever had smiled at him just as radiantly as Petersen smiled at his Asiatic clients.

Petersen closed his burning eyes for a moment, then opened them wide and gazed at Wat Arun on the opposite shore, shining fantastically in glowing clouds. Right from the start the temple had epitomized Siam for him. Its Cambodian towers—*pbra prangs*—expressed the influence of the ancient Khmer people of Siam; the glazed tile that faceted its towers glittered like porcelain, indicating Chinese influences. Yet the temple, standing on the shore of a wide, busy river, exuded the spirit of the land, Buddhistic in style. Petersen had seen Wat Arun in the moonlight once and had found getting down to business again next morning difficult. The bizarre reliquary towers had laid bare an element in his northern German soul that was incalculable. Miss Karin also embodied something alien and dangerous that seduced one into dreaming. "No good," Petersen murmured, and looked reproachfully at the miraculous Cambodian miracle on the west bank. The Far East was constantly mounting major attacks on the common sense of the North. How to explain all this to Martha? A man from Hamburg would rather die than offer as an excuse the powers of fantasy, which in East Asia were stronger than the strongest man. Martha would stare at him through her glasses, baffled, and recommend a cold compress!

Petersen looked at his watch, and to his horror became aware of the fact that he was trembling. The fifteen minutes had elapsed. No ferry in sight. Two rice boats, a coal freighter painted red, and a banana boat glided by. A coolie pushed a cart with sacks of rice on it so close to Petersen that the long jasmine garland lost a few of its blossoms. Petersen jumped aside, cursing. The coolie grinned and stuck a few of the blossoms in his bamboo hat, which was full of holes. His idea of fun! To annoy a foreigner was almost as amusing as an evening at the Chinese theatre.

Petersen lit his sixth cigarette and stared out across the water. He had waited like this on a landing in Hamburg when Martha had gone to Cuxhaven for a week.

He wondered what Martha would look like now. Photos didn't reveal much, and Petersen hadn't seen his wife in so many years that he couldn't really visualize her. All he could actually remember was her shock of blond hair, her sturdy way of walking, and her beautiful strong hands. He wondered if Martha still wore her old-fashioned glasses, or would she have acquired horn-rimmed ones by now? And the little loose wisps of hair behind her left ear...Martha was a wonderful woman, but she didn't know how to do her hair. "I don't have any time to look in the mirror," she said once. Petersen had always felt that women should take time for that. In the Far East this feeling had grown stronger. The Siamese women looked at themselves in the mirror for hours, with the gentle criticism that was so typical of them. The results were definitely pleasing.

In Hamburg Petersen had always remained silent when Martha had clipped her words like that. She was the wise one. She had been expecting her first child at the time. Before her marriage she had been a teacher of mathematics and classical languages in a girls' high school. None of the girls had ever had a crush on Fräulein Doktor Jansen, as they had on the curly haired drawing teacher, for instance, or on funny Fräulein Grimm, but whenever they were in trouble, they had instinctively turned to Martha. She could look sharp as a knife through her glasses, but when one didn't know what to do next, something deep and warm glowed in those cool knowing eyes, and one was wonderfully consoled. Young Petersen must have felt the same way; otherwise why had he wanted to marry Martha? She was five years older than he, and a teacher. Petersen's friends couldn't understand why this handsome, rich young man, who could have had the most attractive girl in Hamburg, had fallen for such a serious and staid women without a trace of chic.

Martha was more astonished than anyone else.

"There's no fool like an old fool," she said drily when she finally accepted Petersen's stammered proposal after rejecting him twice. She had a motto for every situation. Petersen didn't think much of proverbial wisdom. What proof was there that every early bird caught the worm? But on the evening of their engagement, which had been celebrated at the Alster villa of Petersen's grandparents, he had kissed all the mottoes from her rather stern lips. He could kiss marvelously: you had to grant him that.

For the wedding Martha had appeared without her glasses and with the first permanent wave of her life. She had almost looked beautiful; her delicate features were illuminated from within. She had stripped off the school teacher overnight. As if in a prosaic street cherry trees had suddenly blossomed, Petersen had thought, and at once had been ashamed of the poetic simile. His grandmother, who after the death of his parents had taken over his upbringing and education as a prosperous Hamburg merchant, discouraged any poetic inclinations. His grandfather had been a silent man, but he had revered his wife in his coolness. All the Petersen wives were very special women who looked down on their rash but enterprising husbands from an imaginary marble pedestal, solid and firm. But Martha was a woman who read books, something of which Grandmother Petersen's worst enemy couldn't have accused her. Grandmother had a subscription to the opera and to the State Theatre, and until his marriage Petersen had considered this the height of intellectual ambition. Since his arrival in the Far East he had learned to regard Martha's book wisdom more skeptically. One had to start learning all over again here. The experiences of one's ancestors in faraway Europe were useless in an atmosphere where one thought so differently of living and dying.

Petersen didn't know why he suddenly had to think of his wedding. So much lay in between: a world war ...Petersen and Company in Bangkok...Cambodian beauty...and a girl whom a mixture of Sweden and Java suited marvelously...to all outer appearances. But what beautiful girl could compare to Martha?

How happy they had been at first! Petersen had found in Martha the motherly love he had needed without realizing it. His faith in her was boundless, and he began to see many things through her eyes. Martha lived only for her husband. He had begged her to give up teaching at the high school, and from then on she had given only private lessons at home, but without charging for them, which offended Petersen's business sense. Even a friend of mankind should be paid for her services. But Martha helped her lame ducks mercifully through their finals. Nobody could explain an equation like Fräulein Doktor! She remained just that for her girls, who retired blushing and giggling whenever Petersen barged in on their mathematical idyll.

He had come to Bangkok in 1939. Uncle Wilhelm Christian had welcomed him as a matter of course. That was the good thing about Hamburg families—they followed the call of faraway lands. All over the world, a relative was nearly always sitting under a palm tree who could offer you iced coffee and a job. With his customary rashness, Petersen had spoken incautiously about the Hitler regime. He had never become a party member because he wasn't for it, and Martha was against it. In this period of crisis, Petersen had lost his head completely, but Martha had been heroic. As soon as she received a private warning from a devoted friend of the family, she had watched over Petersen, calmed him, and shipped him off to the Far East fast. She hadn't served him any mottoes nor wept any tears, at least not in the presence of her desperate husband. The night before his precipitate departure he had fallen asleep in her arms like a tired child. At five o'clock in the morning, when the garden gate bell rang and Petersen scarcely dared to breathe, Martha had strode to the gate like a dragon, and had accepted a telegram sent from a niece: the young woman had just given birth to twins and the Petersens in Hamburg had to find out about it at 5:00 A.M....

It had been Martha's intention to follow Petersen to the Far East a year later, but their daughter had contracted typhoid fever, and after that the Second World War had made all such plans impossible. Little Charlotte was a delicate child and her recovery was slow. Martha had never been able to grasp the fact that this ethereal child was *her* daughter. And now Petersen was standing on a pier in Bangkok in torturous expectation, trying to build a bridge between past and future. He hadn't seen his family for ten years.

How had the children developed, he wondered? He had known them only as babies. Martha had sent pictures after the war, but somehow Petersen hadn't been able to believe that the bespectacled schoolboy in his shabby suit was his son. And the little girl with the braids, wearing a dress fit only for an orphanage, couldn't possibly be Tiny, his enchanting little daughter with blond curls framing her face with its porcelain features! Chubby, called Chubb now, and Tiny had been rosy-cheeked little elves in fine white woolen dresses and suits in the Hamburg nursery on the Jungfernstieg! The pictures of the children had brought home to him in his tropical paradise the effect of the war in a frightful fashion. If even Hamburg had become a shabby city, then the world was in trouble, big trouble! Petersen had looked at the picture of the children for a long time, and was thankful that Grandmama hadn't lived to see the downfall of the solid citizenry...

A dark spot showed up in the distance, moving slowly in Petersen's direction. The Siamese agent came running. "They're coming! They're coming!" he cried excitedly, bouncing up and down like a rubber ball on the hot wooden planks. He was carrying jasmine garlands too. They were for the pilot of the *Frenonia*, who was bringing his bride from a small Danish town with him. Nai (Mr.) Chuang belied the legend of the impassive Asiatic: he could run like a weasel and coo like a turtle dove. "Is Mem coming to Siam for the first time?" he asked, looking at Petersen with consuming curiosity. Petersen nodded. Yes, Mrs. Petersen was.

He saw the ferry as through a hazy window. He didn't know anymore how many years he had been waiting on this pier for Martha and the children. And then, suddenly, Martha was in his arms, clinging to him as if she never wanted to let him go again, and Petersen was silently stroking her hair, kissing her beautiful strong hands, and hanging the jasmine garlands around her and the children who now were called Albert and Charlotte.

Martha's blond hair had become strangely lifeless. In spite of her sturdy figure and face—red now from the heat—she looked haggard, although Peterson had been sending food packages home regularly since 1945. A wave of love and compassion flooded his customary blithe spirit when Martha, his composed, poised Martha, looked up at him through glasses hazed by tears and stammered fearfully, "Have I grown *very* old, my boy?"

"Nonsense, beloved!" Petersen found it difficult to smile his famous smile, but then he took his wife in his arms and kissed her fervently. Martha was his home! She was the only woman who gave and didn't only take. The joys of their youth and what they had suffered together united them with bonds that held faster than ...than Siamese jasmine. Petersen felt at peace. Now everything was going to be all right. Surely Martha felt it too, because she sobbed once more, wiped her glasses with her old briskness, and at last looked at her husband. In spite of the years in the tropics, Petersen had scarcely changed at all. His eyes, light blue as the sea, still shone

11

endearingly in his suntanned face. His tall body had remained slim and muscular through daily exercise, and he had only five gray hairs! Martha was proud of him.

The children stood holding hands like forgotten pieces of luggage. Chubb had the biggest feet in his class and saw this as an exceptional achievement. The tall elegant stranger in his snow-white pith helmet wasn't his Papa yet. Besides, Chubb's fourteen-year-old dignity was suffering because of the jasmine garland around his short neck. What would his schoolmates say if they saw him now? At this point his passionate wish was to be on the soccer field in Hamburg, but unfortunately there was nothing he could do about that. So he asked Petersen politely if there were radios in Bangkok, and was so furious with himself over the foolish question that he turned bright red when Petersen laughed and said, "But of course, my boy! Bangkok is a metropolis. This evening you can hear any country you like!"

All Chubb really wanted was to hear the results of the Hamburg game, but he was obviously relieved. He had been scared to death all the way over. If Chubb had a radio and his sister, Tiny, he was satisfied. He looked curiously all around him at the tropical pier; nothing escaped his sharp eyes behind their glasses. He had never seen rice being loaded to the accompaniment of singing. You could count the ribs on the naked, shiny backs of the coolies. Why didn't they wash their dirty khaki shorts? Chubb didn't want to ask. Petersen might laugh at him again. And that was the worst thing that could happen to him. The poor boy had no idea what still lay in store for him in this respect as far as the natives were concerned. Big and little Europeans were a traditional object of ridicule in Siam. And Chubb was exactly like his mother—stocky, shortsighted, reliable, and exceptionally intelligent.

Petersen couldn't stop looking at his eleven-year-old daughter. She wasn't wearing an orphanage dress now as in the faded picture, but a white embroidered linen frock which Petersen had sent to Hamburg. She was still tiny, but somehow she had Petersen's elegant posture and Martha's glorious blond hair, and—when she didn't happen to be crying—the most enchanting smile in the world. Unfortunately Tiny cried like a baby at the slightest opportunity. It didn't impress her mother but it distressed Chubb every time. Tiny had to laugh and be happy! Right now she looked radiant. She liked it when her beautiful, merry Papa picked her up and held her high like a doll and set her down again gently on the pier, saying to Martha, "Tiny has turned into a real little lady! My little lady!"

Martha replied, a little sharper than warranted, "Charlotte has nothing on her mind but her appearance. Don't make her vainer than she is already!"

In the excitement of their meeting, Martha's typewriter and one of their suitcases had been left on the ferry of the East Asiatic Company. Petersen and Martha hurried back with the chauffeur. You weren't allowed to carry anything yourself; the servants were there for that. One also shouldn't leave anything of value on the ferries of Siam: things tended to disappear within minutes. "*Mai hen*...seen nothing," was the only explanation they got.

For the first time in her life, Martha had forgotten something, which amused Petersen enormously. He had taken her arm and was talking about the children. Chubb had celebrated his birthday on the ship. It had been "terrific!" But it had embarrassed him that the Danish officers had made such a fuss of him, especially the engineer, who was amused by Chubb's questions. Chubb had a lot of technical know-how.

"He's actually too old for the tropics," Petersen said hesitantly. "Boys in their formative years don't belong here."

"We're only staying a year," said Martha.

13

She would never part from Chubb. He was her favorite child, her only weakness. She would tutor both children. Why else had she studied to be a teacher? Charlotte, unfortunately, could scarcely add two and two; she preferred looking at herself in the mirror.

"Chubb is such a help!" Martha said, full of motherly pride. She still called him by his nickname although he had recently begged her not to. He had been fourteen now for all of four days! "Charlotte is a difficult child," Martha went on. "Very unpredictable. I hope there isn't a mirror in her room. I have tried again and again to explain to her that vanity is at the bottom of all evil."

Petersen said nothing. A trace of irritation had spread like a hazy cloud across his enjoyment. Martha remained a teacher, and right now he was in no mood for mottoes. Not yet! He held her arm closer and looked around the narrow passage of the ferry. No one in sight. His wife was looking up at him in astonishment. He took her in his arms and kissed her passionately. She was so...so *clean*! So clean through and through! "Martha!" His voice was husky, his throat tight with the rare emotional thrill. How had he managed to live without her for so many years? "Silly boy," she whispered. It was her way of expressing the utmost tenderness.

When they returned to the pier, without the typewriter, Petersen was knocked on the head, figuratively speaking. He stared and hoped he was dreaming. Miss Karin was standing beside the children, a jasmine garland in her hand. She had on an old rose sharkskin suit that enhanced her marvelous figure, and her slanting eyes glittered like black diamonds under her white Indian brocade turban. She was loaded down with jewelry in every price category. In this respect the halfcastes of both sexes had no sense of proportion. A strange smile played about her full Javanese lips. She stood motionless, watching Petersen and Martha approach.

"Who on earth is *that*?" Martha asked, her brows raised. She was staring at Miss Karin's elegant suit and turban with the profound suspicion of a frugal housewife.

Petersen lied through a red fog. "My secretary. The stupid woman must be bringing some work to the pier!"

Miss Karin Holm, who didn't speak a word of German, had also been appraising Petersen's wife sharply, and had noted with satisfaction that she didn't know how to dress. Also her hips were too wide. And why didn't the Mem dye her hair? Did she want to look like Petersen's mother?

"Darling," Miss Karin said, in her singsong English. "I have lost your parting gift. So sorry! I wanted to sell the necklace yesterday. You know...my gambling debts. I am desperate! If I can't pay them by noon tomorrow, I shall have to commit suicide. I am so terribly sorry to have to bother you about it here."

Petersen thanked God that Martha had studied ancient, not modern, languages. He said, his lips stiff, "This is Mrs. Petersen."

"So glad to meet you," said Petersen's latest secretary, and looked up in the air.

Martha mumbled something incomprehensible. Her sharp gray eyes behind their glasses were watching Petersen with eerie concentration. "Tomorrow morning," Miss Karin went on, "I'll pick up two thousand ticals at your office." In spite of her despair she was smiling at Petersen, amused and a little malicious. He would *have* to give her the money; otherwise the stern Mem would find out something about her husband she wouldn't like at all. "Tomorrow morning at eleven," she repeated.

"I wouldn't do that if I were you," Martha said, to Petersen's horror, in her slow, correct English.

Had Petersen taken Martha for an idiot? He had written to her often enough that in cosmopolitan Bangkok English was the most frequently spoken language.

15

It was only logical that she had thereupon decided to increase her knowledge of English. She had certainly had enough time to do so.

Martha's tone was so authoritative that Miss Karin was frightened and dropped her jasmine garland. Chubb, an orderly child who fortunately couldn't yet follow an English conversation, picked up the blossoms with the idea of putting them in water when he got home. He liked flowers if he didn't have to wear them around his neck. That was the moment when Tiny started to cry. Surely the stranger with the glittering eyes was a wicked fairy who would put a curse on them all! Tiny knew every fairy tale from Andersen through the Brothers Grimm, and knew also that evil witches sometimes appeared as beautiful young women. Martha's efforts to allay Tiny's fears had been unsuccessful.

Chubb immediately pulled an unbelievably dirty handkerchief out of his pocket and anxiously wiped away Tiny's big tears. He was always astonished that such a little girl could produce such big tears. Tiny didn't have a handkerchief with her. She never thought of anything.

Martha picked up her little daughter and held her like an infant. With her small bones, she was light as a feather. The heaviest thing on her was her hair. "Shush, shush, darling," Martha whispered.

There were dark circles around Tiny's eyes. Having succeeded in attracting her mother's attention, she now sobbed a little harder. If she could only work up a fever, Mama would pay attention to nothing but her. To be nursed by Mama was Tiny's favorite dream.

"Let's go, Johannes," said Martha. "The children have got to rest." She gestured to Chubb and walked stonily to the waiting car. The end of the world between Hamburg and Bangkok had taken place in exactly five minutes. This was not unusual east of Suez...

Petersen followed, white-lipped, his head pounding.

Martha had never called him Johannes, not even after his little stupidity with the glove salesgirl. Miss Karin remained standing alone on the pier, rouging her lips skillfully. She had taught Nai Petersen a lesson. She didn't let anyone stand her in a corner like a parchment parasol. Still, she felt uneasy. Petersen's eyes had been so dead. Or was it the weeping blond child who had fled from her? Europeans were strange. Had Miss Karin's father, whom she had never known, been so incomprehensible too? During the scene on the pier she had experienced a whiff of something akin to the decay that occasionally wafted through East Asia's orchid gardens. Miss Karin brooded: had she gone too far? No. Nai Petersen had deceived her. He had never mentioned that he had a family. Miss Karin had talked herself seriously into the possibility that if she became "very very respectable," Nai Petersen might marry her some day. A friend of hers in Singapore had managed to bring this off. She had saved herself by moving into the white world.

Miss Karin had never introduced Nai Petersen to her Javanese mother. The old woman spent a great deal of her time on a bamboo mat, chewing betel, and with her magical fingers carving tiny figurines. She had no models from her Javanese homeland to go by; they lived in her mind and in her gentle shining eyes. Miss Karin despised her mother's dolls. "Toys for natives!" she called them. Yet she sold them to Bangkok and Singapore antique dealers at quite a profit. Artificially aged and blackened, they were then sold to trusting Europeans as museum pieces. Miss Karin's business acumen was astounding.

Miss Karin awoke from one of the reveries which sometimes overwhelmed her without her volition. In a week she would send the Mem a bouquet of orchids. Then she would know that no offence had been intended. She looked at her wristwatch, a present from the first mate of the *Selandia*, then she hailed a rickshaw.

17

Tonight the Danish officers would be giving a party on board. The arrival of a ship from Europe was always a big, shining event in everyday tropical life. Miss Karin intended to wear a long, seagreen taffeta dress. As her only piece of jewelry she would wear Petersen's gold necklace.

Martha and Petersen sat as if turned to stone in the big open car which Petersen had bought as a surprise for his wife. The children sat beside the chauffeur, holding hands and looking with astonished blue eyes at the East Asian street life. Tiny's little forefinger, which Chubb secretly adored, kept pointing excitedly at the scarlet, green, and gold roofs of temples that towered up into the sky above the clamor of the markets. The skirts and sashes of the buyers mirrored the colors of the Siamese *wats*, the Buddhist temples. A Chinese wedding procession passed by, a drama in red and gold. Siamese mothers carried their naked infants on their hips in bamboo carriers. An Indian with a carmine red turban was driving a water buffalo across a street with flaming red trees. "What's that?...And that?...And *that*?" Tiny asked, and Chubb told her as best he could. He would have liked to ask Mama, but she looked tired. Besides, Tiny had boundless faith in Chubb's wisdom and he didn't dare to disappoint her or she would immediately begin to cry again.

Martha looked apathetically at the flat sampans, fruit boats gliding across the glittering water, mountains of red, yellow and emerald green fruit under the blazing sun. The Gulf of Siam had already astonished her. In comparison with this bright water, her beloved Alster was a pallid river. Hamburg was a matte pastel compared with the glowing landscapes of Southeast Asia. Even the shadows caught in street corners seemed to glow with light and imprudence. How beautiful Thailand was! The extravagant temples had been built with mathematical precision, the trees gleamed with the eternal green found only in monsoon areas. But Martha could enjoy none of this alien glory. The sweat on her brow was cold. From time to time shivers ran down her robust body. The climate seemed to forbid any sort of excitement. Martha's beautiful strong hands clutched her shabby bag.

She had always saved every penny where she was concerned. Chubb's shoes and milk for Tiny had created constant financial problems in the years following the war. After the Japanese occupation, which ended in 1945, Petersen and Company in Bangkok had had to start all over again. The wave of hatred against Germany had penetrated as far as Southest Asia. Moreover, the country had been allied with Japan. The Chinese had at once turned to English and Dutch firms, made fresh contacts with the United States, and ignored the first German imports. But by 1950, with doggedness and honesty, Petersen and Company had succeeded in winning back their most important Chinese customers. Hannes Petersen had opened up new markets in neighboring countries. It wasn't big business yet, but the future looked promising if things remained quiet in Siam.

Petersen's private life, however, didn't look nearly as promising right now. He stared tensely straight ahead when Martha once made a move as if she wanted to push her loose hair behind her ears, but halfway up to her head her hand sank down again. Petersen didn't move. If only Martha would break the silence! Even if only with a motto! "There's no place like home!" Or, "Faith can move mountains!" Oh God, was he going crazy?

He must explain everything to Martha at once. The children were much too busy to turn their heads. They were watching a Chinese coolie wife in blue linen trousers and a jacket of the same material, cutting up a fruit into small pieces with a rusty knife. Her children were each to have a piece. Since the car had to stop frequently in Bangrak, the market district, because of the usual traffic jams, Chubb and Tiny could take in the entire operation.

"The knife is dirty," said Tiny. "Why doesn't she clean it?"

Chubb had the feeling that the question didn't apply in the Far East. He said, "I guess she doesn't have time," which wasn't exactly factual. The anxious Chinese mother had become used to the sight of rusty kitchen knives in Swatow. Her grandmother had cut up fruit with a similar knife for her and her fourteen brothers and sisters.

Petersen wiped the sweat from his brow. He had called it quits with Miss Karin; he had only forgotten that it took two people to call a thing quits. He didn't think things through. But what did Martha know about the loneliness of the European man in the tropics without a wife? What did she know about the helplessness of hot blood? Of the eerie emptiness of a wooden veranda in the moonlight? Had she experienced the endless humid nights, swarming with memories and mosquitoes, in the sober north? Petersen was forty-three years old and healthy as an ox, and yet...he shouldn't have done this to his wife. Not to Martha. How she had clung to him in the moment of their greeting! It was as if she were seeking protection in him for the first time in her life. He knew so little about her life in Hamburg during the war. Suddenly, in glowing script, he could see Martha's letters, written during the first war months. They had contained no complaints of the hunger no food packages could still, no complaints about Tiny's early years, filled with sickness and nervous tension for mother and child. When the sirens had sounded, she had carried her whimpering little girl down into the air raid shelter, silently, to all appearances controlled, Chubb trotting behind her with a small suitcase that contained, among other things, Petersen's letters, written during their engagement. Nothing could happen if Mama was with them! Chubb was convinced of that. Petersen had always been convinced of it too. Martha was the salt of the earth.

Petersen had the dull feeling that the little indiscretions of which he hadn't been able to steer clear in Hamburg either, had been crimes against the spirit of love. He had grown up at a time in which sin had no longer been a reality. For many people of his generation and background, the words *repentance* and *forgiveness* were clichés that prospective businessmen didn't bother with any more after confirmation. He didn't see them as the great truths to which a civilization, mired in materialism, had to reorient itself if it was ever going to find its way out of the Nazi darkness, back into the light. Clichés were mechanical, and their content as unreal to Petersen as Germany's indescribable misery.

Right now Petersen was experiencing only a weak reflex of these truths, but they struck him like a blow. He sensed suddenly that he had been wrong in despising Miss Karin. Hers was a gambler's nature, like his, but she played according to the rules of the Far East. In spite of his years of experience in the tropics, Petersen had grasped of these rules that regulated all human relationships and ties over the heads of the European only the conventional ones that concerned business. In his private life he had been a loser for quite a while. Martha must hear him! Even a murderer on trial got a hearing!

"Martha," he stammered, "I swear..." He stopped. Should he tell her that Miss Karin had never meant anything to him? Did he want to insult Martha's intelligence on top of everything else? A dry sob stuck in his throat. He made fists of his hands so that not a sound should escape him. He closed his eyes like a dying man. He didn't know what to do next.

Martha had come to. All she did was lift the heavy, scented jasmine garland from her shoulders with a tired gesture and let it fall in the dust. But then she did look at her husband, a piercing look. And suddenly something deep and warm lit up her cool gray eyes. She had looked like that at the black sheep in her undergraduate class years ago. The girl had stolen something valuable from the locker room for the second time, and Martha had surprised her at it. When the foolish child, who came from a prominent Hamburg family with a too-strict mother, didn't know what to do next, Fräulein Doktor Jansen had said, after a long pause, "I'll give you one more chance; but you've got to help me."

Martha must have communicated something similar to Petersen now, because with a sigh of relief, he let his head sink down on her shoulder like a tired boy. His dark glasses hid the expression in his eyes. They were looking at a fantasy street with cherry trees. The trees were no longer in full bloom but they still bore the fruits of life... Shyly he stroked Martha's shabby handbag.

Now the car was driving through a street of luxurious gardens. Silver canals snaked along orchid greenhouses and blossoming shrubs behind which loomed villas and bungalows with big verandas. Here Asiatics and Europeans lived in rare East Asian harmony, house beside house. The Land of the Free had never known anything like the European quarters of other colonial lands. Petersen looked around him. Suddenly his soul was filled with a light but by no means heedless serenity which he couldn't express yet. In the end he murmured something only Martha could understand. A Hamburger would rather bite off his tongue than make a declaration of love loudly and clearly. Petersen whispered something even less clear. He didn't look at Martha but seemed to be counting the gardens at the edge of the road. "Don't," said Martha. And her voice was like the night wind over a lotus pond: a lullaby, soft and wonderfully consoling. Then, abruptly, she shook her head. *What* had got into Tiny? The tropical sun was shining on her uncovered, curly head! One couldn't put the child out of one's mind for a minute! "Chubb!" she cried. "Put Tiny's hat on at once! She isn't thinking of anything, as usual!" But just then Petersen's car stopped in front of a large tropical house with four verandas and a park that to Martha looked bigger than Hamburg's Innocentia Park. In front of the gate, which was overgrown with bougainvillea, stood and knelt dark-skinned figures in snow-white jackets and brocade. The white figures were Chinese and Indian; the dainty ones in the long colored culottes, or *phanungs*, were Siamese. The old Chinese cook had grouped his family—one daughter and three grandsons—around him as if they were being photographed for the Chinese New Year. The Siamese servants formed a second group. They were kneeling under a rose-red bougainvillea branch. The Indian night watchman with his high white cap and long bamboo staff stood alone, like a statue on a wide space. Stifled giggles came from the Siamese group.

"These are your obedient servants, Mem," said Petersen.

Martha gave the giggling group a sharp look through her glasses. "They seem to be highly amused," she said drily.

Then, as Martha walked through the gate with the children, the old Chinese cook came to meet her, bowing low. Ah Chang had served many Europeans, but he had remained Chinese. He knew how to behave and gave the giggling *amah* a look in which superiority was mixed with pity for so much ignorance. He mumbled something in a ceremonial tone and handed Martha a lotus flower on a

23

tiny lacquered tray. Martha looked at Petersen, who was standing behind her.

"Ah Chang wishes his honorable mistress prosperity and many sons," Petersen translated with an impassive face.

2

A House in the Tropics

Later, when Martha thought about her first weeks in Siam, she sometimes asked herself: had she really experienced all these strange and contradictory things—the tranquility of nature and the stealthy opposition of the servants against her authority from the day of her arrival? The Mem wanted to make various changes, which all of them accepted as in order. She demanded punctuality, cleanliness, regularity, and reliability. But in the Far East the servants had always taken their own customs and inclinations as a measure for all things. The Siamese cleaned furniture and other objects most unwillingly. Didn't they always get dirty again?

Work organized according to certain hours was abhorrent to them. They cleaned, planted, washed, and cooked when it pleased them. Not earlier, not later. Ah Chang served Petersen's guests an excellent dinner when he felt the time was right for it, usually an hour and a half after the arrival of the guests. In the meantime Number One and Number Two boys handed around drinks and small delicacies which Ah Chang had arranged lovingly on silver platters. Until Martha's arrival, nobody had had anything to say against dinner served at nine-thirty when the guests had been invited for eight o'clock. During her entire stay, Martha was unable to get Ah Chang to have dinner ready two hours earlier, and start to serve at seven forty-five. He wished the Mem prosperity and many sons with all his heart, but he wouldn't let any "female fish" interfere, not even the German Mem, who could look at him so sharply through her glasses. On such occasions Ah Chang mumbled into his pointed white beard: "It is easy to be rich and impolite; it is difficult to be poor and polite." He knew at least as many proverbs as Martha, but his sayings were tinged by the wisdom of Confucius. That these wisdoms made Martha extremely impatient was certainly not the fault of the Chinese moralist.

From the start the old cook declared himself the devoted grandfather of the Little Master. To Chubb's astonishment, Ah Chang overwhelmed him with small charming gifts which Number Two Grandson had to make according to the old man's instructions—a pretty woven fan made of rice straw, a parchment lantern on which Ah Chang himself had pasted a picture of the God of Riches, little figures made of rice flour, an age-old Chinese craft which Ah Chang, with bloodthirsty curses, had taught Number One Grandson (who would rather have been catching fish).

Tiny was treated like air by the old Chinese and his relatives, all of whom ate Petersen's rice. She was destined to become a Mem and demand that dinner be served two hours earlier. "No good," mumbled Ah Chang. When he wanted to, he spoke English; when he didn't want to, he didn't understand a word of Martha's orders.

Although Martha grew accustomed fairly quickly to life in the tropics, the contrast in attitudes did confuse her at first. Time and space were something that East Asia—at least in Siam—could still distribute freely, even in the year 1950. After the bombing of the Alster villa where Martha and Petersen had been so happy, she and the children had had to share the fate of the unfortunate millions who had become unwilling lodgers by losing their homes. Now, overnight, she owned something which in Europe would have been considered a lost paradise: a large house with a beautiful view, servants who functioned if they were treated properly, and time. The house, with its high, light rooms and a covered veranda with chaise longues and wicker tables, stood in a cultivated jungle, a piece of the East Asian Eden as was still to be found in the Menam delta.

In former days the district of Bangkapi where the Petersens lived had been partially jungle. The residue of a silent primeval forest, luxurious ferns and painterly weeds was still alive in the spacious gardens of this idyllic Bangkok suburb. Petersen's gardener, who was simply called *khon suan*, "the man who looks after the garden," considered it to be his first duty that the foreigner, the *farang*, didn't force his ridiculous order on the tropical scenery. The *farangs, khon suan* explained to the *amah*, wanted to make prisoners of the spirits of the trees and bushes. Everything had to grow and thrive where it was ordered. For the Siamese gardener there was no such thing as weeds. Nai Petersen had let *khon suan* do as he pleased, but the new Mem had burst in on their peace and easygoing life style and expected *khon suan* to work. This was very cruel of the Mem, *khon suan* explained to the *amah*. The little Siamese girl nodded. The Mem *was* cruel: she demanded that the *amah* not let the little girl with the golden hair out of her sight. The *amah* had learned to watch over a water buffalo, but a foreign child was something else again, especially when *dek phu ying*, which was the *amah's* designation for the little girl, moved as fast as quicksilver. The water buffalo at home had moved so slowly that the *amah* had been able to ride on his broad back, half-asleep, for fifteen minutes at a time.

The *amah* sighed, and stuck a red hibiscus blossom behind her ear. This little act of coquetry did not escape *khon suan*. He grinned from ear to ear, showing his snow-white teeth. "*Sue maak*...beautiful," he said.

27

The *amah* began to giggle. She found the gardener beautiful too. Unfortunately Number Two Grandson broke up this little idyll to tell the *amah* that the Mem wanted to speak to her *at once*. The *amah* strolled over to the main house in a tempo that would have taken Martha once around the Innen Alster.

Khon suan stood in front of one of the beds and picked his nose thoughtfully. The Mem had told him where to dig some new beds. He had listened to her orders with a broad smile and ignored them, although Martha had made herself perfectly clear in sign language. "*Khao tjai mai?*" she had asked, a dictionary in her hand, just to make sure. *Khon suan* had nodded and smiled. Of course he had understood, but he would plant flowers where and when he wanted to. *Khon suan* didn't garden in the midday sun. He sauntered out of his quarters toward evening and received an eight-hour-a-day salary for his activities. But he had a green thumb. The shrubs and flowers he planted and cared for according to his system grew lushly. If he took a fancy to a certain type of shrub that didn't grow in Petersen's garden, he stole a fine specimen from somebody else's, where he had admired it. Not even the Mem could demand more from a devoted servant.

His pride was his orchid greenhouse, which stood to one side of the main house. Siamese orchids were famous for their variety and color, but they required experienced care. *Khon suan* had transformed the orchid house—which delighted Chubb—from a rotten old wooden arbor into a magical island where rare examples of orchids in pastel shades hung in clay pots on wires from the ceiling and walls, or flaunted their mysterious beauty in huge pots on the ground. But he didn't grow the orchids for his employer alone; he secretly sold a few, the ones he felt he could do without, to a small flower shop on the Silom Road. This, he felt, was his right, just as the cook, Ah Chang, considered what he added to the

28

price of the food he bought daily something that he had coming to him.

Martha never ceased to be astonished over the fact that Petersen seemed to see nothing wrong in these deceptions, as she called them. She never actually came out of her astonishment during these first weeks in the beautiful old house that stood solidly yet dreamily in a cautiously tamed wilderness. She who at home had been a master in the art of dealing with human beings was powerless to cope with the eternally smiling faces of her 'obedient' servants. They came and went as they pleased. The Siamese retreated into the farthest corner of the veranda when Martha raised her voice to give an order for the fourth time. They bowed humbly and didn't obey. It was as if this wonderland of the Far East were trying constantly to remind the woman from the West that in the twentieth century one had to pay a price for a sojourn in paradise.

Wherever Martha looked there was beauty and an eternal blossoming: banana bushes, gleaming flowers, tamarind, and cassia trees grew between giant palms and stretches of lawn. In the early morning hours and at twilight, house and garden went under in an unearthly stillness. All one heard was the chirping of crickets and the cry of the house lizard.

The servants, with their innumerable relatives and 'helpers,' lived a few meters away in low wooden houses, with bamboo mats to sleep on and bowls to eat out of as the only furnishings. There might also be the picture of a Hollywood actress torn out of a magazine and in this ragged condition stuck on the wall with thumbtacks. Ah Chang kept the hens and ducks he raised in front of the kitchen house, and with Chinese diligence planted all sorts of herbs and vegetables which he sold to Martha at a fairly high price.

In the evening the servants sat in their open pile houses, chatting, smoking, and playing games of chance in a world that was arranged to everyone's satisfaction, partly by Buddha and the Spirits of the Air, partly by Confucius. The Indian night watchman slept on the floor of the garage and at unexpected hours cried out to Mohammed for help. He had a habit of dancing in the moonlight and losing money in the daytime. Martha hardly ever saw him.

At the beginning she found it difficult to connect the servants and their respective duties. It seemed to her that strange faces and figures appeared briefly in the house and then disappeared in the servants' quarters. There was the *ampah*, "the girl who looked after the flowers in the morning." This was apparently the only thing she had to do. She was a niece of the washerwoman and had to give the latter sixty percent of her monthly salary. Everybody found this quite in order. Nang Sanit, the washerwoman, had infant twins, and from the money the *ampah* gave her she bought candy for them, and rings and beads. The latter she strung on their fat little wrists and ankles to protect them from evil spirits. As far as the spirits were concerned, Nang Sanit wasn't taking any risks. After all, Deng and Tong—her daughters' names—were in exceptional danger in the house of a foreigner.

Another creature whom Martha saw only occasionally in the morning was the floor coolie, a young Siamese with a naked torso, wearing a red sash and culottes, who pretended to be cleaning the floors. Martha thought he was seventeen. To her astonishment she found out from Petersen that Tanbun was over thirty, and had a wife and five children living in a bamboo hut somewhere in Bangkok. Tanbun never visited his family, yet he asked Petersen every month for an advance to cover the many expenses they seemed to incur. One day Tanbun disappeared. "Why?" Martha asked Number One Grandson, holding up her dictionary reproachfully. Nobody would wipe the floors because that was Tanbun's job. "Tanbun gone away...*pai lao*," the boy replied with an expressionless face. Martha asked two more times for the reason. Number One Grandson replied twice more that Tanbun had gone away. Then Martha gave up. She had grasped the fact that never in her life would she find out why the floor coolie had left the house without giving notice. Not until three days later, when she missed the bracelet Petersen had given her when Tiny had been born, did it become clear why Tanbun had disappeared. Apparently his family wasn't satisfied any more with Petersen's support.

Nobody knew Tanbun's address. The police promised to look for the bracelet, and that was that.

From her bedroom Martha could see the outlines of the *lampu* tree through the mosquito netting. Its filigree branches and blossoms rose into the sky out of the swampy ground. The *lampu* tree stood motionless and magnificent beside the *klong*, the canal that bounded Petersen's property on the south. Fruit and coal freighters passed through it at all hours. Chubb and Number Two Grandson caught fish there, and with the *amah's* help, Tiny picked blue and pink water lilies for her Papa, to whom she was passionately devoted. When Martha saw how jubilantly the little girl ran to Petersen and told him so lovingly about all the little things she had experienced, it gave her a stab in the region of her heart. She had sacrificed so much for this child, and she had eyes only for Petersen...Chubb also experienced pangs of jealousy but bore them with manly dignity and betook himself to his radio. His radio had remained faithful.

For a few weeks now, Mama had been giving him mathematics and Latin lessons. They were sitting on the veranda, looking at the *lampu* tree, and they were happy. Martha hid her weariness as best she could from Chubb's sharp, eager eyes. His thirst for knowledge was unquenchable. If only she had a teacher for him! She had thought educating the children in this climate would be easier. But it would be only for a year, she told herself.

A few months later she found a tutor for Chubb. One morning Professor Berger appeared on the veranda and offered her Viennese baked goods. He was a tall slender man with fine features and eyes in which the suffering of the eternally wandering Jew was mixed with the sparkling vivacity of the Austrian. Professor Berger had taught philosophy at the University of Vienna until 1934 when he had emigrated with his family to Bangkok, via an internment camp in Shanghai. His wife had a bakery in her house and Professor Berger delivered her goods to those Europeans he hoped would not redirect him to their cooks. "I am a philosopher," he told Martha with an embarrassed smile, "and a poor scholar has no place in the Far East. I tried to get into Chulalongkorn University in Bangkok, but the Siamese government is employing fewer and fewer foreigners. In Japan I was considered an enemy of the Axis; now I am living in a country that rejoiced over Hitler. That's the way it is. The emigrant is always in the wrong place."

Martha ordered iced drinks and asked the professor, who was standing there in a sweaty sports shirt, holding his basket of baked goods, to sit down. Nothing in her face betrayed what she was thinking as she looked at this man who after 1945 had had to accept the fate of the white coolies. "Wouldn't you like to go back to Vienna?" she asked cautiously. Vienna, Professor Berger explained gently, was overpopulated with the shades of his beloved dead. Finally Martha asked him to tutor Chubb, and he accepted delightedly. Frugal Martha offered him a far too generous salary and the scholarly man protested vigorously. Then he at least wanted to teach Martha Siamese as well, and she replied heroically that she would love that. The professor asked Chubb several questions and promised to set up a study plan for him. With what Martha was paying him he could afford a delivery boy.

When Petersen heard about it he said, "Now I think you're at home, my love! You have a lame duck again whom you can transform into a swan!"

Three months after their arrival, Tiny would almost have drowned if Martha's instinct and a certain inexplicable feeling of uneasiness hadn't made her walk through the garden to the canal in the middle of the noonday siesta. Tiny had gone to the canal with the *amah* to pick water lilies for her Papa. The *amah* was supposed to help her. Her help consisted of smoking cigarettes and from time to time calling out, "*Rawang!*...Careful!" without looking at the child. A thunderstorm was threatening. Tiny stretched out farther and farther to reach a blue lily. Just as Martha reached the canal, the child slipped into the water.

She was too startled to scream. The *amah* sat motionless on her mat and cried "*Rawang!*" a little louder. If the water spirits wanted to claim the child with the fair hair as their own, she wasn't permitted to do anything to prevent it or the insulted spirits would let her father's rice fields dry up. Martha saved her daughter with one grip of her strong hands. She carried her back into the house, rubbed her forehead with eau de cologne, and laid her under the mosquito net. Then she sat like a salt column beside her bed. They couldn't stay here! But leave Petersen after three months? He needed her and she needed him. Both of them knew that now.

Petersen found Martha unconscious on the mat beside Tiny's bed. The child was sleeping peacefully under the netting. The servants were in their quarters. Number Two Grandson would be serving tea in a few minutes. Meanwhile Martha could have died! Petersen was pale under his tan.

When Martha came to she was in her bed. Dr. Johannsen was standing beside it. The tall doctor from Bremen was just pulling a hypodermic needle out of Martha's arm. "It's nothing, Frau Martha," he said, in his deep voice that reminded her of home. "But Hannes is feeling terrible!"

Petersen didn't say a word. He was staring at Martha, and she saw to her astonishment that his eyes were red. "She was lying there so still," he told Dr. Johannsen, his voice hoarse.

"You should take a vacation," the doctor said drily.

Petersen was himself again at once. "That's impossible! I've got a big business deal pending with Wong and Sons in the next few days, or the Americans will get there ahead of us!"

"Well, thank goodness for that!" said Martha. "Give me a cup of tea, Hannes. Tell Number Two Grandson to bring a cup for Dr. Johanssen too. We'll have tea on the veranda."

The *amah* was sent back to her village. Dr. Johannsen promised to find a nursemaid. In the meantime Ah Chang's daughter would look after Little Missie.

3

The Lotus-Eaters from the Elbe

Petersen stood on the terrace of his house and called for the third time, *"Khon rot! Ma ni reu reu!"* which was meant to convey to the chauffeur that he was to come on the double. Where the hell was he? As usual Petersen had allowed a half hour for the man's morning rice, but Phom could not be punctual. Time was an elastic word in his Siamese vocabulary.

Phom was probably chatting with Nang Sanit, the washerwoman, while his two sons were taking care of Nang Sanit's twins. They were devoted to Deng and Tong, toted them around for hours, and fed them cookies from Martha's cookie jar, which was made of wire netting and had feet that stood on a clay tray in a solution of diluted ammonia, so that the black ants couldn't get through the wood and the netting. The twins loved sugar, honey, and cookies, and sucked and nibbled at sweets all day.

The two boys were called Mu (pig) and Nu (rat). Like any cautious Siamese, Phom had given his progeny these names to deceive the jealous gods. He would never have called his sons Golden Boy, for instance, or Diamond, or the evil spirits would have stolen these valuable children, and Phom would have had nobody to get water out of the canal for him to wash the car. Phom could have got water easily from the kitchen where it ran constantly out of a rusty tap. Ah Chang never turned a tap off—a matter of principle. His family, all of whom followed his example, did likewise. They didn't have to pay the huge water bill at the end of the month.

Electric light also didn't worry this Chinese family. The old cook illuminated the kitchen house and the sleeping quarters of his relatives with an electric light bulb that hung on a wire from the ceiling of his wooden veranda. Sometimes the light burned all night. The Siamese servants lit coconut oil in tiny clay bowls, but usually the moonlight sufficed for them. The rice fields of their fathers hadn't been illuminated either.

Phom, the chauffeur, didn't want to have anything to do with Ah Chang, the cook. He wouldn't fetch water from such a bad person. "And the Chinese are bad," he told his two sons, Mu and Nu, whenever a member of Ah Chang's Chinese family showed up in the garden. With this remark Phom was expressing a native and historic aversion. He resented everything about Ah Chang and his family—their good business sense, the different things they ate, and their presence in Thailand generally. And what irritated him most was the presence of Ah Chang's daughter, Cheng. She was a wonderful cook but never offered him anything. Cheng looked only after members of her family. She laundered well and charged Phom for washing every one of his white uniforms. He didn't let Nang Sanit, the laundress, wash them because she had spat betel juice on them once, and Nai Petersen had been "cruel" about it. The foreigners fussed about every stain on a jacket as if it were a crime. Phom had to cook the rice for his sons when Nang Sanit slept in the morning, which happened frequently when she had drunk too much rice schnapps the night before. Phom's wife had gone back to her jungle village a year ago with no explanation, leaving Phom to bring up the children.

Petersen liked Phom's two graceful boys. They ran around his grounds all day and caught fish in a distant area of the canal where they couldn't meet up with Ah Chang's grandsons, and climbed fearlessly and deftly up the high trees. They picked the green Siamese fruit, which annoyed Ah Chang, and cracked it open with their strong teeth. Ah Chang wouldn't touch the green fruit, but the Siamese weren't to have it either.

This morning, however, Petersen paid no attention to them; he would even have bidden Tiny a very brief farewell. He frowned. "*Khon rot!*" he yelled again in the direction of the servants' quarters.

Phom sauntered up at a snail's pace to punish Petersen for the noise he was making. The Siamese hated loud voices. They could be ever so angry but they always spoke softly and with meticulous politeness.

Martha wanted to ask Professor Berger's advice. Couldn't a teacher be found for Charlotte for at least a few hours a day? Her own efforts to teach the child had failed. A definite animosity toward her recalcitrant daughter lay hidden in Martha's otherwise sensible soul. That she was failing as a teacher seemed impossible. The climate had to be at fault. Or was she too impatient with the child? For the first time she thought of Petersen's warning to which she had paid no attention in Hamburg. Children didn't belong in the tropics, Hannes had written. Charlotte certainly didn't belong in Bangkok, Martha had to admit. She got more and more hectic every day and she let the Siamese servants spoil her. Like an old inhabitant of the tropics she asked for a glass of water in a commanding tone and let Ah Chang's daughter, Cheng, dress her and wait on her, kneeling. One bright smile from Tiny, and the stocky Chinese girl in her satin trousers and snow-white linen jacket fastened up to the neck was ready to go through fire for her little mistress. Cheng was a Chinese mother. Her heart was big.

Martha sighed. When Hannes wasn't there life in

the tropics seemed somehow unreal, a phantasmagoria that could dissolve into thin air at any moment. She had no idea that there were many Europeans who regarded this fantastic existence as real and perfectly natural.

Wilhelm Christian Petersen, head of the firm, also showed all the symptoms of a man who had eaten lotus for years. Martha hadn't met him yet. At the moment he was staying in his summer villa in Hua Hin with his Siamese wife, his children, and innumerable servants. Hua Hin was an elegant Siamese seaside resort south of Bangkok, which could be reached in a few hours by train. But Wilhelm Christian Petersen was coming to Bangkok this weekend with his wife and a few of his children to greet Martha and her children. They were his only relatives; his brothers and sisters in Hamburg were dead. Petersen senior attributed this to the climate in Hamburg of which, after forty years in the Far East, his memory was dim. Martha was looking forward to meeting him. She had never forgotten the fact that Wilhelm Christian Petersen had made a life far from Nazi Germany possible for her husband without saying too much about it, which was typical for Hamburg.

In the meantime Petersen was driving to his office, frowning and looking grim. Petersen and Company had its offices on New Road, Bangkok's main business street. There was buying and selling going on along the side streets of New Road as well. Bangkok was one of the last undamaged mercantile centres of the East. Here you could see the typical factories of the Chinese quarter. New Road also had office buildings with several stories in European style. In between you could still see the ruins from the time of the Japanese occupation when Bangkok had experienced several bombing attacks. The removal of ruins took place in the tropics just as slowly as everything else.

Petersen was used to the sight of New Road, had been for years—it was more familiar to him today than the New Wall in Hamburg. With its noise, its disorder, its bumpy pavement and its active international life, New Road was also accustomed to the expression on Petersen's face. Many Europeans drove to their offices looking grim. They had to smile so much with their Chinese clients that one had to grant them this little relaxation.

Petersen cast an absentminded glance at the Art Academy of Chulalongkorn University which he passed every morning. Its colorful roofs, their ridges ending in gilded, curved, snakelike finials, the airy architecture and the giant palms in the garden in front of it gave the college its specific character. Everything was dignified, attractive, and had a holiday atmosphere, like the Siamese students who studied here diligently. Petersen's friend, His Royal Highness Prince Pattani, had attended this university after years at Oxford and Heidelberg, and liked to associate with the English and Germans residing in Bangkok. Even before Martha's arrival he had expressed with great charm his willingness to show the Mem the Buddha temples of his native city, but he didn't want to set a precise date. One day he would drive up to the Petersens' house in his big American car and expect Martha to get in. Any refusal was out of the question unless Martha was dying or was out paying a call. But the latter eventuality would never have occurred to the prince. He was much too accustomed to everyone being at his disposal. He was a relative of the Siamese royal house and his servants served him his food on their knees. His European guests were served in western style, with a cold buffet and every imaginable type of drink. Petersen was curious as to what the prince would think of Martha. She was very forthright; she criticized tactfully, but—she criticized. It wasn't the thing to do when faced with Siamese aristocracy. Even when their sons had studied for years outside the country, the elite of this strange kingdom expected foreigners to praise the advantages of their country but keep politely silent about any disadvantages, just as they did when away from home.

At last Petersen's car drew up in front of the Petersen and Company office building. The traffic in Bangkok's narrow main street was so dense that Phom had frequently had to stand for two or three minutes. Petersen had been sitting for five minutes in his air-conditioned office with the prints of Hamburg on its bare white walls, when his Chinese boy, with respectful obeisances, ushered in the famous Mr. Wong.

Mr. Wong, head of a renowned East Asian export-import house, was a short, agile old man with a long, ivory-colored face. He greeted "young Mr. Petersen" with ceremonial politeness and inquired at length about Petersen senior, with whom he had been friends for years. Petersen responded to Mr. Wong's courtesies with questions about his incalculably large family in Bangkok, Hong Kong, and Singapore. The branch in Shanghai had been reduced to such an extent because of present difficulties, that a great-nephew of Mr. Wong's had been sent to the United States to study advertising methods there. Old Mr. Wong was of the opinion that one should learn what one could so that the "alien devils" shouldn't prove a match for Wong and Wong. This had never happened, but one couldn't let things reach a point where one day one was a rice sack with no rice.

Old Mr. Wong held forth with practical observations like this while Petersen was trying to make out why his important client was a shade cooler than usual. Hadn't he, Petersen, smiled enough? Had he forgotten to ask how Great-great-aunt Wong in Hong Kong was feeling? No. Everything had proceeded according to plan. But Petersen would have to get to the bottom of this shadowy displeasure; before that he couldn't expect an order for the machine parts and precision instruments which Petersen and Company had already offered Wong and Wong in great detail in writing.

Gradually Petersen found out what he was after. He hadn't been dealing with the Chinese for twelve years for nothing. Mr. Wong was dissatisfied with the new German spare parts for an old Japanese piece of machinery he had taken over from a Japanese factory after the end of the war. The spare parts were "no good." Old Mr. Wong knew just as well as Petersen that his coolies had let the spare parts rust in an unprotected shed, and that the machine was creaking with age, but Wong and Wong couldn't lose face. After astute Hannes Petersen—astute where the Chinese soul was concerned —had brought the latent disharmony to light, the old man began just as stubbornly and obtusely to make demands. Petersen of course smiled as blissfully as if the revelations of the old fox delighted him. In private one could be a lotus-eater, but where business was concerned, Petersen was cautious, just as he had been in the gray bookkeeping offices in Hamburg where, under his grandfather's taciturn direction, he had received his first insight into overseas business. His grandfather's principle never to say a word too much and to let business "simmer" slowly, had helped Petersen in the Far East to unimaginable success. The Chinese valued equally capable partners.

Of course Petersen and Company would provide "technical assistance." This was a euphemistic expression in East Asia for the repair of ruined machinery at no expense. Their expert, Petersen explained over their third cup of green Chinese tea, would be only too pleased to ascertain what was "no good" about the German parts. Old Mr. Wong's face was now restored; in fact he seemed to have gained somewhat in this respect. From now on everybody would know how splendidly the Wong coolies handled their machinery. In the end old Mr. Wong, smiling blissfully, gave Petersen a big order for steel products and tools. Moreover, he had recommended to Petersen junior the most reliable agent for copra on the Siamese east coast. He would write to Mr. Wu personally so that Petersen and Company would receive the same low price as the Chinese exporters. As an afterthought, and as a personal acknowledgment of Petersen's little speciality, Mr. Wong had also ordered a considerable number of typewriters which he intended to sell up country. One had to move with the times. Typewriters had been Petersen's brainstorm. They had been a sideline of the firm but had turned out to be big business because their lifespan was short in the Land of Smiling People. Most Asiatics ignored the necessity of cleaning the machines regularly. The layers of dust, which in tropical countries penetrated and corroded everything in short time, ruined the typewriters, which were never covered.

Petersen never ceased to be astonished over the mysterious animosity between the industrial products of the West and the handmade artifacts of the Far East. The fingers of the Asiatics, which handled the machines of the West so clumsily, became precision instruments as soon as it was a question of carving an ivory box, doing Siamese niello silver work or hammering Indian metal candlesticks. Yet the need for machinery in the newly awakened Far East was increasing constantly. This part of the earth was beginning slowly and unmistakably to exchange its ancient aesthetic traditions for the mechanized civilization of its former masters, although Siam remained an exception. Because the country had never been a colony, it possessed a deeply ingrained, cultural self-confidence. But the Chinese mercantile centers that were training Siamese chemists, engineers and technicians were bringing the machine age with increasing success to the Land of the Yellow Robe. Old Mr. Wong and his sons embodied the type of modern businessman who, although he strictly respected the conventions of his forefathers, still took from the West whatever could be of use to his business. Mr. Wong's business ethics were elastic; he also dealt with East Germany for mining machinery and textiles. He was a go-between in this respect for Red China. One had to insure oneself.

Petersen and Company knew nothing about all this. Old Mr. Wong didn't feel it was necessary to reveal his relations to East Germany. According to Confucian tradition, Wong and Wong stuck to a strictly middle-of-the-road path where business was concerned. Confucius had said once, "I have a system or a golden thread that runs through the middle of all things..." Old Mr. Wong, who had developed his various export-import houses from the humblest beginnings, had used this system successfully for fifty years. In his eyes even the cleverest Europeans were naïve fools.

The old man rose. He drank three cups of tea, never more. Then he walked lightly and with dignity over to the old prints and looked at the Alster Pavilion, drawn in a romantic style. "An attractive teahouse," he said softly. He said this every time. Petersen bowed, smiling, and showed Mr. Wong several other prints of ship models of the eighteenth century. The old Chinese man gazed at the yellowed sheets, then he said he would be pleased to show Madame Petersen his historic water landscapes one day. He hoped the Petersen family would soon honor him with a visit. He withdrew modestly and silently, leaving behind an aura of satisfaction and harmony—satisfaction because of the big order Petersen had managed to get out of him. The harmony was a more complicated matter.

Martha stood on the terrace of her house and cried for the third time, "*Amah!*" She had come back an hour ago from the Royal Sports Club, where she and Chubb had gone swimming. This club, not far from Chulalong-korn University, was the haven of all Europeans in Bangkok. The pool cooled you off and relieved tension. In the evening the tennis court was swarming with happy activity. Behind the green tiled pool with its cabins there was a spacious reading room and vast terraces with English lawns, where East and West met amicably after their sport to enjoy the cool of evening. Here, a few days ago, Martha had met Prince Pattani, resting with an iced lemonade at Petersen's table after playing golf. The Prince did not touch alcoholic beverages. In a soft voice he had expressed his intention to pick Martha up for a visit to a Buddhist temple. He would very soon show Madame some of the sights of Bangkok. "Very soon" meant in a few weeks, perhaps in a few months. Then the prince had risen, looked at Martha for seconds out of his dark, melancholy eyes, and had withdrawn silently in his American car with his two servants, who were carrying his golf clubs.

Martha looked through her dark glasses in the direction of the servants' quarters. She had by now learned how to remind her ten or twelve servants of their duties. One stood on a romantic, flower-over-grown terrace and called. Through her dark glasses she could see Ah Chang's daughter, Cheng, with Youngest Grandson in her arms. The cook's daughter was to instruct the new *amah* in her duties. Until now the new *amah* had exhibited nothing but a dazzling smile, a Malayan sarong and enormous feet to indicate her suitability as a nursemaid. Cheng was doing absolutely nothing to initiate the new *amah* in her duties. On the contrary, she wanted to keep her position as nursemaid of the Little Missie with the golden hair, and intrigued secretly and slyly against the guileless Malayan whom Dr. Johannsen had recommended. As a result, the new *amah* decorated her shiny black hair with hibiscus blossoms, chewed betel and chatted animatedly with the Malayan

44

gardener from next door while Cheng circled like a butterfly around Tiny. Finally she came up to Martha and declared she would have to dress Little Missie herself because the new *amah* didn't feel like it. Martha understood just as little Malayan as Chinese. Her conversations with Ah Chang were carried out by Oldest Grandson, who continued to fill the position of Number One Boy and now translated into English in a whisper. Martha was indignant. "Didn't feel like it" was not in her dictionary! "Tell *amah* to come here!" she told Oldest Grandson angrily. He answered as if shot out of a gun that *amah* had gone away. Actually Cheng had sent her away on an errand Martha had never ordered.

Martha gave up. "Tell Cheng to get Little Missie ready quickly. The master will be here in ten minutes," she told the grinning young man in white livery, in a tone of resignation. Cheng bowed humbly and waddled off with Youngest Grandson up to the first floor where Tiny was already in her bath. They were all going to visit Great-uncle Wilhelm Christian and his wife.

Chubb was catching butterflies in the garden to while away the time. He brought Martha an especially brilliant specimen for his collection. Perhaps Great-uncle Petersen could tell him its name? "Perhaps," said Martha, and stroked his blond hair lovingly. Then she pushed her stray hairs behind her ears. Something must have detained Hannes. She hoped he hadn't let himself be persuaded to stop in Swee Hong, the big Chinese restaurant on New Road, with some friend or other for a drink. This happened more frequently than Martha liked, but you couldn't put a man on a leash, least of all in the Far East, where some of the unpredictability of the Oriental tended to pass over into European husbands.

When the whole family, with Cheng and Youngest Grandson following in a rickshaw, arrived at Wilhelm Christian Petersen's house for lunch, the sun was shining with such intensity that the back of Martha's head ached. She had never had headaches in Hamburg. On top of that there were the mosquito bites which caused her legs to swell. Martha had suffered since her arrival from the bites that plagued all newcomers from the West until their blood had become "less sweet." The diluted ammonia that she rubbed on her legs and arms helped a little, but not enough. "God's mills grind slowly," said Martha, sounding resigned. It was the only saying in her vast collection that seemed appropriate for East Asia.

Wilhelm Christian Petersen received his guests on the terrace of his palatial house in Rong Muang, a district in which you could find large dreamy gardens with pavilions, lotus ponds and flaming trees. The house stood far removed from the bumpy street and the newly erected stadium, where the Siamese youth practiced sports on Sundays. Petersen senior had a house with fourteen rooms, four lotus ponds, three pavilions, and a cement goldfish pool that had served during the war in East Asia as an air raid shelter for the surrounding Siamese and Indians. Shrill tropical birds flew among the trees. From the back veranda, which was meters long, you could see the canal where Siamese children were bathing, their happy cries muted. But for all that, an extraordinary silence pervaded the property where old Mr. Petersen had been living for years. Far back from the main house lay the servants' quarters which housed approximately fifteen servants and their families. There were three automobiles in the garage—one for business and one for the master of the house alone. The third car belonged to his wife, Countess Siri.

Nang Siri was a real estate agent by inclination. She drove around the city frequently in her shiny red cabriolet and dealt shrewdly in real estate, smiling sweetly and always turning a profit. She had her own bank account and her own ideas. She had given Nai Petersen twelve children and left their education to him. Four of the children had died of cholera. During one of his business trips, Nang Siri had forgotten to have the children inoculated. In April, during the hot season, the danger of cholera was acute. When Wilhelm Christian came back from Japan, he cried for the first time in the forty-eight years of his life. He loved every one of his half-caste children with a protective yet helpless affection. What was to become of them when he died?

The sons shied away from work and were pleasant. They had married Siamese girls. They lived in the country and never visited their father. Occasionally they met with Nang Siri when she had something to attend to up country. These young men betrayed their German origin only in their powerful builds, which was a strange contrast to their dark, slanting eyes and delicate hands. The daughters lived obediently and as was proper for young Asiatic ladies in the disorderly palace in Rong Muang. The oldest, Pauline, looked more European than the rest. Occasionally she worked for her Uncle Hannes, whom she secretly adored. She was a big attractive girl with red hair, yellow skin, and a beautiful, sensual mouth.

Pauline Petersen was a very quiet girl and had her moods. In such cases she didn't speak to her father for days, and looked at her dainty Siamese mother with arrogant disdain. All she wanted was to marry a European as far away from Bangkok as possible. Old Petersen fulfilled Pauline's every wish, even the most impractical ones, perhaps out of the obscure feeling that he had to make up to her with material things what he couldn't give this attractive, silent girl—a white skin and a suitable marriage. Unlike Miss Karin, who had turned up so unfittingly on Martha's arrival, Pauline had no male friends. Twice a week she taught little Siamese girls German and English in the convent school of the Ursuline sisters. She spoke both languages fluently. She had converted to Catholicism at the age of fourteen, which had caused her Protestant father to protest vigorously, the only time in his role as father. He was "against Rome" because all the Petersens in Hamburg had been "against Rome." But at the time Pauline had looked at him with her passionate black eyes and whispered that the Roman Catholic church didn't differentiate between races and nations. She was the mother of all peoples.... Old Petersen had told his daughter to express herself in a less highbrow fashion, whereupon Pauline had half closed her eyes, which was what Nang Siri did when silent Asiatic fury rose up in her dainty body. Pauline's father had recognized the warning signal and hastily given his permission: Pauline would become "Roman" and the devil take it!

The old man lived in constant fear for his favorite daughter, who for inexplicable reasons had tried to commit suicide at the age of twelve. After Pauline had thanked her father in meticulous German for his permission to be baptized, Petersen senior hastily drank three whiskeys and sodas one after the other, and ate a double portion of lotus. That was the evening he had doubted seriously whether it had been right to bring twelve children into the world who were doomed eternally to fall between two chairs. In the course of time he had grown big enough to express his personal thanks to the Ursuline sisters for the results of their teaching as far as Pauline and her younger sisters were concerned. Pauline had never again tried to end her life. She knew now that it was a mortal sin.

The second daughter took piano lessons in the convent and sometimes at twilight played old Petersen's favorite song for him: "Am Brunnen vor dem Tore". On such occasions the old man sang the words so clearly and loudly that he could be heard all the way to the canal. Nang Siri would stretch herself like a cat in her wicker chair and giggle while Wilhelm Christian sang. She seemed to find the text of "At the fountain, in front of the gate," which he had once translated into Siamese for her, especially amusing. Even more amusing was Winn's bass. Winn was her name for Wilhelm. The *l* became an *n* for Nang Siri.

Hannes Petersen's car raced through the portal and down the long drive to Uncle Winn's *palais*. Phom wanted to show what he could do. Martha cried out twice, "*Pai cha cha!*...Drive slowly!" which only made Phom accelerate. Petersen laid his hand on Martha's. "We have arrived," he said soothingly. A good thing, Martha thought, because Tiny was just about to start crying. Chubb had already taken out his handkerchief. He was sitting, as usual, beside the driver with Tiny, fearfully watching his little sister's twitching mouth. He wanted Tiny to laugh and be happy, although sometimes she seemed to forget Chubb in the course of Cheng's ministrations.

The tropics hadn't succeeded in changing Chubb yet. His radio and his sister were still the objects of his delight. Chubb was loyal. Besides, he was Mama's support and Papa's somewhat flawed son. Petersen criticized Chubb a good deal. He was too fat. He was a bookworm. He wore his clothes inelegantly. In spite of photographs, Petersen had pictured his son as a younger edition of himself, and in the years of his absence had endowed him with added attractions. "Sit up straight, Albert!" he would say, his tone sharp. Chubb obeyed. At least one member of the family called him by his right name! But it didn't make him as happy as he would have thought...

"Welcome to Rong Muang!" cried Wilhelm Christian Petersen, as he ran down the many steps of his marble terrace with surprising agility. He was a tall, heavy-set Hamburger. He was wearing a snow-white suit which he had put on reluctantly in Martha's honor. Usually he wore black Chinese trousers with a silver belt and a thin cotton shirt that was half open across his wide chest. But his niece from Hamburg was probably prim and proper, *etepetete*, a pejorative expression Petersen senior used for all social conventions of the Far West.

He helped Martha gallantly out of the car, shook hands with Chubb and lifted Tiny up high. "Come in, come in!" he cried, with his stentorian voice, and clapped his hands commandingly.

Martha stared at this legendary Uncle in Wonderland as unobtrusively as possible. Wilhelm Petersen had a very high forehead which seemed even higher because he was balding. Only beside his temples two bushes of white hair grew like a broken halo. His light blue eyes looked out on the world sharply yet veiledly, as if muted by a melancholy mist. He had the straight nose and willful mouth of all the older Petersens. Hannes' mouth was much softer, thought Martha, and looked at her adorable husband with a fleeting sense of motherly compassion. Hannes was a romantic; his uncle was a man of action. Otherwise the older man would never have managed the problem of his children.

In the dark, wood paneled hall with its ship models, which Uncle Winn had brought to the Far East from his family home, stood Nang Siri with her oldest daughter, Pauline. The other children had stayed in Hua Hin. Countess Siri would have liked to stay there too, because she had been on the point of selling a villa with white ants in its beams to an American. She owned four villas in Hua Hin, and did a tremendous amount of business during the hot season. She figured the rentals in dollars. She owned half of Winn's house. She had demanded this gently but firmly when the sale, which she had negotiated, had taken place. She had three passions: money, Siamese ceramics, and gambling.

She bowed low before the strange woman and giggled as she whispered something in Winn's ear. It sounded like, *"Mem farang-uan-uan,"* or, "The strange lady is very fat." A slight flush appeared on old Mr. Petersen's deeply furrowed brow. He whispered something so clearly in Siamese that Hannes Petersen had to smile. Even years of association with Nang Siri hadn't succeeded in muffling Uncle Winn's voice.

Nang Siri now walked up to Martha with downcast eyes, bowed low and prettily, and murmured *"Sawat di,"* as she pressed her slim brown hands together in front of her eyes in greeting. "Happiness and health to you." Martha, her expression friendly, accepted the greeting of the exotic woman.

Countess Siri was wearing a cherry red brocade skirt and a white batiste blouse. She had the childlike sweetness and grace of the unspoiled East Asian. She handed Martha a small ceramic vase, a work of art in itself, with a bluish-pink orchid in it, and smiled modestly yet proudly. The vase was a museum piece—greenish, with black and red motifs. With characteristic Siamese hospitality Nang Siri had parted with her favorite vase.

Martha's eyes were warm with thanks. She laid one arm around the smiling, dainty Siamese woman, and looked with her at some of the other pieces in Nang Siri's collection of ceramics which was famous in Bangkok. Dulled by dust, they stood on dusty teak tables, in danger of being knocked over. With her slender forefinger, Nang Siri pointed out single pieces and told proudly and excitedly what they were worth. Pauline translated what her mother was saying. Nang Siri looked at her daughter several times, suspiciously. Had she really told Martha what the large fruit bowl with the red and blue pattern had cost?

During this display, Martha was watching the twenty-five-year-old daughter of old Mr. Petersen with the unerring eye of a teacher. The young girl was only a guest in this disorderly palace. She belonged in different surroundings. But where? When Martha asked Pauline to come and see her sometimes to look at the books she had brought with her from Germany, she was rewarded with a shy smile and a fervent handshake. Yes, Pauline would like very much to visit Aunt Martha! Were there any art books in her library? Pauline confided that she found Rembrandt *famos*—great! *Famos* was her father's expression for highest praise. As Pauline expressed her admiration for this genius of the West in her absurd singsong German, Martha was overwhelmed by such a wave of compassion that she took the big girl with the black eyes in her arms impulsively. She had never done anything like this before in her life! Hannes, in a corner of the hall where he was reporting to Uncle Winn on his dealings with old Mr. Wong, looked with astonishment at his wife and Pauline, who now kissed Martha's hand with Siamese delicacy. Old Mr. Petersen coughed and drank his whiskey without saying a word. At that moment his niece Martha had won his heart. She was being nice to Pauline. She was a *famos* woman!

Petersen senior seemed suddenly to have been relieved of a colossal burden. He took Chubb and Tiny by the hand and led them out into the garden where five tame monkeys with black faces and long golden hair were hopping around on wires. Chubb and Tiny watched them with loud cries of delight. One of the gibbons was already perched on Uncle Winn's shoulder and had flung his arms around the old man. "Would you like to have him, my girl?" the head of Petersen and Company asked. Tiny was suddenly breathless with joy. Then she smiled as enchantingly as Petersen with his Chinese clients. "If...if I may," she stammered. Old Petersen set the gibbon down on his legs like a child and gave Tiny the metal leash. "You can take him for a walk, my girl," he said, "until it's time to eat. His name is Hummel-Hummel. Pauline will bring him over to you tomorrow."

Tiny jumped up, threw her arms around her great-uncle and kissed him. Her golden curls flew like a breath of the north against his head with its bushy white hair. The old man said, "All right, all right, my girl." The veil over his light blue eyes lifted for a moment. This was how his deceased sister, Pauline, had kissed him when he had brought her a toy from Amsterdam or London.

Meanwhile a lively conversation was going on in the big hall. Nang Siri had disappeared into the kitchen to watch over six of her servants who were preparing rice and curry. She may not have had an eye for dust or cobwebs, but she was an outstanding cook. For Uncle Winn that had made up for a lot. Every Hamburger appreciated good food; it didn't always have to be steak or spring chicken. Curry, with twenty-five highly imaginative side dishes, was a decent meal too, Wilhelm Christian had written to his sister Pauline at the time.

Now he was greeting a couple who also came from Hamburg. Charles Krüger owned a paper factory in Bangkok and was a very rich man. During the First World War, he and his wife had been interned. A period of waiting in Hamburg had followed, but the Krügers had returned to Bangkok as soon as the Germans had been permitted to settle there again.

Doris Krüger was a little white-haired lady with a very red face. As a rule she spoke softly, but on occasion she could voice something important so loudly that not only the sensitive Siamese were startled. She lived in a magnificent house near Dusit Park, dedicated to her husband and her six pedigreed dogs, and was a mother to all of them. She had no children.

"We have no intention of going back," she told Martha with her unmistakable Hamburg accent. "Papa came to Siam forty years ago. It wasn't called Thailand then, but that makes no difference."

"I hear you have a beautiful house," said Martha, just for something to say. She didn't know how to deal with this lotus-eater from the Elbe.

53

"Oh, it's all right," said Doris Krüger so loudly that Martha was startled. "And then there are the dogs. You must come and visit our dogs, Frau Petersen. Or should I say Frau Doktor? Papa tells me you went to university. I *was* surprised!"

Martha assured Frau Krüger that of course she was Frau Petersen.

"Papa!" Doris Krüger shouted. "We're leaving!"

Charles Krüger got up at once and walked out onto the terrace to call his chauffeur, who had disappeared. Just like Petersen's Phom. "Stay for tiffin, do," said Uncle Winn. It was all the same to him whether ten or twenty people partook of his midday rice.

"Many thanks, Christian," said Doris Krüger. "But we've got to go or the dogs won't be fed properly." Charles Krüger said, "Well then, *adschüs*, Christian," in his Hamburg version of "bye-bye." "We'll have another talk about this copra business, Hannes, right?"

He bowed to Martha and gave her two children a fleeting glance for the first time. "Send the kids back to Hamburg as soon as you can. They're not going to get anything out of staying here."

He was right, but Martha didn't like advice from strangers. "We're only staying a few months," she said coolly.

Charles Krüger laughed. "That's a joke! Did you hear, Hannes? You're wife's ready to leave!"

Petersen stood by Martha loyally. "Of course," he said. "My family is here on a visit."

"Well, never mind, Frau Petersen. No offence intended," Charles Krüger said politely. Something in Martha's expression had dampened his hilarity. Was Martha Petersen serious? Didn't she really want to stay? Hannes would certainly remain here, now that he was a partner in the firm. Hannes was great at dealing with the Chinese. "*Auf Wiedersehen*, Frau Petersen," said

Charles Krüger. "We would be delighted if you'd come to see our dogs. Bring the children with you. You can ride one of our ponies, my boy," he told Chubb. " I breed horses, race horses, on a small scale." Then the couple drove off in their new car. They were still living comfortably and stubbornly in the Siam of 1910, the Land of Undimmed Smiles. Instead of revolutionary neighbors they had devoted servants, race horses, pedigreed dogs and unlimited peace and quiet.

Since there was no sign of tiffin being served, Petersen senior showed the children his birds. "That one's name is Nok-Takarb," he explained. "*Nok* is Siamese for bird."

Chubb gave the bird a sharp, knowing look. He had always had good grades in natural science. He put the bird's name and colors down in a small, dirty notebook. Nok-Takarb was a fat, shiny bird with green and blue wings that glittered like precious metal in the midday sun. He also classified a butterfly with his great-uncle's help. Wilhelm Christian Petersen looked thoughtfully at the stocky boy with his blond shock of hair and his kind, clever eyes. A *famos* boy! He had strength combined with a gentle spirit.

"Are there a lot of butterflies in Siam?" Chubb asked, eager to learn.

"About seven hundred different types. The most beautiful ones are in the jungle. Maybe I'll take you along some day."

Chubb scarcely dared to breathe for joy. What would his friends in Hamburg say when he brought them back butterflies from the jungle?

"That...that would be very nice," he said, with his Hamburg reticence. Old Petersen nodded, satisfied. One shouldn't carry one's heart on one's tongue.

Suddenly the veil covered his blue eyes again. He had to think of his own shadowy sons, total strangers, young men whose pleasant behavior just barely hid their intellectual lethargy. They were gentle, but they had no strength. They were broken and split to the core.

"Come, children." His voice was hoarse. "In a minute we're going to have a rice dinner."

As the Petersens drove home again on this eventful day, the conversation in the car was lively. All sorts of surprising things had been decided: Chubb and Tiny were to spend two weeks with Uncle Winn in Hua Hin. There Chubb would learn to ride "tame horses" on the beach under Petersen senior's supervision. Tiny would only be allowed to bathe in the sea when Pauline was present. The child simply had to overcome her fear of the water. Since she had slipped into the canal that day, Martha hadn't been able to persuade her to even walk into the swimming pool at the sports club with her. Pauline had assured Martha that no harm would come to Tiny in Hua Hin. She looked at her little cousin with the curly blond hair with humble admiration that touched Martha to the quick. There was no envy in Pauline's dark, brooding eyes, only astonishment that anyone could be so blond and rosy.

Petersen had to fly to Saigon on business, and Martha was to accompany him. He wanted her to see a colonial city where the sun was setting.

At home Ah Chang was waiting for his masters with an enigmatic smile. He pretended not to see his daughter, Cheng, who was just driving through the gate in her rickshaw. The Malayan *amah* had disappeared! "A very bad person," mumbled the old cook. "Not happy with Nai Petersen." Ah Chang had immediately found someone to help him in the kitchen. His daughter, Cheng, would have to look after Little Missie in the meantime, no?

The new kitchen help was one of Ah Chang's nieces. Martha had seen her often in the distance in the servants' quarters. The woman now stood beside Ah Chang, showing all her gold teeth as she smiled. This was Chung. Chung, Petersen explained to his speechless wife, meant "second sister." Whose second sister the woman was wasn't mentioned. She had brought with her a perfectly beautiful, very young girl, her daughter, whose name was Ah Bue. She was to help too.

"But the *amah* never gave notice!" Martha protested weakly.

"You're not in Hamburg," Petersen replied, sounding a little provoked. "Cheng told the *amah* that you didn't need her. She wants to look after Tiny herself. It's as simple as that."

Ah Chang's new helper bowed low. She was wearing the wide, woven bamboo hat of the Chinese market woman and dusty sandals on her feet. She had on black trousers and a black jacket. Martha didn't like the Chinese woman with her sly eyes and hands that somehow looked greedy, but...she wasn't in Hamburg. Daughter Ah Bue had her mother's eyes and hands. Both of them withdrew with the old cook in the direction of the kitchen house.

So they were rid of the Malayan girl. In Bangkok the cook chose the servants, not the foreign master who didn't even know the thousand herbs and the two thousand medicines of the Chinese. Ah Chang was Number One in the Petersen house. The Mem, with her scholar's glasses and immodest voice couldn't change that. Ah Chang could never get over how loudly and clearly the "female fish" of the West spoke to their husbands. It was a slap in the face to all Chinese tradition, and tradition was as necessary for a family as wings for a bird or water for a fish. Shaking his head, the old man withdrew on the covered path that led to the kitchen house with its eternally running water.

Cheng bowed humbly before Martha and murmured that she would now get Little Missie's bath ready.

She bowed so low that neither Petersen nor Martha could see the triumph in her face. Nobody was going to rob her of the child with the golden hair! Or the nice salary that went with the job. With the money, Cheng's Oldest Grandson could learn so much that his stomach would be full of pencils. Cheng had to be mother and father to her sons. Her husband had been shot long after the Japanese occupation by one of "the yellow dwarfs" who had stayed on in Bangkok. Since then Cheng smiled only when she asked Martha for an advance on her salary.

"Cheng!" Tiny called from upstairs. "Bring me an iced lemonade!" Tiny already spoke Siamese quite nicely, with a German accent. Cheng understood the child with the golden hair as if she had been speaking Chinese. She would teach Little Missie some Chinese when they were in Hua Hin. The Mem had just sent the message that she was to have the child's dresses washed and ironed by the day after tomorrow. Cheng wouldn't let the Chinese washerwoman do anything so important. She didn't iron well enough for the child with the golden hair. For Cheng no work was too much when it was for her little mistress.

Three days later the children drove with their great-uncle, Nang Siri, and a happy Pauline to their summer villa in Hua Hin. Pauline wouldn't let Tiny out of her sight, whether the Chinese woman liked it or not. Pauline also had ways and means of secretly getting her way. She had learned this from her Asiatic mother. Meanwhile Petersen and Martha flew to Saigon.

4

Saigon—City in a Setting Sun

The cities of the Far East, which are suffering a world-shaking cultural and political transformation in the second half of the twentieth century, impress the European with their image of disunity. The past is not yet dead and the future is being born anew every day with tears, mistakes, and the thunder of cannon. Petersen had experienced the old Saigon shortly before the Indo-chinese War, when it was a city of elegant leisure, magnificent colonial achievements, and tropical charm. During the Japanese occupation, he had been to Saigon twice. A melancholy tropical sun had shone on Marshal Petain's marionette theatre. The city was swarming with General de Gaulle's underground fighters.

Martha had a headache, despite which she looked around her with interest. Saigon was very different from Bangkok. When you were driving along its spacious boulevards with their colonial buildings, it was hard to believe that the wild, triumphant winds of revolution were blowing through this enchanting city. The French sense for order and beauty was present everywhere; it ruled over all government buildings, powerful yet unobtrusive, as prescribed by the traditions of the Seine. The Chamber of Commerce was a triumph of classical good taste, so was the Pasteur Institute, the famous Bank of Indochina, with its branches all over the Far East, the exemplary schools and "gardens for children," the fine restaurants and shops in the Rue Catinat. Yes, Saigon was a world in its own right, but a world on which the sun was setting.

French, Annamese, and elegant Chinese women sat in outdoor cafés, as on Paris boulevards, leisurely sipping their aperitifs. Politics were a man's business. They preferred the gourmet foods and champagne in the shops on the Rue Catinat. The fashions and perfumes from Paris offered further delightful distractions. One laughed, one conversed pleasantly to the accompaniment of distant cannon fire or the sounds on the Mekong River, and the vesper bells of the French cathedral. The colony was on the best of terms with the padres and nuns at the mission where the sick were nursed and children were educated quite apart from economic crises and politics, and God was worshiped with French practicality and Christian zeal. In the little spare time they had, the padres busied themselves with Annamese art and legend. Many a valuable contribution toward the understanding of the country flowed from their pens.

At the hotel, Martha took a shower and stretched out for two hours on their double bed. She didn't like to share a bed with anybody. In a short while Hannes was always lying in the middle and had all the covers. But what could you do here against French customs? In the meantime Hannes went to see two customers and made appointments in Cholon, a suburb of Saigon, where the most important Chinese firms had their offices.

During her sightseeing in Saigon and the Chinese settlement of Cholon, Martha was impressed by four things: the polyclinic; an old beggar woman; a fortune teller in Cholon; and the merchants selling delicacies in the markets of Saigon, the likes of which couldn't be found anywhere else in the world.

In the huge, immaculate polyclinic, Annamese and Chinese mothers crouched as far as the eye could see, faithful and resigned, holding up their sick infants to the doctors standing behind long examining tables. The doctors and the nurses in their white aprons and starched caps had light and dark faces, blue and black eyes. Here France had scored a victory which no propaganda could destroy. French doctors and nurses had instructed Annamese and Eurasians so that now they were able to cope effectively with the diseases of East Asia. Many of these young Asiatics had studied in Paris, and all of them were grateful to the unselfish French assistants who did their duty the year round—not a simple task. The Annamese mother's knowledge of hygiene and the practical care of her baby was unfortunately nil. If a medication didn't help at once, it was discarded. And the babies ate everything that their loving mothers offered them on the market place—dusty sweets, cheap tropical fruit already rotting under its shiny skin.

These market places reminded Martha of the teeming life in Bangkok, only the produce being sold was different. It was clean! And delicious! The sellers ran happily through the streets with their baskets and cried in their monotonous voices: "Snails with coconut!" "Snails with rice perfume!" Tonkinese, their teeth gleaming like enamel, offered little shells of banana leaves that held a soft cake made of flour, lard, onion, and a sharp sauce. The name of the delicacy was *ban beo bac*, and it melted in your mouth. And there were other strange refreshments: herb gelatin that you drank from a cup with sugar water and ice; soya bean milk which a fat old Chinese man kept warm on his little stove.

In Cholon the Chinese were in charge. Cholon was the heart and soul of Indo-china's business life. Here you found rice mills, saw mills, dye factories, tanneries, brick factories—in short, everything that Saigon had to offer in the way of beauty and science. It was a long way from Cholon, with its low huts to the elegance of Saigon with its harbor which the Americans had developed: a saga of

61

Chinese diligence and indomitable energy. There was something indomitable about even the beggars in Cholon, or so it seemed to Martha as she watched an ancient Chinese woman standing in the entrance to a pagoda. She could have been seventy or seven hundred years old, a Chinese "mother of pain." Every line in her wasted face with its sharp, slanting eyes under their drooping lids spoke of self-denial and steadfastness unto death. Her wrinkled hands looked as if they could grasp and hold fast; only her bony feet in their torn sandals seemed powerless and weary from wandering, tired of running and serving.

Under the arcades of a Chinese temple, fortune tellers sat at low tables, selling their words of wisdom to coolie women with long braids. There were beggars here too. They were all ears. A little wisdom that cost nothing had always been a Chinese form of enjoyment. The coolie women in their clean white jackets and black satin trousers listened thoughtfully. A brief look into the future could prevent errors in the present. The legendary Emperor Fu Hsi had practiced the "science" of fortune telling. One of his contributions to Chinese civilization was the mysterious *pakwa*, which formed the basis of the Book of Transformations.

Martha smiled. Their French guide was teaching her quite a few things Hannes didn't know. Hannes was too superficial, like his daughter, Tiny, who right now was probably dipping her dainty little feet into the sea under Pauline's supervision, and with Cheng, who was secretly jealous. Children! They were the fruit of life! With this thought Martha felt at one with the unknown "mother of pain" in Cholon.

On the streets of Saigon the Annamese Festival of Death was in full swing. In front of the native houses stood low tables laden with steaming bowls of rice, soup, cake, fruit, and "spirit money" made of gilded cardboard.

Because now, after the sun had set, the hunger phantoms emerged from hell and went to their families to eat until they were full. Every member of the household knelt in front of these little altars with their flaming, smoking candles, praying for their suffering dead. When the smoking candles were almost burnt down, the Annamese strewed rice to the four winds out of a big bowl. That was the Rice of Mercy, which was paid to the shades, after which the hallowed "spirit money" was burnt and the ashes cast into the Mekong River. Thus it was borne toward the nine yellow sources of the realm of the dead. What was left in the sacrificial bowls was given to the beggars of Saigon who all year long looked forward to the Festival of Death.

The carriage with Martha and Petersen and their guide drove past the big illuminated pagoda where hundreds of the faithful were praying to Buddha to have mercy upon their dead. Here too there were rich, sacrificial gifts, incense, and burning candles. The priest in his yellow robe mumbled prayers for the dead and offered sacrificial gifts to an unknown judge for the liberation of souls.

Martha watched, bewildered. The incense, the kneeling crowd with their dark, resigned faces, and the murmuring of the monks transported her into a condition not unlike a trance. With a tired gesture she pushed some stray hairs behind her ears.

In a café they refreshed themselves with ice cream. Martha's fine face, in such strange contrast to her sturdy body, came to life. "But of course we'll go to the movie, Hannes," she told him. "You were looking foward to it so much." One couldn't deprive him of every toy! He didn't seem to have noticed that Martha's iron nerves had suffered considerably during the war years. He didn't think of things like that, like his daughter...

The big, elegant motion picture house was filled with French men and women, Annamese and Chinese.

They were showing a picture from Paris, a medieval legend: *Les Visiteurs du Soir*. The French liked visionary and illusionary themes with a hidden moral. The Annamese were full of admiration for the priceless costumes of the knights and ladies, while the Chinese were trying to figure out how much a yard of the brocade might cost which the castle maid was throwing so carelessly into a chest. How could anyone handle such treasure with so little respect? The silk merchants in the audience shook their heads—the Europeans remained barbarians!

Nobody could say later exactly when the hand grenade was hurled into the orchestra section. The result was indescribable chaos. Screams, groans, a mad crush to get out. A rebel must have crept into the auditorium. There were wounded and dead. Only the Europeans in the balcony were safe. You couldn't throw a hand grenade upwards without being noticed...

The lights didn't function right away. Somebody said, "Don't try to get out now. Wait till they've cleared the downstairs area. No hurry..."

The Petersens flew back to Bangkok in the dawn. One always tried to travel then because of the heat. Although the airport was only a few miles from the center of the city and therefore still within the French zone, one avoided taking off in the dark of night. Until now the Vietnamese guerrillas had avoided any daylight operations. For how long? A few days ago they had set fire to a rice barge on the Mekong River in the heart of the city. Lately French sentries on the outskirts of Saigon had been shot. How was this going to end? The colonial civil servants who hadn't been in Paris since 1946 didn't realize how exasperated the French at home were over the loss of their men and war material. And not only in France. How long were the western powers going to sacrifice gold and weapons for Indo-china? The munitions factories were employing far too many people who would have been needed for the reconstruction of buildings destroyed by the war, and altogether for the industries of peace. Business suffered in the West and in the Far East.

That was what Petersen was thinking as they flew over jungle and rice fields. As far as business was concerned, the trip had been a disappointment. The Chinese in Cholon wanted to wait until they knew which way the wind was blowing. Nobody could blame them for that.

On the tiny rectangular rice fields far below, women and children were moving like toys—a peaceful picture. Martha closed her eyes behind her new, tinted glasses. The old ones had broken, and she had chosen fashionable frames for the new ones, for lack of any other choice. They made her look years younger. But there were dark shadows under her eyes and she was finding breathing difficult. The heat was already penetrating the plane with its hot breath. "Tired?" asked Petersen.

He asked it out of force of habit and knew the answer. "I'll take you to the seashore where the children are," he went on. "You can stay there for two weeks. Uncle Winn has plenty of room."

Martha nodded. Sometimes Hannes really did show consideration, or was he finding the presence of a wife who was always tired a nuisance? But Petersen had taken her hand and was stroking it. "My poor girl..." Suddenly their roles had changed. An experienced father in the tropics was comforting and encouraging his wife. Astonished, Martha said, "I'd rather have a cigarette."

Rice fields...jungle...rice fields...a deceptive peace lay over the Indo-china landscape. Nowadays the peasants had to be protected by tanks against the guerrillas who wanted their rice. These rice fields could tell stories if they wanted to. Young farmers hid in canal boats so as to escape conscription: the harvest couldn't wait. Or they disguised themselves as women. They all wore the same conical bamboo hats anyway, and the women were as slim as the young men. The peasants lived in constant fear of the Vietminh, of the French who needed so many soldiers for an endless war which was gradually bleeding their land. And there were traitors among them, who sided with the Vietminh. There were sacks of rice that suddenly began to move and turned out to be murderers in ragged uniforms. If one wasn't wearing some sort of uniform or screaming some sort of slogan and delivering certain quantities of rice...for whoever controlled the rice controlled the people. And whoever controlled the people would inherit Indo-china. Martha knew nothing about the rice legends of the East, but she sensed that the calm lying over the endless fields was false.

Bangkok received them with its smiling peace. Siam was truly the Island of the Blessed in a seething East Asia. For how much longer?

5

In the Shadow of the Buddha

Martha and the children had been in Hua Hin by the sea for two weeks now. Uncle Winn's spacious house with its view of an ever-changing mother-of-pearl sea, had been a haven of rest for Martha after the eventful days in Saigon. She swam several times a day with Chubb and Pauline, watched over her suntanned daughter as she waded, and in the evenings talked quietly about pleasant things with Uncle Winn. Surrounded by his giggling and obedient daughters, the head of Petersen and Company spent his holiday in heavenly quietude and simplicity. Nang Siri was in Bangkok on business and spent only the weekends in Hua Hin. She lay in a hammock in the garden for hours, peacefully nibbling Siamese sweets made of coconut and palm tree sugar which Mae Wat, the cook, prepared daily for her mistress. They were served wrapped in banana leaves. The ceramic dish filled with sweets was exceptionally beautiful, and there were always flowers standing on the teak table beside the hammock, but the table was never dusted. When ants fell on a scattered crumb of coconut cream, Nang Siri would knock on the table three times with her delicate, bony finger. That was a sign for the ants to disappear. All the Siamese knocked frequently on their teak tables instead of rubbing down the tops with a chemical fluid and removing the stains and crumbs. Martha was in a constant state of astonishment that Nang

Siri could remain so slim and graceful yet eat so many sweets! Not an ounce of fat marred her waistline, thin as a dancer's, with its heavy belt of Siamese silver circling it. Nang Siri lay dreamily in her garden by the sea, in her long, tight sea green skirt with a white blossom in her shiny black hair. It took Martha a long time to find the shrewd tough business woman behind this exotic vision in the palm garden.

Nang Siri was basking in the extraordinary boom that had overwhelmed the houseowners of Hua Hin with the arrival of the Americans. The main attraction was the beautiful golf course. If one forgot the heat and the natives, one could fancy oneself on one's dear old golf course back in the States. When things got too hot for them in Saigon, the foreigners would rent one of Nang Siri's villas and recover from all the excitement in the so-called Paris of the Orient. Members from the American Embassy in Bangkok also favored Nang Siri's villas in Hua Hin. Siam really still was the Land of Smiles. But the one who smiled most of all was Nang Siri in her hammock. Her bank account grew without her having to do much about it. Only the ridiculous people from the West liked to work for work's sake.

Martha and her son took a fancy to the childishly gay and hospitable fisherfolk who lived a few miles from the resort of Hua Hin and honored the traditional and seasonal worship of Buddha. Fathers and sons frequently visited the village temple during the rainy season to spend three months in the shadow of the great Buddha, the Enlightened One, who one day would lead them to Nirvana, the Buddhist paradise. At the end of the rainy season they returned happily to their huts, devoting themselves again humbly to the sea and fishing, filled with a gentle tolerance toward their fellow men and with consideration for all plants and animals. In this remote East Asian fishing village, people and animals rested during the blazing noonday hours on shadowy verandas or under old trees. Hua Hin did not come to life again until early evening. Then the children rode on the beach on tame ponies; the adults played tennis or golf or went to the fishing village where nets were hung on bamboo poles to dry, and the inner parts of the fish, which had been removed, spread a penetrating odor. In the late evening one went fishing.

One day Martha, Chubb, and Pauline took part in a sailing regatta. Pauline was the translator. She chatted and laughed so uninhibitedly with the fishermen— Martha had never seen her like that with Europeans. Even toward Martha who treated Pauline with so much warmth and frankness, the girl was overly polite and strangely reserved. Her soul seemed overcast by an uncontrollable melancholy when she was dealing with Europeans.

One couldn't talk to Uncle Winn about his favorite daughter. When Martha suggested at the end of her vacation that she would like to take Pauline with her to Hamburg for a year, the old man asked if she had suffered sunstroke while bathing. Pauline was to stay where she belonged—period! But where did she belong? Where would she belong when the old man died? One look at Uncle Winn's face and all advice stuck in Martha's throat. And there was Pauline, talking rapidly in Siamese, and the good-natured fishermen, who presented Nang Siri with the tastiest fish of the seven seas, didn't laugh at her red hair and yellow skin and the slanting black eyes of a maverick Asiatic. For them she was Pauline Nangsao Petersen, daughter of the rich and deeply devout Countess Siri, because Countess Siri was an ardent Buddhist, and like the fisherfolk in their huts, celebrated every feast day and ceremony. Every year she donated new yellow robes to the monks in Hua Hin and Bangkok, and spent hours in silence in front of the altars of the Great Buddha, the Enlightened One.

Nobody knew what went on in the soul of this efficient business woman during these hours, least of all her German husband. In the days of his youth he had looked upon her as an enchanting toy; later her sound business sense and attractive dignity had been a constant pleasure, but he knew the woman who shared his life only superficially by her behavior and apparent reactions. He was "against Buddha" in the same inconsequential way as he was "against Rome." This strong old man, who of his own free will had cut loose from the traditions of his homeland, was wrapped in an isolating layer of spiritual resignation. But there was one thing he had learned from the Asians: he enjoyed the present moment with philosophical indifference, and never let trivial things vex him. Only Martha's suggestion to drag his Pauline into the foggy city on the Elbe had excited him. Nobody was to laugh at his girl or shrug her off. Old Mr. Petersen knew, in spite of forty years spent in the Far East, that some dumb cluck, as he expressed it in his mind, would take cruel pleasure in turning up his nose at Pauline's high-pitched voice, her tall body with its much-too-thin arms and legs, and her Asiatic eyes. And it would wound his girl to the core.

Chubb was very happy in Hua Hin. He had thinned down a bit through the riding. Or was it the heat? Anyway, he was slimmer and more muscular. The fishing at night with Pauline and the Siamese fishermen was the greatest experience he had had in the Far East so far. After the color orgy of the sunsets, one rode out to sea under huge stars. Even an occasional storm didn't frighten the Siamese fishermen. They were wearing consecrated amulets or chains; the Great Buddha protected them. On the following morning, Chubb carefully wrote down the names of all the Siamese fishes he had seen, either caught or swimming free. Later, when he was living in Thailand, they wouldn't laugh as much over his ignorance as they did today.

For old Mr. Petersen it was understood that Chubb would eventually live in Thailand. He had grown very fond of the boy. Martha could stay in Hamburg if she wanted to. Chubb and the little girl, who was growing more amusing every day, would then live with Uncle Winn and Hannes in Bangkok. A good thing that the old man never divulged this charming picture of the future to Martha. The harmony that united the Petersen family in spite of all differences would probably have suffered as the result of such a revelation.

According to Martha, she and the children would stay out the year, as planned. After that the best thing would probably be for Hannes to return with them. He could manage the Hamburg export house any time, together with his cousin Hinrich Petersen. Martha had brought this offer to Bangkok with her as a gift, but it had been received with stony silence by her husband. Like a Siamese, Hannes simply avoided any discussion of a change in his way of life. Discussions were *lambag*— mere tedium and vexation. If only all Europeans would finally realize that, Hannes thought secretly. Aloud he said nothing. Martha was older and wiser. At any rate, she had been in Hamburg. But no evasion could hide the fact that after four months, Martha and Hannes found themselves in the conflict in which so many Europeans in Thailand became involved: life in the Far East or in the West? All the men wanted to send their children home and remain in the Far East as long as political events allowed; most of the women tried to persuade them to let the whole family go home. "Stay where you belong and make an honest living there," Martha had said during the first one-sided debate with her husband. He had shrugged. As if he weren't making an honest living right here in Bangkok! Where *had* Martha learned all her sayings?

For the time being they were still living peacefully in their house in Bangkok, which had by now become a real home for Martha and the children too. They had no home in Hamburg. Even Martha shuddered when she thought of the many trips to the housing bureau and everything else that would have to be attended to when she returned. Did she *have* to go back to Hamburg? All her European and American neighbors sent their children home and stayed in Bangkok, where they still managed somehow to get something out of life in these chaotic times. A gentle law between peoples still ruled in Buddha's shadow. Everybody could think and believe what he pleased. From day to night the sun of tolerance shone over this vast land. It glowed as a symbol of perfection on the marble Bangkok temple Martha visited two weeks after her return from Hua Hin, with Prince Pattani and his wife.

The Prince and Princess appeared in Bangkapi unannounced and in their car, and invited Martha to come with them to see this jewel among the temples of Bangkok. The prince was wearing the customary dress of the Siamese aristocracy: a jacket closed at the neck with jewels, and a silk *phanung*, or trouser-skirt in the color of the day of the week. According to age-old traditions, on Sunday, under the sign of the sun, one wore red. Monday prescribed white or silver; it was the day of the moon. On Tuesday one appeared in bright red brocade; Wednesday, the day of Mercury, demanded green; Thursday, the day of Jupiter, permitted various colors; Friday, silver-blue, and Saturday, the day of Saturn, dark blue. The ladies wore jewelry to match, beginning with rubies on Sunday, and then proceeded to glitter throughout the week with moonstones, coral, emeralds, diamonds, and sapphires.

There were not many Siamese families left who still adhered strictly to the traditional color schemes as did Prince and Princess Pattani. Many had done away with the *phanung* as old-fashioned and dressed like strangers from the West, and the jewels to go with it could frequently be found these days at the pawnbroker's. Even in Siam the times weren't what they used to be under King Chulalongkorn. Siam's aristocracy still appeared only at important ceremonial events in the glory of their brocade and jewels.

The Marble Temple lay close to Dusit Park where Mr. Krüger and his wife lived with their dogs and race horses. With its fabulous, gilded portal gable and multiple roofs of glittering gold-yellow tiles and brightly gilded terminals jutting out and up in the ubiquitous gilded, snake-like curves, it was a glorious example of Siamese temple architecture, the Prince explained in his meticulous German. The Princess said nothing. She didn't speak German and she didn't like to speak English. Why didn't these foreigners learn the language of the land if they wanted to live in Siam? In emerald green with matching jewelry, she gave the *Mem farang* an enigmatic look out of her slanting eyes that glittered like jewels. "*Phut Thai dai mai, Mem?*...Do you speak Siamese, Mem?" she asked softly and capriciously in Siamese.

"*Phut nit noi*...I speak a little," Martha replied, accenting every word correctly.

The Princess smiled. She was delighted. This stranger at least made the effort, even if she had no talent. The atmosphere became so relaxed that the Princess spoke to Martha from then on in fluent English. She wanted to know a lot: Where would Martha go when she left Bangkok? Did she prefer Bangkok to "Hambourg?" Surely she did, no? Did she find Hua Hin a more elegant resort than those found in the West? Surely much, much more elegant. And whether one really and truly killed sick dogs or mosquitoes or snakes in Hamburg, which was not in accord with the laws of Buddha...The Princess used the word "murdered." But the last, important question she had put in Siamese, and the Prince translated in a somewhat milder form.

"The Princess is very anxious to learn. She is interested in everything in Europe," His Highness explained

73

gently, but it had to be evident to even the most naïve European that the Princess' interest was negative. She had been in Paris once with the Prince and had found it a poor edition of Saigon. The Parisians spoke much too vehemently and raced like tigers around the Place de la Concorde. Did they drive that fast in Hamburg, the Princess wanted to know as they arrived at the Gallery of the Buddhas? Prince Pattani gave his wife a look. She smiled and was silent, obedient.

Martha gazed in astonishment at the fifty bronze statues in sitting or standing positions. The Prince explained in his soft voice: they were Buddhas in Cambodian style; their crowns were to remind one of the Indian god, Vishnu. Beside age-old Siamese statues, there were also Burmese and Japanese Buddhas. And then Martha recoiled in front of a ghostly sight: on a richly carved altar, decorated with silver vases, candelabras and flowers, a hollow-eyed, ghostly creature was enthroned. You could count its ribs. "The Great Buddha after his forty days of fasting," whispered Prince Pattani. Then he was silent. He couldn't explain to the stranger the beauty of asceticism; he didn't want to. It was none of her concern.

They had tea beside the Prince's lotus pond. Servants in glittering *phanungs* served something that the Chinese restaurant Swee Hong on New Road sold as "European cakes." The Princess ate the same sweets as Nang Siri. She didn't have to ask the *Mem farang* if the sweets in Hamburg were comparable to those in Siam. No wonder these foreigners so rarely smiled. Who could smile over such dreadful delicacies?

The Prince spoke about Heidelberg and how happy he had felt there. He hadn't been back to Germany since his student days and had a picture of endless ruin, starvation, and typhoid. He didn't know Hamburg. Perhaps he would visit the city on the Elbe from London.

It was six o'clock in the evening. A cool breeze was wafting through the trees and across the ponds in the park. The Prince sat gracefully upright in his wicker chair, gentle but aloof. His hospitality and conviviality were sincere but very formal. His fine, gaunt face with its deep-set black eyes was distinguished and relaxed, and gave the impression of an antique cameo. His robe gleamed in the rays of the setting sun. And it was as still around him as it had been in the Marble Temple with its wide halls and courtyards, where Martha had seen figures in yellow robes slipping by, their eyes downcast— the Brothers of the Yellow Robe.

As a young man, Prince Pattani had spent three years in the Marble Temple. With the weapon of meditation he had fought the five *nivaranas*, the five evil tendencies of the human soul, according to the instruction of Buddha. He had knelt at the prescribed hours on a red carpet in front of the Great Buddha picture in the *bot*, the chapel, until the Darkness of the Spirit had been dispelled. The Foolishness of Close Friendship had fallen away from him. Buddha demanded that one attach oneself to nothing on this earth. One should wander alone, yet help mankind whenever one could. Close contact sullied the soul of the ascetic seeking the truth. A radiance of these teachings surrounded this Siamese prince who was drawing Martha's attention gently to the fact that the lotus was the symbol of purity and contemplation. And to Martha it really seemed as if the white and pink blossoms at her feet were rising up out of the swampy pond with their green jagged leaves and an incredibly powerful luminosity. Buddha, in a condition of enlightenment, had compared the growth of the spirit with the development of the lotus flower from its bud, embedded in the mud, to a full beautiful blossom in the sunlight.

"The lotus position is the position taken when meditating. You saw it today in the sitting Buddhas in the

Marble Temple," said the Prince. Then he was silent.

Martha rose tactfully: the friendly audience had come to an end. With a bow, the Princess had retired long ago to the palace at the rear of the park. In front of a lacquered pavilion sat two beautiful young servants, plaiting small flowers into sweet-smelling garlands. They were singing an old Siamese song softly in monotone.

Complete silence accompanied Martha to the prince's car where a chauffeur in uniform bowed low. The silence was light, yet fraught with secret thoughts and complexities. How much denial lay in it! How much resignation blossomed in the shadow of the Buddha! The people of the West attached themselves—probably in heroic idiocy—to other people, and loved them with a pain that Prince Pattani smiled at. Martha drove home, deep in thought.

The Indian night watchman came to meet her, staggering and gray with fright, and mumbling incomprehensible words. The Siamese and Chinese servants were standing in a circle, screaming, bent over a figure lying on the ground, bleeding profusely. The old cook drew away from the group. "The Master...Missie! Our poor master! Dead...quite dead!"

Johannes Petersen was alive, but he was bleeding from twenty-one wounds. A fairly large rabid dog had jumped at him out of the canal. In his panic, Petersen had tried to push the animal back in. Frothing at the mouth, the dog had attacked Petersen and tried to bite him on the neck. In the end Petersen had choked the crazed animal with his left hand.

He had had to fight for his life alone. No one came from the servants' quarters to help him. All of them knew that a struggle with a rabid dog could cost you your life. Even if the dog didn't kill his victim, he could infect him with rabies, which was even worse. If the dog wasn't found and examined, which happened frequently, one couldn't even know if there was a danger of rabies.

Martha didn't waste any time looking at her unconscious husband. She didn't utter a sound of lamentation. She gave her orders with such firmness that the servants obeyed at once. Then she wrote a hasty note to Professor Berger and sent the laundress to him. He would know what to do. The chauffeur had to be wakened first. He was sleeping off a hangover under his favorite palm tree. The children were at the sports club. Thank God! thought Martha.

Petersen had regained consciousness. He whispered, stupefied, "Martha...where am I?"

Martha and Ah Chang had bedded him carefully on a mattress on the veranda. She hadn't dared to have the bleeding man carried upstairs. The old cook had been a real support, once he had recovered from the shock.

At last a car came driving up the broad driveway. A sigh of relief escaped Martha when she saw Professor Berger. He had arranged everything like a general whose services had been needed at last. Dr. Johannsen and a dainty little Siamese, Dr. Charoon from the Bangkok Pasteur Institute, were with him. She was to give Petersen the injection with the serum against rabies immediately. At this time of the evening the Institute was closed, but the little lady doctor always had the capsules against snake bite, rabies and smallpox in her villa, where she resided with her aunt, an old court lady. Dr. Charoon was learning German from Professor Berger because she intended to take a course in bacteriology at the University of Vienna.

Dr. Johannsen disseminated a calm he by no means felt. This was a bad thing that had happened to his friend Petersen. It was not to be expected that the stray dog had been inoculated with antirabies serum. Packs of such dogs were running around Bangkok, death in their jaws, allowed to live by a population who even in the case of rabid dogs took too literally the command of the Buddha to kill no living thing. The Siamese government had of course taken certain measures that were intended to render these mad dogs harmless, but in the shadow of the Great Buddha they were only obeyed halfheartedly. Perhaps if you killed such a mad dog, you would be such a creature yourself in your next life. "Don't worry, we'll fix him up, Frau Martha," mumbled Dr. Johannsen.

If Martha hadn't been so benumbed by the catastrophe, she would have heard the false assurance in her friend's voice. Fortunately she didn't know what Dr. Johannsen and the Siamese doctor knew: the daily injections with the serum were *not* a hundred percent reliable, because one was only building up immunity in the body *after* the dog bite. It was a subsequential prophylactic measure, a ghostly race with the poison that was trying to work its way through to Petersen's brain. One could count on an incubation period of at least two weeks, yet one had also to reckon with a waiting period of months during which the disease might break out. That was the worst thing about it, because the person forgot the danger when it remained dormant for some time. On the other hand, the patient on whom the serum was ineffective died within five days. Dr. Johannsen had had a case like that in Chulalongkorn Hospital. He didn't like to think of it now. The patient, a ship's officer, had been bitten by a small dog on his arrival in Bangkok, but had had the injections given to him only three weeks later. When he began to itch and ran a temperature and was hoarse, he had gone to Dr. Johannsen, smiling, unsuspecting...doomed. On the third day he had been so hoarse he couldn't speak, and complained of unbearable headaches. He couldn't drink because swallowing induced cramps. The end had been a nightmare with the last gruesome manifestation of the illness: paralysis resulted five days later in death. A blessing.

That was what Dr. Johannsen was thinking as he gave Petersen, who was looking around, half-conscious, a tetanus injection. Then the two doctors washed the wounds and bandaged them. Dr. Charoon gave Petersen the first rabies injection. She was skillful and meticulous about it. "Tomorrow we must give him the strongest injections," she murmured, looking at Martha compassionately.

Dr. Charoon spoke fluent English. She had studied in Cambridge and she loved England, but her place was in her own land with its many suffering people whose greatest misfortune was their ignorance, lassitude, and superstition. Dr. Charoon not only combated illness; she also fought against the "spirits" of the air, the water, and the rice fields, who interfered decisively in the existence of the farmers and fishermen of Southeast Asia. Every homeowner should have his dog inoculated for rabies, but how many did so? And one had no protection against these four-legged murderers from the canal, who crept into houses through openings in hedges and garden fences and attacked humans and animals.

"Martha!" Petersen sounded miserable. "I feel awful."

Martha laid her hand on his forehead. He lay there, eyes closed, white from loss of blood, and spoke in a strange, reedy voice. "Uncle Winn...I won't be able to...tomorrow..."

His voice died away in a murmur. It had shot through his mind suddenly that he couldn't go to the office tomorrow. "Shh, Hannes," said Martha, her voice choking. She had taken off her glasses because the tears were blinding her.

Petersen opened his eyes. "Don't cry." He spoke with great effort. "I...I'm not worth it..."

Dr. Johannsen gave him an injection, something for

sleeping; the rest was easy. He took Petersen to Chula-long Hospital in his car. Martha was to stay in the hospital with Petersen for the next few weeks. Dr. Johannsen realized that any plea that she stay home would be in vain.

Professor Berger promised to take the children for a while and keep them busy. Idle children were an even greater problem in the tropics than at home. Ah Chang swore that nobody had to be brought in to watch over things; he and his daughter "with the golden voice" were perfectly capable of looking after everything. It wouldn't be the first time that thieves had fled at the sound of Cheng's voice. And the old cook would drum it into the Indian night watchman that he should attend to his duties properly.

In Chulalong Hospital, which was situated near the sports club, a room had been readied hastily for Nai Petersen, with a couch and mosquito net for Martha. Dr. Johannsen wanted to stay with Petersen at least until midnight; after that he could be reached at home by phone. The young Siamese intern and the night nurse promised to do everything they could for the sick *khon farang.* The doctor had taken one look at Petersen's numerous bandages and murmured, "*Mai di naak . . .* very very bad," but Dr. Johannsen had given him a warning look. The German lady didn't know very much about the illness, he whispered in Siamese. The *farang* was her husband. They had two charming children. Both Siamese nodded. They understood. Their gentle hearts trembled with compassion for the pale, stunned woman with the tears running down her cheeks. Martha rarely cried. Was it centuries ago that she had sat beside the lotus pond and drunk tea with Prince Pattani? The transition from lyrical beauty to a reality like this had come too suddenly. Everything in Thailand happened in the shadow of the Buddha: a meditative life filled with dignity and loveliness, and then the threat of creatures who hadn't been rendered harmless in time.

Dr. Johannsen was called to the phone. Dr. Charoon told him the dog had been found. The autopsy revealed that it was rabid. She was sorry...

"A patient," said Dr. Johannsen as he came back to Martha. "He wanted to know if he should continue with a certain medication..." Dr. Johannsen's voice was hoarse. He must be tired, thought Martha. How wonderful it must be to call a doctor only because of some pills...Hannes had always been such a strong patient, too.

She looked at her husband. All she could see was bandages. His blond hair hung damply over his boyish forehead. "Dear God," Martha prayed. "Help us!"

"Water!" Petersen whispered.

Dr. Johannsen was at his bedside at once. "Drink, Hannes! Try to swallow!"

The fruit juice in the drinking cup ran down Petersen's bandaged neck. He was too weak to say 'dammit!' Martha had dried her eyes. "Don't worry about it, Dr. Johannsen," she said. "Hannes is always awkward with drinking cups." She leaned over her husband with the refilled cup. He was breathing hard. "Come on, my boy," she said, with a trace of her former energy.

Petersen drank all the juice. Dr. Johannsen was looking at him thoughtfully. Somehow he had to prepare Martha for possible complications. "Listen to me, Frau Martha," he said finally. "During the next two days Hannes is going to be given the strongest injections. We hope all will go well..."

"Then is the danger over?" Martha asked.

"Dear Frau Martha," Dr. Johannsen said quietly. "You are a sensible woman. There is no point in keeping the truth from you."

Martha stared at the doctor.

"In most cases," Dr. Johannsen went on, "these injections prevent an outbreak of the illness, but we can only be absolutely sure in six months."

"Six months," Martha stammered. "But...but that is..."

Words failed her, then she pulled herself together. As during the bombing nights in Hamburg, everything rested on her shoulders again. She must nurse Hannes as if no Damoclean sword was hanging over them. And she had to summon all her strength and courage. If the children lost their father...but that was something she didn't want to think of.

"It's very hard on you, dear friend," Dr. Johannsen said gently, "but you know, my grandmother in Bremen used to say, 'Nobody is given a bigger load by the dear Lord than he can bear.' She was a wise old lady, and she knew all about life."

Martha looked gratefully at the man who spoke with a voice that reminded her of home.

Dr. Charoon gave Petersen his injections daily. She also took a special flower and candle sacrifice to the Great Buddha in the *bot* of the Marble Temple for the family who seemed to be so fond of her Viennese friend. Every day she smiled a little more. Nai Petersen was young and strong. In the weeks that followed he showed no symptoms of the illness.

Prince Pattani sent a small Buddha statue from the Ayudhia period. The figure was sitting in the prescribed position on a lotus throne. In a note accompanying the gift he expressed his deepest sympathy over the accident that had befallen his honored friend. The Princess sent a silver basket of sweets "to render a little happiness." When the children were allowed to visit Petersen at the hospital for the first time, he was already well enough to tell Chubb to stand up straight. Tiny was given the sweets from Princess Pattani. She ate so many of them that they didn't render her "a little happiness."

Petersen seemed to have recovered and Martha was filled with hope. But nobody could say for sure that the danger was over. The same fear and uncertainty remained rooted in Martha's heart that had overwhelmed her like the attack of a mad dog during the first night after the accident.

6

Masks and Faces

"Hello, girls!"

The voice was addressing the Misses Black and Macpherson, who had been bored to death in their small American town, and in the Far East had become such important persons overnight that they didn't want to go home again. Letitia Black was a tall, thin journalist with colorless hair and colorless eyes, and a colorless passion for law and order which her Puritan forefathers had bequeathed upon her as well as a considerable income. Jane Macpherson was a photographer from the same small town in New England, and she had nothing but her photography and a yearning for marriage. But she had never received a proposal. She startled every male with her enthusiasm at finding herself in the company of a man. She had just turned thirty and resented it.

The "girls" were breakfasting, just as they did in the States, at 7:30 A.M.—not earlier, not later. Lawrence Desmond had startled them with his robust greeting. Jane Macpherson leapt to her feet, knocking over the cream jug. How sweet of Mr. Desmond to visit them! Desmond was startled too. Jane Macpherson was always knocking something over.

He was nervous. His job at ECAFE—the Economic Commission for Asia and the Far East—was tiring. This heat! And in his private life things weren't in order either. He didn't want to go back to New Orleans. The

Far East had him in its clutches, as it did old Petersen, with whose daughter, a redhead, he had ridden horseback on the beach at Hua Hin.

"What would you say if I stayed in Bangkok? I mean, after my contract with ECAFE is finished?" Lawrence Desmond asked his two friends from New England.

Jane Macpherson stared at him, wide-eyed, speechless. Letitia Black said drily, "You're crazy. What would you do here?"

"Business," said Lawrence Desmond. "There are a couple of fellows here who do great business with the Philippines. Export-import. I had a look around while I was there with the boss. Manila cigars, volatile oils, copal, hemp...export to the States could be increased. I've been studying the market. Besides, right now we can import tax-free. The European countries can't do that. If only I had money to invest. Couldn't you loan me a few thousand dollars, Letty?"

"No," said Miss Black.

"Too bad," Lawrence Desmond said casually. "I thought you were a good business woman. But I forgot, you're Scottish."

"Thank God!" Letty Black said complacently.

"By the way, have you heard anything about the case of rabies?" asked Jane Macpherson, who had never stopped eating.

"A wild story," said Lawrence Desmond from New Orleans. "I know both Petersens. The old man's been living here since the beginning of time. Met him quite by chance at the sports club. Riding. Rides like a berserk cowboy, in spite of his age. He gave me some very good advice about Siamese industry and agriculture. For free, Letty. What do you say to that?"

Miss Black's smile was condescending. "Why don't you ask old Mr. Petersen about the rabid dog incident?"

"I can ask his daughter," said Desmond, strangely absentminded suddenly.

"Which daughter, for heaven's sake?"

"Pauline Petersen. The daughter of the old man. She came to Bangkok for the weekend. I met her at the sports club." Desmond mopped his brow. He didn't respond to Jane Macpherson's smile. His handsome dark face with its scar over the right temple was a mask behind which he hid his thoughts. Why was Jane smiling at him? When the Philippine girls smiled, they looked entrancing, and Pauline Petersen smiled a little secretively, if rarely. When Jane smiled she looked silly. Why didn't she wear a mask like the Asiatics?

"I'll do my best to find out about the rabid dog incident for you," he told the tall, thin journalist. He wanted to please Letty Black because he wanted to stay in the East. But without money that wasn't possible. "Would you like me to introduce you to Dr. Charoon? She works in the Pasteur Institute, and I know her very well. She wants to take a course in Vienna. I told her she'd do better in the States. We have all the new methods and the old scientists from Europe."

"And the money," Letty Black said caustically.

"You don't miss a trick, do you?" said Lawrence Desmond, and rose. He would invite Pauline Petersen to have supper with him at the bar-restaurant on New Road. That way Letty Black would get her rabid dog story and Lawrence Desmond, perhaps, an enigmatic smile.

Petersen's encounter with the rabid dog was still the chief topic of conversation in Bangkok. Visitors poured into Bangkapi. Letty Black and Jane Macpherson turned up with Lawrence Desmond. While Martha ordered refreshments, Jane surreptitiously took a picture of the orchid greenhouse. Quite by chance, Mr. Petersen was in the picture too. It was a little blurred, but still one could recognize a European in Chinese trousers lying on a bamboo chaise longue. Jane didn't make much of an impression on Martha because she declared that they simply had to get Tiny to Hollywood. She had the makings of a child star! Much prettier than Shirley Temple at her age! Martha froze. She at once sent Cheng and Tiny to another part of the garden. Hollywood! That was all the child needed! But Hannes' laugh sounded enthusiastic. "You never can tell," he said. He was very proud of his little daughter with her lovely blond hair, elegant posture, and a smile that won all East Asian hearts. But the strangest visitor of all had turned up the week before.

Hannes had wanted to go to the office, but Uncle Winn, who had come to Bangkok from Hua Hin to initiate a business deal, had begged his nephew to spend one more week recuperating at home. Things were running along nicely without him, although Hannes would not want to recognize that. Finally Uncle Winn had said that after all he had managed somehow to run the firm of Petersen and Company until the year 1939 without his nephew from Hamburg. Hannes had coughed and swallowed another week of vacation. Afterwards he had mumbled that Uncle Winn was a stubborn old man. He, Hannes, had established all the branches in East Asia, hadn't he? Martha had calmed him: Uncle Winn meant well.

When the rickshaw drove into Petersen's garden with the surprising visitor, Martha wiped her glasses. She couldn't be seeing straight! It couldn't possibly be...

Miss Karin Holm, carrying a bouquet of orchids and a small package wrapped in gold paper, was walking gracefully toward the Petersens on their veranda, which was overgrown with blue blossoms. The package was for Petersen, the orchids were for Martha. Karin Holm's smile was ethereal.

"I was so—oo unhappy to hear that Mr. Petersen had been so ill," she said in her singsong English as she handed Martha the orchids, which she had intended to send over after the arrival scene. Four months or eight didn't make much difference in Siam.

Martha said, "Thank you very much."

"Thanks," mumbled Petersen, unwrapping the gold paper.

There was a moment of absolute silence among the three people on the veranda, as if the whole world had suddenly grown still. Miss Karin was much more beautiful than Petersen remembered. She was wearing a dress of gossamer Indian material which revealed her beautiful figure rather than dressed it. Her face, framed by her blond hair, was an almond blossom. She looked more fragile than she had looked months ago. There was a triumphant gleam in her eyes but Petersen couldn't see it; Miss Karin kept her eyes downcast. "A little present from my mother, with her best wishes," she said, as Petersen let the gold paper fall to the floor.

Not a word of admiration, although Petersen had an eye for beauty. The old Javanese woman, who sat cross-legged on her mat, humbly, silently, and was afraid of her blond, passionate daughter, was a first-rate craftsman. Only she didn't know it. There were so many men and women where she came from who could create worldly images with their fingers and didn't think anything of it.

Miss Karin's mother had carved a Javanese dancer and dressed her in classic brocade. The tiny figurine, with its delicately painted face, was wearing a red and green patterned brocade sarong wound tightly around her wooden body. A green, gold, and red sash flowed down over the wooden base; wide, red-gold brocade sleeves, gathered at the wrist, fell from her narrow shoulders. In her left hand she held a silver fan and her headdress was composed of tiny seed pearls and gold thread. The old Javanese woman must have spent days on the headdress alone! The dancer's head showed its curved eyebrows, flared nostrils that seemed to be quivering, and half-open mouth with curvaceous lips that surely would have been humming an age-old melody if the figure had been alive...

The figure *was* alive!

Miss Karin had danced in the same costume on this very veranda a week before Martha's arrival. Only the jasmine garland was missing. Miss Karin had dropped it at Martha's feet. "How lovely!" said Martha. "This is awfully nice of you. Please thank your mother for us."

Martha was really moved. These Asiatics forgot so quickly what they had done to one in their thoughtlessness. And then they brought presents like this! Such rare orchids! They must have cost a fortune! They were bedded in moss in a little basket of plaited silver. The roots were intact. The gardener could plant them. Still Petersen said nothing.

"I'd like to give the gardener the orchids right away," Martha said, and called "*Khon suan!*" But *khon suan* didn't come. He was drinking iced coffee in a Chinese shop on the canal. Martha leaned over the veranda railing. Mu and Nu, the chauffeur's children, were nowhere to be seen either. What was visible was old Mr. Petersen's car, driving full speed ahead through the gate.

"Excuse me for a minute," said Martha. Never had Uncle Winn been so welcome! She had absolutely no idea what to talk about with Miss Karin. They had only one theme in common: Johannes Petersen.

"Uncle Winn!" Martha cried. "You're just in time for tea!"

The old man got out of his car laboriously. His eyes, blue as the sea, were veiled like the North Sea in the rain. His high forehead was streaked with wrinkles. Under his suntan he was pale. In spite of the tropical heat, his hand was cold. "Uncle Winn!" Martha cried, shocked. "Don't you feel well?"

"I have to speak to you alone, Martha. Right away!" said Petersen senior.

"We'll go to the back veranda." From there you could see the *lampu* tree which Petersen senior loved, and the canal with coal freighters and fruit sampans gliding across it from morning to night. Yes, they would have tea there.

"Excuse me for a minute!" Martha called out to the veranda with the blue blossoms and the two Javanese dancers. "Uncle Winn wants to speak to me."

"Don't you want to have tea here?" Petersen asked, his voice pleading.

"Later, later," Martha called out, smiling.

"Don't you want to thank me for my little present, Johnny?" Miss Karin asked, pouting. "You've become very impolite since you've been married."

"Thanks," Petersen said again, in a voice that was dead. He had put the devilish present down on the small teak table beside his chaise longue. "A charming idea."

Irony was lost on Miss Karin—or was it? "You just don't know how charming I am and how much I love you," she said, in a conversational tone. "When is your wife going home? She's been in Bangkok for ages!"

"Please leave my wife out of this," Petersen said, louder than was called for. "Mrs. Petersen is staying in Bangkok."

"How nice for you! Or you'd be very very lonesome, wouldn't you, Johnny dear? By the way, I'm engaged."

"Congratulations," said Petersen. "May I ask when the wedding is to take place?"

In the past Miss Karin had told him so often that she was engaged it was hard to believe her. She had wanted to catch him with it, but Petersen was an old experienced hunter: he did the catching.

"This time it's really true," Miss Karin said naïvely.

Petersen looked her full in the face for the first time. It would be a very fortunate thing for her. "Who is

it?" he asked, his voice friendlier. He had never known a
bride who gave such curious presents.

"You don't know him." Miss Karin looked at her
darling Nai Petersen with her almond-shaped eyes.
"He's a bore. Swedish matches. But rich. And as much in
love as you were once. Tell me, Johnny, do you still find
me a little little bit beautiful?"

"You are ravishing, and you know it, you...you
witch!" said Petersen. Suddenly he was feeling quite
cheerful and reverted to the tone of the Bangkok bachelors. He pointed to the figurine. "This lady is less talkative than you; otherwise you're both perfect."

Miss Karin giggled. When she was married, Johnny
would come to his senses. Mr. Liljefors drank. But he
was a white man. Unfortunately, a fat white man. The
wedding would take place in the Oriental Hotel, a
"white" wedding. Miss Karin's mother would just happen to be away, otherwise it wouldn't do at all in front of
the whole Swedish colony. "Johnny," Miss Karin said,
languishing, "give me an engagement kiss." She came
very close.

Petersen jumped up, throwing off the cover Martha
had laid across his knees. "Good evening," he said
harshly. "*Pai reu reu!*"

How could he have said anything like that? It was
the sort of thing one told the rickshaw coolies: Go
quickly! Go! One didn't say anything like that to a European, not even to a half-caste.

Miss Karin had turned pale under her makeup.
Such humiliation! The white men stepped all over her.
And she had just given Petersen a valuable present
which she could have sold for many dollars. Did he say
pai reu reu to his daughter? Miss Karin was filled with
uncontrollable hatred, hatred of Petersen, of Martha
who had stolen him from her, of the child too, with her
golden hair and blossom-white skin, who possessed

Johnny's false heart! Miss Karin had watched Petersen with Tiny in Lumbini Park. Her heart had shriveled. In her way she had loved Petersen. Not an ounce of fat and only five gray hairs...

"I'm going," she said politely, her face a motionless mask.

"Forgive me, Karin," Petersen said, feeling very embarrassed. "I...I'm nervous."

"What am I supposed to forgive?" Miss Karin asked innocently. "Sick people are always nervous, especially when the poison of a mad dog rests in their brains."

Petersen shuddered. For a moment the mask had slipped from Miss Karin's almond blossom face and he was shocked by the hatred in her eyes. But the best thing was to ring down the curtain on the whole business.

Number One Grandson appeared with tea. He cast a disapproving look at his master's visitor: a Eurasian! What did she want from his master? And Number One Grandson was supposed to wait on her!

"Please stay for tea!" Petersen tried to smile.

"Thank you." Miss Karin walked, gracefully and controlled, into the room that led from the veranda to the gate. "My rickshaw is waiting."

"I'll have you driven home in my car!" Petersen said helplessly. He called, "Khon rot! *Ma reu reu!* Come quickly!"

"*Pai reu reu,*" said Miss Karin, an enigmatic smile on her lips as she got into the rickshaw.

"Karin...please!" Petersen was feeling damned uncomfortable. But the rickshaw had already driven through the gate.

He walked slowly back to the veranda. His head was throbbing fit to burst! He picked up the figurine that an unknown Javanese woman had carved and decorated for weeks. The face, like a mask, seemed to be smiling at him; the parted lips were saying "*Pai reu reu...*"

He must have been holding the figurine too tightly. Suddenly he was holding nothing but splintered wood and tattered brocade in his hand. A cool breeze had sprung up. Peteresen shivered. He felt ill, exhausted, and filled with a dark fear. That was what came of it! As an Indian client had once expressed it, "Throwing rubies away to find glass..." *Where* was Martha? And Uncle Winn?

Oldest Grandson poured tea and served sandwiches which Ah Chang had prepared lovingly with baked liver and bacon. Petersen's favorite sandwiches. Besides, liver would restore Master's lost blood. And now Master didn't touch the hot delicacies but stared straight ahead as if he had seen a ghost. "Take it away!" he said. Did he mean the sandwiches or the broken figurine?

Number Two Grandson silently put both on the tray and withdrew discreetly. "Think twice and say nothing," his grandfather advised him whenever he was in doubt about anything. And grandfather was always right because he was old, wise, and had a beard that ran out into a thin, fine point, like a true scholar's. This beard was Number Two Grandson's ideal. Some day he would have a long, thin, pointed beard like it, and be old and honored. The days and months flew by like a weaver's shuttle. That's what Grandfather always told Mother Cheng when she groaned over how slowly the time passed until she would have saved enough for the education of her sons. Number Two Grandson smiled. Time flew like an arrow!

On the back veranda, time hadn't flown. Time was no arrow and no weaver's shuttle. Time was a stone, lying dead in the river bed.

"You're sure?" Martha asked a second time. "There's no possibility of a mistake?"

"None," said old Mr. Petersen. "Dr. Johannsen has examined Pauline thoroughly. Last week she went to

Hamburg again...I mean Bangkok," he corrected himself. "Pauline doesn't tell me anything."

Martha said nothing. She looked at the canal where the water was flowing silently. The old man had spoken very softly. The suffering in his voice made Martha's heart ache. "Uncle Winn," she said gently, without looking at him. "Pauline is devoted to you. You know that. I guess she...she wanted to spare you the shock."

"She is in her third month," Petersen said, his voice dead.

Martha nodded. If Pauline was in her third month, one would have to find her lover and tell him. "Who is it?" she asked. "Do you know who..."

"I don't know," said the old man. "Pauline doesn't tell me anything." He rose. "What should I do, Martha? You are our wise one." He was trying desperately to make light of it.

"Mother Saint Patrick," Martha said. "You told me that she brought Pauline to her senses once before this."

"I went to Mater Dei this morning. Unfortunately, Mother Saint Patrick is in Ireland right now. She needed a change of climate. She might have..."

"Where is Pauline?"

"In Hua Hin with her mother," old Petersen said angrily. "Where she belongs, damn it all! I told Siri to stop selling houses now and look after her daughter... which is the proper thing to do in a decent family!"

"Quite right." Martha said in an effort to calm him, although she didn't think it was all right at all. Nang Siri had never been a source of support for Pauline.

"Can't you visit them again?" old Petersen said suddenly. "I have to go to the west coast next week on business. Hannes is all right now. I'll take your boy with me. I promised him I would. Perhaps Pauline will be happy to see you."

He hoped of course that Martha would get the stubborn girl to talk. He sensed instinctively the strength and sympathy his niece radiated. Hannes, the dog, had been damned lucky!

"I'll be glad to, Uncle Winn," Martha said. "I was just going to suggest it to you. I'll take Charlotte with me. Pauline is so fond of her."

"Thank you," old Petersen murmured. "Well, say hello to Hannes for me."

There was a slight pause. Uncle Winn was standing beside his car, but he wasn't getting in. He was staring at the palmyra tree under which Hannes' chauffeur liked to doze with his two sons whenever he was needed. "Listen," he said at last, without looking at Martha, "my Pauline is a damned decent girl. Respectable and...and clean. It can happen to the best girls, Martha."

Martha pressed the man's cold hand. "I know," she said. "I know, Uncle Winn. We'll get the thing straightened out. You'll see."

She wasn't at all sure of it, but it was impossible to let Uncle Winn go like that. She had always encouraged her girls in Hamburg right up to their final exams. And perhaps everything would still turn out all right.

"If I find the fellow, I'll break every bone in his body," said old Petersen as he got into his big car.

Martha shook her head. That wouldn't help Pauline. But one would have to find the fellow. Uncle Winn was right about that.

"Could it be our new young man?" the old man wondered, brooding. "I had him with us for a month in Hua Hin. He played tennis with Pauline and really taught her how to play. I mean young Harms from Harms and Company. Very respectable family. Big villa in Flottbeck. Tommy makes a very decent impression. Of course the climate is bothering him some. What do you think?"

Martha knew young Harms casually. Naturally, one never knew...One never knew anything about Pauline.

7

The Tin Island

After rice, tin was Siam's most important export.
Petersen senior and old Charles Krüger often sat on the
veranda after dinner talking about East Asian tin. Both
gentlemen had invested in the metal on Nang Siri's
advice. It had turned out to be excellent advice. Petersen
and Company and Charles Krüger had made a fortune.

After the war, a big demand in machinery for
Siam's tin mines had developed, but Germany wasn't
included. The English were the historic exporters of
mining machinery to Siam and Malaya. The United
States had come in on it. And the Danish East Asiatic
Company, which owned vast concessions for tin on the
island of Phuket, also delivered what the foreign firms
required. But then there were the Chinese. They had
been the first to mine tin on Phuket. Tin vessels had
been used in China for thousands of years.

Hannes Petersen had grasped all this and already
during the Indo-chinese War had formulated a plan to
introduce dredgers from Hamburg. Petersen senior had
laughed. "Get that out of your head, boy! The Danes and
the English have a monopoly on tin. The Danes are still
here and the English will be back. We Hamburgers can't
compete with them. In East Asia nothing changes."

Sticking out his chin just as stubbornly as his uncle,
Petersen junior didn't agree. "When the war's over, I'm
going to get in touch with Hinrich."

Hinrich Petersen in Hamburg was the cousin who had told Martha that Hannes could come back to the home firm any time he wanted to. Petersen and Company in Hamburg were, among other things, agents for machine export. They had been quite important in this respect until Hitler had reduced foreign exports and the port of Hamburg to such an extent that one had to take on minor commissions inland just to break even. At the time they had been doing business with Thailand, then, as in 1950, a land with a positive trade balance. Yes, Hinrich wrote to his cousin in Bangkok, they could start with dredgers, in a small way. Things were coming along in Hamburg.

After various conversations with old Mr. Wong, Hannes had actually taken an exploratory trip to Phuket Island. The Chinese weren't working only as coolies there. All over the Far East there were wealthy Chinese entrepreneurs. Hannes Petersen had discussed the philosophy of Lao-tse and the practicality of machinery in their offices, to which old Mr. Wong had recommended him with a flowery letter.

Mr. Wong's friends had smiled politely and wished Petersen junior luck with his western inventions. But such things had to be considered carefully. Machines broke down more easily than coolies, and they didn't smoke opium either. The Siamese government, which didn't regard the Chinese firms favorably anyway, wouldn't like that. They were making money as it was, if a little more slowly.

"When will your nephew be going to Phuket?" Krüger asked. He had been very interested in Petersen junior's moral victory. The Chinese only liked to buy from old friends or from people recommended by old friends.

"*I'm* going," said Petersen senior. "My nephew has had a little bout of fever. Too many visitors, I presume."

Naturally Hannes had nothing on his mind except

Martha and the children, but Miss Karin's visit had unnerved him. He was extremely sensitive since the dog had bitten him; the injections had enervated him too. So he only went to the office for a few hours every day; travel was out of the question. Business with East Siam could wait, but one of them had to go to Phuket. The Chinese lost face when they were kept waiting too long, and they were the best clients in the Far East because they were also the best salesmen. Business with the Siamese government was much more difficult. The Siamese were aristocrats or farmers. There was no middle class buying and selling internationally.

"So when will you go?" Charles Krüger asked a second time. What was the matter with Christian? He was downright absentminded.

"Next week," he said at last, gulping down his fourth whiskey and soda. It didn't taste right today. Twilight, the most beautiful hour in Bangkok, was falling across the club's wide expanse of lawn. The sun had turned into a ruby bowl wavering between clouds on the horizon. Wilhelm Christian Petersen didn't want to go home to his disorderly house in Rong Muang. He couldn't think of anything but his girl there...

"Is Pauline going with you?" Charles Krüger asked. Pauline accompanied her father on all his travels, as secretary and companion.

"I'm taking our boy with us." "Our boy" was Chubb.

"I like the boy," said Krüger.

"I should say so!" Chubb's grand-uncle growled. "That boy can hear the grass growing! It can only be to his advantage to see a tin mine in Siam. He wants to live here later as an engineer."

"Well, well!" Charles Krüger was astonished. "He's only fifteen, isn't he?"

"Fourteen and a half," said Petersen, who hated inaccuracy in business or in private life. So much depended on precise calculation. "I knew what I wanted when I was his age," he said belligerently.

"And what was that, Christian?"

"Not to stay in Hamburg!" said Petersen senior. "I mean, I wanted to feel a fresh wind blowing through my hair. Of course I didn't know that...that I was going to stay away longer than they'd expected at home..." Krüger nodded. At home they always thought that the sons were coming back.

Three young Americans were walking across the golf course, a tall man with black hair and two women. "Who are they?" Charles Krüger asked. "They're not English."

"Americans. A Mr. Desmond from ECAFE. Pauline rode with him in Hua Hin. So did I. A great rider, even though he slouches when he walks. I don't know the ladies. New ones keep coming all the time."

"Unfortunately. They ruin our prices. Rents have gone sky-high since 1945. By the way, your Pauline came to see us last Sunday when she was in Bangkok to get mail from Hannes or something like that," Charles Krüger said, without any transition.

"What did she want?" Old Petersen's heart began to beat irregularly and the light veil crept over his eyes.

"Nothing, really. She wanted to see the dogs and horses again. And of course my wife. Your girl can ride, Christian! She can ride Alsternixe without a saddle! She wanted to break her in. Mama says I should ask you first. Alsternixe is capricious."

Nothing moved in Petersen's face. Had the girl gone crazy? To ride *now*? Or...

"I say, Christian...my wife said to tell you Pauline should see Dr. Johannsen."

"Why?"

"She fainted while she was with us. I wasn't to tell you. It was beastly hot Sunday. Pauline has the constitution of a horse, still—it scared Mama."

"I'll send her to Dr. Johannsen. Anybody can faint."

"I must say, you're giving Johannsen plenty of business," Charles Krüger laughed.

Petersen was silent. Then he said suddenly, "Charles" ...and paused.

"Did you say something Christian?" Krüger was lighting a cigar. "What is it?"

"Nothing." Petersen got slowly out of his wicker chair. "Well, then, *tschüss!* Remember me to your wife."

"*Tschüss*, Christian," said Charles Krüger.

Old Petersen walked slowly past the softly lighted swimming pool to the garages where the Siamese, Chinese, and Malayan chauffeurs were crouched in a circle, gambling, or talking and laughing. Happy people. As he watched them the old man was overcome by a dreadful loneliness. Lately he had spent more time than ever with his family and Hamburg friends as if their solidarity and cordial reserve offered support now, when things were falling apart. There was no point in reproaching Nang Siri. It had pleased Petersen for so many years that she did not come from Hamburg, but when there was trouble...it was a strange thing about Asiatic women: they fled from a serious face.

Nang Siri simply couldn't understand her husband. Birth was something as natural as the sowing and growing of rice until the harvest. Pauline was twenty-five years old. It was high time that she lived the life of a woman. The conventions of the West made Nang Siri smile. Last week she had given Pauline a house in Hua Him, a small villa, a gem behind bougainvillea blossoms and mango trees. Pauline and *luk chai*, her son, would live there prosperously and peacefully. She had already engaged an *amah* from a rice village in the Menam plain. And after having thus done her share, she had got into her red motorcar and gone about her business in city and country. She would come back when everybody in Hua Hin was happy again.

Old Petersen sighed. "*Khon rot!*" he cried, in his stentorian voice.

His chauffeur, in his white uniform, reluctantly left the circle of gamblers and started the car. The big Indian

100

at the gate opened it and greeted Wilhelm Christian Petersen, who drove back to his empty house in Rong Muang.

They were sailing along the west coast of Siam. Chubb was standing with his grand-uncle at the railing of the freighter of the Thai Navigation Company, a-mazed. From one day to the next they had moved into another world, unlike anything to be found in Bangkok. Mountains rose up out of the sea and changed their color all day long. Valleys appeared, peaceful and un-touched, a strip of golden sand was wreathed by ever-green rain forests, some of which had never been penetrated by man.

"May I have your binoculars, Uncle Winn?" Chubb asked all day and half the night. Uncle Winn slept on deck with the boy. It was too hot in the cabin.

The old man sighed. He had just described the vege-tation of the Siamese jungle—*lalang* grass, moss, giant palms, and the big *mai-yang*, the tung tree, rich with oil, enthroned majestically above the shrubs. Its smooth powerful trunk grew as high as forty meters; only then did it develop its twenty-meter-high crown with the shiny, dark green foliage.

"How do they get the oil out of it?" Chubb asked, always practical.

"The coolies slit open the trunk with a jungle knife, about a meter above the ground. Mr. Steffens can show you all that." Werner Steffens was an engineer from Hamburg. "He'll be waiting for us at the port of Tongha."

"And Uncle Justus too?" Chubb asked, busily writ-ing everything down. He was very curious about Uncle Justus, his Grand-uncle Winn's oldest son, who had mar-ried a Siamese girl. Justus had a small job as foreman somewhere in a Phuket mine. Nang Siri had informed Justus—whom since birth she had never called by any-thing but his Siamese name, Prasert—that *khun paw* (father) was coming to Phuket. Perhaps Prasert would want to meet him in Tongha with Mr. Steffens. That would be *sanuk* (fun) for *khun paw* and Prasert.

"I think Uncle Justus is coming," said old Mr. Petersen. Justus couldn't possibly not come. He was in constant communication with Nang Siri and received money from her when his job as foreman, which he changed frequently, was no longer *sanuk*.

Justus was by no means lacking in intelligence, but he was lethargic, and, at the core of his being, split and broken. What his father didn't know, or didn't want to know, was that Justus-Prasert harbored a slow-burning rage against him and all Europeans. His wife's Siamese family looked upon him as an intruder. They thought just as little of half-castes as did the Europeans who had thoughtlessly given birth to or sired them. Prasert rarely spoke German; he preferred Siamese. He wore the native dress: a white cotton shirt, a checked scarf around shoulder and waist, and a *pasin*, a long skirt, or wide Chinese trousers. He wore European work clothes only at the mine: a khaki shirt and pants. He had not replied to Nang Siri whether he would go to greet *khun paw* in Tongha. To write letters was *lambag*, a nuisance. Besides, Prasert never thought a week ahead, as a matter of principle. There might be a dance festival in the village, something he never missed. He danced the festive folk dances of Siam with a gentle passion. In the *ram wong* one walked slowly in a circle with one's partner and moved one's delicate, supple fingers in meaningful gestures. Prasert had almost succeeded in looking Siamese. He had smooth black hair and dark skin. Only his huge frame betrayed his north German father. And unfortunately one could not discard one's figure like a foreign language or dress. But if his father wished it he would perhaps, but most unwillingly, go to greet *khun paw* and sail back the same evening. They lived in different worlds and had nothing to say to each other.

If Prasert were to take the trouble to analyze his feelings, as the ridiculous *farangs* liked to do, then he would discover that he wasn't merely angry with his father—he hated him. The sight of him, the sound of his voice, made Prasert ill. He had brought misery upon his poor mother. That Nang Siri was very happy, in her way, with "Winn," and would never have let any *farang* or anyone else bring misery down upon her—was incomprehensible to her son. He sought his way out of the imbalance of his soul in hatred.

Eurasians frequently saw life melodramatically. It was a typical trait of those in the Far East who since early childhood had had to accept a hybrid role, racially and socially. That Pauline chose to torture her father by not confiding in him was also Eurasian melodrama. She knew she was his darling—in this respect Martha had been right—but now she was angry with him too, perhaps in her helplessness. Deep down inside her there was a dark longing to torture her father in the Asiatic way—with stubborn silence. Mother Saint Patrick would have been very displeased if she had known how her protégée was reacting to the suffering which, after all, was inflicted on the Christian soul to purify and in the end make perfect. But Mother Saint Patrick was in Ireland. Pauline had never written to her. The converts in the Far East, who were still strangely influenced by their Buddhist mothers, were a problem. And yet, Mother Saint Patrick thought often, the mercy and prayers of the nuns were with these poor dear girls, whether they wanted it or not. And that was what the Mother Superior of the Ursuline sisters in Bangkok had told old Mr. Petersen when he had gone to see her. She was a very energetic English woman and didn't tolerate any "nonsense"—not in her work nor in the spiritual household of the soul. The old man had left her comforted. A very sensible lady, no doubt about it. Perhaps everything would turn out all right after all.

This was what he was thinking in the night as they sailed toward Phuket Island across the Indian Ocean. In spite of his aversion to "Rome," he was pleased that at Mater Dei they didn't take to their heels when faced with disaster, like Nang Siri, who wanted to see everybody happy so that she could be happy.

The night was light. It was very quiet on deck. Chubb had fallen asleep. The old man looked for a long time at this representative of a new generation of his Hamburg family. Asleep and without his glasses, the boy looked like a newborn babe. But he could chatter like a bookworm. A good thing that he had his grand-uncle to get him going on sports. The old gentleman had become so estranged from his homeland that he resented the fact that at the age of twelve Chubb had never sat on a horse nor ridden in the Hamburg Riding Academy, which was what all Petersens had done. Martha had shaken her head when Uncle Winn had deplored her one-sided educational methods. No...in the starvation years Chubb couldn't have ridden. Then he would have been still hungrier, quite apart from the expense and the fact that there were no horses. In those days there was nothing in Hamburg.

Islands with mangrove forests, silence, and the whispering of the Indian Ocean. On the other side of the deck people were speaking in every Asiatic and western language. Old Petersen could hear them—Siamese, Indians, Malayans, Chinese, all talking at once. The largest group spoke English with an American accent. Two gentlemen from the ECAFE and two women.

The Misses Black and Macpherson hadn't let the opportunity slip by to join Mr. Desmond and the head of ECAFE, Mr. Kenneth Portman, on an exploratory trip to the famous tin island of Thailand. Mr. Desmond and Mr. Portman were interested in tin and of course in the economic progress of all the undeveloped lands of the Far East. This country, which was sometimes called Siam, sometimes Thailand, was a gold mine. All it needed was planned management. If the production of the valuable raw materials in Thailand could be increased, why shouldn't the United States profit by their export? And if the living standards of the peoples east of the Suez was to be raised, why not with American canned goods, breakfast cereals, and pressure cookers? Untouched millions were hidden in the peninsula of Siam. The population could easily have a television set, a pressure cooker and tomato soup in a can per person—if they wanted it. But did they want it? That was the question that critical Americans like Mr. Portman and Mr. Desmond asked themselves outside the conference room.

They sailed across a sea of islands. It rained. Rock formations and woodland glowed behind veils of moist air. Every now and then junks and flat sampans and motorized ferries crossed the Indian Ocean. All bore cargoes of something they were bringing to unknown villages and ports. "Copra," old Mr. Petersen told his grand-nephew, pointing to a forest of coconut palms. The flesh of the dried fruit was a vital resource of worldwide trade, and with better exploitation offered great possibilities. The industrial nations of East and West transformed the dried nutmeat into raw material for the oil industry and fats. Tongha, on Phuket Island, was the most important copra port. For years old Petersen had tried to persuade his son Justus to go into the copra export business. His wife's family owned a quite valuable plantation of coconut palms on the west coast. Justus had declined politely. Too much trouble, too much hard work...

Mr. Desmond came to stand beside Petersen senior. He liked to talk to the old man. "I can see a chance for great economic development in Thailand if one explained it properly to the people," he said. "For instance, ECAFE is going to recommend the planting of jute. I

105

must say, the government in Bangkok has its ears wide open for suggestions."

"But the people in the country don't," said Petersen senior, suppressing a smile. "And over ninety percent of the people in the country are employed in agriculture." Nice, this young American with his enthusiasm and theories.

Lawrence Desmond was silent. Something about the old man reminded him of his daughter, Pauline, with whom Desmond had gone riding in Hua Hin. Was it the height? The stubborn chin? For a fleeting moment he could see this strange girl, who happened to understand a lot about business. Pauline Petersen could be so gentle, quite different from Jane Macpherson or his fiancée, Adrienne, back in New Orleans. Desmond still had a letter from her in his pocket, unopened. "How is Miss Pauline?" he asked. It sounded absentminded.

"Thanks," old Petersen said stonily. "She's fine."

Engineer Steffens from Hamburg-Othmarschen was waiting for them at the port of Tongha. He was watching the big dredgers in the water where the mining of tin had already begun below sea level. Steffens was employed as engineer by the biggest Chinese firm on Phuket; it was his job to supervise the various machines and methods for mining tin on the peninsula. But at the moment he wasn't thinking of tin. A few days before he had taken his wife to a nursing home in Bangkok. She was expecting her first baby any minute now. Usually calm, Werner Steffens was dreadfully nervous. If it hadn't been old Mr. Petersen arriving, no power on earth could have kept him on Phuket right now. His only wish was to be with Mathilda. Perhaps his son had already arrived and a wire was on the way! But when he had come to Siam years ago, Petersen senior had put him up for weeks in Rong Muang and had introduced him to a man who knew all about mining in Siam. They had traveled to Phuket together, and the direct result had been a job for him with some Chinese friends. No, he had to be there to receive Petersen senior. It was the thing to do.

Steffens was of medium height, fat and jolly. His bristly blond hair stuck like a brush out of his round head with its big blue eyes. He always looked surprised. Unconsciously he opened his eyes wide like a child that doesn't quite grasp the world it lives in. There was nothing false about Werner Steffens. Naturally he wasn't as polished as the Hamburgers in Bangkok; the mine and the jungle saw to that. But in the evenings, when a primeval silence lay over the island, he liked to play Beethoven. And played very well. But only for his own pleasure. Mathilda was allowed to listen. Mathilda was allowed to do anything. If only she could go on enjoying life here a few more years, until the little one who was just arriving in Bangkok had to go to school in Hamburg.

"Hello, my dear Steffens," said old Petersen. "This is our boy from Hamburg."

"Hello my boy," Steffens said pleasantly, but he wasn't feeling comfortable, that was obvious. What was wrong with him?

"Albert wants to be an engineer too," said his grand-uncle.

"*Famos!*" said Steffens. "Great! I can show you a thing or two. Should I say '*sie*'?"

"No." Chubb sounded regretful. "Everybody's still saying '*du*'." He was shifting nervously from one big foot to the other, just as he had done on his arrival in Bangkok. Chubb couldn't bear to be the center of a conversation. But Steffens wasn't really paying attention. Now it had to come...and it came.

"Where is Justus?" asked Petersen senior, looking around the pier. "Is he so busy that he has to be late when I come to Phuket once in fifteen years?"

"Justus...I heard from him today. He has been prevented...he's very sorry, Mr. Petersen. Maybe he'll come tomorrow..." Steffens' face was as red as a beet. Damn it all! It wasn't right.

"My dear Steffens," said old Mr. Petersen, looking at his former protegé thoughtfully. "You should have started lying as a boy in Othmarschen. You're not going to be any good at it now."

Steffens said nothing. Like every Hamburger when faced with a crisis, he had nothing to say. Petersen senior probably knew anyway that Justus hadn't excused himself. He just hadn't turned up. It was as simple as that.

"So that's that," old Petersen said calmly. "Come along, gentlemen. How about a little rice dinner? Where are we staying, my dear Steffens?"

"With me...if that's all right with you, Mr. Petersen," Steffens mumbled, not looking at the senior member of the German colony in Bangkok. "It isn't too orderly right now, with Mathilda away, but my cook makes great curry."

"*Famos*!" said old Mr. Petersen. "Come along, my boy," he told Chubb, who couldn't take his eyes off the ocean. "Do you feel like rice and curry?"

"And how!" cried Chubb. He couldn't think of anything better.

"So there you are," said Petersen senior. "Thanks a lot, Steffens. Glad I'm going to see your new house. I guess your firm's been generous."

"We're going to have dinner with 'my' Chinese tomorrow," said Steffens. "Yes, they're generous, all right, when one knows how to handle them. Have you ever eaten Chinese food, son?"

"Papa never takes me along when he goes to Hoi Tien Lao with Mama. He doesn't think I'd appreciate it."

"Hm," growled his grand-uncle. Hannes was a lousy father!

"And tomorrow we'll talk business, right, Mr. Petersen? I've ordered a car so that you can ride around the island with the boy. We'll eat tiffin together. And in the afternoon I can take the boy along to the mine."

"*Famos!*" old Petersen said for the second time. He was suddenly hoarse, as if talking tired him. And his eyes looked like the North Sea when it was stormy...

The four Americans from Bangkok were guests of the Siamese government in Phuket. A secretary who spoke English, two cars, and a villa with a garden had been put at their disposal. Their young Siamese guide was exquisitely polite. He explained to the *farangs* from America that the Siamese government was very pleased with the income derived from the tin island. The entrepreneurs had to pay a small amount to the government for the yield of every *picul*, or sixty kilograms, exported. This small amount added up to three million ticals in five years. That was *sanuk*—fun. At least that was what Mr. Kenneth Portman gathered from the radiant smile of the Siamese secretary in his snow-white uniform.

"Not bad," murmured Portman, head of the ECAFE in Bangkok. He was a larger than lifesize, tall, thin, bespectacled New Englander, reserved, critical, and hardworking. He was a Harvard man, which in Jane Macpherson's opinion automatically made him one of the greats of this earth. He was also a brilliant national economist. That evening, on the veranda of the villa in Phuket, Mr. Portman made it clear to his co-worker, Lawrence Desmond, that further progress in this enormously rich land could only be achieved if one succeeded in developing the mentality of the Siamese. For instance, ECAFE shouldn't just be handing out concessions, levying taxes, or, where industry was concerned, depending solely on planting rice and cultivating coconut palm plantations. They should be educating technical experts for the mines, at any rate to a much greater degree than they were doing now.

"And how do you suggest going about that?" asked

Mr. Desmond. "I just had it explained to me by an old German gentleman who's been here forever that the Siamese plant the rice and leave industry and technology to others, and that's the way it is. And the government doesn't seem to be doing badly in Phuket." Larry Desmond, who also didn't like to work more than was absolutely necessary, could sympathize with the Siamese standpoint. But the expression on Mr. Portman's face became tense.

"We are here to develop things, not to sympathize with outmoded traditions." His voice was cold. "Will you please keep that in mind, Desmond?"

He never addressed his colleagues or acquaintances by their first names, only his friends, and he had only one or two of those in the whole wide world. Spending an evening with Mr. Portman was no fun.

The Misses Black and Macpherson had meanwhile driven around the island and penetrated deep into its interior. They found Phuket enchanting in its way. They had stopped at a fairly large coconut palm plantation. It had been still and green there. Jane Macpherson took some beautiful pictures. A farmer and a woman had walked out of a solidly built farmhouse. The woman was wearing a red *phanung* and a blossom in her shiny black hair. The man had looked strange, not at all Siamese. A giant of a man. But his face had had an Asiatic look. His skin was golden brown, his eyes were black and dreamy, but his forehead was high, like a European's, and his smooth shiny hair stood up on both sides of his forehead like a dark halo. In the middle the hair was missing, which made his forehead look even higher.

"Letty!" Jane Macpherson whispered, breathlessly. "Look at that farmer! Is he an Asian? He isn't the least bit graceful. And his forehead! I don't know, it's stupid, but he reminds me of..."

"It *is* stupid," said Letty Black. "Do stop bothering me with your resemblances!"

110

Jane Macpherson was silent. Letty was nearly always right but this time her photographer's schooled eye had seen correctly. The unknown man on the coconut palm plantation *had* resembled a tall old European whom Jane had seen for quite a few days on the ship that had brought them to the tin island. He was Justus Petersen, who was hiding from his father in the interior of the island.

Again they were sailing across a sea of islands, but this time they were headed for Bangkok. Accompanying old Petersen was a radiant middle-aged compatriot who sometimes opened his eyes very wide. Steffens was the happy father of twins. He was absolutely crazy with joy. His presence on the ship did Petersen senior good. It was nice for a change to have a happy man around, especially comforting now, after something had again broken down for him on the tin island, something that had been a weak ray of hope. Wilhelm Petersen had intended to suggest to his oldest son that he turn over a new leaf. He wanted Justus to come into the Bangkok firm and work his way up under excellent conditions and with experienced direction. After all, *khun paw* wasn't getting any younger, and nobody knew if Johannes Petersen would stay on indefinitely after Martha and the children had left. Except for Petersen senior, all of them were guests in Thailand. They came and went away again.

As far as business was concerned, the trip to Phuket had been a success. Was it a sign of the times or the fact that a man with white hair carried more weight with the Chinese than blond Johannes Petersen? The head of the firm Tscheng Hua had given a very decent order for pumps and compressors. Steffens, who had explained everything so beautifully to the Chinese gentlemen would get his percentage of the deal. Petersen and Company didn't accept favors.

Chubb was overwhelmed by everything he had

seen and learned. He had smelled the jungle. He had been to the mine every day with Mr. Steffens. His decision to work as an engineer in the Far East after the trip to the tin island was firm. Besides, he had discovered within himself the taste for foreign lands that was common to all Petersens.

"I think I'd better marry a Chinese woman," he told his grand-uncle. They were standing at the railing, watching the mangrove woods beyond the blue ocean. Sampans, laden with mangrove rind, were plying in the direction of Penang. Big junks were transporting bamboo baskets and wood coal, an agreeable business from island to island, from century to century.

Chubb's remark astounded Petersen senior. "Why a Chinese woman?" he asked.

"I like them best," Chubb said innocently. "I really don't have much use for girls, except for Tiny, of course. They giggle so dreadfully, don't they? Our Ah Bue in Bangkapi never giggles. And she doesn't talk much. I like that." He had rarely said so much about himself all at once, but he had such confidence in Grand-uncle Petersen, who treated him like a grown man.

"Well," said Petersen, "that's nothing we have to hurry about."

"Of course not." Chubb sounded very sensible. "I was just thinking." He manipulated the binoculars. "What's that?" he cried. On the shore he could see little plaited bamboo objects in the golden sand.

"Magical protection against crocodiles," Petersen explained. "The natives think some crocodiles are evil spirits. The Chinese send up fireworks. That makes such a beautiful noise. And crocodiles are very nervous creatures."

"Did you ever go on a shark hunt, Uncle Winn?"

"Many times," replied Petersen. "It's very dangerous."

He stroked a blond curl off the boy's hot forehead.

112

Such eagerness, such quick intelligence—this unused *strength* that had developed under a sober sky. The tropical air was too balmy, too humid. It was probably not Justus's fault that he was as he was. He should have sent him to Hinrich Petersen as an apprentice before the Second World War, to live under a gray sky in brisk air, in the Chile House office in Hamburg, where things were disposed of and accounted for efficiently. But Justus had already lost interest in Penang. He had boarded a coastal ship and, smiling as if everything were all right, had sailed back to Phuket to his wife, his coconut palms and his tropical peace. Justus dreamed the typical dream of all Eurasians: a big, important position or nothing. His poorly paid job in the mine irritated him so much that he sometimes stayed away for days. Nang Siri simply sent more money when he didn't enjoy his job any more. And he always had rice and fruit. He couldn't understand or sympathize with his father's craving for activity. To make money, a lot of money, fast—that even Justus would find fun. But to sit day after day in an office—*mae lambag*—what a nuisance! Petersen senior sighed. What had Chubb wanted to know? Oh yes...about sharks...

Jane Macpherson was having cocktails with Lawrence Desmond. In a week they would be in Bangkok again. If Larry didn't propose in these romantic surroundings, he never would. They were alone on deck. The rock formations were ghostly islands in the moonlight.

Jane didn't look at all bad this evening, thought Larry Desmond. Altogether, she had changed; she wasn't so effusive any more, and she was an excellent photographer. She showed him her pictures from Phuket, and the one of the coconut palm plantation with the strange man who had looked neither Asiatic nor European. Larry Desmond racked his brains...of whom did the man remind him? Suddenly it hit him. During their dinner in Bangkok, when Larry Desmond had asked Pauline Petersen about the rabid dog incident, her father's pending journey to the island of Phuket had been mentioned. Of course! This had to be the legendary brother who lived on a coconut plantation on the island, the Petersen family's lost son! Pauline had the same high forehead and dreamy eyes, and she was gorgeously built, in Larry Desmond's opinion. His fiancée in New Orleans, Adrienne, was small and thin. She had written that they were going to be married as soon as he came back to the States. That would be in three months. He had torn the letter into little pieces and thrown them into the Indian Ocean. Why were fiancées little and thin?

"I don't have the negative any more," Jane was saying, pointing to the picture of Justus Petersen. "But the story should be interesting, with this shot illustrating it. Unfortunately the farmer didn't speak English."

Larry Desmond must have been hit by a tropical frenzy, because he grabbed the precious picture, of which there was no negative, out of Jane Macpherson's hand, quick as lightning, and let it fall into the sea.

"Larry!" she screamed. "How could you be so clumsy? I told you I have no negative!"

"I'm terribly sorry, Jane," Desmond mumbled. "I was slapping at a mosquito and it slipped out of my hand. Never mind, darling; you have loads of pictures of Phuket."

Jane Macpherson was so delighted that Larry had called her darling, that she at once got over the loss of the picture. She looked at Larry adoringly, and a strange shyness was reflected in her slightly protruding eyes.

Kenneth Portman, enjoying the moonlit night by himself, walked by. His cold eyes behind their glasses sized up Jane's look and attitude correctly. He went on walking. His long shadow fell lonely and disapprovingly on the wooden deck.

Old Mr. Petersen sat with Jane Macpherson's photographs on a deck chair and showed Chubb the tiny island once more, this time in pictures. "Wonderful!" cried Chubb, and reddened at once. Was he being gushy, like a girl? But Grand-uncle didn't respond. He was looking with his slightly veiled, sharp blue eyes at the disappearing rock formations and woods of Phuket, where there was so much that was precious and unused.

8

Fireflies

In Wilhelm Christian Petersen's villa in Hua Hin, one shining day passed like the one before and after. Martha felt completely relaxed, and wondered how she could get Pauline to talk. Pauline was as silent as the snow in the north, which she had never seen. Her melancholy laid a pall across her gentle good humor, even penetrating her silence and the little she had to say. Just the same, every now and then she sought Martha's company. She sensed instinctively the warmth and strength of this woman from another world. Yet even Martha's ability to place herself intensively yet critically in the position of another human being seemed to fail in the face of this girl's obduracy. Still Pauline tried to make friends with her aunt in the ingratiating manner of the East. She had noticed what Siamese food Martha liked and ordered the servants to prepare time-consuming exotic delicacies for Mem Banghapi. The servants called Martha the Strange Woman from Bangkapi, just as Doris Krüger was the Strange Woman from Dusit. The cook couldn't tell the many European guests who came to the villa by the sea apart any other way. Mae Wat found that the women from the West all looked alike. But they weren't all alike. All of them treated their servants differently.

"Mem Bangkapi understand," Mae Wat explained to her niece, Sangvien, a young girl from Mae Wat's rice

116

village, as she began to prepare a meal for Martha that Pauline had ordered three days before. Mae Wat did anything outside the daily routine of her meal schedule when she felt like it. *Kanom kang kao* was a dish that required time and love.

"Why didn't you do it yesterday?" asked Pauline.

"No prawns at market," Mae Wat replied, her face expressionless. Pauline accepted the gross lie with a friendly smile. "Maybe they'll have some tomorrow," she said. "Mem Bankapi loves *kanom kang kao*. She says nobody prepares it like Mae Wat."

Mae Wat beamed all over her wrinkled face and shifted her wad of betel from one check to the other. *"Mem Bangkapi mi khwam khit,"* she said, expressing with satisfaction the fact that the foreign woman from Bangkapi was clever.

Slowly she strolled over to the kitchen house to prepare *kanom kang kao* for the clever Mem. She had simply forgotten Pauline's order. Now she sent Sangvien back to the market with a long list. Sangvien was to bring prawns, grated coconut, garlic, parsley and orange leaves. Then Mae Mat went to work. Sangvien had to help by running to get the things Mae Wat had forgotten on her first list. This was a customary Siamese and Chinese cooking procedure. One never bought in advance, but went to get an herb or anything else when it was needed for a specific dish. No servant ever said to a cook, "Why didn't you ask me to get that in the first place?" Only the simpleminded foreigners asked questions like that! There was always time enough for marketing, and you got the dinner on the table when it was ready. Mae Wat found it incomprehensible that the foreign ladies made such a fuss about having meals on time. Mae Wat and Sangvien ate whenever they felt like it, and then they didn't eat the good rice dishes quickly as the foreigners did. Rice eating was an important event, and one didn't want to be disturbed while eating. Mae

Wat and Sangvien admired Martha because she never tried to make them leave their dinner to go on some sort of errand.

"*Klua mai mi...* we have no salt," said Mae Wat, and Sangvien ran to get it. Meanwhile Mae Wat baked the prawns in a big black cast-iron pan that had a deep hollow in the center. The foreigners' flat pans, for which the Old Master had sent to Hamburg, stood untouched on the shelf. They were too beautiful and too impractical for cooking. Behind the largest unused pan stood an ugly shell box with "Greetings from Cuxhaven" spelled out on it. Mae Wat had been so enchanted with the box that one day she had taken it off the Old Master's desk and put it for safekeeping in front of her on a kitchen shelf for three days, "to dust it." Since nobody had missed it, it now rightfully belonged to her. She looked at it in the evenings and wondered what the word *Kluxhavenn* meant.

"*Nam man mu mai mi...* no lard," she told her helper when she started to bake. No sooner had Sangvien returned with the lard and two packs of cigarettes for herself and Mae Wat—the price of the cigarettes was added to the other items—when Pauline called impatiently, "Sangvien! Come here! Fan me!" which meant that Sangvien was to fan Nangsao Pauline, who had made herself comfortable in Nang Siri's hammock. It was going to be hot. Nangsao Pauline was always fanned when she wanted it. Old Master's orders. It hadn't surprised Martha at first, but it dawned on her gradually that Peterson senior might have been right when he had so definitely rejected Martha's suggestion to take Pauline with her to Hamburg for a year. Who would fan Pauline in Hamburg?

"Who bandaged your toe?" Pauline asked indolently, looking at Sangvien's big toe. It was cleanly and efficiently bandaged, and Sangvien was just as fascinated by it as the cook with her shell box.

"Mem Bangkapi," she said proudly. She had stepped on a piece of glass when she had gone for the chili Mae Wat needed to make rice and curry. Martha had noticed the wound when the girl had served bananas. Sangvien hoped the wound wouldn't heal for a long time. Mem Bangkapi had such beautiful hands, and they had treated the injured toe so gently. For thanks Sangvien had cleaned Martha's room with special care. This meant that she had decorated every object on Martha's dressing table with flowers. Orchids bloomed in her powder box; an enchanting but poisonous blossoming twig was stuck in her bottle of mouthwash, and branching wide and exquisitely from the ceramic jug filled with rain water, which was used for washing, were the dirty branches of a sugar palm. It was not the height of hygiene but the epitome of submission and beauty that Martha found in her bedroom that evening. Cheng, who slept next door with Tiny, removed the flower garden Sangvien had arranged so solicitously, cursing with malicious pleasure. Martha threw away the bottle of mouthwash, but Cheng retrieved it and kept it. Everything thrown away pained her Chinese soul. She didn't use the mouthwash but stood the bottle beside her bamboo mat in a place of honor—such a beautiful bottle, with a silk ribbon!

While Sangvien fanned her, Pauline read a foreign book, a novel set in New Orleans. Mr. Desmond, with whom she had ridden so often in Hua Hin, had given it to her. Pauline shut the book and threw it on the grass. Sangvien would pick it up and take it to her room. A Siamese lady didn't carry anything herself; the servants were there for that. Pauline closed her eyes. Her thoughts wandered. How would it be if she told Martha the truth? Pauline felt abandoned. She could feel the new life in her womb...the child with no father. It had all been a dream, but now the shades of fear and shame had fallen on the sunny villa by the sea. Aunt Martha wasn't at all *etepetete*, or prudishly formal, as Papa had feared she would be, and she seemed to like Pauline in the quiet, reliable way Papa had always loved her.

Papa! For a moment Pauline opened her eyes and looked at the fiery sea of blossoms in the garden. Papa was angry with her. Or was she imagining it? The big strong protective figure of her father appeared fleeting in her mind's eye. Papa had always comforted her. For Pauline he had been the embodiment of loyalty and of a love that was utterly reliable. But now everything was changed. Papa didn't talk to her any more. Pauline didn't realize that he couldn't talk to a mute daughter. A shy alienation had developed between them. No, she couldn't talk to him. So, preferably to Aunt Martha. Perhaps she would find Aunt Martha alone? No, Aunt Martha had a visitor from Bangkok, Aunt Kathy, Professor Berger's sister-in-law.

Katharina von Kinsky was a fragile little woman who had followed her sister, Theresa Berger, into exile of her own choosing. She had an indomitable will and a shining sense of justice. She and Martha had understood each other at once. Both had strong family feelings, and that was a bond. They were discussing how one could bring Pauline to her senses. In Aunt Kathy's opinion, Pauline was a problem, no doubt about it. And Martha felt that no daughter had the right to torture a father who lived only for her, with stubborn silence. On his last visit, the old man had looked dreadful. One could only hope that seeing Justus again would give him a lift. But there had been no mention of Justus in Chubb's report on their trip.

Pauline had received a letter from her brother. Justus offered her his home and his love. Pauline could come to him right away if she wished. And her son would live a life in and with nature, as was fitting for a Siamese. Pauline had written to Justus at once and thanked him. Perhaps...she didn't know yet. Papa might prefer it if she just disappeared. But she wasn't sure of that either, because Papa was angry and didn't talk to her.

This news didn't surprise Justus. *Khun paw* was a hardhearted *farang*. What could you expect from him?

Martha knew nothing about this correspondence between Hua Hin and the tin island of Phuket. Meanwhile Aunt Kathy had left; Martha was alone with Pauline. This suited the girl very well. In the presence of Katharina von Kinsky she had been aloof and arrogant. Aunt Martha had horrible friends! *Farangs!* But Martha hadn't been offended by Pauline's bad behavior. Nearly all half-castes in the Far East were either arrogant or depressed. They had no feeling of security socially, the poor girls.

Pauline had closed her heart and mind against the West, yet it had been a man from the West who, a few months ago during an hour on the beach at Hua Hin, had made a woman of her. In the Far East passions flared like fireflies, in nights intoxicated with love. Passions were brighter and more fantastic than under the pale sky of the West, and were snuffed out just as abruptly as tropical fireflies in the dark. This was what happened to Pauline. But what did Aunt Martha know about fireflies? What did she know about a girl to whom a man had said for the first time that she was beautiful, more beautiful than any girl he had ever known? He had spoken words the likes of which an Asiatic, always conscious of the conventions, would never have been capable—romantic, tender words. A firefly love had flared up, as happened a thousand times between a white man and a daughter of the East. Pauline had only begun to think when she had realized that she was going to bear the white man's child, the fruit of their passionate and thoughtless lovemaking.

But Pauline was not a flower girl who gives the

121

white man his satisfaction as a matter of course if he looks after her and spoils her. She was the daughter of Wilhelm Christian Petersen from Hamburg, and that was a problem. Besides, Pauline was a Christian. She had been taught that marriage was something sacred, an unbreakable bond, a sacrament, even if it was being scoffed at and trodden in the dust in many parts of the world. A child needed a mother and a father. Everything had gone wrong for Pauline.

So there she sat in front of Martha, a stubborn, unhappy child, tall and beautifully built, and more helpless than Chubb was today at fourteen and a half. Her red hair, with its smooth, straight parting, fell down either side of her rounded forehead, giving her a new and touching beauty and accentuating her dark, melancholy eyes. It framed her face with its high cheekbones and lovely, full, sensuous mouth. A Mary Magdalene in the tropics. Her short nose, the nostrils a little too flared, was Siamese; her chin was the firm Petersen chin, so quickly stuck out when one wanted to make a point. And in the same way Pauline was spiritually attached to two worlds. She could move quickly from one level of experience to the other. Even Martha found it difficult to follow Pauline. This was further complicated by the fact that her changeability of mood and spirit was all part of a morbid sensitivity that, like her stubborn silence and Justus's hatred, had grown out of the social insecurity of those trapped between two civilizations. They were the stigma of the half-caste. All one could do was love Pauline and surreptitiously try to guide her.

"My dear child," Martha said gently. "It's no use. You've got to do something about it."

They were the right words. For the first time Pauline looked at her aunt, honestly and helplessly. There was no resisting Martha, not in the long run. And when Martha saw the expression in Pauline's eyes and read the lethargy that was her Far East heritage, she challenged the girl boldly. "Pauline!" she said, her voice firm. "Who is it?" And when Pauline dropped all resistance just as suddenly as she had raised a wall of silence between Martha and herself, Martha found it difficult to suppress a cry of astonishment.

The situation was more difficult than she had supposed. A Siamese father would have given a clear picture of the future. As for young Harms—as Petersen senior had declared, he would have broken every bone in the fellow's body and then demanded in no uncertain terms that he marry Pauline at once. But Mr. Lawrence Desmond from ECAFE was a very different story. He was engaged. In three months he was to be married in New Orleans. And his impoverished family depended on the marriage. Petersen couldn't break every bone in his body and force him to marry Pauline, especially not since Pauline had made Martha swear not to tell her father anything. Martha had never broken a promise.

"Does he know that you are expecting his child?" she asked after a long pause.

"No." Pauline was staring straight ahead. "And he is not to know. I don't want to make him unhappy."

"My dear Pauline," Martha said emphatically, "that is utter nonsense!"

That night Martha sat for a long time on the veranda with its view of the sea. There was no moon. It was a night of flickering shadows and tropical humidity. In her bedroom Tiny was sleeping naked under a mosquito netting; Cheng was asleep on a bamboo mat in front of the bed, Youngest Son lying quietly and contentedly beside her. He would succeed, with modesty and diligence. Cheng would serve the *farangs* until she was finally served by her daughters-in-law, as had been the custom for generations. The new China was propagandizing a slackening and eventual dissolution of the Confucian family ethic that had not yet penetrated to Cheng. In exile the old honorable family customs were still valid. It was the same all over the Far East.

Tiny tossed restlessly in her sleep. At once Cheng was up, speaking tenderly in Chinese to the child with the golden hair. With a fine batiste cloth she wiped the sweat off Tiny's delicate body. Cheng hoped that the child with the golden hair would stay in Thailand for a long time. The others could leave—she would weep no tears for them.

Martha looked at the sea. For the first time she was all alone in this Southeast Asian world with its flickering shadows. A huge pile dwelling...the murmuring sea- ...fireflies in the dark...and an unproblematic life for the sons and daughters of the land. But only for them! Martha thought of Pauline. A light was still on in her room. The poor child. Her problem couldn't be solved melodramatically as those members trapped in the realm of two races tried to solve them. Pauline felt insecure. It had taken a lot of patience and firmness on Martha's part to normalize the girl's views. But she had succeeded in making clear to her that she owed her father and her unborn child a more realistic solution. For Pauline had the same strange indifference with which Eurasians constantly faced the rest of the world, and it worried Martha. Only their own problems, usually in connection with a specific man, and the urge to self-destruction that slumbered in them and had already once led to a suicide attempt in Pauline's formative years, played a part. Eurasian! A vast world of neurotics, constantly faced with the choice: West or East? And most of the sons, like Justus Petersen, chose the East. The daughters were Europeans only in appearance. They dressed and spoke like white women, but they had not inherited the energy and sobriety which was the support of even the most average white woman in the Far East, at times also in a marriage for an Oriental man. But the finale was more often than not an endless struggle over traditions, conventions and religion.

Martha got up and fetched a package from the veranda. Aunt Kathy had given it to her on leaving: the unfinished treatise on Plato in relation to the present day, which her brother-in-law, Professor Berger, was working on. "He is a genius," she had murmured. Would Martha like to have a look at it?

Martha opened the package and read halfway through the night. If genius was a mixture of diligence, sound erudition, passion, and some of the trappings of a prophet, then Professor Franz Berger was a genius.

Next morning, after a restless night, when Martha was breakfasting with Pauline, she asked casually, "Linchen, would you do me a favor?"

Pauline looked at Martha adoringly, rather like the black sheep in her undergraduate class. "Look," said Martha, "your English is excellent. Mine isn't good enough to do any translating. How would you like to translate the first chapters of this manuscript into English? I'd be very grateful if you did, dear child."

Pauline took the manuscript eagerly. Aunt Martha had praised her! "I'd love to," she said happily. "I have nothing to do now."

Martha hesitated for a moment. How to express it? Pauline's eagerness was genuine, but it was a little like the fireflies that flared up and went out... "Linchen," she said. "It would mean a lot to me to get the chapters soon. You're quick and you know how to concentrate. What do you think?"

Pauline was neither quick nor did she know how to concentrate, but Martha was an experienced teacher. She knew that girls who were hungry for praise and recognition developed the characteristics one attributed to them in advance praise.

"I'll start this evening." Pauline said firmly. "You'll get the translation just as quickly as I can do it."

And Pauline actually did work conscientiously on the manuscript which a few years later was to become a sensation in the western world. She also wrote a letter to Lawrence Desmond of ECAFE at his hotel in Bangkok, to please Aunt Martha and to please the child alive in her womb now for three months. But she still didn't want to have anything to do with her father.

During the same night, Jane Macpherson and Larry Desmond were on board ship, not far away from Bangkok. Jane Macpherson leaned against Larry Desmond. He was such an attractive man. "Larry," she said dreamily, "what are you thinking about?"

"Oh...all sorts of things," he said, and moved away a little. He was thinking of a girl with bright red hair and a gentle tenderness, a beautiful and good girl. And with good business sense. She knew the methods and business traditions of the East inside out. That she must have inherited from her father.

Larry Desmond stretched. This morning he had written a letter to his fiancée in New Orleans, a girl called Adrienne, whom he was supposed to marry in three months. But he loved another girl; he was in love for the first time in his life. Pauline hadn't written to him and just that made it perfectly clear to Larry Desmond that she was the only girl he wanted, and that he wished to stay in this alien land. Let his sister in New Orleans work if she wanted to live in luxury. Her brother had no intention of sacrificing himself for his family by marriage to a wealthy girl. The Far East put everything into the right perspective.

"Good night, Jane," he said gently. "I'm tired."

Jane Macpherson watched him, speechless, as he walked to the other side of the deck and sat down in a chair beside old Mr. Petersen. She controlled the tears that in her case flowed so easily. Her slightly protruding, unseeing eyes were fixed on a glittering flying fish, swooping up and down through the dark. There weren't any flying fish in New England. Suddenly there was a tall shadow behind her. She started. Mr. Portman. What did he want at this time of night?

"Miss Macpherson," said the head of ECAFE. "You shouldn't pay so much attention to Mr. Desmond. Don't you know that he's engaged to a young lady in New Orleans? They are going to be married in three months, just as soon as Mr. Desmond's contract with ECAFE ends."

Jane gasped. This was the first she had heard about it. There had to be a mistake. She said, "If that's so, Larry would have told me. Please mind your own business."

The muscles in Mr. Portman's fine, pale face tightened. He should have known. This girl was totally lacking in common sense. "It shouldn't happen again, Miss Macpherson," he said coldly. "I wanted to prevent you from making a fool of yourself in the colony. Naturally you can do as you please. But I hope you'll give some thought to our prestige in the Far East. We don't have a very good reputation, socially. Too much drinking, too many indiscretions by those who lose all sense of discipline away from home. I know the climate plays its part. But in the Orient we should stick to the conventions, or the Asiatics will hold us in contempt. Good night."

Jane Macpherson watched Mr. Portman go, her mouth agape. She didn't reply to his good-night. Another one of those Puritans from whom she had fled to the Far East. An arrogant spoilsport, Bible in hand. She hated him!

9

A Wedding in the Tropics

Ten days after old Mr. Petersen's return, Pauline was married to Lawrence Desmond. The wedding was celebrated with a small circle of friends and relatives, with all the festiveness and beauty for which a tropical garden with pavilions and Chinese lanterns is the correct backdrop.

Nang Siri had hurried back to Rong Muang from her business in Bangkok, and spent days preparing Siamese sweetmeats, garlands of flowers, and lanterns. On long tables decorated with flowers, the guests from East and West would find all the delicacies that made Siamese celebrations so wonderful: rice and curry steaming on little stoves which the servants in brocade *phanungs* would fan to an even glow. A festive curry had many side dishes—finely minced chutney, tomatoes, small fried fish, paper-thin fried potatoes, pickles, sweet and sour pineapple, roasted coconut, baked bananas, and all the other culinary surprises which western guests couldn't stop staring at, it was all so exquisitely and colorfully arranged in Nang Siri's priceless ceramic and silver bowls. There would also be a choice of European foods wreathed in jasmine—roast chicken, roast beef with herb mayonnaise, salmon, and many other dishes that Petersen senior had been served in the old days in his Hamburg parents' home. The silver bowls with Siamese dancers and gods engraved on them held the blessing of the tropics. Mountains of cake—Siamese and German—would be piled high on crystal platters, and on a huge silver plate with the flight of the Princess Sita engraved on it, the wedding cake would stand. The Petersens' Viennese friends were stirring the batter at this very moment, a present from the Berger family, who had received one of the invitations that had been sent out in German, Siamese, and English with great joy, since all the years they had been in Siam, they had never before been granted the privilege of attending such a celebration.

Nang Siri smiled all the time. Everyone was happy. Family life was what it should be again. Nang Siri was by no means heartless. She was as happy as a child that Winn seemed to have been relieved of his incomprehensible sorrow. But he looked tired. Nang Siri whirred around him like a dragonfly.

Her personal generosity and the Siamese tradition of hospitality were boundless. Tradition demanded that every guest receive a present—flowers or fruit—just as the peasants offered rice to their wedding guests. Nang Siri readied powder boxes, paper knives, vases, and jewelry made of niello silver for her guests. The latter was a Siamese specialty that entranced all Americans who hadn't been in Siam long, and led to cries of delight and gratitude. But all of them had been in Thailand long enough not to reject the presents with words, "Oh, that is much too valuable for me!" That was an insult Nang Siri would never have forgiven. One gave presents in Siam in a quite different way. There were no parallels to the fairy-tale splendor and riches presented with charm and as a matter of course at Indian and Southeast Asian festivities.

A stage had been erected near the house. Classical Siamese dances were to be presented after the ceremony as a finale to the celebrations. The wife of the English doctor, Dr. Tyler, had asked her aunt, Princess F., to lend her own dance ensemble for the garden party. The group had never danced in a strange house. The princess had said she would attend. It made so many of the aristocrats happy to give their guests from the West an idea of the ancient aesthetic Thai traditions in this charming fashion. Petersen senior had thanked the princess in a formal note written in Siamese. Nang Siri and he would never forget the princess's kindness.

Near the four lotus ponds, surrounded by palms and tamarinds, stood old Mr. Petersen's *sala*, his private pavilion, a dainty garden house with white columns and a Siamese roof. You could find *salas* like this all over Siam—inside the temple district, at streetcar stops, anywhere in the woods. They were places for rest and meditation, protection from the glowing fires of the sun god Phra Suriya. And here, in this little garden house with its bamboo walls and a painting by a Japanese artist, *The Elbe in a Storm*, as its only decoration, Wilhelm Christian Petersen spent the evening before Pauline's wedding.

It had all gone too fast.

The old man had passed silently and unbowed through a purgatory of torture the likes of which Nang Siri and Pauline had never known. And then, suddenly, it was all forgotten. Nang Siri was radiant because Winn had got his way and Pauline was going to be married. Pauline was radiant because Larry had written to her before she had to put moral pressure on him, as she had promised her aunt she would. She had eyes for nothing but Mr. Desmond. She had given her father a fleeting and thoughtless kiss, and had cleverly managed to avoid any serious discussion with him. Everything was all right again, everybody was happy! Why didn't *khun paw* look happy? Pauline and Larry would fly to Manila after the wedding and stay there. Mr. Desmond had managed to get a friendly release from his contract which had only had a few more weeks to run anyway. His successor had already arrived in Bangkok, an old man with spectacles from Boston. Portman was pleased to note that he was married.

The ECAFE in Bangkok had presented their colleague with a Siamese silver tea set and intended to turn up en masse, with the exception of Jane Macpherson, at the garden party in Rong Muang. Miss Macpherson had sent her regrets: she had a fever. Whatever Mr. Portman thought about this surprising marriage of his closest colleague, he kept to himself. To jilt a fiancée in New Orleans three months before the wedding could only be termed highly improper. That Mr. Desmond had never mentioned that he was attracted to Miss Petersen Mr. Portman found in order. He himself behaved the same way. He was interested in a certain American lady in Bangkok, but so discreetly that even the lady in question knew nothing about it.

Mr. Portman liked Petersen senior a lot. On the voyage to the tin island he had conversed with him about East and West, and had admired the patience of the old man who came from such an impatient nation. He sensed that Petersen's exceptional tolerance stemmed from the consciousness that he had deviated from his own traditions.

Wilhelm Christian Petersen had deviated when he had joined his fate with Nang Siri's, and it had never seemed so clear to him as on this evening before Pauline's wedding. He had as little to do with the festivity as his daughter now had to do with him. He would have liked nothing better than to go and see Martha tonight. He would have looked at the *lampu* tree on her veranda. But he didn't want to let even Martha, who had managed somehow to straighten out Pauline, to know how lonely he was. Soon after the wedding, Hannes and Martha would go on a fourteen-day trip to Ceylon for Hannes to recuperate. Old Petersen had booked the tickets. It was his way of saying thanks. He didn't accept favors without reciprocating, not even from Martha, of whose eventual departure he thought with a sadness he wouldn't even admit to himself in the *sala*. She was the salt of the earth. Hannes, the rascal, was damned lucky!

The old man rose and gazed broodingly at the Japanese painter's *The Elbe in a Storm*. He had had it copied from a painting he had kept for years in a drawer of his desk. He had declined Mr. Portman's invitation to dinner, and Nang Siri still had a lot to do to transform garden and house into a magic kingdom by tomorrow evening. Her giggling and soft chatter penetrated across the garden and into the *sala*. And Justus Petersen, who had come from the tin island to attend the wedding of his favorite sister, had joined the happy people in the house and garden. He had greeted his father in Siamese, but wasn't keeping him company this evening, the only evening they could have spent together talking. After fifteen years he had nothing to say to his father. Tomorrow he would sail back to Phuket.

What had Wilhelm Christian Petersen done to turn his children away from him? He had tried to educate them and make them happy to a far greater degree than Nang Siri, and now, on the evening of his life, he stood there with empty hands. His daughter had eyes for no one but the young American, who without realizing it had caused the old man the worst hours of his life. There was something of the adventurer about Larry Desmond. He was too easygoing. The wisdom of the Far East attracted him less than the good life and the exotic backdrop there. Old Petersen hoped he wouldn't make his girl too unhappy. He would have liked to tell her that she could always count on him, but she hadn't given him the chance. Would she write to him from Manila? Pauline didn't like to write letters. But perhaps she would remember her father once she had settled down. She was a good, sweet girl, only a little thoughtless.

Petersen senior would also have liked to tell his

daughter that she shouldn't be so humble toward her husband. In love Pauline was suddenly an Asiatic—her man's word was law, and his pleasure in her a measure of her value. One could only hope that everything would go well. Anyway, Pauline was going to stay nearby, and life in the Philippines wasn't so different from life in Bangkok and Hua Hin. And she had her own house. Possibly Nang Siri was more farsighted than Petersen senior had assumed. Pauline had her own fortune too. Her father had insisted on property separation. The gentleman from New Orleans had agreed to anything Mr. Petersen wished. He had taken out a loan from his father-in-law, a much larger sum than he would have received from Miss Black under the best circumstances. Petersen senior was willing to set his son-in-law up in business, but he was a shrewd and perspicacious calculator. He didn't invest in anything risky. Mr. Desmond's export-import plans for the Philippines were sound. In this respect the old man, who guarded the happiness of his beloved child jealously yet helplessly, was not worried.

The moon had risen over the tall trees of Rong Muang. Petersen senior thought of his homeland. Everything would have been different if he had married Florence Krüger, the sister of his friend, Charles. Like him, she had always personified the Hamburg ideal of permanence. Even today, after the war and the postwar years had done away with so much permanence, Florence would be sticking stubbornly and heroically to this ideal. Feelings, business, even life itself was worthwhile only if it included the quality of permanence. So under the influence of this ideal, young Wilhelm Christian Petersen had tried to give permanence to his tropical paradise. Tonight it seemed to him that with all the sober intellect and fortitude he had inherited, he had been a fool on a grand scale. Nothing and no one could give permanence and stability to the unreal existence of the alien lotus-eaters. Those were blessings of the north, which Petersen senior had left behind forever. Even if in the north the old order had collapsed, and a benighted spirit had hovered for years like a dark cloud over the Elbe, he was sure that in Hamburg they were still dreaming the old righteous dream of the permanence of private life and the new constitutional state, and they would realize this dream slowly and doggedly, and turn it into reality. He would not be with them. He was living in a cultural and private exile. In the structure of Siamese-Buddhist society he was and remained an onlooker. But the old man in the *sala* did not choose to analyze his dilemma. He stuck out his chin and ignored it. As long as Pauline needed him, he was in the right place—and that was that.

A car drove up to the gate. It was around midnight. Petersen senior didn't move. That had to be Pauline. He peered with his sharp blue eyes into the moonlit garden. Lanterns and chains of flowers everywhere. And truly it was Pauline, coming home arm in arm with Larry. Five minutes later Larry reappeared, whistling cheerfully, and drove off.

And then the unexpected happened. Pauline was suddenly in the *sala*. She had swept in like a ghost in her full silver gown. The stiff corkscrew curls Martha hated, justifiably, again covered her small head with its little ears and prominent cheekbones. They had reappeared with her happiness. And then Pauline was sitting at her father's feet as she had done as a child and a growing girl. And with the startling change of mood that occasionally overwhelmed her like a monsoon wind, she clung to Petersen senior and whispered, sobbing, "Papa! Dear Papa! I...I want to stay with you forever! I...I'm afraid!"

For a moment the old man's heart seemed to stop. Had the girl gone crazy? But no...everything was all right just as it was. His Linchen hadn't forgotten him completely.

He took his big handkerchief out of his pocket and wiped away her tears, one by one. That was what he had always done. And he spoke the same words he used to say to little Pauline when she had come running to the *sala* with her childish anxieties. "Don't! Don't, my girl! I'll see to it that nobody harms you!"

It was a strange thing for a father to say to his daughter on the eve of her wedding; it was even a ridiculous remark. Mr. Portman would have shaken his head over it. But Pauline seemed to feel that the remark was all right, because she looked up at her big, powerful father with tears in her eyes and said obediently, "Yes, Papa." Then the two walked arm in arm, as they had done always, to the disorderly palace where Pauline's childhood and youth had run their course. And Petersen senior, reassured, decided that now one could celebrate the wedding.

Pauline and Larry were married in the chapel of Mater Dei. It was a small wedding; only immediate members of the family were present and Mr. Portman functioned as best man. Mother Saint Patrick had returned two days before from Ireland and sang with her girls like an angel. They were dainty, prettily dressed Siamese who obediently forced the foreign hymns out of their throats somehow, but it was all very beautiful and touching. Mr. Portman, who ordinarily didn't approve of "Rome" either, conversed animatedly with the English mother superior. An atmosphere of peace emanated from the little chapel, decorated with orchids and garlands, with its new organ and the many happy faces which even the bride's Buddhist mother appreciated. Nang Siri knelt reverently near the altar. This too was characteristic of the tolerance and tact of the Siamese people.

Toward evening the festivities in Rong Muang began which no one present was to forget. Martha decided that she had never seen anything so perfect: a vast floral island in an ocean of everyday life. Guests of all nations and races strolled on the trimmed English lawns. One could be united so pleasantly and unconstrainedly only in Bangkok. Old Mr. Wong and his daughters, swathed in brocade, promenaded with Charles Krüger and Dr. Tyler, who told the fine old Chinese man age-old jokes. Martha sat for a long time in a fairy-tale pavilion with Mr. Portman and Miss Black, whom she began to like more and more. Professor Berger and Aunt Kathy were conversing seriously in Siamese with Princess Pattani, who was asking graciously if they had mangoes and durian fruit in Vienna. She had never met such charming Europeans. They spoke Siamese very nicely and never complained once about the heat.

Miss Karin Holm was among those present, with her Swedish fiancé. They were going to be married in eight days. The invitations had already been sent out. Miss Karin couldn't keep her eyes off Hannes, who remained very much aloof. He had evidently not got over the Javanese dancer's last visit. He was talking to a pretty young Siamese girl whose *pasin*, a Siamese wrap-around skirt, was ornamented with real sapphires.

Pauline looked beautiful and happy. She walked among her guests arm in arm with her husband and father, and helped Nang Siri talk to the foreigners present. Tall hurricane lamps, candles and lanterns in the shape of lotus blossoms hung over the buffet. Boys dressed in white passed around trays of drinks.

The most memorable guest was the old Siamese princess who had contributed her dance group to the festivities. She sat as was proper for her rank in a seat of honor beside Prince Pattani, on a small raised platform decorated with flowers and Siamese brocade, waiting for the dance drama to begin. She was a tiny, shriveled, filigree figure, and she was wearing the traditional *pha-nung* and priceless jewelry with casual dignity. Nang Siri

136

personally brought her Siamese delicacies in gold bowls, with Petersen junior's old cook, Ah Chang, watching discreetly from the distance. The bowls were real gold, and thieves could be everywhere. Ah Chang's grandsons were serving with the other boys who had been recruited from friends and from the Chinese restaurant, Swee Hong. But all the food and the European dishes which Martha and Aunt Kathy had helped to cook and arrange had been prepared in the house. This was a rule of Siamese hospitality and the greatest satisfaction to the hostess. Martha gazed in astonishment at the fragile Siamese sweets: flowers and blossoms of spun sugar, works of art in jelly or ice!

The entire German colony was present. Good old Steffens, who had given Justus Petersen hell in Phuket, was among them. Mathilda and the twins were doing very well. Steffens would stay in Petersen's house in Bangkapi until Hannes and Martha came back from Ceylon. Hannes still needed to recuperate, and he didn't want to travel without Martha. The children would stay with Uncle Steffens, and the Berger family would help to look after them. Naturally Petersen senior would visit the children daily. Something was missing in his life when he didn't see Chubb and the little girl, who became more droll every day.

Wide-eyed, Chubb and Tiny watched the fairy tale that Nang Siri had created magically in house and garden for just one night. It grew dark. The lanterns and hanging lamps were turned on. The old princess was still sitting in the place of honor and eating with an incredible appetite. One couldn't imagine where that much rice and sweets could find room in her ceremonious little body. A gong sounded. The Chinese boys put out the lights. Now only the stage was illuminated, and the moon had risen. Behind the stage, palms and tamarinds stood in its silvery light, and on both sides sat the musicians with cymbals, drum and xylophone who began the classical accompaniment to the *lakon*, the famous classical Siamese ballet. And the *lakon* dancers, dressed in brocade and real jewels, and instructed by the old princess, entered. They wafted out of the natural wings like Asiatic elves, in gold and sea-green brocade, moving their gold-brown limbs, decorated with costly bracelets, in festive and exciting rhythms. Here the mystery of the Far East had taken on shape and immortal beauty. The heads of the dancers bent like lotus blossoms in a dreamlike wind; their high, pointed, jewelled headdresses swayed a little on their delicate heads. The name of the ballet was *Rama's Plaint*. The dancer who played the part of Prince Rama, seeking his bride, Sita, in the jungle, embodied grief, longing, and loneliness in the exquisite movement of her body and fingers. She was wearing the highest *mukata*, or crown, the crown of kings. Her face was a white mask; only her rouged mouth and her black, almond-shaped eyes gave her life and dramatic tension. Women had been playing in Siamese dramas only for the last two hundred years. Before that boys had played the parts of princesses and court ladies. But the delicacy and serpentine grace of the Siamese women had made the female *lakon* a high point of Siamese classical ballet also in contemporary Thailand. With shining eyes the old princess watched the dance drama she knew so well. For her it was more than a drama. *Lakon* was the lotus bridge that led back to her past at the Siamese court. "Beautiful, is it not?" she whispered.

Prince Pattani nodded. His father had known the princess when she was young. Both of them had participated in the festivities at the royal court, the great festivals to honor the Buddha, the traditional Harvest and Moon Festivals, the *lakon* nights under a full moon. What did the young people and the many foreigners watching the dance tonight know about the soul of this land, its spirit, its traditions, its unalterable love of beauty and dignity? The young Siamese of today no longer knew anything about the art of making flowers, of which Nang Siri and her family were still masters. The prince looked around the garden, at the pavilions, and nodded, satisfied. This was what a ceremonial flower decor should look like. It had to be carried out with fantasy and patience. Nang Siri and her family had taken the flowers apart, blossom by blossom, and with silver wire had put them together again in new, stylized forms, creating transitory and exquisitely perfumed works of art that would bloom for only one night. Never could the West produce so much patient craftsmanship! Two silver bowls stood on either end of the teakwood table from which the old princess and the Pattanis had eaten. Nang Siri had filled them personally with damp clay and had transformed flower petals in every color in the rainbow into a scented mosaic. It was an act of homage for her illustrious guests, and had been suitably appreciated. But Nang Siri had created her masterpiece on the stage itself. In the background, between two wooden columns wreathed with flowers, there hung a whole curtain of blossoms which Siri and her helpers had put together with silver wire, flower by flower. They had worked on it until four o'clock in the morning, then other helpers had sprayed the curtain with water and kept it fresh until the festivities were to begin. For a few hours a magic curtain had been created to heighten the magic of the *lakon*.

Nang Siri sat with her daughter and her American son-in-law in cushioned wicker chairs and asked suddenly, shyly, "Are you satisfied, little one?"

"Oh, Mother," whispered Pauline. "It is indescribably beautiful!" She pressed her dainty little mother's hand so hard that Nang Siri had to suppress a cry. Pauline had Winn's handclasp, just as she had inherited his tall figure and his chin.

Pauline looked at her husband. Larry was in a trance. He was staring wide-eyed at the glittering gold vision of dream and discipline that was still in motion on the stage, festive and mysterious. This strange dance drama had none of that hint of decay which clung to so many plants and objects in the Far East like a fatal perfume. This classical Siamese ballet was the immutable century-old embodiment of beauty which Larry Desmond had experienced until now only in transient things—in flowers, in Asiatic girls, in a sunset over a temple roof, in the metallic gleam of fireflies that blinded you for a moment, then was gone. What Lawrence Desmond experienced that evening was a union of tradition and beauty, the eternal wedding of the East. And this son of the new world recognized in the golden glittering wave of dancers in front of the transitory flower curtain the inflexibility and seductive strength of this part of the world to which the woman beside him belonged irrevocably, for better or for worse, in spring and in autumn, in the sunshine of fulfillment and the destruction of the monsoon. During the last months Pauline, like Prince Rama, had been a mute lamentation; now she was tacit jubilation—trusting, yet in her innermost self a stranger, inheritor of a lotus flower culture which would not permit itself to be trampled on by the merchants of the West.

Pauline looked at her husband, her eyes half-closed. For the first time in her life she was proud of her Siamese heritage.

Weddings in the tropics are major events. Soon there would be another wedding, this time in the Swedish colony. Mr. Bengt Liljefors was going to be married to Miss Karin Holm at the Oriental Hotel in Bangkok with cocktails, a buffet with Swedish specialities, American jazz and Swedish songs. Again, some people wouldn't be able to come to the wedding "because of illness." Miss Karin's Siamese mother had known six days in advance that she would spend this gala day in her daughter's life in her little pile dwelling on Silom Road. Karin had decided it. And the shy old Javanese woman, who lived in constant fear of her vehement daughter, had agreed without a word. She didn't want to stand in the way of her daughter's happiness; still she found it incomprehensible that she should have to miss the celebration. In her camphor chest there was a priceless Javanese gown which she had worn at her wedding to Eric Holm. At this ceremony too, which had been celebrated in the bride's Javanese village, the emerald mirror of bliss had been dimmed. Eric Holm was a foreigner and a Christian, and the wedding had taken place without the honorable Javanese rites. A signing at a registry office, and that had been all. Still Sita had worn her most beautiful gown with a batik *kain*, a long Javanese skirt. She had designed the pattern herself and printed it on the material in gleaming colors: a sun of flowers that played around her slender hips.

For a wedding present, her grandfather had given her a dagger that had been in Sita's family for generations. This *loksampana* had a blade in the shape of a serpent. An inherited dagger gave the owner strength and made him invulnerable, and that was what Sita's father wanted to give her, because she was leaving her home, the Hindu temple and the scene of her dancing.

Engineer Eric Holm had spent a holiday on Java and had married Sita on the spot. He took her to Siam where they lived in the jungles of the north for the first few years. Then Holm, his wife and little Karin had moved to Bangkok. They had lived in a hotel, and one day Eric Holm had disappeared. He left his wife a bankbook and his best wishes for the future. And so Sita gradually grew old.

She bore her fate with patience and the ability to endure suffering which is indicative of the stoical yet proud Javanese women. She carved dancing figures, looked every now and then at the inherited dagger, and bowed humbly in front of her daughter who was occasionally violent, at other times generous. Miss Karin sometimes spoiled her mother. She would bring her rare fruit, an old piece of brocade, a vase with flaming red flowers. She was the best daughter as long as there wasn't a European in sight. But since Karin had become engaged to Mr. Liljefors, she had paid no attention to her mother. And now she had forbidden her to put in an appearance at the Swedish colony. They were planning to go to Sweden right after the wedding. Bengt's contract had expired and he was anxious to go home, which pleased Miss Karin. He wasn't too young and not very slender, but he was a white man, and he was rich. According to Miss Karin, *all* white men were millionaires.

Three days before the wedding, Miss Karin drove to the Oriental Hotel. There was still a lot to be settled. Bengt wasn't feeling well. He had written to her from his bungalow, which he shared with three other Swedes, that she should attend to everything and not come to see him. The doctor had prescribed absolute rest if Mr. Liljefors was to be fresh for the wedding.

The owner of the Oriental Hotel was considerably more polite to Karin than she had been before the engagement. She was a French Swiss who had lived in Bangkok a long time and knew everybody. "A letter for you, Miss Holm," she said, smiling, and handed Karin a letter with Bengt's handwriting on the envelope. For a moment a shiver ran through her. What could Bengt have to write about three days before the wedding? Was he feeling worse?

"Just a minute, please," said Karin. "I would like to see what my fiancé has to say. He hasn't been feeling well."

"I'm sorry to hear that," the owner said politely, hiding her impatience. Couldn't the lady read her love

142

letter after their conversation? "Please excuse me," she said to Miss Karin. "I see some new guests. I'll be with you in a minute."

Miss Karin sat down in the lobby with its decorative palms and a view of the river, and began to read. It was a long letter and she read it twice, as if she found it hard to grasp. At this very moment Mr. Bengt Liljefors was in a plane on his way to Sweden. He made it clear to her in many carefully chosen words that she would never have been happy in the cramped family home in his native Swedish small town. It was all his fault. Karin should please forgive him but he had realized suddenly that she would prefer the tropics to Swedish everyday life. With all best wishes and the plea, again, to be forgiven...

Miss Karin got up and, head held high, walked out of the Oriental Hotel. Her face was a mask. Her hand, with which she crushed the letter and stuck it into her expensive alligator bag, was ice cold. She might have known it. She had had the wedding invitations printed and sent them out against the wishes of her hesitant fiancé. The Swedish consul had been invited as guest of honor. Unfortunately the guest of honor had advised his esteemed compatriot to get out from under as fast as he could. He had made inquiries about Mr. Liljefors's fiancée. It seemed that she flirted with every ship's officer who happened to land in Bangkok, and flirting was putting it mildly. She had had an affair for months with a German; the arrival of that man's wife had put a stop to that. She was not a woman one married. Moreover, the mother of the Swedish millionaire had written to him that she could only give her blessing to a marriage in the tropics to a Javanese girl with a heavy heart. Bengt was her only son; they were very close, closer perhaps than had been good for Bengt. He had never been able to make up his mind at home to get married; he wouldn't be able to do so in the future. But the main obstacle was his wife's Javanese blood which had frightened his mother to death. In Bangkok everything might look different, but one only lived in the tropics for a while.

Miss Karin called a rickshaw. Her voice was harsh yet expressionless. She drove to Silom Road. There was her mother, sitting on her mat, carving hateful symbols of submission, Javanese figurines, toys for natives!

Miss Karin walked across the swaying, rotting wooden bridge between flaming trees and palms, into the little pile dwelling. There was a whirlwind in her head. Her black slanting eyes seemed to be looking through blowing sand at the scene of her fearfully hidden yet dominant private life. Everything that the old Javanese woman, sitting on her coconut mat, personified had toppled the cheap European background Karin had built up so painstakingly again and again. Her imagination, activated now by shock, didn't even grant her the hiatus of despair, which is the right of every disappointed creature. On the contrary, behind the motionless mask of her face, her brain was working with feverish but faulty intensity. The room, her mother, the carved figurines dressed in scraps of brocade, and the spider on the wooden ceiling all took on the dimensions of a nightmare. In a few hours, this girl, who had no father like old Petersen to protect her from the inimical stupidity of the white world, had lost all feeling for the measure and value of things.

In manic exaggeration, Karin saw the East Asian element in her existence as a demonic power that had had a destructive effect right from the start. A power emanating from vengeful Javanese spirits had planted itself scornfully between her and the white world. Not even as a child had she been permitted to inhabit the sphere of innocence legitimately. Her fate had been sealed from birth. There was no free will for her because she hadn't been fighting individuals but an abstraction: the bias of the white world against the half-castes of the East, a struggle that began anew with the birth of every

144

half-caste and ended only with death. Tragic, senseless, and for the western witness, embarrassing. Because frequently this element of exaggeration was part of the struggle, as in the case of Karin Holm, an exaggeration that manifested itself everywhere—in the wild, tropical, primeval expressions of nature and under the unbridled East Asian sun. And it was under the influence of this manic element that the figure of her mother, the figurines, the spider on the ceiling, were distorted into a gruesome, spectral vision.

Karin screamed so shrilly that the unsuspecting woman on her mat, who hadn't heard her daughter coming, jumped to her feet with a cry of pain. In her sere old hand she was holding the Javanese warrior who was to be a wedding present for her incomprehensible daughter. "What is the matter with you? Has something happened?" she asked gently.

Karin stared at the old woman, her mouth open wide. As if through a veil of sand she could see the demon who lived in this gentle frame. Still under the spell of a tropical frenzy, she grasped the figurine and began to beat her mother with it. The old woman stepped back, numb with shock. Her daughter's distorted features filled her with a deadly fear. And then Karin began to laugh. It sounded even more dreadful than her scream. She walked up to her mother, laughing, and smashed the other figurines which the old woman could have sold at a good profit. Still the old Javanese said nothing. Like her brothers and sisters at home, she shrank instinctively from violence. Her almost superhuman ability to endure and suffer prevented her from doing anything about the fury of her possessed daughter.

Karin stopped. The oppressive silence in the simple, clean wooden room quite suddenly brought her to her senses. She threw the ruined toys for natives on the floor and looked at her mother calmly in a frightening change of mood. And then she said something that no daughter may say to her mother under any circumstances, in any language. She spoke Javanese, so that there could be no doubt about the meaning of her blasphemy.

The old Javanese woman listened to her daughter in silence. She wasn't afraid any more. She nodded, strangely solemn. Honorable Grandfather had been right. The gods punished those who obeyed the white robbers and left the Island of the Blessed. The goddess of death had punished Sita with the degenerate fruit of her womb.

Still the old woman said nothing, but she stuck her wrinkled hand inside her batik breastband and drew the dagger out of it quick as a flash, the *loksampana* with the blade in the shape of a serpent. Karin raised both hands, terrified. "No!" she whimpered.

The last thing Sita saw was her degenerate daughter who didn't possess an ounce of Javanese dignity. It was a long last glance. Pride was in it, contempt for the West, and compassion for ignorance. This daughter, who was trembling for her life didn't even know that a Javanese can no longer live when his own flesh and blood sullies his dignity. Sita's sisters had been dancers at the sultan's court. They had preserved their strength and dignity. They lived now in their village in the new nation of Indonesia, in the old peace, surrounded by sugar palms, volcanoes, and respectful daughters and grandchildren. To be sure, Sita had taken the inherited dagger with her into her marriage with the white man. The dagger had given her, as it had to according to the beliefs of her nation, strength and invulnerability. But there was one situation in which the magic of the dagger was ineffective: when a mother was wounded by her flesh and blood. So that was why Sita silently forced the dagger into her breast before Karin could stop her.

On her wedding day Miss Karin sat in the Chinese dance hall Hoi Tien, in Bangkok. The screams of the neighbors, the burial of her mother, the cowardly flight of a white man whose face she could scarcely remember—all that lay so far back, as if it had happened years ago. Karin was meticulously dressed and rouged. On her face a static smile, the smile of the Asiatic taxi dancer, had erased every other expression. Jasmine blossoms were threaded through her beautiful blond hair. She looked enchanting, just as she had looked on the veranda where she had danced in the moonlight for Johannes Petersen. That was a hundred years ago too.

"Do you know Hong Kong?" her partner asked. Mr. Yu was a rich business man from Hong Kong.

Miss Karin replied that she would simply love to see Hong Kong. Mr. Yu's plane left very early the next day.

Next morning two Bangkok couples were at the airport: Petersen and Martha, and Mr. and Mrs. Charles Krüger. They were flying to Ceylon to meet Charles' sister, Florence. The Petersens weren't staying in Colombo, but after greeting the lady from Hamburg, they were going on to Mount Lavinia, where Hannes was to spend fourteen days recuperating. The Krügers would bring sister Florence back to Bangkok.

A strange couple entered the airport—a fat little Chinese and a tall blond with slanting black eyes. Doris Krüger looked at Miss Karin curiously. It had been a real Bangkok scandal. The Swedish consul had cancelled the reception for Mr. Liljefors and Miss Holm at the last minute. He had tried to reach as many as he could of the guests outside the Swedish colony whom the bride had invited, among them Petersen junior and his wife, but Miss Karin had the list and nobody knew her address... not even the owner of the Oriental Hotel, who sent the Swedish Embassy a bill for the preparations already made. She wasn't going to be the one to suffer when a Eurasian had again been jilted.

"Isn't that. . .?" Doris Krüger whispered excitedly.

"Yes," said Martha, and spoke at once of something else.

Miss Karin boarded the plane for Hong Kong with Mr. Yu without even so much as glancing at Nai Petersen. She was chatting loudly and her laughter was shrill. An Englishman, traveling on the same plane, turned to his business colleague. "Russian," he said. "They always overact."

Then the huge bird flew off in the direction of Hong Kong and the other huge bird flew with the Petersens to Ceylon. The two planes quickly put as much distance between them as now lay between Nai Petersen and Miss Karin.

10

The Dark Moon of Ceylon

On the flight to Singapore, the four Hamburgers didn't indulge in much conversation. Two days before her departure, one of Martha's Chinese servants had mentioned something that had taken place while she was in Hua Hin trying to straighten Pauline out. But right now wasn't the time to speak to Hannes about it. There would be time enough after the few days in Colombo, when they went to Mount Lavinia for their holiday. Hannes had some business appointments with Singalese firms in Colombo. A big city in the blazing tropical sun was not the place for domestic conversations. Martha pushed the stray hairs behind her ears.

Hannes was sitting there, blissfully smoking one cigarette after the other. He was looking forward to showing Martha Colombo. He loved Ceylon best of all the island nations in the East, an undamaged isle that had safely withstood the storm of war. Ceylon had not experienced Japanese occupation. An Island of the Blessed in a restless continent.

"Please don't smoke so much, Hannes," Martha said. She was very pale.

Petersen laughed and lit another cigarette. "Do you think I'm like Chubb?" he asked. "Your old man knows how much he can take!"

That was exactly what Hannes had never known. Martha shrugged and said nothing more.

"Is the flight bothering you?" asked Petersen. "You're so pale."

"When do we get to Singapore?"

Petersen looked at his watch. "In about fifteen minutes. We'll board ship right away. Is that all right with you? You can see Singapore another time."

It was very much all right with Martha. She was looking forward to the trip from Singapore to Ceylon. Altogether she felt best on a gently rocking ship. She watched Hannes for a while in silence. She wouldn't feel at peace until she had spoken to him about it. One's Asiatic servants, of course, lived on their love of intrigue. It could be a fairy tale, to vex the Mem a little. But it was strange that Hannes hadn't said a word about it, not even after Pauline's wedding. When all of them at last got back to Hamburg, an orderly life could begin again.

Martha had already allowed two more months for Bangkok. She hoped to persuade Hannes to come home too, but somehow had the feeling that he wasn't giving a thought to returning with them. Since her arrival in East Asia, her entire existence seemed to be hanging in the balance. Except in her own soul, Martha could feel stability nowhere. All those families that arrived in Bangkok and left again...except for the Viennese family, who were condemned to go on living the lives of the white coolies if somebody didn't find the right place for the professor. If only Pauline had finished translating the manuscript! But she had given up after the first chapter. It was too difficult...Aunt Martha should please excuse her...and she had to go to the Chinese tailor so often right now before the wedding. But Martha didn't give up so easily when it was a case of helping a friend. In Colombo she would talk to Florence Krüger. The Krüger sisters had had an English grandmother, and Florence had spent a part of her childhood and youth in England. So she spoke English and German.

She would certainly be glad to translate the first chapters.

Martha looked out of the plane onto the waterscape below. The mountains and villages were tiny interruptions at the edge of the ocean. From the air this Asiatic paradise seemed just as much in suspension as the lives of the Europeans in East Asia. Two months ago war had broken out in Korea. In Bangkok life went on as usual. The Siamese enjoyed the limited bliss of an existence which was a fruit of Buddhist philosophy. All things passed. The "little war" in Korea would be over one day too. If there were any political anxieties in Thailand, then they would be about one's immediate neighbors: Indochina and Burma. That was where direct danger might come from. That was what Prince Pattani had told Martha at Pauline's wedding. Then he had watched the classical Siamese ballet again and enjoyed every minute of his limited bliss. In their silent way the Siamese were truly experts at the art of living, Martha thought. They meditated in the shadow of the holy fig tree and were in no hurry to exchange this existence for the next. She would find the same spiritual ambience in Ceylon, the cradle of Buddhism.

Petersen had closed his eyes. Martha was cool to him. Why? What was wrong? She was probably very tired. Wild horses wouldn't have dragged Petersen to moody Pauline in Hua Hin; Martha, however, was always looking for lame ducks who took her time and strength. But she had a husband and children who had a right to her time and strength. Pauline's marriage to the gentleman from New Orleans would turn out badly. Petersen was sure of that. Pauline was jealous. And she could hang onto a grudge for years. In this respect she was like Miss Karin. But just as Petersen had arrived at this lady in his reflections, the plane came down on the airport of Singapore like a tired bird. Not a moment too soon.

After days of peaceful voyage in the Indian Ocean, the Island of the Happy rose out of the blue waters. Martha was standing at the railing with Petersen. He had laid an arm across her shoulder. With his free hand he raised his binoculars to his eyes and excitedly watched the shining pear-shaped island with its mountain peak which Buddhist pilgrims had been visiting for years. The Adam's Peak of Ceylon was as famous in the Far East as the Golden Stupa of Nakom Pathorn in Siam. Pilgrims from all over the world traveled to it.

Petersen always felt this strange excitement when approaching an island. He had aimed his binoculars just like this as a boy on the island of Helgoland, and had felt at the time like Columbus on sighting the American continent. One sailed toward adventure from across the sea. His grandfather had put his arm across the shoulders of his young grandson and had said, "Yes, my boy, there's something about an island..." Chubb too had been excited when he had sailed toward the tin island of Phuket with his grand-uncle. All the Petersens had a thing about islands. But Chubb was too shy to mention it to his father.

"Next year we'll sail to Java and Sumatra, if business remains as good," Petersen told Martha. She couldn't believe her ears! Java? Sumatra? Next year all of them would be going to Blankenese if she still had something to say in this marriage! But Martha was too clever to bring it up now because they were just entering the port of Colombo, and Florence Krüger was waiting for them on the pier. The Krüger's English cousin, who had spent the last thirty years in Ceylon, was waiting with her.

Florence had already been in Colombo two weeks. She had wanted to look around herself first, and couldn't drag her brother into any museum or temple. "Hello, how are you?" Charles Krüger asked his sister. Then he introduced their English cousin, pipe in mouth, to his Hamburg friends.

Dr. Philip Conway was very tall, very thin, and his

hair was just as wild as Dr. Tyler's in Bangkok. And he was as hospitable as all the English in the Far East. He at once invited the Petersens to dinner on the following evening. Florence and the Krügers were staying with him. He nodded when Petersen said that he and Martha would be going on to Mount Lavinia in a few days. "A nice place," he said. Then Petersen and Martha drove past the Dutch church and the cinnamon gardens. The shadow that Petersen didn't notice or didn't want to notice, drove with them. It hung, dark and mysterious, over the white city of Colombo.

"May I speak to Mr. Petersen from Bangkok?"

The desk clerk gave the woman questioning him a look out of his shrewd, evaluating eyes. Her white tropical suit was shabby. It had been washed too often, and by Chinese who frequently treated linen like leather. And the woman hadn't spent much money on her hair either. The poorly dyed curls looked like a home permanent. The White Russians in the Far East hadn't had any jewelry to pawn for years, and when they had passed thirty, as this woman certainly had, they couldn't hope to get much out of a man.

"Mr. Petersen has already left," said the desk clerk. "But Mrs. Petersen is still here. Do you wish me to announce you?"

"No, thank you," the woman replied. "How long is Mr. Petersen staying in Colombo?"

"That I can't say," said the desk clerk, who knew very well that Mr. Petersen intended to leave for Mount Lavinia in three days, but discretion was a part of his profession.

"Thank you very much," said Tatiana Boulgakoff, in the harsh English of the White Russian. "I'll come back."

"As you wish," said the desk clerk, without too much enthusiasm.

Just then Martha walked into the spacious lobby.

153

The Russian woman stared at her for a moment. Johnny's wife. An expression of unfathomable amusement lay in her eyes, as if she knew a lot more about Petersen's past in Bangkok than Martha did. One couldn't just strip off one's past like a snake's skin. In her Russian Restaurant on Suriwongse Road, Petersen had met all the ladies who had dispelled his loneliness during the long years of separation from his wife. Miss Karin had been a guest in her restaurant too.

Martha also looked thoughtfully at the Russian woman. Where had she seen this shabby creature with the heavy makeup over a skin tanned by the tropical sun before? On the plane to Singapore! The Russian woman had sat motionless the whole time, staring down at the fleeing landscape and smoking. On her hard face, with its prominent cheekbones, there was as little expression as on a death mask.

After the war, Madame Boulgakoff's restaurant had gone downhill rapidly. She had made a lot of money during the Japanese occupation. Swedes, Norwegians, Danes, Germans, and Swiss, all of whom enjoyed freedom, were steady customers in Bangkok in those days. But in 1945, everything had changed. The Americans didn't go to Russian restaurants. They had their club for American businessmen, the Rotary Club, and their private cocktail parties. Some Germans had been deported— the British military had discovered that they were Nazis. They had disappeared together with the last German ambassador in Bangkok, back to their ruined country, to internment camps where they were to be denazified, to a starvation hell. Johannes Petersen had been able to prove that he had fled from the Gestapo. Petersen senior had sworn to the fact under oath. Otherwise Hannes would also have been deported in 1945. Martha kept thinking more and more if it might not have been for the best in the long run. Hannes always had to be forced to decisions. His inclination to let things slide had found a philosophical basis in East Asia. The fatalism of the Asiatic met this inclination halfway.

At first Petersen had been a frequent guest at the Russian Restaurant on Suriwongse Road. With Martha's arrival, these visits had stopped abruptly. Miss Karin had given Tatiana a colorful report of the scene on the pier. They had drunk a lot of vodka and laughed a lot. "He'll be back," Madame Boulgakoff had said. "They all come back."

And they usually did. The Far East had its own rules where love affairs were concerned. Yet it did look as if Petersen had definitely turned his back on the Russian Restaurant after Martha's arrival. "Just wait," said Madame Boulgakoff.

Miss Karin had giggled, then she had become engaged, and now she was in Hong Kong, from where she had written her Russian friend a long letter that had made the Russian woman smile. She found intrigues just as amusing as did Martha's Asiatic servants. They were such a fun pastime after reaching the years when one could only incite men to fury. Madame's arrival in Ceylon was a coincidence, not a happy one. She had been offered a Singalese place to run. The owner had been in Bangkok on business and had suggested she take a look at it, with which Madame Boulgakoff had finally landed among the natives.

Martha watched her leave, yet one more person whom the East had conquered. The Russian woman's arrogant expression hadn't deceived Martha: her dark, almond-shaped eyes were filled with a fatalistic despair, the hard demonic despair that the White Russians had brought with them to East Asia after 1920. One took one's revenge on all Europeans who were successful in business and had brought their families into the luxury of the tropics, away from a continent grown shabby.

"Is there a message for me?" Martha asked the desk clerk. She was expecting Florence Krüger. Hannes had left early to keep his business appointments. Up to now the German expectations of trade with Ceylon had not been fulfilled. A source for the import of vital raw materials had opened up for them recently, but as far as the sale of German manufactured goods in Ceylon was concerned, things were practically at a standstill. Laws were even being considered that would again restrict German and Japanese imports by insisting on licensing. Since the Ceylonese had taken their fate from the British crown colony into their own hands, a great many economic problems had arisen. West Germany was powerless as long as it lacked a diplomatic representative in Colombo. Only a German consul general could strengthen the friendly relationship to the present Ceylon government, inform the government tactfully of German trade expectations, and see to it that they were carried out. Petersen junior was planning his own agency in Ceylon. He had already corresponded about it with Hinrich Petersen in Hamburg, and suggested that Hinrich bring pressure to bear wherever possible on the powers that be to see to it that the German representatives yet to be appointed should be knowledgable in business matters.

Johannes Petersen had the makings of an economic pioneer. He was familiar with vast areas of the Far East. He felt that the next years would offer great possibilities for the export-import firm of Petersen and Company. If Martha couldn't see that his place was in East Asia right now, where one could reconstruct in so many different areas, then...then what? Petersen couldn't think of an answer to the question on the morning after his arrival in Colombo, as he discussed a future exchange of material with two influential Ceylonese. The children had to go back to Hamburg; he had said so from the start. And he was still saying it now seven months later. And in this respect he was right. He couldn't understand Martha. He couldn't grasp the fact that since she had never left Europe before, she hadn't had time yet to make the

156

standpoint of the so-called colonial parents her own. For years she had protected and educated her children; she knew that both of them needed her influence, especially Charlotte, whom Petersen spoilt in an absolutely senseless fashion. And now things had reached the point where Tiny wanted to go to a party almost every day! She had made a lot of young foreign friends in Bangkok.

Martha was thinking of her daughter when Florence Krüger walked into the lobby, tall, slender, and dressed with unobtrusive elegance. Florence had experienced the downfall of the solid middle class in Hamburg from the beginning to the bitter end. Like her parents and grandparents, she was a traditionalist, but she was also a woman who paid tribute to the present. She was a leader in important women's organizations which, after 1945, worked for social and international progress; she frequently visited the refugee camps and orphanages in and around Hamburg. A wholesome and animated friendship existed between the two women, born of a certain similarity of natures. But Florence had less patience with her fellow men.

"Charles and Doris will be the death of me!" she declared as soon as she walked in. "They have nothing on their minds but dogs and horses and the indolent life of the tropics. If Charles hadn't begged me in every letter, I'd never have come!"

Martha smiled. All families were the same. They rarely understood each other, and joined their families in exotic countries out of a purely misconceived sense of obligation. "Martha!" Florence said now. "You've changed. Have you lost weight, or is something bothering you?"

"Both," said Martha. "And what's new in Hamburg?"

"Waiting for your return. When are you coming back, anyway? I guess with me."

"Maybe. I can't tell you that today. It's all much more complicated than I thought it would be. Hannes..." she paused. She had never discussed Hannes with any of

157

her friends. And what should she tell Florence who was looking at her slightly ironically?

"The mysterious East?" asked Florence. "Is he carrying on again? He should have outgrown that by now."

Florence was ten years older than Martha and felt she could be frank with her. Hannes had always been a great fellow except for his little indiscretions. All the male members of the Petersen family inclined toward such little indiscretions, except Hinrich, who was a stuffed shirt and surely had fish blood in his veins.

Martha didn't answer right away. Florence had screwed up her left eye, which she always did when she felt she was on the track of something. "Hannes doesn't want to come back to Hamburg," Martha said suddenly.

You could rely on Florence. Her irony was more on her lips than in her heart. It was the irony of a disappointed woman. Florence had been in love with Wilhelm Christian Petersen, but she had lost him to the Far East before you could say Jack Robinson. You couldn't rely on the Petersen men—not where women were concerned, at any rate. Her disappointment had made a decisive impact on her life. After one night of love she had come to a decision—never to depend on a man. And she had been strong enough to stick to it. A wound had remained, and she spoke with the slightly sour sense of humor that irritated her brother Charles and his wife.

"Hannes doesn't want to go back?" she said, in a tone of utter disbelief. "Has he had a sunstroke?"

"Oh Florence!" Martha pushed her stray hairs behind her ears with a tired gesture. "I'll tell you all about it another time."

Florence understood, but she was worried. Martha had never been tired or resigned. Were the tropics enervating her? Or was Doris Krüger's bit of gossip correct?

Florence glanced at her watch. "Let's have a look at Colombo," she said energetically.

They got into Dr. Conway's car. The chauffeur, a

Jaffna-Tamil, grinned at the two *Mem sahibs*. He had come to Ceylon from south India, and all European women amazed him.

"We have time until this afternoon," said Florence. "Colombo is an enchanting city, not nearly as dusty as Port Said."

Martha enjoyed the drive immensely. A little of the splendor of the crown colony still permeated the snow-white highway that ran along the ocean. The luxurious colonial life which Martha had already witnessed in Saigon had an English face in Colombo. The Victoria Bridge, the world-famous port itself, the cinnamon gardens, the many villas with carefully tended lawns and flower beds—everything still bore the label: British Empire. Ceylon had only been an independent member of the commonwealth for two years; it had been a British colony for a hundred and fifty. And everywhere there were memorials and traces of earlier colonial periods. Martha looked at them with astonishment. The Portuguese and the Dutch had strewn their churches and family names across the island. It was they who had started exporting cinnamon and founding factories. The Dutch burghers, whose places of business and residences could still be found in Ceylon today, had a strong mixture of Singalese or Tamil blood in their veins; and all races and nations—the Indian Moors, the ancient Veddas, the Singalese, and the many Tamils from neighboring India—had lived peacefully in the crown colony side by side, just as they lived today under the tolerant regime of the Buddha.

Florence had seen and learned a lot from her English cousin, Dr. Conway. The harmony of the races here had made a deep impression on her. Europe, and especially Germany, could learn something from it. Florence had found the organized intolerance of the Hitler regime torturous. "What is the position of the Germans in the Far East?" she asked.

"Not easy," Martha said, after giving it some thought. "But Hannes can fill you in on all the details. You see, we are still reaping what the Nazis sowed, and the new arrivals in Bangkok look at us skeptically. 'Germans... former Nazis, of course.' One can't let everybody know that one's husband was also a refugee, and that one... well, Florence, you know."

Florence Krüger nodded. She had found a home for two Jewish students of Martha's and their families with her English relatives and friends. And she had also been able to help her own friends leave Germany as long as it had still been possible, but of course it had all been a drop on a hot stone. If everyone who could have helped then had helped...

Florence was looking at the palms in the English garden. "We are the heirs," she said slowly. "Nothing we can do about it. But just because of that we must support an understanding of democracy and international cooperation. It's strange how few Germans have an appreciation of such matters. In Hamburg you'll find more understanding than anywhere else. Hannes could explain a thing or two to his compatriots, I think."

"And he will. You can depend on it," said Martha, with her old energy. Florence's presence was doing her good.

When Martha got back to the hotel at around five, Petersen was in the bar. He had found her short note and was annoyed that she hadn't come back for lunch. When Petersen was in a bad mood, which was rarely, then he was just as obnoxious as only charming men can be. "Nice of you to come back at all," he muttered. "Do you know what you look like? For God's sake, pay some attention to your hair, at least occasionally! Those stray hairs of yours have been driving me crazy for weeks!"

"Did you have some interesting talks?" Martha paid as little attention to Petersen's outburst as if he had said nothing at all. One couldn't say that the first stop of their holiday was being a success. Hannes was chain-smoking again, fifty cigarettes a day.

"We talked plenty," Petersen replied irritably. "We have to go to dinner in two hours. By then I hope you'll have done something about your hair."

"That's quite likely." Martha's voice was cold. She found it provoking when a forty-three year old man behaved like an ill-bred boy.

Petersen looked up. Martha was paler than on the plane. "I'm sorry," he mumbled. "My desire for your company is becoming a nuisance. I apologize, *Mem sahib!*"

"That's all right, Hannes."

There was the sweat of exhaustion on Petersen's forehead. Martha had never been completely free of worry since the dog had bitten him. How difficult it was to convalesce in the tropics! Hannes was hardened by sport, but the shock and the many injections had weakened him.

"How about a pink gin?" Petersen stroked Martha's beautiful, strong hand tenderly. He had a way of being able to appease a woman in seconds. But Martha was just leaving. "Until later, my boy," she said. Then, frowning a little, she went off to the hotel beautician.

She wanted a massage for her migraine. You couldn't get anything like it in Hamburg. Massage was an East Asian art. And she had to do something about those stray hairs. In Hamburg Martha had never had time to look in the mirror. In East Asia she definitely had too much time...

Petersen drank his fourth pink gin. Really, he had to do better at controlling himself. Martha had been through plenty with him. He didn't dare to tell her that he had written to Hinrich Petersen that the children would be leaving in four months. Dr. Johannsen was taking his vacation in Europe and would take them with him. Petersen had asked if the children could stay with Hinrich and his wife, Lisa. Or one would have to put them in boarding school. Hinrich should make inquiries.

Petersen ordered his fifth gin. He could drink and drink and one didn't notice anything. He was not the silly boy who had let Martha influence him. That might have applied in a destroyed Hamburg of over a decade ago, but today he was a mature man who knew the world from both sides, and he had no intention of letting Martha go again. He needed her for himself and as a protection against all other women. They can go to the devil, he thought. But the ladies didn't go to the devil, not on order, and especially not in East Asia. Not one woman east of Suez seemed to realize that Petersen was finished with his indiscretions. The past was one of the strongest elements in the Orient, a power that was sometimes constructive and sometimes destroyed.

"Good evening, Mr. Johnny," said a harsh voice.

Petersen swivelled around in his chair. I'm a bundle of nerves, he thought, frowning. And this was all he needed! The White Russian woman from Suriwongse Road. He had felt dizzy when he saw her at the airport in Bangkok, but then he had thought all she had wanted was to say goodbye to Karin. And then the woman had got into the plane for Singapore.

"I have received an airmail letter from Karin," Madame Boulgakoff explained. "She doesn't like it in Hong Kong."

Petersen rose. "Excuse me," he murmured, not looking at the heavily rouged face with the cruelly amused eyes. "I have to change. I have a dinner engagement."

"*Just* a minute, sir!" said the Russian woman. "Give me a little of your valuable time, please, or I shall have to speak to your wife."

"You leave my wife out of this!" A vein protruded suddenly on Petersen's forehead with his fury. "Otherwise something's going to happen!"

"Something is certainly going to happen if you don't

help old friends," the Russian woman said softly. "Why are you so excited, Mr. Johnny?"

"How much?" Petersen asked furiously. "I don't have much time. So...how many English pounds?"

"None," Madame said, to Petersen's surprise. "Our little Karin wants to come back to Bangkok. She would like a job as your secretary."

"Until now our firm hasn't hired any nightclub artists," Petersen told this lady out of his past. He was so furious that he could only speak English with difficulty. "The two of you must be absolutely crazy!" He said it so loudly that the bartender looked up. A little blackmail under the rising moon of Colombo. An old story, as old as the European's love for the half-caste.

"I have no intention of letting you blackmail me," said Petersen. "I wasn't born yesterday."

"Nobody wants to blackmail you," the Russian woman said seriously. "But Karin thinks you'd better do something for her. She's expecting a child."

So that was the game they were playing. And Petersen was cast as the idiot. As always in a crisis, Petersen thought fast. "Then I think Miss Karin should turn to the Swedish man who jilted her," he said, forcing himself to remain calm. If Martha came into the bar now to remind him that it was time to dress for dinner, he was in trouble.

"Don't fool around with me, Mr. Johnny. I know you. Karin is a respectable girl. She never loved anyone but you. You seduced her and then left her...cruelly, in spite of the fact that only a short while ago she was still visiting you every evening in Bangkapi. She sensed how lonely you were. Your wife was in Hua Hin for weeks. Karin has a soft heart..."

"Soft as a hard-boiled egg," said Petersen, harshly. He had to put a stop to this thing and get down to business with this woman. He wasn't a superlative sales-man for nothing.

"Tatiana," he said ingratiatingly. "You're the cleverest woman between Europe and Asia. Let's deal with this thing practically. You won't come out of it badly. The restaurant on Suriwongse Road is doing all right, isn't it?"

"If I had ten thousand ticals and Karin as the major attraction, I could build it up again. I took a look at a place here today. Dreadful! The Singalese spit all over the place. My restaurant in Bangkok is clean as a whistle, isn't it?"

"It certainly is," said Petersen, knowing better.

"No native guests in *my* restaurant," the Russian woman declared with naïve arrogance. She seemed to have no idea how much the Siamese despised impoverished White Russians.

"Three thousand ticals when I get back to Bangkok," Petersen said softly. "And my wife is left alone."

"And my return fare," the Russian woman added. She had been counting on two thousand ticals.

"With the first boat tomorrow morning," Petersen suggested. Madame Boulgakoff was in what for her was practically a state of animation. She smiled in her way, without any participation by the rest of her face. Quite a trick!

"And how does our little Karin get from Hong Kong to Bangkok?" she asked.

"No idea," Petersen said casually. A murderous fury was rising in him all the way up to his throat, and he never stopped smiling. A fine vacation! "Have a good trip, my dear."

Madame Boulgakoff understood and rose. "I'm broke," she said.

"So am I," said Mr. Johnny. "My bank account is in Bangkok," which meant that he wouldn't pay until she had kept her part of the bargain. "And one more thing," he went on, "if your valuable time permits. If you or Karin so much as show your faces in Bangkapi or anywhere else in my wife's presence, then I will have the license for your restaurant revoked. Is that clear? The Bangkok police close down unlicensed gambling joints. In that respect they can be very disagreeable."

Madame Boulgakoff gave Petersen a look of such hatred out of her melancholy eyes that he stepped back for a moment as if he had been struck, but he pretended not to have noticed anything.

"To talk is silver, to be silent is gold, they say where I come from," he said dreamily.

"One lives and learns," said Madame Boulgakoff. "Perhaps you'll come to see us some time when Mrs. Petersen has gone?"

"Good evening," said Mr. Johnny, and strode out of the bar smiling radiantly.

"Where have you been, Hannes?" Martha cried. "You've got to change!"

She was wearing a silvery evening dress. The hairdresser had worked wonders. Her hair was shaped in attractive waves around her fine little head. At the nape of her neck it was knotted in a way that had no relationship whatsoever to the tight little knot she twisted hurriedly every morning. She had taken off her glasses. To please Hannes she didn't wear glasses when they went to a party. She had never worn such a beautiful dress as this one which the Chinese tailor on Suriwongse Road had made for her; she had never spent so much money on herself. She looked extraordinarily attractive, yet with the dignity she always personified. "Madame is cool, cool beauty," the hairdresser had murmured. "Madame always wear hair very soft."

Martha looked at Petersen expectantly. What would he say to her new hairdo? It really did make her look ten years younger. The cherry trees in a prosaic street had blossomed suddenly. During the war Martha had experienced terrible times in Hamburg. There wasn't a woman in those days who had done anything about her appearance. They had lugged coal and potatoes in sacks into their makeshift homes. But in the Far East a woman was still a luxury item. This Martha had found out, to her astonishment. And tonight in the bar it had dawned on her: she had had no idea that her loose stray hairs irritated Hannes. There were a lot of things she hadn't known about her husband.

Petersen stormed past Martha to the bathroom. He had given her only a fleeting glance and hadn't said a word about her hair.

Martha looked at the tall palm trees in the hotel garden. The shadow between Petersen and herself grew sky-high. What had happened? She had a new hairdo and her husband hadn't noticed anything! A few weeks ago he would have been delighted. Was it too late? In the last two months, Martha had had the impression that Hannes and she had never been so happy together. He had matured a great deal and seemed to realize what had happened to her. And when she had come back from Hua Hin he had said, "Thank God you're back! I won't let you go again!" He had been strangely excited and had looked at her almost imploringly. And then, two days before leaving for Ceylon, the old cook had come to her and in his Chinese way, with many digressions, had mumbled in pidgin Engish, "Mem better never go away. Gourd sometimes have bitter leaves; guest sometimes have bitter tongue."

Martha had had the certain feeling that Ah Chang knew Petersen had told Martha nothing about any "bad guest." Had Hannes done something foolish again? Could that be possible? The atmosphere in the Far East was full of temptation, illusion, and threatening powers. Martha knew too much about life not to be able to see that wealthy, handsome men were the desirable prey in a hunt in which she could not and would not participate. She had patience and understanding, but Hannes had to play his part. Marriage was an agreement. And while Martha gazed at the tall coconut palms it seemed to her as if again the rug had been pulled from under her feet. By whom? Never had Hannes spoken to her as he just had done in the bar. And never had he been so full of reservations. He seemed to have two or three lives: the smart, cool, calculating business man; Martha's devoted husband; and a sporadic father. The children didn't seem to be a necessity to him. Perhaps he had been separated from them for too long. But then Petersen had always been spoiled by women. She didn't know this man. She, the prudent one, the mother-beloved, couldn't for the life of her fathom the secrets of her husband. She couldn't ask him who had visited him; he had to tell her that himself. She could lose everything, but she would not gamble with her dignity. At that moment Martha decided that no woman in the world really possessed her husband, except perhaps for the woman who was indifferent to him. Just then Petersen appeared in black trousers and the white dinner jacket of the tropical gentleman. The short jacket enhanced his elegant figure.

He laid the Siamese brocade cape across her shoulders while she walked to the waiting car that was to take them to Dr. Conway's house. Martha didn't feel at all like a dinner party. Social life in the Far East took its steady course until a catastrophe threw cocktail glasses and guests in a heap. The English had been having their drinks in the sports club in the early morning of December 1941, on the day the Japanese occupied the city. Hannes had told her that.

Dr. Conway's dinner was served in a large dining room. Singalese servants in full white skirts with tortoiseshell combs in their hair, served food and stimulating drinks. Martha sat beside her host. Doris Krüger still couldn't get over the change in Martha. She was speaking softly, then suddenly she blared out, "I hardly recognize you, Martha! What do you have to say about your wife, Hannes? Ten years younger with her hair done like that!" Dear Doris had about as much tact as a rhinoceros. "Do be quiet, Mama," whispered her husband.

Martha pretended not to have heard but went on talking to Dr. Conway. He was telling about the years of instruction he had taken from a *swami*, a Hindu master or spiritual teacher. Dr. Conway knew all about the supernatural powers that could enter into the yogis through their teaching. "I did a few exercises with the *swami*," he said. "But of course I am only a beginner in his disciplines."

Martha listened with great interest. She didn't know that many Englishmen, arrogantly looked upon as cranks by superficial compatriots, busied themselves on lonely tropical evenings with the spiritual recognitions of the Indians. The longer one stayed in the Orient, the stronger the urge for knowledge that was inaccessible to the West.

Later they sat on the big veranda and breathed the scent that wafted across to them from the cinnamon gardens of Colombo. A big moon hung in an ink-black sky. Petersen and Krüger were discussing business problems connected with Ceylon. Florence, making an effort to control herself, was talking to Doris. Dogs, dogs, and more dogs! If only she hadn't let herself be persuaded to come, but Charles had been so persistent in every letter...

"I find the teachings of yoga a little eerie," Martha was saying. "I wouldn't like to spend my life among these Hindu wise men. Aren't they really taking the ground from under your feet?"

"Yoga gives you the ground under your feet, Mrs. Petersen," said Dr. Conway. "It is a purifying bath for spirit and soul. I don't mean only the breathing exercises and the exercises for concentration and correct posture, which I learned just by watching my teacher. I mean the power that gives you control over your senses and emotions. One has to become invulnerable; then one can master one's own fate and the fate of others."

Martha held her breath for a moment. Was he right, this Englishman speaking with his eyes half-closed? Was there such a thing as an invulnerable woman?

"A *swami* can walk across thorns without feeling pain by sheer will power alone. He can go without food for six days and feel no hunger because he is concentrating in a very specific way. He can achieve absolute freedom through spiritual isolation," said the pleasant voice of the man sitting beside her. "A very useful science in a world that moves from one slavery to the next."

Just then there was a scream from the servants' quarters. "Oh," said Dr. Conway, "you must excuse me for a moment. My cook's grandmother is ill. They have sent for a devil dancer to drive out the illness."

"Don't your servants let you treat them?" Martha asked, astonished.

The doctor laughed. The grandmother wasn't his patient, and all the servants in his house trusted the devil dancer rather than the white man who had only landed on the island a hundred and fifty years ago. "If we go and stand behind the hedge without making any noise, you can see something strange," Dr. Conway suggested to his guests. "Something you'll find only in Ceylon."

What they saw took place on the outer fringes of the present. Ceylon had the most modern harbor in the East and the oldest devil dancers. Ceylon lay on the direct route between the Suez Canal and Calcutta, Rangoon, Singapore, and it was on the route to Australia; Ceylon tea, rubber, copra, and coconut oil went to all these places, but the devil dancer in Dr. Conway's garden in Colombo was unaware of all this.

He wore a white robe embellished with palm leaves, and he danced to the accompaniment of a dull drum in front of a little house altar that was covered with sacrificial gifts: rice cooked in coconut milk, betel nut leaves, areca nuts, and flowers. His assistant sang songs of exhortation. The dancer moved wildly yet formally, like a marionette driven to ecstasy by some unknown power. Bracelets jingled on his dark withered arms. He began to tremble. His eyes threatened to pop out of their sockets. His dank black hair hung disheveled around his dark face. He was horrible and he was grotesque. Suddenly he screamed again and sank down in front of the little altar. The cook and the other servants revived him by spraying water on his face. The devil dancer moved and stared with unseeing black eyes in the direction of the hut where the old woman was lying. Then he rose and carried a clay pot into the hut. When the grandmother drank the holy water from the hands of the devil dancer, the demons of sickness would leave her body.

"These superstitious people must give you a hard time," Martha said later, when they were back on the veranda again.

"I don't know," said Dr. Conway. "People are superstitious in Europe too. And I must say I prefer my cook's devil dancer to the gyrations of our politicians in the West."

Petersen smoked his next to last cigarette of the evening. He had smoked over fifty cigarettes that day. It was late. He was talking animatedly to Dr. Conway. The doctor was a typical representative of the former power of British civilization in the Orient, a power that was gone. But the art of compromise was what made Dr. Conway's existence possible in independent Ceylon. The English had become guests whereas before they had been fatherly protectors. But business flourished between London and Colombo, and between the devil dancer and science. There were plenty of Singalese and Tamils who sought Dr. Conway's treatment of malaria.

"If we Germans could only learn not to put all our eggs in one basket," said Petersen, putting out his cigarette. It was time for them to leave. He wanted to get up.

But what was this? Suddenly the moon was beginning to shine darkly. Was there going to be an eclipse? Now it was a black ball that moved with an eerie power toward Petersen's forehead, and all this was enveloped by the uncompromising night. The dark moon shot close, a demonic mask that reminded him vaguely of Madame Boulgakoff. Gruesome amusement and behind it a void of despair...

Why didn't the others notice anything, Petersen wondered? A feeling of panic rose up in him, making him dizzy. He was plunging into a fiery glowing void, into a tropical purgatory of palm trees, blurred figures, and a glass with some whiskey in it danced on Dr. Conway's wicker table. Then the glass disappeared in the raging moon-sea. Petersen tried to reach Martha with a look but he couldn't penetrate the dark to the clear light that had to be her face. He had the feeling that this was the end: a merry life and a lonely death. This was his fate. Martha was not to cry for him. That was what he had said to her when the mad dog had bitten him. And hazily he thought that he had never said anything more sensible.

He could still think, but he couldn't see. He stretched his hand out through a black emptiness. Only, please, not to be blind... He had to see the Cambodian towers on the Menam River once more.

He screamed without making a sound. Now the moon was lying on his face, a glowing disc that was pressing the life out of him. Goddammit! He couldn't breathe any more. "Air!" he gasped. "Air!"

When the dark moon had drifted away again into the cloudy night, Martha, in her beautiful silvery dress, leaned over Petersen. "It's nothing, Hannes," she murmured.

"I can't see you."

Petersen tried to grope his way through the black curtain in front of his eyes. Martha's hand found his from a mysterious distance. "Everything will be all right again very soon. But you must be patient, beloved."

Somebody plunged a dagger into his arm. But it was only a hypodermic needle. Petersen could see the tropical background as if through a veil. "You just fainted, that's all," said Dr. Conway. "I think I'd better drive you to the hotel as soon as you feel better. I'm sorry, Mr. Petersen."

Petersen tried to smile. "And I'm even more sorry," he said softly. "Silly of me..."

Half an hour later Petersen was ready to leave, although there was still a veil over his eyes, which irritated him. He wanted to get up with his usual energy but something held him fast in his wicker chair. "I...I can't walk, Dr. Conway," he stammered. "How stupid!" It was as if he had been struck suddenly by paralysis.

Martha's face was white. The threat that had been hanging over Hannes ever since the dog had bitten him...it couldn't possibly happen now, after so many months? Petersen had dismissed it as nonsense, and Martha had been so happy over his quick recovery that she hadn't thought seriously about it any more either. But the six-month incubation period wasn't over yet!

Martha controlled her fear because Dr. Conway had given her a warning look. While Petersen was unconscious she had hastily told him about the accident. Dr. Conway called for an ambulance and Florence Krüger deposited her horrified brother and sister-in-law somewhere else in the house. Meanwhile Petersen's left arm and leg became immobile. When the ambulance arrived, they lifted him in and Dr. Conway brought Petersen to his clinic.

"I'll observe him for at least eight days," the doctor said, frowning. He ran his fingers absentmindedly through his thin hair. "Please, Mrs. Petersen, don't visit him during the first days. He must have complete rest."

Martha nodded. This time Hannes would have to journey through this night without her. And that was the bitterest thing of all.

"Has he had any excitement during these last days?" Dr. Conway asked.

"Not that I know of. He was looking foward to his vacation. It's almost impossible to get him away from Bangkok. What's wrong with his eyes, Doctor? Is it an aftereffect of the fainting spell?"

"I don't know yet," Dr. Conway said. "I'm going to consult a colleague. We'll do our very best, Mrs. Petersen. But you know, every case has its surprises. If the next five days pass without any further disturbance, then it can't be connected with the dog bite."

"Shouldn't I spend the night with you, Martha?" asked Florence. Poor Petersen, she was thinking. What a dreadful fate!

"Dear Florence," Martha's voice was a whisper. "I...I want to be alone."

Florence Krüger understood. She would breakfast with Martha tomorrow? Yes, that would be nice. Martha pressed her hand. Friends were a comfort. Then she drove back to her hotel. Five towers of silence rose up all around her.

11

Affliction in Paradise

Martha had never felt the paradisiac beauty of Ceylon as strongly as in the days and nights following the collapse of her husband. A sapphire bow with garnet rims arched every evening from the coconut palms along the coast to the gardens and mountains with their Buddha temples and ruined royal cities. Martha had spent five moonlit nights in silence and prayer. Every now and then Dr. Conway let her look through the door into the sick room. Most of the time Petersen slept. A dark bandage covered his eyes. During the first two days he couldn't move his arm or leg, but gradually there was a change.

"It seems to be a serious circulatory disturbance," Dr. Conway explained on the fifth day of the crisis, "And your husband is also suffering from nicotine poisoning. That's responsible for the sight problem, but I'm sure this will improve in time."

They were sitting on Dr. Conway's veranda, facing the big *surya* tree. The crickets had begun their incessant concert. An ambience of fever and subtle decay hung in the damp air. Young Singalese girls with antelope eyes were strolling by, singing and expectant in the blue evening. They moved with meditative grace. Innocent and fatalistic passion were expressed in the way they walked.

"How long may I stay with him tomorrow?" Martha asked. It would be her first visit.

"As long as you like. In three or four days you can go to Mount Lavinia. There's no point in making an invalid of your husband."

Dr. Conway knocked the tobacco out of his pipe and went on hesitantly. "Something that excited him terribly must have taken place. He should only see people he likes. After his delirium during the first night, it seems to me that certain Russian friends are not good for him."

"We don't know any Russians," said Martha, surprised.

"Then...I don't know. Anyway, he needs a lot of rest. He seems worried about you and the children. He's very reserved. Just the same, I asked him yesterday if anything was worrying him."

"Actually my husband tends to be blithe," said Martha. For some reason or other the conversation was making her feel very uncomfortable. Dr. Conway was being so cautious.

"I suppose he's always been very lucky," he said now. "He isn't...shall we say, trained...to cope with ...hmm...serious difficulties. I am counting on your influence."

"Dr. Conway! Please tell me what's really wrong with him. I can take a lot. He's over the worst, isn't he? I mean now, this nervous breakdown. I'm so happy that it isn't..." She couldn't bring herself to say the word "rabies."

"Mr. Petersen may be left with a lame leg. We don't see much improvement in the leg. The arm is doing nicely."

"You mean...he won't be able to ride anymore?" Martha stammered.

"We will be very glad if he can walk without assistance. He tried for the first time today, a little impatiently, like all sportsmen." Martha stared silently into the dark evening. "I hope the leg will gradually improve," Dr. Conway went on. "I shall come to see you in Mount Lavinia."

"Thank you, Dr. Conway." Martha's lips were pale. "In these few days you have become our friend."

Dr. Conway coughed, embarrassed. "Well," he murmured, his eyes on the bamboo trees moving in the evening wind. "You'll manage, Mrs. Petersen, I'm sure."

"Shouldn't my husband go back to Europe?"

"A vacation there would do him good, but he won't hear of it. Why not, do you suppose? Are things still very bad in Hamburg?"

"No, Dr. Conway. That's not it. My husband can manage on very little when he has to. I don't know why he's so reluctant to go back. I've been hoping all this time that he'd want to return with us, but if he isn't well now...I can't leave him here alone."

"No, you can't," said the doctor. "Of course, you must send the children back. By the way, Mr. Petersen told me that he had made arrangements in this respect. And that's quite right."

Martha couldn't bring herself to ask what arrangements. Things were getting more complicated all the time. Had Hannes lost all confidence in her?

She drove back to the hotel deeply upset. Had she imagined life in Bangkok would be simple? Had she thought that after more than ten years, she and Hannes could pick up where they had left off in Hamburg? Actually she had no idea what had happened to Hannes in the long years of their separation. "Bad guests," Ah Chang had mumbled.

A curse had fallen on the Petersen family, and Martha, usually so alert, had failed to see it coming.

Could that be Petersen walking toward her?

A tall, stooped man, wearing dark glasses to protect

176

his formerly bright eyes, stopped dead as Martha handed him a bouquet of tropical flowers. He hurled them out onto the veranda of his sick room. "You can wait with the flowers until they bury me!" he said. "Won't be long now. Would be for the best, anyway."

"Sit down please, Hannes," said Martha, and helped him to his wheelchair. "Or would you prefer to sit outside?"

"Whatever you like."

Martha pushed the wheelchair out onto the veranda. A Singalese nurse brought tea. Petersen was silent, a silence that weighed leaden on Martha's heart. "I'm so happy to be sitting here with you again, my darling," she said softly.

Petersen didn't respond. Dr. Conway was right. Hannes had never been conditioned to accept misfortune.

"Dr. Conway tells me they're very satisfied with your progress," she said. Every word hurt. If only Florence were here! Or Doris Krüger, to talk about her dogs! Hannes had always laughed so heartily over her stories. But the Krügers had gone back to Bangkok, and Martha hadn't let Florence stay with her.

"Hannes." Martha broke the silence. "I was quite surprised to see how well you were walking."

Petersen laughed. "Oh Martha, stop being so goddamned tactful! You get on my nerves. Forgive me, but I think it would be best if you went back to the hotel."

He swallowed. He took off his glasses, took his handkerchief out of a pocket in his Chinese robe and wiped his tired, dull eyes clumsily and ashamedly. He had last cried when his grandfather had lain in his coffin and he knew the old man would never sail to the island with him any more.

Martha poured tea as if she didn't notice. "Nonsense, my boy," she said, as in their best days in Hamburg. "You smoked too much and worked too hard. And now you are going to recuperate. But you've got to cooperate a little. After tea we're going to walk three times around the room and the veranda."

Petersen looked at Martha through his dark glasses. "Martha," he said haltingly. "Do you think that...that I'll be able to ride again...later...as I used to? I mean, when I'm...when you..."

"Certainly, Hannes."

Later, arm in arm with Dr. Conway and Martha, Petersen made his big outing around the room and the veranda. Martha was so sensible. It did him good. Fortunately she didn't pity him. In her presence the feeling of isolation, of being suddenly separated from the world of the fortunate and healthy, was dispelled. The dread fear of being pitied and the urge to withdraw into the jungle like a wounded tiger was very manly. Manly emotions were honorable and sometimes a little silly...

When Dr. Conway visited the Petersens two weeks later in Mount Lavinia, Petersen came to greet him with a cane, without Martha's help. "How about going for a sail?" he said.

"Sounds good to me," said Dr. Conway. "Nice place you have here." He was observing Petersen surreptitiously. He's going to make it, he thought. He's got over the shock. Mrs. Petersen is a capable woman.

Mount Lavinia—a blissful silence broken only by the sea, palm trees, sea air, and a summer hotel in English style. Singalese servants, a hotel bazaar with ivory elephants and tortoise-shell combs, a huge terrace with parasols, and the music of the waves. "There's nothing like an island," said Petersen.

Martha came out onto the terrace with some letters. "Mail from Bangkok," she cried, and greeted the doctor who had so quickly become a friend.

"It can wait," said Petersen, with a trace of his former blitheness. "Or have Chubb or Tiny written?"

Martha held up a letter. "You can read it to me after lunch," Petersen said contentedly. "We're going for a sail first."

He still couldn't read properly. The nicotine poisoning had affected his eyes. But Martha said that would get better. He had told Martha about his arrangement for the children. She had agreed with him that they certainly had to go back to an orderly life in Hamburg. She hadn't said what she thought of the arrangement, not yet—Hannes had to be in better shape.

"Would you mind very much if we sailed another time?" said Dr. Conway. "I feel terribly lazy today. Big outbreak of malaria. Here on the terrace it's always so beautiful. I'm not quite as young as you, Petersen."

Hannes Petersen was a polite man. He had learned as a boy that you let older people have their way. "Whatever you say, doctor," he replied. "I like the terrace too. And you?" turning to Martha.

She answered quickly, "You know you can't get me away from it." She loved to swim, but although Petersen had urged her to, she hadn't swum since they had arrived. And to sail in the narrow Singalese boats would have been a treat. But how was Hannes to get into the boat without the help of at least three men? Hannes didn't think things through. He was like his daughter Tiny.

12

The Elephants of Kandy

Since Petersen had come to East Asia he had wanted to see the elephants on the Katugastota River near Kandy. Now he had been in Ceylon for three weeks. He had recovered in Mount Lavinia, slowly but surely. Even his eyes felt as bright as ever. He still used a cane when walking and he didn't know whether his leg would ever be well enough for riding, but his sudden collapse, which had shaken body and soul doubly after so many years in the tropics, had enforced a rest that the hectic life in Bangkok had never granted. When he sat with Martha on the ocean terrace in Mount Lavinia, the conflicts of his life in Bangkok seemed unreal. He still hadn't told Martha that Miss Karin had visited him on the veranda with the blue blossoms. He hadn't asked her to come, but he hadn't told her to go away either. He was not as old or wise or content as the sacred elephants of Ceylon, but he was just as uncommunicative.

And now they were going to drive through the jungle to the Katugastota River to see the temple elephants of Kandy. Petersen had once listened to Prince Pattani talk about his pilgrimage to Kandy. The elephants bore the famous relic—the sacred tooth of the Buddha—across the island. Dancers and music accompanied the colorful processional. The prince had walked with the other pilgrims and trodden the path of the elephants; in the evening he had meditated in the Queens Hotel in Kandy.

In the peaceful surroundings of Mount Lavinia, Petersen had studied the *dhammapada*, the teachings of the Buddha. For the first time in years he had had the time and relaxation to do so. The little English edition was a present from the prince. His Highness had given it to Petersen at the sports club before his departure. "Holidays are times for reflection," the prince had murmured. Petersen was truly calm and content, and let Martha read aloud to him from the *dhammapada*.

In these relfective hours beside the sea, Petersen became conscious of the special magic of his wife. Martha provided peace, not excitement. And it seemed to Petersen as if every woman who could not make her man's world peaceful and harmonious had missed her vocation, especially in a day and age when calm and warmth had disappeared in such a startling fashion. He looked at Martha. She had changed in East Asia. Her strength and gentleness were present now in a different disposition. In Hamburg Martha had often spoken to him sharply. "I don't have time to look in the mirror," she had said impatiently when Hannes had asked her to tuck the stray hairs behind her ears. By the way, where were those stray hairs? Martha's hair was suddenly wavy, and she wore it in a loose knot at the nape of her neck. Her hair was shiny. Why hadn't he noticed it all this time?

"Martha," he said, with the old impish smile that had always stood him in such good stead with the ladies. "I always thought you were a black sheep. Now I see that you're not different from all other women."

Martha looked up. "And what do you mean by that?" she asked pleasantly.

"You got yourself a new hairdo because you were so miserable over my illness," he said. "That's what all women do."

Martha actually blushed.

"Suits you marvelously," he went on. "Why on earth haven't you always done your hair like that? You look adorable!"

For a moment Martha said nothing. Hannes hadn't paid her a compliment in years. He was looking at her as he had looked when on a prosaic street the cherry trees had burst into bloom overnight. It was the little expressions of love that made all the difference in a marriage. One evidently needed a cup of tea to cry...an isolated moment on an island...a new hairdo.

"Silly boy," Martha whispered.

They drove through the jungle to the former royal city of Kandy in a happy mood. Dr. Nari Talaiyar sat beside the driver. He was a young teacher and a friend of Dr. Conway's, a slim, medium-sized Singalese who let his English, which he had learned in a missionary school, melt on his tongue like a bonbon. Dr. Talaiyar was an ardent and ambitious representative of the new independent Ceylon. Day and night his glowing black eyes saw the vision of a hygienic, flawless model island where every citizen could read and write. There was something touching about this young patriot whose innate gentleness and Buddhist resignation had vanished in the stormy winds of the times. He was looking forward to the outing to Kandy. He would show Dr. Conway's friends the elephants and the Temple of the Sacred Tooth. Both belonged to the old Ceylon, to which the young patriot remained bound by a thousand ties. His grandfather had been a *mahout*, an elephant driver in the immeasurable jungles on the island. The young man in his snow-white tropical suit of the westerner had inherited understanding and respect for the "Prince of the Jungle" from his grandfather.

The drive to the elephant river led over hills and through valleys. Now and then rice fields and tea plantations could be seen between a chain of hills. Martha saw the land that led to the great jungle, which tolerated no automobile roads. The jungle actually began beyond Kandy but its character was presaged already by the rank vines, the immense thornbushes and cacti. In the villages crocodiles bathed in swampy streams, and behind them and the flooded rice fields lay the primeval forest, motionless, a timeless green pyramid, a mute superfluity of tropical nature.

"Martha," said Petersen. "I have been wanting to tell you something for a long time. Nothing important. It happened while you were in Hua Hin."

Martha leaned forward. Would Hannes tell her at last who the "bad guests" had been whom the old cook had mentioned?

"Do you remember the two servants Ah Chang got for us after Tiny nearly drowned? I mean Chung and Ah Bue."

"Of course. I didn't like Ah Bue." Martha had suddenly lost her soft voice.

Petersen wiped his dark glasses. Then he said slowly, "That was a crazy thing. I mean Ah Bue. She's a very attractive little beast. I'm sure you noticed how she was after me all the time, presumably to wait on me."

This was the first Martha had heard about it. In her presence Ah Bue had never waited on Petersen. However, according to him, Martha had been gone a week when Ah Bue had turned up in Petersen's bedroom every evening with gentle Chinese doggedness, to console the master over the absence of his wife. Or something to that effect must have been on her mind.

"That's unbelievable!" Martha exclaimed. And again it was a daily occurrence of which neither Ah Bue nor Chung, her mother with the gold teeth, thought anything. Chung was only obeying the customs of the Chinese when they tried to pass off their beautiful daughters advantageously. Not forever; just for a little while, naturally. Chung herself had been sold by her father to a rich family where she could mull at her leisure over the misfortune of having been born the eleventh daughter of a poor tailor. Chung had never been beautiful, merely diligent and greedy. She had found it very nice of her father that he hadn't drowned her at birth, which happened occasionally in Chung's native village. Chung was still afraid to this day of the river spirits. Her daughter Ah Bue was afraid of nothing, not even of Nai Petersen's wrath. But he hadn't liked the offer. After a talk with the old cook he had fired Ah Bue and her mother.

Ah Chang, who usually had great influence over Petersen, couldn't make any headway with him this time. He had intimated that his niece and her daughter might take some sort of revenge which he would be powerless to prevent. Petersen had laughed aloud. Unfortunately Ah Chang had lost much face through his master's laughter. He had waddled back to his kitchen, muttering to himself, and had been sick, presumably, for three days. Petersen had extricated himself from the affair by raising Ah Chang's salary.

"I wanted to tell you," Petersen said, "so that you wouldn't wonder about it. I didn't know whether you would notice the absence of the two women when you came back from Hua Hin."

"I'm not allowed to enter the kitchen house," Martha replied, "or Ah Chang might think I was trying to check up on his supplies. But I'm surprised about something else."

"And what is that, *Mem sahib?*"

"I'm surprised over what the women in the East seem to see in you," she said, smiling.

A burden had fallen from her. For a moment, during her talk with Ah Chang she had thought the "bad guest" might have been Miss Karin.

When Dr. Talaiyar and Petersen reached the Katugastota River, the princes of the jungle were just having a bath. *Mahouts* with naked torsos and shining cloth headdresses were watching over the small and large elephants taking their holiday in the water. The mighty

184

animals promenaded thoughtfully and pompously through the glittering river with its view of the dense jungle and hills of Kandy. Dr. Talaiyar told his guests many things about the artistry of the *mahouts*. They had to treat the elephants with great caution after they had been captured in the jungle. Many perished; they died of sorrow after their first months of captivity. The *mahouts* stroked the elephants with long, thin bamboo branches to acclimate them to the outside world so that they could bear a human foot on their skin without going wild and tearing off, bellowing crazily. But it was a long way from the taming of the jungle prince to the temple elephant of Kandy.

"I hope I can ride again soon," said Petersen. "Then we'll come here again, or go to North Siam. When I was a boy I longed to ride an elephant one day."

He was staring at the sacred animals, entranced. The landscape along the river seemed to belong to them and the *mahouts*. They moved with arrogant calm in front of the giant ferns along the banks. "A man should have as few wishes as the elephant in the forest. That's what the Buddha said," Dr. Talaiyar told them, and Petersen wondered what it would be like to have so few wishes.

Petersen couldn't say later why he finally succeeded in telling Martha in the Temple of the Sacred Tooth about Karin Holm's visit on the veranda. In Mount Lavinia they had been in complete harmony for the first time in years, and perhaps that was why he had suddenly felt the urge to confess. They had wandered, astounded through the temple gardens, and had seen the sacred swans in the blue lake of Kandy. Then Dr. Talaiyar had led them inside the temple. The way to the cell where the relic for pilgrims and strangers from every country in the world was stored led through gilded bronze doors that were ornamented with ivory carvings.

"The Tooth of the Enlightened One has made Kandy the center of the Buddhist universe," Dr. Talaiyar whispered. He had become very quiet suddenly, as if the patriot and statistician had been transformed into a pilgrim. He had met a friend from Colombo and had excused himself for a few minutes. Petersen and Martha had walked on through the temple halls. Singalese women with almond-shaped eyes whisked by silently and laid down flowers and sacrificial candles. And that was when Petersen, his face turned away, had owned up to everything, except Madame Boulgakoff's effort to blackmail him.

"Let's not talk about it," Martha said. It took an effort to say it.

"When you are with me, everything's all right," Petersen mumbled. "You are my..."

Martha raised her hand to stop him. "But I won't always be with you," she said softly.

Petersen turned pale. "Are you angry with me?" he asked, as in the old days.

"No," said Martha. "Where you're concerned, I'm used to trouble."

She forced a small smile. It was a clever imitation of a true smile. As they drove to the Queens Hotel for lunch, she wondered what Hannes would come up with next. At the same time she decided to go back with the children. She hadn't forgotten the children in the happy hours in Mount Lavinia, but for the first time in her life she found herself thinking more about herself than about Chubb and Tiny.

Next day the Petersens drove back to Colombo. On the following day they were embarking for Singapore, away from the sacred elephants of Kandy. In Colombo a fat letter was waiting for them. It was from Hinrich Petersen in Hamburg. Martha opened it in a strange state of excitement, and as she read her eyes widened with astonishment.

13

Hannes Petersen—Private

"Well, Hannes, what have you decided to do?" Martha asked.

They had been in Bangkok now for a week and Hinrich Petersen's letter stood inimically between them. It was strange that Hinrich, who according to the opinion of experts had fish blood in his veins, could have created such a stir among the Petersens in Bangkok. Hannes and Martha hadn't had a chance yet to discuss Hinrich's suggestion because Mathilda and Werner Steffens, with the newly-born twins, had been staying with them. But now they had returned to the tin island of Phuket, twins and all. There was no further excuse for Petersen to shy away from a decision. His health was much improved. His eyes were still slightly irritated, but he could read and write again. There was no question that he was perfectly capable of answering Hinrich Petersen's letter, which had been addressed to him.

"Hinrich is crazy!" Petersen said indignantly. "I never heard of such an insane idea! That would just suit him! But it's *out*!" Then he got up to drive to his office, frowning.

On the terrace he called loudly for his chauffeur. Instead, Phom's twin sons, Nu and Mu, put in an appearance. They were picking their noses vigorously and informed Petersen that their Papa was *mai sabai*, very ill. So he's drunk, thought Petersen. That was all he needed.

At that moment old Mr. Petersen's car came driving up, the one used for business. In it sat a young Hamburger with very long legs and a rosy, completely expressionless face. It was young Harms, whose bones Petersen senior had threatened to break without any justification whatsoever.

Young Harms, from Harms and Company, Hamburg/Fuhlentwiete, had "a hell of a lot of respect," as he liked to put it, for Petersen junior. Hannes was his ideal. Even if Thomas Harms could never hope to smile as winningly as Hannes Petersen, he *was* quite a few years younger. Tommy was twenty-six. In his eyes Hannes was an old-timer, not only because of his experience but also because of his years. Forty-three was a biblical age for young Harms. At Petersen and Company he was known as Baby Face. There was something naive and innocent about him. Thomas Harms, on the other hand, considered himself seriously a ladies' man. He was about to become engaged, and had written to prepare his parents in Flottbeck near Hamburg for the announcement. His fiancée would fit into his home town of Flottbeck like a tiger in a girl's boarding school. This was one of the more drastic comparisons that young Harms would admit, but only to himself. Perhaps one might have a little talk with Petersen junior on the subject? But Petersen junior hadn't come back from Colombo in much better health. He still walked with a cane. Well, thought young Harms, that's age for you...

"I've come to pick you up, Mr. Petersen," he said, bowing stiffly and formally to Martha. "Mr. Petersen isn't going to use this car."

"Thank you, my boy," said Hannes, with dignity. "Until later, Martha. We'll talk about it."

"Mr. Petersen," said young Harms on the way to New Road, "while you were away, Wong and Sons cancelled the order for the three thousand typewriters. They wrote that they could get them cheaper from the United States."

188

"Well then, didn't you make them a cheaper offer?"

"Of course not!" Young Harms sounded indignant. "You said before you left that you'd given Mr. Wong the lowest possible figure."

"But there's *always* a lower price! You'll never learn, my dear Harms. Mr. Wong was only cancelling pro forma. He's expecting a new offer from us. Wasn't my uncle there to attend to it?"

"Mr. Petersen senior was in Hua Hin. Miss Krüger was coming for a visit."

Petersen accepted this bit of information in bitter silence. Florence Krüger and Uncle Winn had grown up together in Hamburg. At age eighteen, according to the family chronicle, they had shared romantic feelings. Of course, Uncle Winn's private life was more important than business! When the junior partner decided to take a little holiday after twelve years, everything went to pot! Hinrich's idea *was* crazy! At the thought of Hinrich Petersen, Hannes saw red.

At his office he immediately put through a call to Wong and Sons. He would be very honored if Mr. Wong could see him today or tomorrow. The soft lisping voice of a Chinese secretary gave him a time for that afternoon that was suitable. Mr. Wong would be delighted to see Mr. Petersen. "Fine," replied Hannes in his private office, where young Harms fortunately couldn't follow him. Mr. Wong could certainly be made to change his mind. The cancellation of a contract was always a pretense. Young Harms had been in East Asia for months now and still believed everything he was told. "Idiot!" his boss muttered. Then he took Hinrich's letter out again, put on his new tortoise-shell-rimmed glasses, and stared at it as if reading it for the first time.

Dear Hannes,

Many thanks for your letter. I was very sorry to hear that you had been bitten by a rabid dog. Why don't they vaccinate dogs with antirabies serum in Bangkok? I hope you make a splendid recovery. Be careful after the many injections. We're not all that young any more!

"We!" I like that! Petersen was furious. Good old Hinrich was all of ten years older than he!

He skipped the passages about business, although they interested him, but he had already answered them. "As for your suggestion," Hannes had written at the end of his business reply, "I'll have to speak to Martha and Uncle Wilhelm Christian about it. I don't think it likely that this idea of yours can be realized."

For a second time he read the incomprehensible suggestion that this stuffed shirt of a Hinrich had put down on the long-suffering airmail paper.

Of course Lisa and I will be happy any time to have Chubb and the little girl stay with us and look after them until you and Martha are ready to leave the tropics. I have already begun to make inquiries about private schools, in case you still want to send the boy to one. I personally am against boarding schools. Even if Lisa and I aren't used to much noise and confusion, we would be glad to have the children with us. Don't worry about expenses; I'll keep accounts.

Petersen paused, skipped a page—Hinrich's description of their vacation in Westerland. It was always the same: Hinrich complained about the cost of everything but always wanted the best; Lisa played bridge. Petersen supposed that was what all childless women did—played bridge from morning to night. Martha had never played cards. Petersen wondered what Martha would say if he answered Hinrich right away. Damn it all! She couldn't possibly be serious about going back with the children! She was used to trouble where he was concerned; she had said so in Kandy, and smiled a little. Martha was a wonderful woman, just a little cool. Petersen refused sternly to think of Karin Holm when she said "Johnny…," and looked at him out of her almond-shaped eyes, so gently and innocently, and falsely. One sensed the bewitching aura, the ambience of great adventure of which an Indian poet had said, "And a rain of flowers fell from the Himalayas." Frowning, Petersen applied himself again to Hinrich Petersen's letter.

Finally, after giving it a lot of thought, I would like to make a quite different suggestion and hope you won't reject it without thinking it over. I have been in Hamburg all my life and would rather like to feel a different wind blowing through my hair before I grow too old for a little adventure. How would it be if you, Martha, and the children came back to Hamburg and I took over your job for a few years? After all, I know a lot about overseas business, and from your letters have learned that the Chinese, who remain our best clients, are strict realists. I am sure your success rests primarily on something I like to see, from a business standpoint as a Hamburg virtue: namely, honesty in word and deed, the ability to make cool decisions, and a strict reserve in all private matters. Lisa would like to come to Bangkok too. She was thrilled with Martha's account of our niece Pauline's wedding. Even princesses were there! I personally am more middle-class in my reaction to titles. They don't mean anything to me if the person behind the title doesn't justify the advantage of birth. In Hamburg we have never thought differently. But the ladies fall for that sort of thing. I imagine that young Harms has enough experience by now so that he could be useful to me in the beginning. And then, after all, there's Uncle Wilhelm Christian, who built up everything...

Never had a sentence outraged Hannes Petersen as much as Hinrich's declaration that Uncle Winn had "built up everything." Petersen lit a cigarette, an exception. It didn't satisfy or calm him. And young Harms as an expert on the Far East! It could make a crocodile laugh! That's what they thought at home! Hinrich, with his prehistoric ideas on virtue! Strictly realistic and ignorant, like Baby Face from Harms and Company, Fuhlenwiete.

There was a knock on the door. Petersen's new secretary, a Eurasian, age thirty-five, entered the room soundlessly. Ulla Knudsen, daughter of a Danish captain and a Siamese, was a splendid secretary. She had the right approach to life. She was more interested in her salary, which was high, than in romance. She supported her mother and her four younger sisters. After office hours, which ended in the tropics between four and five, Miss Knudsen dealt in real estate. Before the Japanese occupation she had worked for an English lawyer and gained insight into the practices of the Bangkok real estate agents. Miss Ulla Knudsen was tall, blond, and faded. She spoke with a shrill voice but she was a first-rate secretary. She spoke Siamese, Danish, English, Chinese, and Malayan. Young Harms always turned to her for information. Petersen junior was too impatient to explain the business with Wong and Sons properly.

"A visitor sir," whispered Miss Knudsen. "A lady."

"Well, now!" Petersen was surprised. "A lady! Miss Knudsen, please ask her what she wants. You know that during office hours we don't talk to ladies!" He smiled at his secretary, medium strength. She functioned still better when one turned on the smile full force. It was that way with every person with Siamese blood. A smile was the basis on which one could start to build solidly.

"The lady says it is a private matter." Miss Knudsen was looking at her boss with consuming curiosity. Curiosity was her only failing. She lived on the experiences of others. The greed for a private life of her own was what drove her to illumine the lives of the people around her with the bright light of her curiosity into the farthest corners of their souls. She had always been fascinated by Karin Holm's stormy career. All Eurasians in Bangkok knew each other and lived in a social and psychological community of fate. They had their own tennis club, their own dances, and their own morality. Through his acquaintance with Karin Holm, Petersen junior had become the object of intense interest to his ostensibly strictly neutral private secretary. She knew very well who the visitor was, but she wanted to see Petersen's face when he saw the lady. "She has very little time," said Ulla Knudsen.

"Have her come in," said Petersen, in a sudden decision. He had the feeling that he'd better receive this visitor. He had just caught sight of her through the half open glass door. "Good morning, sir," said Madame Boulgakoff in her harsh English.

Miss Knudsen retired, satisfied. Her boss had turned pale. She tried to look through the keyhole, but her boss had drawn the green felt curtain in front of the glass door. He wasn't born yesterday.

"What do you want?" Petersen's voice was cold. "I must ask you to be brief. I have a conference in fifteen minutes."

He didn't offer his visitor a chair but stood facing her, full height. It made Madame Boulgakoff feel uncomfortable. She had a long torso and short legs and looked better seated.

"You don't mind if I sit down?" she said, settling in Petersen's desk chair so that now, with Petersen standing opposite her, it looked as if she were in charge. Shameless bitch! he thought, and waited. That was something he had learned in many negotiations. One was at a disadvantage at once if one started a conversation with a difficult client.

"I came to get my three thousand ticals." Madame Boulgakoff was smiling. "All you have to do is write the check and I'll leave."

'I don't know what you're talking about," said Petersen, sounding innocent.

Madame Boulgakoff stopped smiling and jumped to her feet. Petersen took the opportunity to sit down in his chair. His checkbook, a picture of Martha and the children, and a revolver were in the top drawer. Petersen had a gun license. Not everyone in Bangkok did.

"I think you know what I'm talking about. You promised me the money in Colombo. Karin Holm and I...but I have no intention of wasting my breath. Karin is in Bangkok. She came back three days ago and is staying with me."

"I have no intention of writing Miss Holm's biography," Petersen said softly. "You must excuse me, Madame, but I am not on vacation, as I was in Colombo, and we can't continue our little bar conversation in my office. You couldn't seriously have believed that I was going to hand out any such sum to you."

Petersen felt victorious. What a good thing he'd told Martha all about it in Kandy. Let the women come running! Martha had grasped the fact that they were molesting him. He stretched out his fine-boned hand to ring for his secretary to show his visitor out. He rose, leaning lightly on his cane. "Good day, Madame. It has been a pleasure."

"Just a minute, and you will have every reason to be pleased," said Madame Boulgakoff.

She opened her shabby bag, which contained everything she possessed that could be carried around—a few hundred ticals and the picture of a Russian city before the revolution. "Do you know this letter?" she asked. "It will interest your wife."

Petersen stared speechless at the yellowed pages the Russian woman was holding up at a safe distance from him. "You wrote this letter to Miss Karin Holm in 1946," she said. "In case memory fails you, in this letter you accepted certain responsibilities for Miss Karin..."

"How much?" Petersen's voice was hoarse. He knew exactly what he had written in that letter.

"However much it is worth to you," said Madame.

A cruel amusement sparkled in her eyes, and she prudently looked down.

Petersen named a sum that was more than Madame Boulgakoff had expected. He must have been out of his mind when he had written that letter! Not even young Harms would have expressed himself in such an indescribably irresponsible fashion as Petersen had done at a time when his mental picture of Martha and the children had faded. The absurdity of it was that Petersen hated to write letters. It was a family trait. One wrote that one was doing well, fairly well, or not especially well, meaning very badly. Business was so-so... thanks... greetings from house to house... your Johannes. And then, on a moonlit night in Bangkok, he had sat down and let his emotions run rampant, as infatuated as a high school freshman! Not only that—he had written that he would always look after Miss Karin. He knew that it was his fault. An idiot, that's what he'd been. If there was anyone who knew how to handle a seduction scene on a tropical night, then—in spite of her extreme youth—it was Miss Karin. Today she was twenty-three, still too young to be... to be so businesslike! But together with the Russian woman, with whom she had been living since her mother's death, Karin exploited faded emotions to the hilt. If Martha saw this letter, even though written long ago and no longer valid, she would write Petersen off. Not publicly—there were the children to consider. But Martha couldn't and wouldn't forgive this letter as she had done his other follies. All that was missing was a promise of marriage, and he had been on the point... How could he have forgotten what Martha and the children meant to him? And today he was nervous when Martha left him for three hours. There was no excuse for it. For the first time in his life he had betrayed Martha.

Petersen wrote the check and handed it to Madame

195

Boulgakoff. Then he tore up the letter and burned the small pieces in a big Chinese clay ashtray. It was decorated with a dragon design—very appropriate! Then he rang for his secretary.

"I don't want to be disturbed, Miss Knudsen," he said calmly. "I have to go through the Wong and Sons correspondence of the last two months. Do you have the files handy?"

"Of course, sir," said Miss Knudsen eagerly. "Do you want me to take dictation?"

"Later. First I have to see the correspondence between Wong and Sons in Hong Kong while I've been away. Maybe I'll have to go there. I thought the typewriters had been ordered long ago."

"Young Mr. Wong wrote that he'd rather deal with you personally," Miss Knudsen replied. She was looking at her boss sharply but couldn't discover anything in his face that indicated he was upset. And the Russian woman had left without saying a word.

Miss Knudsen returned to her office and put through a phone call to the Russian Restaurant. It was her duty as a friend to look after Karin Holm's interests to some extent. She seemed to have had a bad experience in Hong Kong and since her return had suddenly been very reserved. What was the matter? A new man about whom Miss Knudsen was to know nothing? She would find out. She always did.

"Karin?" Miss Knudsen asked in the cracked voice of a sprung trumpet. "I would like to invite you to have lunch with me at Chez Eve. Oh? You're ill? I'm sorry to hear that. The doctor won't allow visitors? But I'm not a visitor, darling. All right...as you wish. Bye-bye!"

Miss Knudsen hung up, disappointed. On the other hand she had saved money. A lunch at Chez Eve was actually beyond her means. Her mother and sisters could eat rice and curry for three days with what it would have cost her. She didn't believe for a moment that Miss Karin was ill. That was an excuse she had used far too often herself.

Petersen had buried his face in his hands. A shame that the green felt curtain hid this sensational sight from his private secretary. The correspondence with the Wongs lay untouched on his highly polished teakwood desk. Petersen was taking a look at his private self and was finding the sight dismal. Not only had he betrayed Martha, he had for a moment also forgotten his son and daughter. Today he couldn't understand it. And while a part of him sat in the small dark cell of his shame, he realized that the promises he had made Martha after her arrival had been made lightly; otherwise he would have sent Karin away that time before Pauline's wedding, when she had appeared on the veranda with the blue blossoms. The wicked restlessness which he had believed dead had crept up on him again and he had lost his head. Now he had exiled himself finally from the street with the cherry blossoms. He was suddenly sure that Martha had understood him in Kandy very well and had rung down the curtain on their relationship. Even if she were to send her children back to Hamburg alone, which was what Petersen was hoping, she too had changed. She had probably given up on him as she would on a student who, despite generous extra coaching, could not achieve the goals of his class. And she was right. She would still stand by him publicly, but the cherry blossoms were definitely gone.

Petersen suddenly realized that Martha would always do her duty with kindness and intelligence, but her disappointment, which she bore silently, created an autumnal landscape in the midst of the East's sea of flowers, a landscape full of shadows. That was his doing, after the happy days in Mount Lavinia. "Where you're concerned, I'm used to trouble," she had said in the temple in Kandy. Yes, but not to endless deceit. And now there was no way back to Martha's radiant warmth. Nothing was left but his duty as her husband and the father of his children, who had already been in the Far East far too long. He had to write to Hinrich at once.

Dear Hinrich!

Many thanks for your explicit letter. I'm very relieved that you are willing to take our kids. That's very decent of you. Of course it's understood that I assume all costs. Many thanks also for your questions about my health. I am feeling fine again. Uncle Winn is with Florence Krüger and his wife in Hua Hin. He is getting old and not entirely equal to the increasing pressures of business in this aftermath of war. But this is strictly between us! Of course he has a tremendous amount of experience and does all the Bangkok business with his former vitality, but I take care of our connections with the other East Asian markets. And it isn't simple, I can tell you! Germany is in a difficult position, a hangover from the Third Reich. We'll get there though, slowly but surely. What is more, Uncle Winn is a very rich man, who quite justifiably doesn't have to pay too much attention to business. He owns a lot of property in the name of his wife, Countess Siri. I'm a poor devil who started from scratch here, and am at last beginning to put a bit aside, but the standard of living in postwar Bangkok is so high, I'm afraid not much would be left over if I were to go back to Hamburg now. Your suggestion, dear Hinrich, shows you are not quite clear about the situation here. Please don't resent my candor. I am speaking solely from a business viewpoint. Nobody values your qualities as a business man more highly than I do, but it is just these qualities—reliability and candor—that can occasionally be a handicap in the Far East. I'm afraid you see the trade relationship between us and our Chinese clients too simply. Certainly big, famous firms such as Wong and Sons are thoroughly realistic, but in the Chinese sense of the word. It would take too long to explain in a letter what I mean by that. One can't explain in twelve pages what one has experienced and learned in twelve years the hard way. Apart from the fact that I've never written a twelve-page letter in my life and in my old age have no intention of getting into the habit. I'm going to be forty-four—a sobering thought!

If you don't feel boarding school would be right for our boy, then I'm for his going back to the Johanneum. Albert rides very well now and he isn't such a bookworm any more. I would like him to continue the traditional sport of our family. Please see to it that he doesn't start on grandmother horses! That Uncle Wilhelm Christian's sister fell off her horse and unfortunately broke her neck is no reason that from here on all Petersens have to ride ancient nags! The separation from the children is a hard nut for both of us to crack, but there's no getting around it. Please tell Lisa that Tiny is a child that needs a lot of love.

Young Harms is an ass! He believes whatever an Asiatic client tells him at eleven o'clock in the morning. Hopeless! But please don't mention this to the old Harmses in Flottbeck. In this respect parents can be funny. And you recommended Harms so warmly to me! In his own surroundings I suppose he does all right. I'm for his returning home, but he's crazy about the East, which is understandable because Bangkok is an enchanting city—I mean privately!

Once again, many thanks for your friendly offer to take our children. There's nothing like family. One finds that out when one is far away. Here in East Asia everyone is on his own. You wouldn't like it, Hinrich. You like the steady life of a burgher and a community spirit, don't you? Perhaps I'll feel that way too when I'm ten years older.

With very best greetings from house to house,
Your JOHANNES

P.S. Martha sends heartfelt thanks and greetings. She has been urging me to write but so much business accumulated while I was in Colombo that I had to attend to immediately.

Petersen rang and gave his secretary the airmail letter. Now he still had to tell Martha about his decision.

Madame Boulgakoff did not proceed to the Russian Restaurant right away. She was very pleased that Mr. Johnny had paid Karin's gambling debts. He had been very understanding. He probably realized that there were a thousand ways in which one could still damage him.

Like all White Russian refugees, Madame Boulgakoff had experienced the Far East in all its cruelty. She had come to Shanghai in 1920, a nine-year-old girl. In those days all Russian emigrés were allegedly princes and countesses. Then her parents had died. She had come to Bangkok with other White Russians and had cooked and helped a White Russian general and his wife in their restaurant as kitchen maid. They had been constantly in debt until they had opened a gambling room at the back. The couple were killed during the Japanese occupation in a bombing raid on Bangkok.

Madame Boulgakoff hadn't remained a kitchen maid long. She was the owner of the restaurant now. The old people had spoken of nothing but Czarist Russia and had treated all their comrades with Slavic *grandezza*. In Madame Boulgakoff's opinion they were fools who couldn't grasp the fact that in East Asian exile you had to make money if you didn't want to be crushed by the Chinese. Madame Boulgakoff had a few beautiful Russians and Eurasians working for her. They were waitresses but also "entertainers," as they were called in Bangkok. These girls, who were not prostitutes, were to see to the good spirits of her guests and drink with them. Most of them were taxi dancers on the side, or hairdressers or salesgirls. They were only engaged at the restaurant by the hour. Miss Karin had been the sensation of the postwar period. In 1946, one year after the defeat of the Japanese, she had appeared at the restaurant selling Javanese dolls. But none of the dolls had pleased the owner of the Russian Restaurant as much as the girl selling them. Karin was seventeen at the time. Her luxurious blond hair shone as brightly as if she weren't living, like the other girls and women in the place, on the dark side of the moon.

Tatiana Boulgakoff had always lived on the dark side of the moon. Everything in the Far East was torture for her: the poverty she could never get used to, the mosquito netting and clothing that constantly needed mending, the cheap fish and fruit that the Asiatic merchants at the markets contemptuously shoved her way. A foreigner was expected to send her Chinese cook to the market; she didn't go herself and demean herself by haggling about the prices. There were the years of constant fear that her rent would be raised, which, eventually, it always was. First the Japanese had driven prices up in 1945, and since then the Americans had bought the whole city for a few dollars and had further complicated life.

Madame Boulgakoff called a rickshaw and said in her harsh Siamese, "Drive me to Talat Noi." The small market was only a short walk from Petersen's office on New Road, but she was exhausted. The midday heat lay on her chest like an iron chain. But she had a check, of which nothing would be left over for Karin. She had to pay her own gambling debts first. Then she could have her place painted, and pay her rent. She already owed three months. Yet everyday life remained unchanged, the unbearable everyday life of the White Russian refugee in Bangkok, made up of sweat, humiliation, and uncertainty.

Madame Boulgakoff put on her dark glasses. For a moment she had forgotten Petersen. She would think of him when the time came to tap him again. When it came to plans and intrigue, her brain was tireless. Her own fleeting love affairs with compatriots and later with Japanese officers of the Occupation lay behind her. She had been difficult and unbending with her lovers, even in an embrace still filled with the dark fury that had accumulated within her against the rich and the fortunate. Johannes Petersen embodied everything she hated: he was rich, without a care in the world, and weak, but he could become brutal when attacked. A good thing that Karin had shown her the letter after the arrival of Petersen's wife, the letter he had written in a moment of mental aberration. Karin had wanted to tear it up, but Madame had snatched it from her. "We're going to need that letter," she had said, and laughed. Karin had understood. In spite of her nineteen years she already knew all the tricks of the trade, not so much from experience as from instinct.

Madame Boulgakoff stepped out of the rickshaw into the cavernous building that housed Talat Noi, swarming with people and penetrated by innumerable odors. She was looking for a kitchen maid who could also serve when necessary. She had to be young and pretty like the rest of her personnel.

A Chinese vegetable woman was crouched in a corner. She had on a wide plaited bamboo hat and her eyes were sly, her hands looked greedy. "Have you anything for me?" Madame asked in Chinese.

The woman, Chung, showed her teeth in a greedy smile. She pointed with her bony hand with the broken nails at a beautiful girl. Her daughter, Ah Bue, had lost her job. She had been employed by "first-rate," which meant rich foreigners, and had had to leave because of illness. "Is she healthy now?" asked Madame. "I don't have any money to support sick girls. My place isn't a charity institute."

Chung grinned. Ah Bue, whom Petersen had fired, bowed low and prettily. She was wearing black satin pants and a clean high-necked jacket delicately embroidered with peonies. Ah Bue was an artist when it came to needlework. She hid her vexation over the job with the white woman in the shabby linen suit. A *Mem farang* who had to ride in a rickshaw! An aura of defeat and misfortune emanated from this new mistress as from the turtle, which spat out its illness with its saliva.

"Come," said Madame Boulgakoff. "My rickshaw is waiting."

Ah Bue nodded sullenly. A foreigner who rode in a rickshaw with her servant was way down low on the social ladder, and Ah Bue had the blond foreigner who had fired her so heartlessly to thank for it. All she had wanted to do was comfort Nai Petersen in his loneliness, at her mother's order. Her mother had already heated the Chinese wine over the fire. Ah Bue hated Petersen. It would have been a good job for mother and daughter.

They drove through the merry noise of the market to the Russian Restaurant. Life was truly strange and ironic. Because in the creaky rickshaw with its stained and torn upholstery sat two women from different worlds who had nothing in common but their hatred of a rich and privileged foreigner. Neither Madame Boulgakoff nor young Ah Bue were aware of it, but in their chance meeting there lay the germ of a tragedy that was to develop slowly but inevitably under the tropical sun.

"Can you cook?" Madame Boulgakoff asked the young Chinese girl.

"I used to help my uncle in the kitchen. He's still in the big house in Bangkapi."

"What was the name of your mistress?" the Russian woman asked, suddenly interested.

Ah Bue thought for a moment. She hadn't a good memory for foreign names. Then she said the name in syllables, like a child. "Mem Pe-ter-sen." Just then they drove past Petersen's office. Ah Bue pointed to the big brass plate with the firm's name on it. "That name," she said in Chinese. "Very good Mem...very very bad master. Ah Bue serve quick quick. Master push servant away with foot. Ah Bue cry. Help mother on market in Talat Noi. Ah Bue good girl. Master Petersen very bad master."

Ah Bue was acting out the tragedies of her life for her new mistress with the innate theatrical genius of the Chinese. The past became present again. Petersen was a cruel tiger who trod little yellow flowers underfoot. What a wonderful drama!

"Stop talking nonsense!" her new mistress in the shabby linen suit scolded, but her tone was friendlier than her words. Bangkok occasionally presented one with entertainment. A strange city...

On the afternoon of the same day Hannes Petersen was sitting at the sports club, resting after a day at the office. His visit with old Mr. Wong had turned out as expected. They had discussed Ming porcelain and drunk tiny cups of green tea. Gradually they had begun to talk business. Mr. Wong had given a new order and they had come halfway to terms on the price of the typewriters. Finally they had discussed the Wong business in Hong Kong. Old Mr. Wong was also of the opinion that Johannes Petersen should go there one day, with an introduction from the Wongs in Bangkok. Yes, thought Petersen, when it came to dealing with the Chinese, no one could equal him. Hinrich would have been dazzled if he'd listened in on today's conversation.

"May I join you, Mr. Petersen?" Young Harms had spotted his idol in the garden. This might be the moment to talk about it. But his boss was very impersonal. He informed Baby Face, not without self-satisfaction, of the outcome of his negotiations with old Mr. Wong. All of them were invited to a big dinner, including Harms, who wasn't very enthusiastic about it but didn't show it. He had already noticed that Petersen didn't value any personal opinions of his very highly.

"What'll they feed us?" he asked. "Baked toads? Something like that?"

"Just wait, my good fellow. Chinese cuisine is the most exquisite in the world. And if you don't like it, please don't make a face. Then our host would lose face."

This was unfair of Hannes. No one could accuse young Harms of too much facial expression.

"Mr. Petersen," said young Harms, "may I speak to you about a personal matter?"

"What's on your mind?" Petersen heroically suppressed a yawn. Baby Face probably wanted to tell him about his latest taxi dancer. "So go ahead," he said, ordering another whiskey and soda.

"Mr. Petersen...I'm going to get married."

"Well, well. This is very sudden, isn't it?"

Young Harms nodded. "I was going to ask if...if in consideration of this you could raise my salary."

There, it was out. Young Harms had rarely said so much all in one go.

"Hmm," said Petersen. "We can talk about it. Who is the fortunate lady? I take it you'll want to go back to Hamburg." Young Harms's plan to marry suited him. It just might make the boy less dumb. Petersen's marriage had certainly helped him to pull himself together.

"There she is!" cried Harms. "She's only nineteen," he whispered. "Parents dead. Her father was Swedish, her mother French. A...a wonderful girl! Excuse me for a moment. May I bring her over to meet you?"

"Certainly," his boss said politely, looking in the direction of the terrace where a whole swarm of young girls had appeared. Today there were swimming races, with prizes. The young people had invited their friends. Harms leapt up on the terrace to fetch his fiancée to meet Mr. Petersen.

Through his dark glasses Petersen saw the young couple walking toward him. He was much too vain to put on his prescription glasses. The dark pair would do. And in a few minutes he would be looking young Harms' intended over more thoroughly. She was tall, slim and blond. A nice pair, thought Petersen as Baby Face came toward his table, arm in arm with the young lady. "May I introduce..." said young Harms. "Mr. Petersen...my fiancée, Miss Holm."

"Excuse me, Tommy," said Miss Karin, after a glass of lemonade—Karin and lemonade! thought Petersen. "I have an appointment. Shall we meet tonight at the Russian Restaurant?"

"Of course," stammered young Harms. He was disappointed. Why did Karin want to leave so soon? Didn't she like his boss? The two had scarcely exchanged a word.

"I must see my tailor, my lamb," his fiancée explained. "I don't have a thing to wear. And I want to order my wedding gown."

Young Harms was consoled. "That, of course, is more important." He laughed boyishly and a little foolishly. Like a halfwit, thought his boss.

Petersen stared straight ahead while the young man accompanied the daughter of a Swede and a French woman to a rickshaw. This was preposterous! Young Harms wasn't his cup of tea, neither in business nor privately, but suddenly Petersen felt responsible for this guileless heir to the firm in Hamburg. He would have to go to the Russian Restaurant today whether he liked it or not. He would give Karin a fat check to get her to Hong Kong. He couldn't sit back and watch a decent fellow, in East Asia for only five months, being ruined.

"Isn't she sweet?" asked young Harms, looking as radiant as was possible for him.

"Why did she run off so fast?" his boss asked, instead of answering.

"Karin is very shy. She thought we were going to be alone here. But I thought it would be nice if you met her, Mr. Petersen."

Hannes didn't answer right away. Although he was a master at negotiations, he didn't know how to begin. This was serious business. In any other case he would have asked Martha to take over, just as Uncle Winn had done about Pauline. "Where. . .where did you meet the young lady?"

"In a Russian hotel-restaurant on Suriwongse Road. A funny sort of place, Mr. Petersen. I mean. . .for young people. Karin likes it too."

Suddenly a startling stream of words issued forth from the young man. He had carried it all around with him for months. "Karin has been through a lot," he said somberly. "She was engaged to a Swede, and just before the wedding she found out that he had tuberculosis. A hopeless case. I'd been crazy about her for quite a while, but one has to do the right thing, doesn't one? Karin's former fiancé was very old. Over forty." Young Harms blushed furiously. His boss was forty-four.

"Well?" said Petersen.

"Well. . .the Swede had a lot of money, and after all, I'm just starting out in life. First I was a Russian, then an English prisoner. And then Papa said one day over a stiff grog that I'd come back from the war in a daze and I needed to have a new wind blowing through my hair. And then. . .then I got my chance through Mr. Hinrich Petersen. I'm going to work very hard from now on, Mr. Petersen. I have responsibilities now."

Baby Face looked around excitedly out of his watery blue eyes. He could evidently already see himself in the role of husband and father of numerous children. But nothing was going to come of *that*! Petersen would see to it personally.

"You can't keep an elegant lady like that on your

salary," he said drily. "If I were in your place, I'd think it over very carefully, my dear Harms. One falls in love often but one marries rarely."

Young Harms didn't have a trace of a sense of humor. He didn't even smile at his boss's feeble joke. What did Mr. Petersen know about love? A settled man with a wife and two children...

"Karin cares nothing about money," he said.

Petersen swallowed hard. "Well," he said diplomatically. "We'll talk some more about it. Have you let your parents know yet?"

"Mother is very happy about it. She wrote that the daughter of a French mother would certainly be a good cook. Father would like to know more about her."

Petersen got up. "Well, I've got to get along home," he said in an exaggeratedly jovial tone. He felt terribly old suddenly, as if he weren't forty-four but a hundred and forty-four. He drove straight to the Russian Restaurant, but he sent his chauffeur to Bangkapi with a message for Martha: "Must go to an important conference. Don't wait dinner." The chauffeur didn't have to know that Petersen was going to pay a call on a spurious hotel-restaurant that young Harms found so "funny" and felt good in. His fiancée liked it there so much, she even lived there. One drank vodka instead of grog and ate Russian specialties. Everything in Bangkok enchanted young Thomas Harms.

In the early evening hours, the Russian Restaurant was deserted. Only one Chinese girl was at the bar, washing glasses and lamps and filling them with candles for the evening. "I would like to speak to Miss Karin," Petersen said, without looking at the girl.

"Just a minute, Master," a familiar Chinese voice answered, and he was looking into Ah Bue's smiling face. Strange, he thought, and asked how long she had been working there. "Since today," she replied. "Ah Bue very very sad that Master hate her."

Petersen laughed out loud. "It's not all that bad," he said amiably. "Go fetch Miss Karin for me, little girl."

Ah Bue disappeared, bowing politely. With the unexpected appearance of the blond master she had become conscious of her humiliation all over again. Time was slow and strong as the turtle...that was what Great-uncle Ah Chang in Bangkapi said. Ah Bue thought of the red silk clouds of happiness and the sharkfin soup of which the master's cruelty had deprived her. Then she called the half-woman, which was her secret name for Miss Karin. She too thought she was sitting on top of the jade pass on the road to wisdom because the blond master loved her. Ah Bue was of the opinion that Nai Petersen couldn't exist without Miss Karin. It was like that in all the dramas she saw at the Chinese theatre three times a week. In the end there were always corpses and mournful singing. Ah Bue hummed such a Chinese song as she went to fetch the half-woman. Of course Miss Karin had not gone to the tailor, which Petersen had grasped at once. She just hadn't enjoyed his company.

"What's the meaning of all this?" Petersen asked, his tone sharp as Karin Holm strolled into the bar, irritatingly slowly. "You let that boy alone or you'll come to a bad end."

"Jealous, Johnny?" Miss Karin was evidently amused.

Petersen was ready to flare up, but then he noticed that in the beautiful girl's black eyes something akin to panic was fluttering. Karin was only pretending to be amused. Actually she was afraid.

He tried another tactic. "Karin," he said gently. "Think it over. Young Harms is an infant. He can't give you jewelry or offer you any sort of life."

"Don't worry about me. We're going to get married.

Why don't you want it? Am I not good enough for one of your compatriots?" A dangerous light glowed in her eyes. "*You* found me very nice once," she added maliciously. "Anyway, you wrote once..."

"Let's get down to business," Petersen interrupted her. The letter was burnt to ashes, like Martha's love for him. "I'll pay your fare to Hong Kong and two months in a hotel until you've had a chance to find something. You'll make both of you unhappy otherwise. Be sensible, girl."

"Don't you really understand, Johnny?" Miss Karin asked softly, her eyes lowered. A great silence hovered suddenly over these two people who centuries ago had thought they loved each other. And Petersen understood. It was a moment in which past and future melted away. Only the present was important. The incomprehensible had taken place: apparently Karin Holm loved young Harms. She really wasn't thinking of jewelry, money, or the future. The panic in her eyes offered no other explanation.

Everybody would vilify her for dragging a naïve young man into an abyss. Because it was an abyss, and everybody knew it: Madame Boulgakoff, who had introduced Karin to attractive Hannes Petersen years ago; Petersen, who had Karin to thank for the estrangement in his marriage; and perhaps Karin herself. She had to know that for her there was no way back. Now she felt grief and was filled with the fatal Asiatic stubborness: she intended to challenge fate.

"It can't end well," Petersen said again, then he added hastily, "Give me a brandy."

Karin walked behind the counter. Even when she was unhappy she moved like Aphrodite, a slightly shopworn Aphrodite, Petersen thought. And as he silently watched the girl from between two worlds getting his drink, moving between bottles and glasses in her robe of thin Chinese silk, twenty-three years old, with classical

210

breasts, and the whole sweet creature one rotten temptation, something happened to him that happens to every man once, unexpectedly—suddenly and unequivocally he knew that he was growing old. Not because of the cane, which he was still using, not because of the few gray hairs he noticed at his temples sometimes when he was shaving, but because of the new frightening feeling that overwhelmed him as he watched Karin. For the first time he felt sorry for her, with her youth, her tragic stubbornness, her hopeless love for a young fool which she hoped would purify her and which was doomed to fail. And as Petersen looked clairvoyantly into the soul of the girl who had destroyed so much in his life, he experienced the death of passion. He didn't know any more what had attracted him so strongly to Karin Holm only a few months ago so that he hadn't been able to tell her to leave the veranda. She was no concern of his any longer. She was young and foolish and pitiful. Petersen stared at her. She was smoking a cigarette in a long green holder and was lost in the bitter silence—of the Far East. Ten years more...and how quickly time passed...and Tiny would be almost as old as Karin was now. Petersen emptied his glass in one gulp. "I'll have another," he murmured. Dear God in heaven! If someone came along then and treated Tiny as men had treated Karin, Petersen would commit murder! But Tiny, whose name would then be Charlotte Christiane Petersen, lived in another world. And she had a mother who watched over her constantly. But she was in danger too. All of Tiny's potential lovers were Petersen's natural enemies. But Karin hadn't had a father who would have saved her from Petersen. Karin too was looking at the man who for so many years had kissed and then discarded her. She didn't know how well Petersen suddenly understood her.

Never would Petersen be able to explain to Martha that in a dive on the dark side of the moon, he had said

farewell to his youth. It was a farewell without senti-
mentality and without jasmine garlands. The autumnal
moon that shone over the jade pass of wisdom spread an
infinite beauty. Petersen had experienced it over endless
cups of green tea with his Chinese friends. In ten days
all of them would be celebrating the Moon Festival at old
Mr. Wong's house.

Karin poured herself a brandy and drank it down
fast. She was looking at Petersen, but in her mind's eye
she saw a blond young man with long legs and a rosy
face that was honest, trusting, and a little simple. He
was young...young... Suddenly Karin had the feeling
that nothing was impossible for the young. Hers was a
world of dancing, of embraces, and birds singing beside a
river. Now, hand in hand with the young man, she
would pass across Europe's meadows and mountains in
the coral dress Tommy loved so much. "You look like a
schoolgirl in it," he had said in his touching English. A
schoolgirl...And Karin wanted to be a wife, like the tall
pale foreign woman who always won out with Mr.
Johnny.

"What do I owe you?" asked Petersen. This time he
meant the drinks. Karin figured the sum out in her head
with a little extra for service. She could figure very well,
large and small sums. Petersen pleaded softly, "Think it
over again, Karin. Nothing good can come of it. Call me
at the office when you want your ticket to Hong Kong."

Neither of them was aware of the fact that they
weren't taking young Harms' feelings into consideration
at all. And with that they were making a big mistake.

When Petersen got back to Bangkapi, Martha was
sitting on the veranda, looking at the *lampu* tree. The
moon had already risen and suffused the orderly wilderness of the garden with its light. Martha was sitting
very still. What was she thinking of?

"You're late, Hannes," she said, her tone friendly. "Do you want your dinner right away?"

"A little later. I want to talk to you."

Martha seemed to read his thoughts because she asked if he had written to Hinrich. He showed her the copy of his letter. "I think you'd better read it yourself."

Martha read while Petersen, feeling uncomfortable, watched the expression on her face. She looked paler than usual this evening. Her fine lips were pressed together. "So it's settled," she said, and gave back the letter. And that was all Martha had to say about Petersen's decision.

14

Round Cakes from Canton

On the morning of the Moon Festival, Martha took the children to the Chinese quarter of Bangkok. Before they went back to Hamburg, Chubb and Tiny should see how this colorful Chinese feast was celebrated in Sampeng. Martha wanted to take the memory of it with her too. She had talked things over with Hannes. Lisa Petersen, one of the most celebrated bridge players between Europe and Asia, was not the one to take care of Charlotte. Lisa wasn't used to children, certainly not growing children who had been unsettled by their experiences in the Far East. Hannes had listened to Martha without saying a word. After a long pause he had said, "Then for God's sake, go back with the children! I suppose I'll turn up in a few years."

"Hannes," Martha pleaded. "Don't you see that..."

But Petersen didn't let her finish. "I see everything. The children naturally come first." He sounded tired.

Petersen drove to his office, tight-lipped. He had known all along what Martha's decision would be. And why should she stay? They were like all other married couples now—polite, with a sense of duty but with no zest. What was more, Martha looked terrible. The climate was taking its toll more and more every month. But was it only the climate? Petersen couldn't tell because Martha gave him no opportunity any more to build a bridge over past follies. Martha's withdrawal into herself was totally undramatic. No one except Hannes noticed that the warmth in her clever gray eyes was snuffed out when she spoke to him, and that it came to life when friends visited her.

Petersen went at once to Uncle Winn's private office. The old man was getting more difficult every day. It was as if he were disappointed that Hinrich wasn't going to take over Hannes' job. Why wasn't he in his office? Petersen rang for his secretary. How stupid that Uncle Winn wasn't there! They had important things to discuss today before celebrating the Chinese festival of middle autumn at old Mr. Wong's house. Never had Hannes envied anyone as much as old Mr. Wong whose family was still ruled by the laws of Confucius, according to which the master of the house made all family decisions. Although they tried to change the decisions of husband and father in subtle ways, the "female fish" obeyed. But Petersen would have liked to see old Mr. Wong's face if his wife had decided to go back to Canton with oldest son and six daughters!

Miss Knudsen came in so softly that he started involuntarily. In all these years he hadn't grown accustomed to the silent steps of the Asiatics and Eurasians. Amazons on felt soles. Karin Holm had the same silent, startling way of appearing suddenly in a room like a ghost. Once Petersen had complained about Martha's firm way of walking; he thought differently about it now. It was better to know if someone had entered the room, especially when one was looking out of the window, lost in thought, and couldn't tell how long Miss Knudsen had been watching with malicious pleasure. Why didn't the woman knock? But it was Petersen himself who had told her to skip such time-consuming formalities. Ulla Knudsen had been so hurt about the knocking ban that she now appeared in front of Petersen's desk with her steno pad like an airborne Siamese spirit. The woman knew no moderation.

"Will you please see if Mr. Petersen senior has come yet," said Hannes. Why was Miss Knudsen grinning?

"Mr. Petersen senior isn't coming to the office today," Ulla Knudsen announced. "I went to fetch him this morning and he let me drive here in his car. Mr. Petersen senior is always *so* friendly! He often lets me ride in his car," with which remark Miss Knudsen wanted to indicate how much more thoughtful her senior boss was. The occasional trips in old Petersen's limousine were highlights in her life. When she sat back and drove through New Road, teeming with people, sounds, and smells, she was for one incomparable moment mistress of the world and every rickshaw coolie in it. Driving in Petersen senior's car brought an element of magical fulfillment into the life of his private secretary, who never failed to look at the sweating rickshaw coolies with incredible arrogance through the closed windows of the car—ridiculous, greedy ants! As a matter of principle she would walk on foot to the disorderly palace of her senior boss if only to scornfully reject the rickshaw coolies. "No, I won't ride in your rickshaw!" Or, "Get out of my way! My car is waiting!" Or, "What do you charge to go to New Road?...*What?*...*Much* too expensive!" Ulla Knudsen, otherwise so sensible, could never get enough of this petty game. Then she would tell her astonished and giggling Mami how she had made a fool of her archenemies again.

Was Miss Knudsen thinking of her mother when she smiled so brightly at her junior boss? He wasn't drumming with his fingers on the top of his desk, nor was he showing any other signs of the western impatience which the Asiatics found so hateful. How many business deals had *not* been consummated in the merchant city of Bangkok because the partner from the West had jumped up suddenly to telephone or because he had looked absentminded or had interrupted his client!

"The old gentleman has a lot of trouble."

Miss Knudsen paused for effect as she studied her junior boss's face. Good! Petersen had started slightly and his lips had tightened. Had something happened to Pauline? he was thinking. But the baby wasn't expected for months.

"It's about young Mr. Harms," Miss Knudsen finally admitted hesitantly. Unfortunately there came a time when one had to reveal the news. "It looks very bad, and just on the day when all of you have been invited to Mr. Wong's house," she added. It was an eternal secret how she always knew where her boss was invited.

"What's wrong with Mr. Harms?" asked Petersen. "Is he ill?"

"He has gone! Disappeared! We don't know where he is!"

Miss Knudsen identified with the case of Harms and Petersen to such an extent that she used the plural we. "I mean," she went on hastily, "Mr. Petersen senior doesn't know where Mr. Harms has gone. He left no forwarding address. Dreadful, isn't it?"

"Not in the East," Petersen said coolly. "After all, one can go away once in a while."

Miss Knudsen admitted unwillingly that rich people enjoyed a considerable amount of freedom. "Mr. Harms wrote to Mr. Petersen senior that one shouldn't try to find out where he was. He was *never* coming back to Bangkok."

"Did you read the letter?" Petersen asked, softly but snide.

Miss Knudsen blushed and replied evasively that she had heard about it in Rong Muang. The old gentleman had told his wife about it in Siamese in such a loud voice that the girl who arranged the flowers in the morning had heard everything.

Petersen nodded. Miss Knudsen had not found it beneath her otherwise so carefully preserved dignity to ask Mae Wat in the kitchen why Petersen senior had driven to see Nai Charles Krüger. Things must be bad.

Petersen senior had received a telegram from Hamburg the evening before from August F. Harms, Hamburg-Flottbeck. Unfortunately neither Mae Wat nor the girl who arranged the flowers in the morning could decipher the German telegram. The old gentleman had responded to the news from the north with a suppressed curse and had thrown the telegram on the floor where Nang Siri found it two hours later and tore it up. After that Uncle Winn had driven to Bangkapi, but hadn't found Martha and Hannes at home. Oldest Grandson hadn't known where they had gone. Actually he had known that Master and Mem were spending the evening with Dr. Tyler, but the old master had spoken to him so loudly and impatiently that he had to be punished. Number One Boy had lost a lot of face because he had been spoken to so rudely.

"Do you want me to take dictation?" asked Miss Knudsen. She hadn't had so much *sanuk* in a long time. Her boss would of course tear off immediately to the Russian Restaurant to find out if Karin Holm had taken off for Hong Kong with Baby Face from Harms and Company. It had been Miss Knudsen's experience over the years that in every crisis Europeans shouted for their chauffeurs and didn't stop to think things over. But this time she was disappointed. Unlike Baby Face from Harms and Company, Johannes Petersen hadn't arrived in Bangkok only a few months ago. He knew exactly what Miss Knudsen was expecting him to do and he didn't do her the favor. He was not going to deliver more material for gossip. He dictated all morning with a stony face. Then, after assuring himself that his very competent, deeply disappointed secretary had gone to have noonday rice with her mother, he drove to the Russian Restaurant.

Earlier that morning he had received a message

from his uncle which he had not opened in front of Miss Knudsen. Petersen senior informed him that Mr. August F. Harms had begged him by cable to send his son home on the next plane. "Tommy's marriage impossible. Writing," the worried father had thundered across the seven seas. Mr. August F. Harms had also spent his *Sturm und Drang* years in a few exciting cities east of Suez. He had therefore recognized from a picture of Baby Face and Miss Karin that the young lady did *not* have a French mother, and also did not fit into Flottbeck in other respects. In the course of these deliberations it was noteworthy that everyone—Johannes Petersen, Karin, and Mr. August F. Harms from Flottbeck—thought he or she could dispose of a long-legged young man with a totally expressionless face as if he were a child or a package.

Petersen ordered the girl Ah Bue to announce him to Madame Boulgakoff. He had to find out if and where Karin had disposed of Tommy Harms of Harms and Company in order to devour him tooth and nail. While Petersen was thinking what to do, a girl in a pink travel suit appeared in the lobby of the restaurant, which was decorated with Russian lithographs. Petersen stared at Miss Karin as if she had been an apparition. Hadn't he thought she had kidnaped Baby Face?

"Where is Tommy?" His throat was so dry that it was hard not to ask for a whiskey and soda, but one didn't touch alcohol before five in the afternoon.

"I have no idea," said Karin Holm, powdering her nose, as absorbed as if she were alone in front of a vanity table. She treated Petersen like a tiresome Chinese who was trying to sell her a flawed wall hanging.

"I thought you were going to get married in eight days." Petersen spoke exceptionally gently.

"And we are! But in the morning poor Tommy has to work like a dog for a pittance in your office. You always send him off to the horrible Chinese." Karin was melting with pity for this sacrificial lamb of Petersen and Company.

"Tommy has disappeared. He's been gone since yesterday," said Petersen.

The young lady let out a scream that would have been worthy of the heroine of a Chinese drama. She stepped up close to Petersen and hissed, "And it's your fault, you devil! Poor Tommy! He must have committed suicide. You don't pay him enough to keep body and soul alive!"

It was characteristic that in spite of her cry of despair in the moment of her bitter loss, she could not free herself from questions of salary. Petersen stared at Thomas Harms's beautiful, unhappy fiancée. Could he ever have felt passion for such a stupid little fool? He was so sobered that he couldn't even feel fatherly pity for her any more. The girl was nothing but a malicious and not very intelligent gold digger.

"We've got to look for him!" cried Miss Karin. "Give me money for a taxi! I'm going to call in the police!"

"You're crazy," Petersen said calmly. "A scandal for the papers? That's all we need right now. All the firm can do is hire a private detective. Please don't do anything on your own."

Karin Holm gave Nai Petersen an enigmatic look. Then she said quietly, "The best bloodhound is Nai Ketaki. But he charges a lot. He's an Indian. He lives on the corner of Silom Road, near the Mohammed Temple."

"I know the man." Petersen sounded thoughtful. "But I have somebody of my own." Instinct warned him not to join forces with Miss Karin.

"If Tommy comes back, will he get a larger salary from your firm?" asked Tommy's fiancée.

"First he's got to be here," Petersen replied cautiously. Suddenly he thought he saw a light. Did Tommy and Karin intend to blackmail the firm? Was the young man already a helpless tool? No—the son of August F.

Harms couldn't possibly go in for such dirty business. But what should one write to the boy's father? Petersen had to find Uncle Winn at once. He left the Russian Restaurant in a hurry.

Miss Karin watched him go. In seconds her face crumpled as if a mask had crumbled away to expose the naked face, a desperate face. A thought flashed through her mind. She looked at her gold wristwatch. There was just enough time to pay a call. Karin needed money. Ulla Knudsen had money, even though she haggled daily with rickshaw coolies. She owned two quite valuable pieces of real estate and some fine jewelry. It wasn't really necessary for her to live in a dilapidated pile dwelling behind the Hualampong Klong. Karin took a letter out of her pocket. Thomas Harms had written to her. She couldn't remember how many times she had read it; she only knew that he must have gone crazy.

When Karin arrived at Ulla Knudsen's house she found the latter, an influential lady in her circles, having lunch. Miss Knudsen was usually very hospitable, but she hated anyone to watch her eat. And Nang Sanit, her little "Mami," was so startled that the sago pudding with palm sugar sauce almost got stuck in her throat. Nang Nom was easily frightened and pathologically shy in the presence of her daughter's elegant friends. Only the knowledge that Ulla, in spite of her washed-out cotton dresses, was much richer than Nangsao "Kalin"—she pronounced the r like an l —calmed the shy old Siamese lady down again. Just the same, she rose from her mat immediately when Karin entered the room and crept away humbly to a summer house in the little garden.

Miss Knudsen rose, frowning, and picked up the pudding dish without greeting Karin. "Mami, Mami!" she cried, so shrilly that Karin started nervously. "Don't you want to finish your pudding? You like sago pudding so much! And Ulla has another surprise for Mami. But she won't get it until tonight for the Moon Festival unless she is good and eats up her pudding now." And Miss Knudsen carried her mother's pudding with palm sugar sauce and her infinite love out to the summer house with the dark red bougainvillea blossoms.

When she came back she looked a little more friendly as she said, "Mami musn't be disturbed when she's eating. It upsets her."

"Ulla," said Karin. "Do you have a minute?"

"Unfortunately, no." Miss Knudsen had still not forgiven Karin for refusing her invitation to Chez Eve. "I have to massage Mami. I'm the only one who knows how. Goodbye, Karin."

"Goodbye," murmured the girl in the elegant pink suit.

"And please don't disturb me again at lunch!" Miss Knudsen called after her former friend as she left. Unfortunately the exemplary Miss Knudsen had a slight character flaw, like a cracked piece of jade: she liked to give a dog a little kick when it was down.

Karin Holm called a rickshaw and drove to the thieves' market of Nakorn Kasem. An old Chinese lived there who knew every European who had ever got into financial difficulties. Uncle Ho might know if Tommy had sold or pawned anything. Uncle Ho smoked the water pipe which was now outmoded and accepted Karin's moon cake with a deep bow. He sniffed the package, asked, "Cantonese cake?" looked pleased, and laid the expensive present on a valuable, very dirty marble counter. Unfortunately Karin could find out nothing from him. He kept to himself the fact that two days before a long-legged young man with a totally expressionless face had brought a gold watch to him, an heirloom. A half-hour ago the watch had been picked up. Inside the lid there had been an inscription: *Thomas Harms. Hamburg 1822.* The inscription had interested a pudgy old gentleman who lived with his wife and a lot of pedigreed dogs and horses in the Dusit district so much that he had bought it. Then Charles Krüger had driven out to see Uncle Winn, who had suffered a slight heart attack. Dr. Tyler, the English veterinarian was sitting beside him in the *sala*, trying to cheer him up. Hannes had in the meantime gone to the big travel bureau on New Road to find out if young Harms had bought a ticket for a ship or plane.

While old Mr. Petersen stared, first at Grandfather Harms's gold watch, then at the picture *Storm on the Elbe*, Hannes came rushing into the *sala*, breathless. "He's flown to Hong Kong, the idiot!"

"Then we'll find him," said Petersen senior, sounding somewhat relieved.

"Like a needle in a haystack," said Dr. Tyler.

He knew Hong Kong. It was a place in which you could disappear. Or travel on to the colony of Macao. In Macao there were many gambling dens and hiding places and the Portuguese police didn't exactly lose sleep over it.

"So what are we going to write Father Harms?" asked Hannes.

Old Petersen looked up and thrust out his chin. "The truth," he said.

"Did...did the little Holm girl go with him?" asked Charles Krüger. "Then we could put two and two together."

"I don't know," answered Johannes Petersen.

This was followed by an uncomfortable pause, which was interrupted by the arrival of Dr. Johannsen. No, Uncle Winn was not to go to Mr. Wong's dinner that evening and out of politeness eat indigestible moon cake, roast goose, fish in sweet and sour sauce and other Chinese delicacies. "Impossible!" Petersen senior argued. "My dear Johannsen, Mr. Wong would hold it against me for the rest of his life if I didn't turn up. Since..." He stopped. He didn't want to tell Dr. Johannsen what had happened. Not yet. Tommy might come to his senses before all the porcelain in the china shop was broken. It would be embarrassing enough to have to excuse young Harms at the Wongs' with a sudden attack of dengue fever.

"Impossible!" Petersen junior repeated, in rare agreement with his uncle.

Dr. Johannsen had lived too long in the Far East not to know what the result of a refusal would be. Above all one shouldn't excite an old patient and friend further. He came to a quick decision. "What time is the invitation?" he asked.

"Eight. We'll eat around ten."

Dr. Johannsen silently deplored the damned Chinese custom. Many of his western patients, especially those past sixty, suffered from stomach complaints as a result of the late, opulent meals. "I'll give you a tranquilizer now," he said. "If you feel well enough, go to the dinner. I'm relying on your common sense."

Good old Johannsen knew only too well that common sense was a rare commodity among the male members of the Petersen family, but he wanted to leave the old gentleman the illusion of having made the decision. He knew that Wilhelm Christian Petersen would spend the night of the Chinese Moon Festival in his own house.

Meanwhile Karin Holm proceeded to the Bangkok Indian quarter where gold and silver shops baked in the tropical sun. She walked into the shop of Nai Ketaki, whose family lived on the corner of Silom Road. There Nai Ketaki had a beautiful house which his business as a dealer in jewelry and private detective had made it possible for him to buy. Karin needed money for a plane ticket to Hong Kong. Madame Boulgakoff wouldn't give her a cent. Karin was the pièce de résistance of the Rus-

sian Restaurant. That was the reason Madame Boulgakoff had decided to play fate a little. It was she who had
cautiously enlightened young Harms on several points.
She had told him about Karin's mother and her past, in
which Johannes Petersen figured tactfully as "a gentleman from North Europe." Because Petersen could have
her place, where there was illegal gambling, closed if he
wanted to. She had also told Tommy Harms the true
reason for Karin's failed marriage to the rich Swede. He
had listened attentively to everything and had left Bangkok the following day. Madame Boulgakoff had calcu-
lated correctly. The miserable young man had sold his
gold watch in order to buy a plane ticket to Hong Kong.
For a long time he had been spending every cent of his
monthly salary and had begun quietly and impeccably to
go to the dogs. Hong Kong would finish him off. The
thought made Madame Boulgakoff smile. How nice
when for once a person with social advantages landed on
the dark side of the moon. When she imagined how
Petersen would have to write the young man's parents
the bitter truth, life had its compensations. And she
would keep Karin.

   "Do you have a reliable man in Hong Kong?" Karin
Holm asked the tall Indian with the blood-red turban,
dressed all in white. She had sold him her gold watch
and now got down to business. Of course Nai Ketaki
had his people in Hong Kong and Macao: Chinese, cun-
ning. But it would be very difficult to find the young
foreigner. Tommy had written in his letter that he was
determined to make his living in Hong Kong on his own.
Not a word about who had enlightened him as to her
"true nature," as the young man had put it dramatically.
But what did Tommy think he could do in Hong Kong?
Even experienced businessmen who knew the East like
their own pockets and had plenty of capital to invest in
today's Free State of Chinese intellectuals and capitalists
were ruined faster there than anywhere else. The Asia-

tic population had overflowed the former European residential quarters and business districts. A white man would have to be smart as hell to get by.

Karin shivered in the topical sun. She felt a slight pain in the region of her heart. Petersen must have told Tommy about her past. He had practically threatened her to leave the boy alone. How she hated Petersen! She hoped she could one day do something to him that he'd never forget for the rest of his life! But what? Well... she'd give it some thought.

She had pretended to know nothing in front of Petersen in order to be able to think better. It hadn't occurred to her right away that Nai Petersen, who after all hadn't been born yesterday, would simply inquire at the Bangkok travel agencies. But she was positive that sooner or later he would fly to Hong Kong to find Tommy. She had to get there ahead of him. That was why Karin Holm sold her gold watch on the day of the Chinese Moon Festival in order to be able to fly to Hong Kong the day after tomorrow and talk to Nai Ketaki's agent. In Hong Kong her money problems would be over. Mr. Yu was there, the fat little Chinese whom Karin had enchanted in the Hoi Tien dance hall on the evening of the wedding that had never taken place. The former harbor coolie was an influential businessman in Hong Kong, and for the time being madly in love with Karin Holm. Karin would pay Nai Ketaki's agent in Hong Kong with Mr. Yu's money. What a pity that the wrong people always had the money, thought Tommy's fiancée as she walked back to the Russian Restaurant.

Madame Boulgakoff had arrived on Yawarat Road in a rickshaw. She proceeded on foot to a winding alleyway that branched off Yawarat. On the ground floor of a certain house there was a restaurant for coolies. A thin Chinese child, wearing patched blue linen trousers and a jacket to match stood on a rickety staircase. She answered to the name of Brocade. She greeted the Russian woman with a shy smile and received in return a rigid stare out of half-closed eyes. "Is your father home?" asked Madame Boulgakoff.

The child nodded and ran upstairs giggling.

Madame Boulgakoff walked into an establishment in which wild disorder ruled supreme. An old Chinese woman crouched in a corner in front of three tiny coal stoves. Provender—vegetables, fish, herbs, and a sack of rice—lay strewn in front of the little stoves. The room had one small window with wooden shutters. A few torn bamboo mats, an oil lantern with a shade that showed a smeared drawing of a Chinese landscape, and spider webs in every corner completed the décor. Hair, beards, and ribbons lay all over the place. Mr. Lu, the father of the thin, sly child and owner of the workshop greeted Madame Boulgakoff with a medium-low bow. Eight children were sitting around the old woman who was preparing the midday rice with the groping hands of the blind. The children were busy making beards for the theatre. Mr. Lu was a specialist in this traditional art. He delivered the prescribed classical beards to the actors in the Big Chinese theatres on Yawarat Road, who according to the shape and style of their beards conveyed to the audience who and what they were. Naturally, as a smart businessman, Mr. Lu wasn't satisfied with just manufacturing beards for the theatre, the sale of which he occasionally helped along by instigating little fires in the dressing rooms.

Because they were the cheapest workers on the Chinese market, Mr. Lu bought children; that is to say, he bought little girls. The children seated so cosily around his blind mother were all bargains. When they reached the proper age they would be rented out for the night to the less exacting bordellos. Brocade was Mr. Lu's only daughter and reported to her father all the misdeeds of the other little girls who from six o'clock in the morning until late in the night cheerfully and artistically made beards for the theatre. A Chinese orphan was satisfied when it got its rice and not too many beatings. It was really too bad that the League of Nations didn't once look into Mr. Lu's establishment which Madame Boulgakoff would never have found without the help of her servant, Ah Bue. Mr. Lu was distantly related to Ah Bue's mother.

"Do you have the stuff for me?" Madame Boulgakoff asked.

Was she buying beards for the theatre? Oh no! All Madame Boulgakoff wanted was a little bit of opium for which she paid in installments. Opium was better than moon cake. It didn't lie heavy in your stomach but freed your spirit so that you could strip off the chains of reality for a few hours. Tonight Madame Boulgakoff would see the shining moon from her little private veranda and travel into the past. Only Mr. Lu could give her the passport into this dream world of the White Russians.

"It's gone up in price again," he said, smiling gently. "And it's getting harder and harder to find. The Siamese authorities are passing high jail sentences for opium smugglers."

"How much?" asked Madame Boulgakoff.

Mr. Lu kicked one of his little girls, none too gently, and named his Moon Festival price. Madame Boulgakoff paid and left without saying a word. The devil take Mr. Lu! But what could one do? Life was a big and onerous business, and for Madame Boulgakoff, without the poppy of forgetfulness it was unbearable.

When she got back to her restaurant, Ah Bue had already left. She was going to celebrate the Moon Festival with the rest of her family and Uncle Ah Chang in Bangkapi. Madame Boulgakoff was very annoyed over this sudden outburst of family feeling, but years of experience had taught her never to interfere with or make any demands of the members of a Chinese family. Karin would just have to help serve if Ah Bue had to admire the moon in Bangkapi.

Karin was lying under the mosquito net, smoking a cigarette. Her eyes were red. "Shouldn't you be getting dressed? We're expecting guests this afternoon."

"I have a headache."

Madame gave the object of her little intrigue a sharp look. "Still hankering after that long-legged young fool? Don't be ridiculous, Karin! I've got something good for you. He's got money and he's quite young."

Karin didn't seem to be listening. She had had a long talk with Ah Bue while Madame had been away. The name Petersen had come up frequently in their conversation. Yes...one might be able to take one's revenge like that when the time was right. Ah Bue had had a wild suggestion and Karin had nodded. This was something Nai Petersen wouldn't forget as long as he lived! It couldn't go wrong because Ah Bue was a clever, cautious girl. She had received a little present from Miss Karin, something that had delighted her—a necklace of red beads. They were neither valuable nor large, but Ah Bue had declared she had never seen anything so beautiful. "For your Moon Festival," Karin had told her, smiling. And Ah Bue had smiled innocently too, as if she knew why the half-lady had given her the necklace. You got nothing for nothing in the Far East—not even revenge.

Ah Chang and his daughter Cheng were working feverishly on the preparations for the Moon Festival when Ah Bue arrived in her emboidered jacket and new satin trousers. Cheng had just mixed cinnamon with onion extract and was steaming the mixture. Ah Chang was cooking a turtle he had found in a pond five days before. The brain of the turtle, together with Martha's cinnamon and Cheng's onion juice, would result in an essence that prolonged life. Every grandson would get some of this essence tonight from his grandfather. Daughter Cheng found it in order that her father reserved this recipe for the male members of his family. *She* would live to be a hundred years old without turtle, she decided in a disrespectful moment.

The appearance of Ah Bue did not arouse great joy. Ah Chang couldn't abide her. He had lost face by the dismissal of Chung and Ah Bue, and would never forgive either of them. But the resentment of her old relative was a matter of total indifference to Ah Bue. "Where is Little Master?" she asked.

Ah Bue had to repeat the question before Cheng pointed in the direction of the canal. Out of loyalty to her honorable father, she treated Ah Bue like a leper. It would never have occurred to Cheng that Ah Bue was the result of her mother's upbringing. She seemed to have forgotten that it was she herself who had installed these unpleasant relatives in the Petersen house. Cheng was a perfect example of daughterly devotion and general injustice.

Ah Bue sauntered over to the canal where Chubb was fishing with Second Grandson, who was thrilled to be fishing with Little Master. He would fry all the fish that he could catch with Chubb's help. Ah Bue walked up to Chubb so softly that he didn't hear her. "Young Master," she whispered. "Ah Bue bring poor, tiny little present. Tonight is Moon Festival." Suddenly she was embarrassed and looked down.

"Oh! Ah Bue!" Chubb was surprised. "That's nice of you."

He opened the package. Ah Bue had saved her miserable salary to buy expensive moon cakes for him. Chubb didn't know what to say. He shifted from one foot to the other. "Thank you very much," he mumbled finally. "But that's much too good for me."

"Ah Bue would give Young Master white jacket if she had more money."

Chubb found the offer exaggerated, but he said nothing. He had never received a present from a girl before. He looked at Ah Bue shyly out of the corner of his eyes. He thought she looked wonderful in her fine embroidered jacket, closed up to the neck but leaving her golden arms bare. "Did you embroider those chrysanthemums yourself?" he asked.

Ah Bue nodded. "Would Young Master like to count them?" She touched a little chrysanthemum on her breast very gently and looked at Chubb from the side.

"That's silly, Ah Bue," said Martha's son.

For a moment Ah Bue didn't know what to do. Was young master angry? She had only wanted to give him pleasure. All the young gentlemen liked to count the flowers on her delicate little breasts, but Chubb was looking at her frankly and trustingly through his glasses.

"Say, Ah Bue," he said, in his meticulous Chinese, which he occasionally mixed with Siamese words. "When I come back later, you've got to keep house for me."

"Perhaps Young Master marry Ah Bue?" the young lady suggested.

Chubb laughed. The thought of marriage at this moment seemed irresistibly funny, even though he had said once to Grand-uncle Petersen that a Chinese girl would be very useful as a wife. "Well, you know, Ah Bue, we have a long way to go before that," he said. "First I still have to go to school and work hard."

Ah Bue said nothing. Again she looked at the big blond boy from the strange land. Nobody had ever been so nice to her. Young Master had never beaten her. He had often brought her delicacies from the main house. He had even taught her a few words of English. He would never crush her underfoot as his cruel father had done. In her Chinese imagination she had already made a tiger of Nai Petersen. Young Master was her only friend, she decided, and with that Ah Bue wasn't so far wrong. Blind devotion lay in her eyes and the grief of resignation. Young Master would be going away in a few months and she would have to go right on working in the Russian Restaurant.

"Ah Bue will die of grief," she said seriously. "Young Master will forget bad, stupid Ah Bue very fast."

"But Ah Bue!" Chubb was indignant. "How can you say that! I'll never forget you!"

Ah Bue lowered her eyes. At that moment she was a lonely child who knew nothing any more about the ugly plans for revenge she had thought up a while ago with the half-woman. As a Chinese she lived good and bad moments intensively, whereby she forgot the bad ones quickly and kept only the good in mind.

Chubb saw Ah Bue's sad face and suddenly stroked her arm gently. That was what he always did when Tiny wanted to cry. But when he touched the slim arm of the pretty little Chinese girl, he suddenly felt hot and cold, and a strange trembling that evidently emanated from the girl's cool, smooth arm. He turned first red, then pale. He had never felt so confused.

A pallid moon appeared on the horizon. In the night it would be in full glory. The glory was not for boys.

"Thank you very much for the cake," Chubb murmured. "It was...it was very nice of you. Yes...and..."

Ah Bue didn't move.

While Chubb shifted from one big foot to the other and didn't know what to do, his parents drove through the gate. "Ah Bue must go," the little girl said quickly. "All five blessings for the Young Master."

Chubb tore into the house. Ah Bue was a good girl. What did his parents have against her? Ah Bue had wished him the five best things in life: a bed, a candle to read by, a pipe, good stories, and hot food. And she had brought him moon cakes...

15

The Guests of Mr. Wong

Rickshaws and motor cars wove their way between trucks that were late, all hurrying under the fluttering, silvery light of lanterns. In the evening all Bangkok seemed to get into the means of transportation of East and West to rush after a dream in a garden or on a veranda. Nobody seemed to spend an evening at home. Even the rickshaw coolies deposited their fares only to hurry on to the scenes of their nocturnal pleasures: in an opium cellar in Bangrak, in a secret gambling den, or in a narrow vined alley next to a canal where a girl with a flower in her smooth black hair was waiting with a pot of rice and curry. Only the lame, the blind, and leprous stayed home, along with refugees whom the politics of various countries had wafted to Bangkok.

But tonight life on the streets seemed even more hectic than usual. The oil lamps on the rickshaws flickered across festively dressed Chinese families driving to their friends for the Moon Festival. The tropical night was falling. Hunger and passions intensified...at five o'clock next morning the struggle for a bowl of rice would begin all over again.

Petersen inhaled the night air. The nocturnal drama on the street entranced him. "Won't you miss all this?" He made a vague gesture that included the whole Southeast Asian spectacle.

"Yes, of course," Martha said quietly.

She was thinking of Uncle Winn, who had become so attached to her and the children. The pending separation undoubtedly weighed on him, even if he never mentioned it. Martha noticed only too well that the veil of melancholy which occasionally dimmed his light blue eyes had grown heavier during the last weeks. "What's wrong with Pauline anyway?" she asked.

"No idea. Did Uncle Winn say anything about her?"

"He hasn't had a letter from her in a long time. It's a shame. Pauline knows very well that the old man lives only for her."

"He's spoiled her rotten. I can't understand anyone making such a fuss over a child."

Was Hannes serious? "People in glass houses shouldn't throw stones," said Martha. She still had a motto for every situation.

Hannes laughed and stroked her hands that were folded motionless in her lap. "Oh, Martha...you don't change." He sounded gentler than he had in months.

"Thank God!" Martha replied energetically. It was necessary that at least one member of the family still act sensibly. She would write to Pauline tomorrow. Martha couldn't imagine why the girl suddenly didn't write, and she certainly would never have been able to imagine that after two postcards depicting the city of Manila and a rice village in the Philippines, Pauline hadn't written to her father again. This Wilhelm Christian Petersen had not told his niece; this concerned only him and that damned girl of his in Manila!

Mr. Wong's house lay near the old Phya Thai Palace on Rajavithi Road. According to the trend of the times, the palace had been a hotel for years, but the big new hotels on Rajadamnoen Avenue that were fully occupied after the war had put the old palace, which even as a hotel had still radiated some of the aura of its former royal residents, out of business. But the spacious lawns, the enchanting flower beds, miniature waterfalls and pavilions for the classical dancing that the Siamese princes considered requisite, were all intact. The palace was roomy, forlorn, exquisite, and old, and Mr. Wong had settled himself and his family close by because he liked old and exquisite things after office hours.

He had rented his house from old Mr. Petersen's wife in November 1940, shortly after the arrival of the Japanese, and here too the typical spirit of the Far East that equated beauty with lavish space and rare choice furnishings ruled supreme. But the hallmark of Chinese culture that had turned the house in a strange land into a real home for the Wong family was the garden. Petersen and Martha loved it. During their first visit, old Mr. Wong had explained to them that according to Chinese concepts, house and garden were not things apart but a harmonious entity, a *yuancheh*, or garden-home. And house and garden really seemed to coalesce because what was hanging in the rooms in the way of water landscapes was repeated artistically in the garden in miniature. Pavilions with dainty roofs and huge, priceless porcelain vases filled with flowers contributed to the elegance of the *yuancheh*.

Old Mr. Wong's guests were assembled in the largest pavilion after a banquet that had taken place in the dining hall at round marble tables. Twenty courses of daintily garnished dishes with the elements of sweet and sour, crisp and soft, intermingling according to traditional recipes. Little Chinese girls, the beautiful daughters of old Mr. Wong, moved between the guests, giving orders to the servants who were serving mocha, whiskey, lemonade, and moon cakes on lacquered trays. The guests from China and the West looked for a moment at the moon in honor of which the feast was being held. The mistress of the house was not present. Old Mr.

Wong had excused his wife. A slight indisposition. Madame Wong would watch the shining moon happily and undisturbed on her private veranda.

It was a small group of guests whom old Mr. Wong had invited, among them Miss Black and a Mr. and Mrs. Spark. David Spark was Larry Desmond's replacement in the little family of ECAFE. As happened so often in Bangkok, Mr. Wong's guests came from various lands and spheres of activity. But the focus of the evening was the pride of the family, the oldest son, who had arrived with his fiancée from San Francisco the day before. Young Wong was studying economics in San Francisco. His spirit was imbued with such things as canned salmon, chemicals, and import rulings for tea, rice and coal. He had three passions: chewing gum, American jazz, and his fiancée Pao-Chai, meaning Priceless Virtue. Whatever the priceless virtues of the young Chinese girl in her elegant evening dress were, and where and when she presented them to the world, was not obvious, at any rate, not in the house of her future father-in-law. Miss Pao-Chai spoke a lot and very quickly, and to the horror of her well-behaved little sisters-in-law to be, broke into the conversation of the men and showed her future husband not the slightest respect. If old Mr. Wong was displeased with his son's choice—and actually he should have been, if only as a matter of principle, because he hadn't personally chosen the mother of his future grandsons—he didn't show it. He treated the young lady with reserved politeness and a gentle irony so that nobody except perhaps old Madame Wong could have sensed any disapproval. But Madame Wong was sitting contentedly and unruffled on her veranda. The old lady watching the moon, frail and unassuming in her black silk jacket, would gently but thoroughly bully Priceless Virtue after the wedding until the girl had learned in her Bangkok home the manners she now so noticeably lacked. But Madame Wong had already told her oldest son that he was not to appear in her room chewing gum. And the business-like, confident young man, who besides studying economics was making connections for the House of Wong in San Francisco, had looked at his mother sheepishly and had humbly promised to mend his ways.

Martha was conversing with a fat little Chinese from Hong Kong and his daughter. She was trying to think where she had seen the man with the sharp eyes and good-humored double chin before. Suddenly she knew. He had been introduced to her as Mr. Yu at the Bangkok airport. At the time he had been flying to Hong Kong with Karin Holm. His daughter had not been with him. Of course not, thought Martha.

Mr. Yu seemed totally absorbed by his daughter, Phoenix. Like Uncle Winn, thought Martha, and for a moment was angry with Pauline again. Mr. Yu smiled broadly, as only a Chinese father can, whenever Phoenix answered Martha with intelligence and charm. She really was like a golden bird that had risen out of the ashes of a coolie existence. In Mr. Yu's workworn hands, which to this day bore the scars of hard labor in the port of Hong Kong, he absentmindedly held a brocade purse that belonged to his daughter. He always had to hold something that belonged to Phoenix: a postcard she had written to him as a child; a faded red hair ribbon that at this moment was lying on his desk in Hong Kong; or the brocade purse he had given her for this trip to Bangkok. Phoenix found the purse too colorful and ornate, but never would she have caused *tai-lac-yeh*, or Big Old Father, to lose face by putting his overly ostentatious gift in the camphor chest. Her glossy lacquer-black hair was done up in a very becoming style, and her long Chinese brocade dress glittered pink and silver.

Mr. Yu couldn't take his eyes from his daughter, nor from the rectangular piece of opalescent jade that hung like a little glowing cloud on a platinum chain around her neck. It was very old and priceless, and the former coolie had bought it in an auction in Hong Kong. Old Mr. Wong, who liked old and priceless things, had congratulated his business colleague on the piece of jade his daughter was wearing so casually around her neck, and Mr. Yu had admitted to the unheard of price he had paid for it in a whisper, yet loud enough for everyone to hear. In this way the former coolie had at once won face.

Old Mr. Wong had inquired sympathetically about Uncle Winn's honorable health; he had *not* inquired about young Harms, and had reacted to Petersen's excuses for the young man with silence. He sat very quietly in his chair. Not many foreigners understood that by the light of the autumnal moon a Chinese experienced the poetry, maturity, and wisdom of life so intensively that right now Mr. Wong could contemplate with indifference the era of anarchy into which the world had been plunged. Mr. Wong was a Taoist, and the autumnal moon was a friend of those Taoists who no longer existed in Mao Tse-tung's China. Yet the old man hoped, as he looked at the moon, that the red storm roaring across his country would also leave room for the old wisdom that had fortified the Chinese people for centuries. A little pleasant corruption might also be permitted to crop up again, old Mr. Wong thought privately, not as much corruption as before the red storm but not as little friendliness and talent for compromise as today.

The old gentleman with the face of a wise man, who understood so much about business, rose from his chair and begged Johannes Petersen for permission to show his wife the pictures of ancient Chinese calligraphy. He showed his honorable guests from the West only a few choice things in his garden-house—once it might be vases, another time watercolor landscapes, bronzes, or the mandarin coats in the camphor chest. And this evening he wanted to show Martha his most valuable treasure. Because Madame, as the head of the House of Wong had finally found out, wanted to go back to Europe with her son.

The other guests had risen too and now began to walk through the garden with their host's daughters. Quite by chance Hannes found himself suddenly beside Miss Black, although he would much rather have had a bit of fun with the amusing little thing who was going to marry the oldest son of the house. Because although Hannes was an older man now who was hardheartedly letting his family leave him, he did still get a lift out of conversing with young ladies who, like Priceless Virtue, were quite willing to help him pass the time coyly and a little deceitfully. But Miss Black had a few interesting things to say. She told Hannes that Mr. and Mrs. Spark had been in Manila recently and looked up Lawrence Desmond. "Compatriots like to visit each other in foreign countries," said Miss Black, who had never visited a compatriot in a foreign country and didn't see herself doing so in the future.

"How is our Pauline?" Hannes asked a little too eagerly.

"She seems to be extremely disagreeable," said Miss Black.

Hannes nearly stumbled over a root in his surprise. "What do you mean?" he asked.

"I mean that your niece can't get along with people," Miss Black explained impatiently. She thought she had expressed herself quite clearly.

Hannes was speechless. Who were the people with whom the apple of old Petersen's eye couldn't get along? But he couldn't ask Miss Black or the Sparks that.

While the other guests were enjoying themselves in the garden, old Mr. Wong had returned to the reception rooms with Martha. For the festivities he had hung the walls with choice masterpieces of calligraphy on bamboo rolls. He changed these pictures constantly, as he did his water and hillscapes. He would never understand how his honorable guests from the West could bear to live all their lives with the same two or three oil paintings..

Martha examined the scrolls on the walls. Her aesthetic senses were attuned to Gothic art, and she preferred simple, noble lines. Thus she experienced a certain satisfaction at sight of the scrolls. Something in her clearly defined spirit responded to this ancient Chinese art form. The calligraphy reminded her faintly of the number pictures of her beloved mathematics, as if mathematicians suddenly wanted to produce an aesthetic effect.

When she told her host what she was thinking, his face brightened. Instead of replying, he took out of a carved chest a calligraphic masterpiece which had the same shape as the wall hangings. It was very old and was the epitome of the vitality and chastity of this art form. They went to his private room. The furnishings in his bamboo den were ascetic: a wall chest containing thin porcelain cups with no handles, and a few choice examples of Chinese paintings on the walls. Everything was simple in this room and filled with the ambience of meditation.

The old gentleman pointed with his thin scholar's hand to several landscapes, and explained to Martha how akin the representation of cloud masses, of bamboo and rock outlines were to the sparse strokes of the calligraphist. Suddenly he interrupted his explanations. A light disturbance lay like a cloud over his serene forehead. Martha felt an inexplicable change in the atmosphere. Old Mr. Wong gestured to her to sit down. Then he rang an old copper bell. An enchanting little Chinese girl appeared. She was half-child, half-woman, and she was wearing black trousers and a high-necked smock of light, flowered silk. Something about the girl reminded

Martha of the six daughters of old Mr. Wong. Actually she was also his daughter, but her mother was not the almighty Madame Wong sitting relaxed and undisturbed on her veranda, watching the moon and making plans for her family; Ping-erh, or Patience, was the daughter of an embroiderer, attractive, obliging and, as her name implied, patient. She waited mainly on Mr. Wong who seemd very fond of her.

"Ping-erh," old Mr. Wong said gently. "Prepare tea for my guest and me."

Patience made a formal little bow and scurried out humbly in her little embroidered slippers. It impressed Martha that the old man had spoken exceptionally lovingly to this little servant, more so than to the six daughters of Madame Wong who, as was correct for rich legitimate daughters, lived only for their own pleasure. After Ping-erh had brought the lacquer tray with the tiny cups, placed it on a bamboo table, and left soundlessly, old Mr. Wong began a conversation which he had prepared several hours before.

It was quiet in the bamboo den. The moon cast its silver light on the cups with their green tea, on the old man, and on the foreign lady who was wearing a dress the color of the moon. It was the same silver-gray dress Martha had worn in Colombo.

"Madame," said old Mr. Wong. "Is your honorable uncle very ill?"

Martha replied that all Uncle Winn needed was rest. He would so much have liked to come tonight, but a slight weakness of the heart...

"Is it because of young Mr. Harms?" the old gentleman asked.

Martha reddened. What should she say? She had used the excuse of illness so that all of them might save face. Hannes would be beside himself if she contradicted herself now.

"This young man is not as ill as it seems." Old Mr. Wong interrupted the embarrassing silence as he carefully poured tea into Martha's tiny cup.

Still Martha said nothing. She was baffled. Had their host seen through the thin excuse? It seemed impossible. No one outside the family, Charles Krüger, and Dr. Tyler knew about Tommy's headlong flight. "Madame," whispered old Mr. Wong. "Consider me your friend."

Experience, suffering, and wisdom lay in his eyes, but perspicacity and a spark of impishness also glowed in them. "Young Mr. Harms came to see me before he flew to Hong Kong," he explained.

"To see you?" Martha stammered.

"Yes. He borrowed money from me. He would like to make himself independent. A very praiseworthy decision."

Martha thought she must be dreaming. Was it possible that the expressionless young man whom everyone had disposed of could have had more confidence in a stranger than in the Petersen family? It seemed so. And it would add one more drop of bitterness to the many Uncle Winn had tasted since Martha's arrival.

"Did he borrow a lot of money?" Martha asked practically. "Of course my uncle and my husband will..."

The old man raised his hand. "Please do not worry, Madame. You see before you a man who has never lost money, but who also has the patience to wait weeks, months, even years for the repayment of a debt." He said it serenely, as if there were nothing he enjoyed more in the world than to wait for the money owed him by Thomas Harms of Harms and Company.

"Mr. Thomas is the grandson of a banker," said Bangkok's most influential financier. It seemed a foregone conclusion to him that he would get his money back from the descendant of a man in whose gold watch were engraved the words: *Thomas Harms. Hamburg 1822.*

"I loaned him a third of what he wanted to borrow, since I decided this was the sum young Mr. Harms could sensibly expect from me. Unfortunately he had already sold his gold watch, but I am sure your uncle can buy it back at Nakorn Kasem."

Martha was wondering why old Mr. Wong wasn't telling Hannes all this. Probably he thought that Hannes would lose too much face if one could prove that he had lied, albeit a white lie. But perhaps the old Chinese had other, deeper reasons.

"Mr. Wong," said Martha, in a sudden decision. "Why did Mr. Harms come to you instead of us? Frankly, I can't understand it. My husband would certainly have advised him if he hadn't wanted to excite our uncle."

This consideration for the senior boss of Petersen and Company had been far from Thomas Harms' mind, but Martha, who was always trying to think her way into the feelings of others, couldn't know that.

Old Mr. Wong replied calmly, "I would be inconsolable, Madame, if you were to excite yourself unnecessarily. The young man came to me because he knew you would not understand him. He was wise enough to run away from an unbearable situation rather than let it ruin him. He loved a girl who was not suitable." The old man smiled. "All our wise men advise us to flee from the unsuitable partner. The safest way to escape danger is to run away from it."

Martha stared at the old man.

"To be sure, to run away is perhaps not what is considered heroic in the West," the old man went on easily, "but it is extremely practical."

Now Martha had to smile, although she didn't feel at all like it. She had to admire the urbanity with which her host had been able to move from the concerns of art to the concerns of everyday life. The old man looked at Martha for a moment in deep silence. With her understanding she had given him exceptional pleasure. What was more, she had a wonderful son whom old Mr. Wong had invited twice to go fishing with him. But she was overcast with worry. This was perhaps because of her departure in a few months.

"You are wondering why I did not try to keep young Mr. Harms in Bangkok, am I correct?" he asked casually.

Martha started. Her host had read her mind in an astonishing fashion. "It would quite possibly have saved all of us and even Thomas himself a lot of trouble if you had used your influence in this respect, dear Mr. Wong," she said. "All the more since he seemed to feel that you understood him." She said the last words without bitterness. She had accepted the fact that Tommy found the Petersen family lacking in understanding, but old Mr. Wong had left out something, she thought. She was not for running away, even if all the Chinese philosophers and Mr. Wong were for it. She made this point clear, cautiously and politely. Why hadn't old Mr. Wong called up Hannes so that he could have persuaded young Harms to stay in Bangkok? Tommy was so inexperienced. He would come to a bad end. He had only been in the Far East a few months.

"He will get to know the Far East from bottom to top, and that will be of value to him all his life," answered old Mr. Wong with such authority that Martha was silent. Never had she felt so perplexed.

"Please give me his address, Mr. Wong. We must write to him. His father wants him to come back to Hamburg."

"I don't have his address, Madame. I told Mr. Harms to stand on his own two feet. He will either fall or climb up the ladder. Only the future can tell us that."

Now Martha was really speechless. Her gracious host had to have a heart of granite if he had let a desperate, stupid young man leave for Hong Kong with a little money and the advice not to check in again. And still Mr. Wong had asked Martha to look upon him as a friend of the family. His voice was soft and his eyes betrayed an understanding that wasn't expressed in his actions. And when Martha now said honestly, "I don't understand you," old Mr. Wong tried patiently to enlighten his good guest as to why he hadn't interfered actively in the fate of young Harms, and why he did not intend to do so in the future. Such action would be alien to a Taoist. Not to interfere, even if one was tempted to, was the first commandment in the Chinese wisdom of life. The *wu wei*— passivity, no action—of Lao-tse was the principle by which Martha's host abided. And he had traveled well with it. The decision to let fate take its course demanded strength and discipline, old Mr. Wong said gently in conclusion.

He was looking at Martha now with such extraordinary friendliness that she felt warmed. In his narrow, shiny eyes lay an expression of profound understanding that made her feel marvelously safe. A stream of limitless sympathy seemed to flow into her from the old man on this magical moonlit night, saturated with legend and memory. Across worlds and beliefs, from a wise grandfather to a beloved and prudent granddaughter.

"It is up to you if you keep your family together or not, Madame," said old Mr. Wong. He seemed to sense that Martha was the backbone of her family, but that in spite of her strength and discipline she found herself at this moment in the most difficult crisis of her life. She wanted to go back to Europe with her son. Mr. Wong had been told about it a few weeks ago and had accepted the news silently. Naturally he had no intention of interfering in the decisions of his friends. He would certainly not do so now in this fleeting moment of mutual understanding.

He rose from his bamboo chair and walked lightly and with dignity up to Martha, while taking a very small, very precious piece of white jade out of the pocket of his jacket. "It is an old custom to give a dear guest a small gift on the Moon Festival," he said ceremoniously.

"In my country the lotus root, which has the color of white jade, is considered the symbol of loyalty. Please give me the undeserved pleasure, Madame, to accept this piece of jade as a souvenir of an evening that has been precious to me."

Martha thanked him, overcome. She didn't use those figures of speech with which the people of the West, overpowered by the generosity of the East, frequently offended. "Oh, I can't accept that!" Or, "I can't rob you of such a treasure!" Martha took the present in her hand. The moonlight falling through the two oval windows in her host's private room fought to rival the rich glow of the jade, lying on its brocade cloth. "How magnificent!" she whispered.

"A poor little gift," old Mr. Wong said politely.

It was long after midnight when Hannes and Martha brought up Mr. Wong's party again on the veranda with the blue blossoms. It was an old habit of theirs which hadn't been touched by the change in their lives. Hannes had accepted surprisingly calmly the news that Tommy had been to see old Mr. Wong. Why his old friend hadn't interfered further was perfectly clear to him. Again Martha was astonished over how thoroughly and correctly Petersen knew the Chinese.

The evening in the garden-home of his oldest Bangkok friend had refreshed him enormously. And still under the influence of the calm that had prevailed in the moonlit *yuancheh*, Hannes asked his wife for the last time if she didn't want to reconsider her decision to go back to Hamburg with the children in the beginning of the year.

"But we have taken everything into consideration, my dear," Martha said tenderly. "Believe me, there is no other solution. Of course it . . . it is very difficult for me."

Petersen looked at the moon. It was no use. But he tried once more. Martha had spoken lovingly. The light

246

from the moon was caught in her hair. The knot lay like a heavy piece of silver on the nape of her neck. The relaxation in Bangkok had given her a beauty she had never possessed in the north. Her fine face with the big gray eyes was of a shimmering pallor; the wrinkles that the fear and hunger of a dreadful war and postwar epoch had drawn were only fine lines now. Hamburg would probably transform Martha back into the sober, rushed, efficient woman who hurriedly twisted her hair into a tight knot and never wore a silver dress, only serviceable gray suits. In the Far East Martha had blossomed because only much time and rest could give a women the lasting beauty that triumphed over all cosmetic tricks. Everything austere in Martha had become gentle restraint. She rarely spoke in the clipped and sharp manner that she had used in Hamburg because in the Far East the short and sharply spoken word found no echo. Martha herself knew nothing of the change, but Hannes had recognized it even through the glass wall of their estrangement, and he loved her now as he had never loved her in his youth. But the wall still stood between them. And Hannes, whose initiatives were all directed toward the outward appearances of things, was too shy or too awkward to rebuild the bridge he himself had torn down. "Martha," he said, still lost in thought, "do you realize that you have become a beautiful woman here?"

"Silly boy," said Martha. She hadn't said that in a long time. Was Hannes trying to wear her down? It wouldn't be the first time, but rarely had anything good come of it.

Petersen sat down close beside her. He lit a cigarette for them both. First he took a few puffs of hers, then he lit his own, "at Martha's breath," as he put it. It was their traditional foreplay—silent, tender, and familiar to them both. And as they sat there together in the moonlight, Hannes spoke haltingly, his face turned away, of things he had held back for weeks. It was, so to speak, the ninth marriage proposal that he had made to Martha in the course of the years. He expressed himself poorly, because all the Petersens were clumsy when things became serious.

But Martha understood him. Hannes was far more familiar to her when he stumbled over his own words and feelings as when he played the man of the world who turned people's heads. "Don't," Martha said, in her lullaby voice. "I know all about it."

She did. But that Petersen had recently said farewell to his youth in the Russian Restaurant—that she didn't know. A man had to come to terms with that by himself. But Hannes, hesitating and stammering, betrayed such honesty and hidden anguish that Martha finally said, "Why do you torture yourself and us? Why don't you free yourself at last from the tropics?" And when Hannes said nothing, she added, "We need each other, Hannes."

And now everything would have been all right if Hannes had obeyed the voice of reason. But no male member of the Petersen family ever obeyed reason.

Petersen threw his cigarette in a wide arc into the garden and looked at Martha helplessly. Hadn't she just said that she too needed him? Strangely enough Petersen was so modest where Martha was concerned that this had never occurred to him. He had always needed her.

"Why are you going away?" he asked. "It can't be only because of the children."

"No," she said, to his surprise. "It isn't only because of the children." She was silent for a moment as if she, who always knew what to say, were seeking the right words. It was so important that Hannes understand her now, when the old intimacy and warmth had come to life again within them. If Martha had explained to her husband that the company of old Mr. Wong had removed her last doubts, he would have stared at her uncomprehendingly. He didn't think as fast nor see connections as quickly as she did. Besides, he had the male distaste for unpleasant truths which on closer look became even more unpleasant.

"Hannes," she said finally. "I can't stay here any longer. We live in Bangkok in a vacuum—without roots, without ties to a landscape or a civilization. We are only guests here, isn't that so?"

"Naturally. And what do you have against it? You have even been given a piece of jade that museum curators would give their eyeteeth to have. Or think of Pauline's wedding. Did you ever see anything like it in Hamburg?"

"I know, Hannes. Guests are treated royally here, and I am just as fond of my Bangkok friends as you are. But one can't be a guest forever. Even the most polite host expects his guests to leave one day."

"Martha!" Petersen sounded tortured. "I am not as wise as you are. Or a bookworm like you. Forgive me, beloved, but I said that without thinking. I don't want to hear any of it! I want...I want you to stay with me. Is that so difficult to understand?"

"I *can't* stay here, Hannes! This evening has made it clearer to me than ever."

"I make clear, you make clear, he makes clear...I have a right to my wife! You don't have to make anything clear to me!"

"I looked at old Mr. Wong's guests tonight," Martha said, as if she hadn't heard his outcry. "Not one of them was born in Bangkok or at home here! Exile remains exile, even if one makes a paradise of it. Oh my darling, have you really forgotten your home? Doesn't Hamburg mean anything to you any more?"

For a second Petersen saw the banks of the Elbe... Big Michel, who greeted homecoming sailors from far off...his grandfather's *Stammtisch*, the table always reserved for him in the Ratsweinkeller, with its unique aroma of Burgundy, respectability, and tradition. And then...a great gap. A flag with a swastika which was actually an Indian fertility symbol, but the gentlemen hadn't known that. Scarcely any of them had ever let the wind blow through their hair like Johannes Petersen. His flight to Siam...Uncle Winn and Nang Siri...old Mr. Wong...the Cambodian towers of Wat Arun... beautiful girls and Siamese gentleness and tolerance... No, you couldn't turn time back. Even Martha couldn't. His homeland had become a memory. Hamburg? A gray city in fog! And the Elbe in a storm...Of course Johannes Petersen remained a Hamburger, but he had burned his bridges behind him.

"It's no use, Martha," he said. "We're not at a patriotic meeting. I stay here. Let it be. I don't want to talk about it anymore. It's a question now of you and me." He stood up to end the conversation in his own way. He leaned over Martha and drew her out of her chair. He held her close and his lips brushed her cool white throat down to where her breasts began. "Martha," he stammered, "stay with me!" Again he was overwhelmed with how chaste and strong she was. The only woman who always gave and never presented a bill.

Martha was very still in his arms. Hannes' love was like a flood with the ensuing ebb tide. She could cope with the flood, as she had done in Mount Lavinia, but the ebb tide, which during the long years of her marriage had always followed the flood with the power of natural law, had left Martha more resigned and sensible every time. This time she got away before the flood could overwhelm her.

She freed herself of Hannes' embrace with a gentle gesture and at the same moment felt a dreadful pain. It was an echo of all past pain and a presentiment of the future. It was saying goodbye to the man who meant everything to her, with his many good qualities and weaknessess, for which she loved him all the more deeply. One didn't weep one's bitterest tears over the master pupils of marriage. Martha knew and felt everything in this moment that would take place in a few months on a tropical pier. She couldn't bear Hannes' kisses, his arms enfolding her, for another moment. "Good night, beloved," she whispered. "I am very tired."

She looked at Hannes for a moment with eyes that glistened with unshed tears, then she walked slowly, as if burdened, to the glass door that led to their bedroom.

Petersen remained on the veranda. From the servants' quarters you could hear laughter, chatter, and the clatter of dishes and bowls. The old cook was still celebrating the Moon Festival with his family. It was 2:00 A.M..

When Petersen walked into Martha's room, she was lying quietly under the mosquito netting. The room smelled clean and had a beauty that had been created by orderliness. Three things stood on Martha's bedside table: a picture of Hannes and the children, taken shortly after Tiny's birth; a palm leaf fan that Second Grandson had woven for her, and on a little brocade doily, the piece of white jade, a symbol of resoluteness.

The moonlight fell on her pale face. She wasn't asleep. The tears were pouring out of her eyes that in daytime saw things so soberly and cautiously. She didn't wipe them away.

"Why are you crying?" asked Petersen, although he knew very well why.

He took Martha in his arms and spoke comforting words to her, awkwardly. And neither of them smiled because Hannes had to comfort her for her resoluteness.

The Elbe in a Storm

All the Petersens, including Wilhelm Christian Petersen in Bangkok, had instinctively married capable and hospitable women. The only exception was Hinrich Petersen. Perhaps he had thought he was capable and hospitable enough for two, for shortly after Hannes' flight to East Asia, Hinrich had married Lisa Thorsten who was fifteen years younger than he. He was fifty-three now and had little understanding for "frivolity," as he called every expression of levity. Lisa, on the other hand, was very much for frivolity, and since she couldn't get anywhere in this respect with Hinrich, she had taken herself off to the bridge table and there was no getting her away from it. Hinrich succeeded in swallowing all his reactions; you couldn't tell by looking at his long, thin face with the watery blue eyes what was going on inside him. On the day the Hannes Petersens had celebrated the Moon Festival in Bangkok, the Hinrich Petersens had indulged in their longest discussion in months. Martha's letter had triggered it. It had arrived the day before and since then Hinrich hadn't known a moment's peace.

"Martha will stay with us, of course," he said, "until she finds an apartment."

"That's impossible, Hinrich! You know how visitors unnerve me. It will be bad enough to have their horrible children with us, but Martha is just one too many. The schoolteacher can stay with her best friend, Florence Krüger, if Florence decides to come back to Hamburg."

Hinrich ate a piece of toast thoughtfully before he replied. It was a beautiful September day. They were sitting in the garden of their old house on the Elbchaussee. In the garden you were safe from your tenants. Hinrich hated strangers on his private property, but he treated his tenants with exemplary politeness, always ready to be helpful. He was—as Hannes had correctly surmised in his Bangkok office—a gentleman. His tenants were refugees from Silesia. As far as he was concerned, they were foreigners. He had managed to redeem two rooms on the second floor of the house for himself and Lisa, and had installed a bathroom and a small kitchen for the foreigners on the third. And now Martha and the children were to move into the two rooms on the second floor. It wasn't easy to find an apartment these days. Lisa sighed. She had taken an instant dislike to Martha the minute she had set eyes on her.

She poured herself a third cup of tea and said, "What's the matter with you, Hinrich? Cat got your tongue? Don't be such a...such a bore all the time!" Her eyes, as fixed as a china doll's, glanced at the phone. Since Hinrich seemed to have lost his powers of speech, she just had to have a chat with one of her friends. "Why doesn't Martha stay in Bangkok?" she asked, frowning. "I thought it was paradise."

Lisa still hadn't recovered from the fact that she and Hinrich were not going to Siam just because Hannes begrudged Hinrich the chance to have a fresh wind blowing through his hair. Lisa was convinced this was the reason, and she had dished it up to her husband at every meal ever since the rejection had come from Bangkok. She had talked such a lot about their move to Bangkok at the bridge table that the turn of events had been a blow to her vanity. Lisa was a snob. She couldn't get the princesses Martha had written about in connection with

Pauline's wedding out of her mind. Lisa felt she was definitely more suited to hobnob with Siamese princes and Chinese millionaires than "that schoolteacher."

Lisa looked in the mirror of her powder compact, which she always carried with her. She was one of those women of whom one said she must have been enchanting when she was young. Her hair was still blond, a little touched-up now; her figure was still dainty and chic, and she still had the naïve oval face of the young girl who had induced Hinrich to indulge in frivolity on a stormy cruise on the Elbe—unfortunately.

The sight of Hannes, Martha, and the children had always made Hinrich feel lonely. He wanted children. In his thoughts he had visualized a tall blond boy, sitting at a desk, looking out at the grandiose view between the Chile House and Sprinkenhof. But nothing had come of the dream. And to his astonishment, Hinrich had discovered in the course of years that he was lonelier with Lisa than he had been without her. So all he had now was his work, his important collection of Hamburg memorabilia, which he had managed to save from the bombing and fire raids, and the Elbe. He had a very intimate relationship with the river which connected Hamburg with the rest of the world. It had begun when he had strolled through the harbor with his father. In the evenings, in this very house which today he had to share with the Silesians, they had watched the river from the big veranda. During his apprenticeship in England he had been homesick for Mama and the Elbe. Then Mama had died quite suddenly, so Hinrich had had only the river with its indefinable aroma of fish, petroleum, nostalgia, and stability.

"I am sure Martha has her good reasons for wanting to come home with the children," Hinrich said coldly. "And by the way, I want to ask you . . ." but he never got to asking anything because Lisa rolled her doll's eyes and moaned, "I've got stomach cramps!"

Lisa's stomach cramps were something that she could apparently order like a cake or tickets for the theatre. But they never failed to upset Hinrich, who had an iron constitution. He went at once to get her pills, her eau de cologne and a down pillow for her chaise longue. Meanwhile Lisa powdered her nose and groaned softly when she saw Hinrich reappear in the garden. After a while she said, "So that's settled. Martha stays with Florence Krüger. I suppose I'll have to take on the children for a while."

"Martha is staying with us! I'm going to write to them now," Hinrich said in a voice Lisa rarely heard. It expressed profound indignation and astonishment that a Hamburg woman could disregard the tradition of hospitality and the iron will of the Petersens once they had made up their minds about something.

Having made himself clear, Hinrich, his chin thrust forward, looked at Lisa coldly. Then he walked slowly into the house and wrote to Martha how much Lisa and he were looking forward to seeing her and the children. Of course they would all live with them, no trouble at all. He sealed the letter and rose to go and say goodbye to Lisa. It had been his intention to sit in the garden with her, but she would only try to make him change his mind.

He couldn't understand why Lisa couldn't get along with Martha. Martha was a *famos* woman, and so sensible. It never occurred to him, who was strong on export but weak on women, that this was just why Lisa couldn't stand Martha, who, on top of that, had two children. Hinrich usually came to life whenever Chubb or Tiny turned up at the house on the Elbchaussee.

If Martha had known with what joy Lisa was looking forward to her return, her decision to leave Hannes behind would have been made easier. But after all, she had been right in telling Hannes that one couldn't leave Lisa in charge of the children for any length of time. In

Martha's opinion, Lisa was a woman in constant search of the phantom of her youth. That was Lisa's problem. But Chubb and Tiny were Martha's problem. They would have to stay with Hinrich, of course. For his sake.

After sending off the airmail letter, Hinrich drove to the Landungsbrücke Restaurant in St. Pauli. He still had two hours before he had to attend a town meeting. From the restaurant he had a view of the harbor and the Elbe. Both were in motion, but somehow stable in a sort of twilight. The weather had changed. The Elbe under a stormy sky made him think of faraway lands...a whiff of Siam, for instance, which now he wasn't going to see. He hadn't admitted even to himself that Hannes' rejection of his plan had hurt him, for quite different reasons than Lisa's, who dreamed of a horde of servants and parties with princes. Hinrich had considered a change of land and people tempting. The Hamburger was born with a longing for faraway places. So Hinrich Petersen sat in the Landungsbrücke Restaurant like a captain without a ship as his pale blue eyes watched the heavens grow darker. "There's a storm coming up, Mr. Petersen," said the waiter whom Hinrich had known for years.

"Yes," said Hinrich Petersen. He sounded content. "There's going to be a storm."

He paid and walked slowly to the harbor, got into a small boat and rocked for a while between tugs, lighters, and barges. When he finally got to the town hall, he had calmed down. But he would have liked to see Uncle Wilhelm Christian again. He entered the town meeting refreshed and ready to wrestle with any civic problems in an orderly fashion. It was a good thing if one could bring a knowledge of storm and harbor into these hallowed halls. Bonn and Hamburg were different worlds. In Bonn they didn't know the age-old consonance of typewriter clatter, stock exchange tickers, and foghorns on an age-old yet eternally young river.

Old Mr. Petersen too would have liked to see his nephew Hinrich again. He had counted on Hannes returning to Hamburg with his family. Twelve years was a long time. The old man had never expected Hannes to settle in Bangkok permanently. And that wasn't the way Hannes saw it either, not even now. Another three years, then he would surprise his family in Hamburg and go home to stay. Three years, he had told his uncle; but one always stayed longer than planned. The cities east of Suez had that effect. Hannes' reasons were obvious: he wanted to amass a small fortune before he went home. His children had to have an education; the cost of living in postwar Hamburg was frightening. And he wanted to expand the Bangkok business. There were good prospects for German exports to Indonesia and Hong Kong. There was nothing to be said against any of it.

After the Chinese Moon Festival, old Mr. Petersen sat for eight days alone in his *sala*. He looked at the picture of the Elbe in a storm. His wife was in Petchaburi. Some of his daughters were with her. Two were in Hua Hin, and the youngest was visiting Justus on the tin island.

Justus now worked exclusively on his wife's coconut plantation. He had stayed away from the mine too often to keep his job there. Engineer Steffens had broken the news to old Petersen as gently as he could. Justus-Prasert never wrote to his father. His wife gave him pocket money; that was all. Why should he work more than necessary? He was housed and fed and had enough money for a bit of gambling in the Chinese coffee shop. That was all Justus-Prasert demanded of life, and if his father couldn't understand it, that was his fault. But Steffens spared the old man this bit of news.

Right now however old Petersen wasn't thinking of his son. He was wondering with whom it was in Manila that Pauline couldn't get along. He was expecting Florence Krüger. She was going back to Hamburg in three days. Petersen had hoped she would stay in Bangkok at least through the Christmas festivities, but Florence was planning to celebrate Christmas in her own way by giving a party and presents to refugee children in Hamburg. Old Petersen shook his head. He needed Florence much more than the refugee children did. He knew her longer, and they knew the same people in Hamburg. Well...the guests came and went in Bangkok. Sometimes one got the impression that one was living in a huge railway station. He didn't want to think of Martha and the children's departure in January.

The garden shimmered in the afternoon sun. The pretty roof of the *sala* seemed to tremble in the air. He would have tea with Florence here. And then, when the disorderly palace in Rong Muang was wrapped in twilight, and the sun—a hurrying purple ball—sank behind the high hedges, then they would eat in the big empty dining hall and drink the champagne from Saigon which Dr. Johannsen, who wasn't satisfied with old Petersen's heart, had forbidden.

Old Petersen was just going to ring for his Siamese cook when Mae Wat appeared outside the kitchen house, smoking, and came sauntering over to the *sala*. What had happened? It wasn't like Mae Wat to make a move for nothing. She had to cook a big dinner tonight, with European and Siamese dishes.

After the conventional greetings had been exchanged, a nod from the master, Mae Wat kneeling, her hands touching in the Siamese greeting, the struggle began.

"Master Pe-ter-senn *very* good master," Mae Wat said, looking at her good master slyly out of her jolly little slanting eyes. "All market people offer Mae Wat *big* job. Mae Wat always say: Master Pe-ter-senn very good and rich master.

Old Mr. Petersen expressed his thanks formally for

Mae Wat's good opinion of him. He knew exactly what was coming, but he didn't hurry her. That would have been impolite.

"Mae Wat wonderful cook. Do everything first-class," Mae Wat went on, as if speaking of a quite different lady. "Mae Wat save and save for Master Pe-ter-senn, but Master say: *Pai sia.* Go away! Master say: bad food today. Go quickly to another house."

Old Petersen protested vigorously in Siamese against such ingratitude on his part. He reassured Mae Wat that she was the best cook in Rong Muang.

"In Dusit Park too," Mae Wat added ambitiously. "Strange Mem from Dusit Park say tonight: *Aroi, aroi*—delicious delicious. Chicken very soft and ice cream very hard."

Petersen said how much he was looking forward to the meal.

Mae Wat was silent for a moment, as if lost in admiration of her artistry. Then she murmured, "Mae Wat very very sad. Cannot cook for Master Pe-ter-senn tonight."

"Why not?" asked Petersen, unperturbed.

"Chicken too expensive on market. Bad Chinese not give Mae Wat big chicken. 'Go away' cry bad Chinese chicken man. 'Much too little money!' Mae Wat weep loudly. All servants laugh because Mae Wat not given enough money. 'No money, no chicken,' say angry Chinese man. Mae Wat must go far away. Nai Pe-ter-senn have visitor. Strange Mem. No chicken. No dinner. No curry. No custard. Nothing..."

The threatened prospect of not being able to offer Florence anything to eat left old Petersen cold. He had seen Mae Wat coming home from the market with beautiful chickens and the finest vegetables in her bamboo basket. He had given her a considerable sum of money for the shopping expedition but not as much as Mae Wat had wanted. He had wisely held back six ticals and pretended not to notice the sudden eclipse of the sun on Mae Wat's round, shrewd face.

"What would the best chicken cost if you went to the market right away?" he asked. Mae Wat mentioned the sum she had received that morning, plus four ticals. The good master took six ticals out of his wallet, six single bills. Mae Wat counted them carefully.

"Mae Wat most honest cook in Bangkok," she said complacently. "Master make mistake. Give Mae Wat two ticals too much. Mae Wat count: one, two, three, four, five, six! Mae Wat say two ticals belong to Master, four ticals belong to bad chicken man. Nothing for Mae Wat. Not for temple market in November."

"The two ticals are for Mae Wat because she is so honest," said old Mr. Petersen.

Mae Wat rose, radiant, and bowed. "Everybody offer Mae Wat *big* job," she repeated dreamily. "Double pay than with Master Pe-ter-senn. But Mae Wat say: leave me in peace. Master Pe-ter-senn *very* good gentleman, very rich. Go away everybody! say Mae Wat."

"Florrie," said old Mr. Petersen, "why for heaven's sake are you going back to Hamburg? Don't you like it in Bangkok?"

They were sitting in the *sala* over mocha. The moon had risen and was shining mildly and slightly ironically on two old Hamburgers who years ago had almost married. Wilhelm Christian was always in good spirits when Florence was with him. She never drew his attention to anything unpleasant. She didn't seem to notice the dust on the priceless teak tables. She satisfied in the old man, who once had caused her pain, his need for an orderly existence. Without even mentioning Hamburg, she was for him the bridge between two basically different ways of life. When Florence was with him, the evening was lighter; the bleak thicket of his thoughts cleared; his

260

loneliness, which after Pauline's wedding only Martha had been able to ease, no longer caused him the grief that coursed from his heart through his entire being and resulted in a dulling of the brain. He wasn't in the least aware of all this. It would never have occurred to him to observe or analyze his reactions. All he knew was that it did him good to be with Florence, and with the childish egoism and inflexibility of all Petersens, he wanted her to go on visiting him in the *sala*. The "women's clubs," as he termed the women and mothers' organizations in which Florence was active, could surely do very well without her. Old Petersen didn't seem to look upon the fact that he had never written to Florence and after one night of love had decamped to the Far East as anything reprehensible.

Florence didn't reply. She was leaving for Hamburg in three days, period. She was an independent woman, and since she had never married, had been master of her decisions for a long time. But Chris, as she called him, worried her. She had spoken to Martha about him at length. Why did his children behave so badly to him? Martha had written to Pauline but still had received no reply. She had been against Hannes telling the old man that Pauline "couldn't get along" with a certain mysterious person. But Hannes had considered it better to tell Uncle Winn about Pauline's foibles before she quite possibly turned up one day with her possessions and moved back into her parents' house in Hua Hin. With Pauline you never knew where you were at!

"Chris," said Florence, "why don't you go to Manila and see for yourself what your daughter's up to?"

"If she wants me she can write to me," he said angrily. Florence shook her head. Wilhelm Christian was behaving more like an aggrieved lover than a father, but that was his business.

By now it was dark in the garden. Big stars had appeared in the sky. The palm trees were swaying languidly in the cool night wind. Florence hunched her shoulders as if she were cold. Chris got up at once and took a brocade shawl out of the camphor chest that stood beside his bed. It was dark blue, woven in an artful and legendary Siamese pattern in silver and old rose. Florence, who dressed in subdued Hamburg style—blue suit, white blouse and nondescript felt hats—thought she had never seen anything so bold yet so harmonious. "A little farewell present," said the friend of her youth, and laid the precious shawl across her shoulders. It had been designed on a starry night in Lampang, the city of silk weavers in North Siam.

Florence was overwhelmed. "I'll use it as a throw on my piano," she said.

Old Mr. Petersen stared at her. A throw on a piano? He could see a medium-sized Hamburg room. Instead of almond trees and blue birds of paradise, he saw a potted palm and a canary in a cage, and suddenly he knew why he had fled years ago, before Florence could smother him under a piano throw.

"Would you like a cup of coffee, Florrie?" he asked gently. For the first time he felt sorry for her. She was an unconscious enemy of all the beauty that was offered for its own sake alone, east of Suez. Nang Siri's white-haired monkeys screeched in a corner of the garden.

"Why are they making that noise, Chris?" Florence asked. She sounded tired. A crippling weariness that she had never felt in Hamburg had struck again, like a beast of prey.

"I don't know." Old Petersen thought of the calligraphy scroll old Mr. Wong had sent him on the evening of the Moon Festival. The first two verses of a poem by Liu Ch'ang-ch'ing from the T'ang dynasty were inscribed on the parchment scroll:

The guests went away. The monkeys scream.
Now dusk is falling across the stream.

Man is destined a heart that bleeds;
Water is destined to flow in silence...

And with the flowing water old Mr. Wong had probably meant that pain also flowed away.

"What a strange picture!" Florence said just then. *"The Elbe in a Storm."* She had risen. It was time to say goodbye. Her throat was dry. What would become of Wilhelm Christian? "When will you visit me in Hamburg, Chris?" she asked.

But old Petersen didn't answer. He had taken *The Elbe in a Storm* carefully down from the wall and was wrapping it in the piece of silk that the artist had used. No well-bred Japanese ever offered anything wrapped in a colorless piece of paper. "Give this to Hinrich Petersen for his collection," he said. His voice sounded a little husky. Florence had told him a lot about Hinrich's collection of Hamburg memorabilia which he had managed to save through fire and brimstone. "It may amuse him to see how a Japanese master visualized the Elbe," he added shyly.

"But Chris! You can't part from that! It's a museum piece!"

"Let it be, Florence," her old friend said quietly. "I know what I'm doing."

Long after Florence Krüger had gone back to Dusit Park old Petersen was still sitting in the *sala*.

It was very quiet now in the garden. The monkeys had retired into their house and were sleeping like spoiled, tired babies, their little heads under their arms. Only the crickets were chirping. The light in the *sala* was out. Wilhelm Christian Petersen had gone into the house. He was standing, tall and yawning, looking with eyes that were glazed with weariness around Pauline's big, almost empty room. Only her bed, her small desk, and the empty teak cupboards were left. He often went to Pauline's room, but only when Siri was gone and the servants were asleep. Then he would sit for a while on the hard bed or look through the mosquito netting on the windows, out into the garden. He didn't know himself what he wanted at night in this empty room.

He rose laboriously and sat down at the desk. There was still some writing paper and envelopes in the drawer. He began to write:

Dear Pauline,

Mother and I haven't heard anything from you in a long time. We hope you are well. Are you having any trouble? Do you have a good doctor in Manila? Do take care of yourself, my darling. Your mother is already looking forward to her grandson. I am too, naturally. Mother is in Petchaburi with Susanne and Grete. They must be having a good time there or they would have come back long ago. They've already stayed three weeks longer than they had intended.

I guess Aunt Martha has written to you that she is going back to Hamburg with the two children. Uncle Hannes is staying in Bangkok for the time being. I had a visitor from Hamburg too, an old friend, but that wouldn't interest you.

You might tell your husband to write to me when he has a chance. I'd like to know how his business in Manila is doing. After all, I've invested quite a lot in it and wouldn't like to lose my investment.

Sangvien's fiancé is supposed to have caught a white elephant in the jungle. If that's true there'll be no more peace in the house. Sangvien was supposed to serve dinner tonight but she just up and left to celebrate. But it's always like that. Do you remember when you cooked a wonderful dinner because Mae Wat had gone gambling and we had invited old Mr. Wong? You've always been my good girl.

Sometime when you have nothing better to do, you could write to Mother and me to say how you are and what I can send you from here. Are you eating enough?

I am all right. Dr. Johannsen fusses about my heart but that's what doctors are for. Everything is in order at home. I see to it that Sangvien dusts your room now and then in case you ever come to see us.

I guess that's all. Best regards to your husband from both of us. And write if we should send you the comforter. And a check, in case you need money.

Very best greetings,
Your old Papa,

WILHELM CHRISTIAN PETERSEN

17

Pauline and Prasert

Ulla Knudsen's party to celebrate Mami's seventieth birthday was in full swing. Mami was utterly intimidated. She had never seen so many foreigners assembled in her entire life. Ulla had invited everybody—business friends, friends of her friends, and many rich and influential Eurasians. The atmosphere was like in a Turkish bath. The overflowing rooms and veranda of the little pile dwelling on the canal gave the impression that all Bangkok was assembled there. Among the distinguished guests there was a lady whose presence caused old Mr. Petersen to leave the party.

It was Thanom Chandrayarat, the wife of his oldest son. Since Thanom had married Justus Prasert eight years ago, old Petersen had heard nothing from him. It was Thanom who had prevailed upon him not to greet his father on the tin island. She had been opposed to her husband's European father from the start and in the polite but relentless way of the Asiatic had broken the last weak ties between father and son. If there was anyone of whom it could be said that she had caused Wilhelm Christian suffering, then it was dainty, smiling Thanom, who had just arrived with a wrinkled old servant on Ulla Knudsen's veranda.

"Khom," Thanom told the crippled old Siamese, "give Nang Nom our birthday present." Khom was carrying a large package which turned out to be a coconut cake baked according to an old Siamese recipe. Thanom had spotted her father-in-law standing beside a tall blond European woman and had nodded a Siamese greeting to which he had responded. "Excuse me, Martha," he said. "I must speak to my daughter-in-law."

What daughter-in-law? Martha wondered. And where was she?

"Where is Justus?" asked old Mr. Petersen after working his way through the crowd to Thanom, who looked at him silently out of her slanting eyes, as astonished as if *pho ta*, Father-in-law, were talking about an absolute stranger. She knew no one called Justus. "I mean Prasert." Old Mr. Petersen broke the embarrassing silence, controlling himself as best he could.

Thanom slowly nibbled a sticky sweet made of rice and palm sugar and gazed at the canal. "I don't know where Prasert is, Father-in-law," she said finally.

"What do you mean?"

"Prasert isn't here."

"You mean my son has stayed in Phuket?"

"I don't know, Father-in-law."

Thanom yawned politely, her hand in front of her mouth, and began to take off in the direction of Ulla Knudsen's pretty sister, Betty, whom she wanted to invite to Phuket. Like all Siamese, Thanom was hospitable.

"Just a minute, Thanom," Old Petersen would have liked to stop his uncommunicative daughter-in-law by holding her back by the arm, but he knew that one did not touch a Siamese. Thanom turned politely. Hadn't Prasert told his parents what had happened? Or had he only written to his mother? Thanom didn't know and couldn't have cared less. She frowned. A trace of anger lit up her eyes, a small flame. Thanom had come to the party to have *sanuk*, fun. The *likay* players were already assembled on the lawn; those marvelous Siamese clowns in their grotesque costumes, waiting for the sign to start. And as they began their inimitable Chaplinesque foolery, old Petersen gave up all hope for Justus. His daughter-in-law had just informed him that she had divorced Prasert. Why? Justus Petersen, who was named after the founder of the family, Alderman Justus from Buxtehude, had stolen two hundred ticals from his wife. He hadn't worked on the plantation either, but gambled in the village and consumed enormous quantities of whiskey. A *kamoi*, a thief...yes, Thanom had had a lot of *lambag* with Prasert.

Old Petersen watched the pranks on the lawn with unseeing eyes. His face was white; the light in his sharp blue eyes seemed to have died. This was the end. His oldest son, with the blood of honest Hanseatics and an old aristocratic Siamese family in his veins, had been driven from his wife's home as a thief. "I will pay the sum of course," he said, his voice hoarse.

Thanom laughed and looked at the old *farang* evenly. "Nang Siri has paid it," she murmured. "I guess she didn't want the whole village to know..."

"That's all right," said old Petersen, although it was anything but all right, and as Thanom wanted to go on speaking he said authoritatively and with dignity, "Be quiet!"

So that was why his wife had stayed away so long! Justus had probably fled to his mother in Petchaburi, and Siri had tried to find a job for him. Or perhaps Justus had hanged himself. Suicide was nothing unusual for the disturbed Asiatic soul. He had to wire Siri at once. This dreadful Siamese reserve! Siri had never discussed their children with him. She endured everything alone.

Thanom gazed at her father-in-law. He looked frightful. He is ignorant, she thought. The *farangs* wanted the wheel of fortune to stand still for them. That was unreasonable. Because everything in this world—birth, blood, deterioration, and death were *anicca*, or mutable. "Forget it," said Thanom with unusual gentleness.

It is too much, thought old Petersen.

It was months now since he had heard from Pauline. And then, suddenly, with the vehemence of a monsoon, confusion, dark secrets, and deadly fear wafted through his *sala*. He looked at Pauline, sitting there benighted by melancholy and obstinacy. Not a trace of the exuberance and vital triumph that had illuminated her at the wedding. Pregnancy had already stamped her body. Her face was thin, her eyes stared grimly straight ahead. She was expecting her child in three months, and was quite heavy. The cloud of melancholy and stubbornness that had overshadowed this beloved girl of his since birth threatened their unexpected reunion like a thunderstorm.

"Why didn't you send me a telegram, Linchen?" he asked. "I would have fetched you at the airport."

"I made up my mind quite suddenly. I am going to stay with you forever, Papa!" And as her father said nothing, only looked at her silently, she asked, "Aren't you glad?"

"Don't ask stupid questions, lass! Why did you run away?"

Pauline thrust out her chin and sank back in her chair in sullen silence, the silence her father had always feared. It had an effect on him of percussion instruments and drums. Suddenly the old man felt terribly tired, but he couldn't afford to be tired now. He had to bring Pauline to her senses and send her back to Manila as soon as possible. Children were temporary gifts. One owned them for a short while, then one lost them to dangerous, wicked, dreadful, marvelous life, somewhere beyond the *sala*.

"Why are you here?" he asked for a second time.

Pauline began to cry. She still cried like a little girl, licking away the tear drops and swallowing them.

No, thought Wilhelm Christian Petersen. She just wants to soften me up. She knows I can't bear to see her cry. "Do you have a handkerchief, Papa?"

Of course, Pauline never had a handkerchief. Everything repeated itself. Just as he had done at her wedding, the old gentleman took out his big handkerchief and wiped away her tears one by one. "Everything is going to be all right, lass," he murmured.

Pauline laid her little head on his shoulder. A red curl fell across her forehead. It lay there, lost, until her father stroked it back. He raised her gently. "It's getting cool out here. Let's go in and have something nice to eat, what do you say?"

"I'm not hungry, Papa."

"Nonsense! You're always hungry, lass. I've ordered *khao thom* for tonight."

Khao thom was a light tasty rice dish with boiled chicken, herbs, vegetables, and *nam pla*, the spicy Siamese fish sauce that is poured over the dish. Pauline dried her tears and smiled for the first time. "I'll eat a few spoonfuls," she said. "Nobody cooks *khao thom* like Mae Wat."

Old Mr. Petersen walked to his disorderly palace arm in arm with his problem daughter. Mae Wat and Sangvien had decorated the big dining room table with orchids. The dessert was already in the refrigerator, Nangsao Pauline's favorite. A frothy, snow-white cream made of the tiny Siamese fruit, *noi na*, had been prepared in a great hurry. It tasted of strawberries, vanilla, and East Indian tomato. Sangvien had pitted the fruit, her eyes red from crying. Old Mr. Petersen pretended not to notice Sangvien's puffed face. Damn it all! Every woman in the house seemed to be conspiring to cry for him! He didn't have to ask; he knew—the white elephant was gray. He would raise the girl's salary a little; that would console her.

"Well, does it taste good, lass?" he asked.

"*Famos!*" said Pauline, helping herself to a third portion of the national Siamese dish. Old Petersen ate next to nothing. He was satisfied to see how his girl enjoyed her meal at home.

Pauline's room had been readied. Her dressing table was in the usual wild disorder that Pauline created wherever she went. The servants were there to keep it tidy. She lay with her arms crossed behind her head on her old bed. There was no mosquito netting. Her father had had a little enclosure made of wire netting around her bed. There was room in it for a bedside table and a small chair. In this way one could leave the windows open at night and let the wind blow in. She was lying in her tropical wire netting house, peaceful and protected, when her father opened the door cautiously, and sat down heavily on the edge of her bed. All you could see were Pauline's thin arms and her pale face with her flaming red hair framing it. Her body was covered with a light white blanket of *chieng-mai* wool, but her gently swollen contours were visible under it. Old Petersen had never seen anything more touching than Pauline's thin, melancholy little girl's face and her blessed body.

"I am not going back to Lawrence as long as that woman is there," said Pauline. She didn't say "Larry," and her voice was calm but without timbre, which startled her father. But he was thankful to hear her talk at all.

"What woman? For God's sake, girl, don't let me drag the words out of you one by one!"

Wilhelm Petersen was so horrified that he scolded her. Another woman, of course—an American. Mr. Desmond must have discovered that an American suited him better than Pauline. But nothing would come of that. Pauline was expecting his child. Desmond had a responsibility toward her and fortunately Pauline had a father who saw to it that no one could harm her. But this time the old gentleman was wrong. Pauline closed her eyes in abject horror.

"I am talking about my mother-in-law, Mrs. Annette Desmond. *Maman!*" The French word burst from Pauline as if it had been an invective, which it probably was supposed to be. Old Petersen would have laughed with relief if Pauline hadn't looked so miserable. And then it all came out, everything Pauline had silently stored within her. The old absurd story! The mother-in-law who didn't want to give up her only adored son...a struggle between two women that made any quarrel between men, however tough and bitter, seem tame in comparison. Pauline had fought this arrogant, unsympathetic woman from New Orleans with the weapon of the Asiatic—passive resistance. *Maman's* background was French. She was frugal, lively, and tidy. From her mother Pauline was accustomed to a happy, easygoing life and a lavish household. *Maman* wore a girdle, even for breakfast; Pauline dressed sloppily, ate when she felt like it, let the Philippine servants serve her at all hours, and spread chaos whenever she appeared. She didn't like intellectual conversations. In the heat they were *lambag*. The result was an endless, exhausting struggle for a young man who loved his mother and his wife and didn't want to hurt either of them.

But everything was much worse than the usual duel between mother and daughter-in-law. *Maman* came from New Orleans, from a society that looked down with offensive arrogance on the many half-castes—mulattoes and octoroons—living in the area for centuries. *Maman's* husband, now deceased, had lived for years with a beautiful quadroon. This family tragedy had resulted in a

272

pathological feeling for "caste." And now her son had married a girl who, to be sure, didn't have Negro blood but was a mixture of Europe and Asia. *Maman* detested miscegenation of any kind. She had not attended the wedding.

Pauline made her mother-in-law nervous. *Maman* gave little dinner parties for the Americans in Manila in which Pauline did not participate. She boycotted everything *Maman* did with the obstinacy and silence that were her Asiatic heritage. But this obstinacy had a tragic core. In her heart Pauline longed for recognition from her clever and amusing mother-in-law, and when she couldn't get it, not even when she got up early in the morning to breakfast with *Maman*, she developed an antipathy against this self-confident woman that swelled up in her like yeast, just as fast as *Maman* destroyed Pauline's small store of good humor and self-confidence. *Maman* managed to do this not only with clearly expressed words but also with subtle intimations, and Pauline couldn't defend herself. She couldn't even say exactly how the woman did it.

"Your mother must leave," she told her husband after four weeks had passed.

"What do you have against *Maman*, Polly?" Larry Desmond asked, all innocence. "She keeps telling me how delightful you are. I thought you were good friends!"

The abyss of male naïveté. Or did Larry believe what he wanted to believe? Actually, while Larry was away on business in Singapore, Pauline had wanted to do something to please her mother-in-law. *Maman* was giving one of her little dinners, and Pauline had put on an exquisite dress to take part in it. But just as she was about to enter the room where the Japanese houseboy was serving cocktails, she had heard *Maman* say to one of her American friends in her high, silvery voice, "My daughter-in-law *was* going to honor us with her presence this evening, but either she'll turn up three hours late or not at all. You know how these half-castes are. You can't depend on them."

Pauline had sent the boy to *Maman* with the message that she didn't feel well, a very polite note. Next day she had flown to Bangkok. *Maman* would have a good scare, as would Lawrence, and the thought pleased Pauline very much. She was independent. She had her villa in Hua Hin. There she would live in peace with her son, just as Nang Siri had planned. She would gradually forget Lawrence. The prescribed fate of the half-castes had become Pauline's fate.

She told her father everything except the remark that had driven her out of the house. During her confession she had looked at Papa once. He had looked odd, as if he were ill or in pain. For the first time in her life, Pauline showed more consideration for her father than for herself. He had always been so good to her.

"Is that all, lass?" And when Pauline nodded silently, Papa stroked her hands and said, "You don't have to tell me any more. I understand. You don't have it as easy as other girls. But I...I..."

He wanted to say that he had always desired the best for her, that all his thinking had been directed toward making her happy, but you couldn't say that sort of thing. His daughter had been insulted. He had known from the start how it would end. He had expected that sooner or later the lady from New Orleans would betray her feelings about people with mixed blood. Intolerance was the worm in the paradise apple of the world.

Pauline and Justus! Life evidently put them to tests that were too severe. He didn't want to think of Justus tonight. Tomorrow he would send a wire to Petchaburi and find out if the young man was with his mother. Did everything go wrong in his children's lives because they weren't loved enough? He couldn't protect them from

274

the world all by himself. People today didn't love their partners, they loved their prejudices, or the prejudices of their parents. That was why there were so many broken marriages. Was there still love that was compassionate without prejudice? And today, all human beings were somehow pitiable if you looked at them in a strong light, especially Justus and Pauline, who had to overcome the prejudices of two worlds. Thanom wanted a man called Prasert; *Maman* wanted to make Pauline into a respectable woman of the West, a woman with ambition, with as much spirit and housewifely circumspection as herself, who could help to make her husband's business and social life a success. Success was the fetish of the American, just as *sanuk*, fun, was the fetish of the Siamese. Whatever had happened, old Petersen felt in every bone of his big, weary body that his lass hadn't been treated right in Manila.

Pauline was in a dilemma. She didn't want to and couldn't go back to Lawrence unless he asked her to. She still loved him with the tremendous pride and indescribable humility of an Asiatic Juliet. She was carrying his child. Was it to grow up in the social no-man's-land of Hua Hin? Old Petersen decided no. His grandchild was not to grow up like that. He had to speak to Martha. Perhaps she could persuade Pauline to go back to Manila. He stroked Pauline's hair and picked up a cigarette stub from the floor of the little screened room. He was, when it came down to it, just as orderly as his enemy, *Maman*. But he had never been able to impress his orderliness on the tropics. He would have had to spend the whole day bending down, picking things up, putting them where they belonged, and dusting, if his palace was to look like, for instance, Hinrich Petersen's villa on the Elbe. Siamese servants were not Chinese. Ruling, not serving, was in the blood of *khon Thai*, the People of Freedom.

"You must go to sleep now, Linchen," said Petersen.

"Papa," she whispered. "If it's a boy, shall we name him after you?"

"You must be out of your mind, lass. There are much prettier names."

"It is the most beautiful name in the world," Pauline murmured, and nestled her soft young cheek in her father's hand. "Perhaps...then the boy would be like you...I mean...I don't want him to be afraid...ever..."

As she spoke the last words she fell asleep. She had closed her eyes and was breathing regularly, like a child who feels she is being cared for and loved, a child full of pride and fear.

Old Mr. Petersen looked at her. Beloved face! How quickly her hair had grown again, because Lawrence had wanted it long. Soon it would reach to her waist, a red waterfall. In this heat! But a totally strange young man had only to express a wish and Pauline obeyed like a lamb. Nang Siri had never been a lamb. Her gentle charm had wound its way around his iron will and softened it.

"It's the most beautiful name in the world," his girl had said. Old Petersen tiptoed out of the room. The months of worry and waiting were nothing now that he knew his Linchen still loved him.

He picked up her silk blouse from the floor and put it away, folded carefully, in the cupboard with its open doors. He hated open doors, and in the tropics the ants just got into the underwear that much quicker. He shut the doors softly. She could be a little tidier, he thought, as he closed the door to her room.

Justus Prasert was staying with his uncle in Sukhothai. He had come a long, hard, confused way and was now resting with Phya (Count) Sri. Gradually the cloud of dull despair that had darkened his spirit lifted. His mother had been afraid he was going mad. He had fled to her in Petchaburi after the catastrophe on Phuket. He had talked like a man whose heart was sick and his spirit benighted. Prasert was unsteady by nature. Cheap Thai whisky, Thanom's cruelty, and the shame of it all had destroyed him. Nang Siri and her daughters hadn't been able to do anything with him. He was contemplating suicide. He sat motionless in front of his bowl of rice and shook his head with its high European brow from which his shiny black hair grew on both sides like a dark halo. Every now and then he would murmur, "*Mai di...mai di maak...*bad...very bad." One didn't know if he meant the food, life, his wife, or himself.

The first thing Nang Siri had done when the dreadful news reached her—she hadn't even known that the couple were legally divorced—was to refund the money Prasert had stolen. Then, without a word, she had gone to the oldest section of the city of Petchaburi, past the homes of the rice farmers, the orchards and the swaying bamboo trees, with sacrificial gifts for Wat Yai Suvarnavaram, the Big Gold Temple. She had knelt for a long time in front of the Buddha picture in the *bot*, the main chapel. Her grief was like a fish in a dry stream, because the grief for one's firstborn son is greater than any disappointments related to one's later children. It is the same torture that a fish must feel in a stream gone dry. Every Siamese put a grounded fish back into water if he possibly could. Prasert, too, his mother felt, had to be returned to his element. But where was his element? What was his destiny? That was what Nang Siri asked herself as she rose and looked silently at the small statue of an abbot who had been born in Petchaburi and had built this shrine, Somdech Chao Taeng Mo, the honorable Lord Water Melon. He was holding three lotus blossoms in his raised hand, a symbol of pure wisdom. And as she gazed upon the statue of the abbot, a shadowy recognition streamed into her soul, like water into a dry riverbed, and she realized that Prasert's life had taken a

277

wrong direction. Her son should travel slowly and cautiously back to the sources of Siamese existence; his European heritage had brought him nothing but conflict. At that moment of decision, Nang Siri wasn't thinking of Winn, who had meant so well by a "Justus-Prasert," who existed only in his wishful dreams. Winn had Pauline; Prasert had to drink from the source that had nurtured his mother. He should live for a while in a place that had founded a nation centuries ago, a nation that had preserved its pride, its age-old traditions, its warlike courage, and Buddhist gentleness, a nation that still demonstrated these qualities in the last ruins of palaces and temples, hidden from the eyes of strangers by the jungle.

That was why Nang Siri sent her distraught son to Sukhothai. In the year 1238, the Thais had founded their kingdom in a region they had wrested from the Cambodian nation in battle. And the Siamese had given the Cambodian capital the name Sukhothai—Bliss of the Thai People. There, in the house of Nang Siri's oldest brother, Prasert would come to his senses with the help of Phya Sri, who lived in a beautifully cultivated palace with a large garden that ran all the way down to the river. Phya Sri was a high Siamese official, now retired. He was writing a history of Sukhothai and drove regularly to the old ruined city a few hours away. Prasert, according to Nang Siri's suggestion, was to work for him for a while as his secretary, for a small salary which she would pay, because a man had to earn his rice or he became heartsick.

Prasert had accepted his mother's suggestion without the usual *mai di.* For the first time in months, his dreamy black eyes had come to life. He had bowed his huge body low in front of his dainty little mother and had thanked her.

Prasert stayed three months with Phya Sri in Sukhothai. After that he knew what he had to do.

Pauline had been in Bangkok now for ten days. She was lying on a chaise longue on the back veranda, sleeping. Sangvien was kneeling beside her, fanning her vigorously. The little servant looked up at her young mistress with awe: soon she was going to give birth to a son. Pauline was dreaming. She was back in Manila. A smile played about her full, passionate lips. "Nangsao already have rice," Sangvien whispered, and old Petersen, disappointed, sat down to his tiffin alone. The house lived for Pauline. Her father was always especially happy when she slept. By sleeping she would renew her strength.

Pauline was only half-asleep when Petersen senior drove back to his office. Sangvien had gone back to the kitchen house to eat her rice. The girl who looked after the flowers in the morning was attending to the fanning. Pauline was still smiling. She was dreaming of something that had taken place before *Maman* had come to Manila: her first weeks with Larry in the new yet familiar surroundings, because all tropical lands had an aura of abundance, indolence, overwhelming beauty, and indescribable misery. The waterfront of the Pasig River had enchanted her. On the ship, leaning on Larry's arm, she had dreamily watched the mountain tops rising up into the deep blue sky above the volcanic islands. The island of Luzon, where they were to live, was a region of mild earthquakes and violent typhoons, just as were played out sometimes in Pauline's soul. At first she hadn't written to her father because she had been too happy to write, and after that she had been too unhappy. Now, in her dream, she was happy again. She was strolling with Larry through the old city with its many reminders of the Spanish settlers, and Larry was calling her "Polly"...

She awoke out of her half-sleep. A tear fell from her long lashes onto her embroidered blouse with the shoulder straps, which she had put on over her green silk *pasin* because of the heat. She was overwhelmed by a dreadful longing for Larry. She looked at the girl who arranged the flowers in the morning as if she had been a stranger. Suddenly the girl dropped the fan and let out a soft cry, like a frightened bird. "What's the matter, Meh Chan?" asked Pauline.

Then she saw for herself. A tall young man with a dark restless face that twitched nervously was tearing up the steps. "Polly!" he yelled. "Where the hell are you?"

Pauline's hand flew to her heart. "*Pai sia*," she told Meh Chan. "Go away." She didn't want the little girl to be present when Lawrence Desmond greeted his wife after a short, unexpected separation.

Larry was beside himself. He had flown from Singapore to Manila and from Manila, after a talk with his mother, to Bangkok. He was so confused that he had driven to Mr. and Mrs. Krüger's house. He had mistaken the Dusit district for Rong Muang. And the end of the world lay in between. He knelt down beside Pauline and laid his head in her lap. "How could you do this to me?" he stammered. He was trembling. And the more excited he got, the calmer was Pauline. Happiness had always calmed her.

"I don't know, Larry," she said finally, although she knew very well, but she couldn't even tell Larry what had driven her out of the house.

Larry rose and tossed his black hair off his forehead, "If you ever run away again, Polly, I'll . . ." He couldn't say what would happen. His kissed Pauline's hair, her eyes, her trembling lips. His long fine hand passed gently over her swollen body. "I only have you," he whispered.

Pauline laughed softly. She hadn't known that Larry needed her just as much as she needed him. "I'll order tiffin for you," she said.

"For heaven's sake, I feel sick, darling."

"Nonsense!" said Pauline, unconsciously adopting her father's tone. "You can always eat, Larry."

And while Larry Desmond ate the rest of the tiffin, which in a tropical household is so lavish that six European families can eat of it, he told Pauline about Singapore and his prospects of a job with UNESCO. Perhaps in March. In Bangkok...

"Oh, that would please Papa," said Pauline, beaming. She didn't ask about *Maman*. She had forgotten her.

That evening old Petersen had a talk with his son-in-law in the *sala*. That was where he usually had his talks. Pauline was in her room, writing, according to her father's wish, to her mother, Nang Siri in Siamese.

Dear Mother!

It is nice here with Papa. We have a lot of fun together. I hope you and the girls are well. I hope Justus has come to his senses again. It is *very nasty* of him to show Papa so little consideration. Papa doesn't know what to think about Justus. He would be glad to try him out in the business again when he has recovered in Sukhothai with Uncle Sri. You're to please write him that. Papa can't write himself, he's too busy.

Larry came today. We're going back to Manila just as soon as we've seen you here. Papa says you are coming back to Bangkok end of the week, with Grete and Susanne. There's time enough until March of next year to fix up my house in Hua Hin. I'll tell you all about that when I see you. I'm terribly proud of Larry. He is *famos*, just like Papa...only, of course, different.

Health and happiness wishes,
Your devoted daughter,

PAULINE

That evening Petersen senior and his son-in-law became friends. Like most Americans, Larry was very frank, but he stuck to his story that *Maman* had decided all on her own to go back to New Orleans. Whatever he had said remained buried between mother and son. It had been the worst hour of his life, but it had made a man of him. He had always been afraid of *Maman*; now he understood her and felt sorry for her, a quite new and protective love. *Maman* must have felt it. She had not been bitter. Her French practicality had prevailed. She had realized that she had to create a life of her own for herself. Perhaps she had also recognized that her son now wanted to live his own life, that her duty had been fulfilled long ago. Moreover *Maman* had not only retained her composure; she had written Pauline a generous and sensible letter. Old Petersen had to respect the woman. It couldn't have been easy for *Maman* to give up her beloved son to such a strange girl. He would have liked to keep his Linchen too.

His son-in-law was no stranger to him any more. They got along marvelously, the way a younger and an older man can get along when they have a strong emotional bond. They both came sauntering into the *sala*, looking radiant. Pauline had the typical gift of the East to prolong a happy moment creatively, so that it continued far beyond an evening, a week, even a year, and fortified the spirit during periods of stagnation and darkness. Pauline's father couldn't prolong such moments of happiness. The thought that in a few days Pauline would leave him and he would be alone in the *sala* again was already depressing him. Only a cosmic stopwatch could have consoled the old man. He could have sat there forever in his tropical kingdom, his lass at his side. "Are you sure you'll be coming to Bangkok?" he asked.

"It's very likely," Larry replied cautiously. "It depends on a lot of things, on the political situation especially, but it certainly looks as if I'll be staying in East Asia for a while."

He's right, thought the old man. Beyond his garden feverish change was going on all the time...the new China, and Thailand's precarious borders. Pauline had to have security, that was the main thing.

Tokay, the big house lizard, let out a cry. The three people in the *sala* listened. If Tokay cried seven times it meant luck for the owners of the house. It was an old superstition adopted by Thailand's guests. While the young couple whispered to each other, the old man counted the cries. Later he would remember that Tokay had only cried four times.

18

A Young Man in Hong Kong

Three days after Pauline's departure for Manila, Hannes Petersen flew to Hong Kong, partly to explore the possibility of new markets, partly also to try to persuade a long-legged young man with a totally expressionless face to return to Hamburg. He knew where to find Thomas Harms. Mr. Ketaki's agent had got in touch with a certain Father Mollman, a German and an escapee from the prison in Tsingtau, and with Mr. Yu. Both had been called on by Tommy but neither had been able to get him on a ship to Europe. Mr. Yu hadn't really tried very hard. He had discovered traits in young Tommy that he thought might be useful to him. This of course he hadn't written to Petersen and Company in Bangkok, but he had reported truthfully that young Mr. Harms did not wish to return to Hamburg. Martha thought it odd that Hannes should get so excited about it. After all, he didn't want to go back to Hamburg either. She thought people in glass houses shouldn't throw stones. She hadn't lost her old penchant for mottoes.

Bangkok was getting emptier all the time, Hannes thought on the plane. Now the young Desmonds were gone too. Aunt Kathy had boarded a ship a while ago and left Bangkok forever. She wanted to experience spring in the Vienna Prater once more, she had explained. Hannes had become very friendly with Miss von Kinsky. It was strange how everyone in East Asia who spoke one's mother tongue almost became a relative, and how every departure became a hard, even if unadmitted, loss. But the biggest shock had been when Hannes had found out one day before his trip to Hong Kong that Dr. Johannsen, who had looked after the German colony in Bangkok for years, was going back to his native city of Bremen. He had booked a cabin on the ship Martha was leaving on, and would travel with her and the children in January. "But who on earth is going to look after Mama?" old Mr. Krüger had asked indignantly. Nearly everybody felt it was very inconsiderate of Dr. Johannsen to want to spend the rest of his days in his native city.

The plane approached Hong Kong. The jewel of the Far East loomed up out of a veil of sunshine. The British crown colony, with its magnificent banking houses in Victoria, behind which rose steep, narrow Chinese alleys, was a haven of freedom for thousands of Chinese intellectuals and merchants from the People's Republic, who didn't want their sons to march in the Red Army and had no inclination to do so themselves. Perhaps there was a chance here for West Germany, thought Petersen, as he went about finding Thomas Harms, who had run away like a wild jackass from a little whore with dreamy eyes and blond Swedish hair with nothing but a camera, a loan from old Mr. Wong and his own fat head. But Hannes Petersen was wrong. Thomas Harms had something else: skillful hands. Wood, iron, screws, hinges, and locks became pliant when he touched them. And that was a big thing in East Asia. Petersen had overlooked the fact that young Harms was a passionate Mr. Fix-it. He had been on the point of entering the Institute of Technology when Hitler's war had made that impossible. But a lot of strength and dexterity still rested in his hands, and he was the right man when it came to straightening out what was bent or setting a plank precisely level with the one next to it. It was something he didn't have to learn, but a gift, like the ability to think just thoughts or cook

285

fine Chinese fish in sweet and sour sauce. Madame Yu, the wife of rich Mr. Yu, whose junks and sampans in the harbor of Hong Kong rocked a lot of little businesses into one big business, could cook fish like that. Tommy had eaten her fish and after dinner, with a few simple manipulations, had made a rosewood box that wouldn't close behave itself. Mr. Yu and his daughter, Phoenix, had watched his long nimble hands breathlessly. And it gave Mr. Yu an idea.

He began to question his guest, whom Father Mollman had brought to him. Ten days later Thomas Harms was supervisor in one of the repair shops to which Mr. Yu's junks and sampans brought their wares from all over the world, and shipped them off again when they were repaired. For this the former coolie paid the foreigner a disproportionately high salary, not because Thomas Harms was a white man—nowadays the Chinese were not inclined to pay a bonus for color—but because Tommy's old, buried passion to make broken things whole combined very well with the Chinese passion never to throw a screw or the smallest piece of wood away.

In Hong Kong a career had opened up for Tommy that required no examinations, recommendations, questions, or any formalities whatsoever, as can happen only in East Asia from one week to the next. After the evening in his home, Mr. Yu had taken the young man to his workship in the harbor, had shown him a junk with a broken mast and asked him, "Can you mend it?" Young Harms had looked at the junk for quite a while. It was a narrow boat that sometimes moved smuggled goods, but that didn't concern him. That was Mr. Yu's business. Then Thomas had nodded and said in pidgin English, "Can do, mister." He had worked on it one whole day. Everybody stood around grinning while the foreigner foraged around for tools that were either not there or had rusted, and then set to work with what he could find. He worked with obvious pleasure, and after a while the coolies had begun to jump up and down and help eagerly with a lot of shouting. If one didn't shout as if one were being tortured while one was working, how could things turn out right? And so Hannes Petersen found a young man in Hong Kong who still had long legs and an expressionless face but who otherwise had nothing more in common with the old Tommy. When Hannes Petersen looked him up in the repair shop, he had just finished work and some good-natured scolding. "Hello, Mr. Petersen. How are you?"

"How are *you*? asked Hannes Petersen.

"Just fine," said Thomas Harms, and lunged after a screw that was about to escape. "Sorry. The boys never put anything away."

"Why didn't you write to your parents, or us?"

"Well, you know, Mr. Petersen," said the new supervisor of Yu and Sons, "that wouldn't have been much use. Mama would have had a fit, and you would only have wanted me back in Bangkok."

"Don't overestimate my longing for you, my dear Harms. As you can see, I've managed without you."

"And how!" said young Harms, gazing at his former boss with knowing eyes. "No more cane and ten years younger!"

Petersen couldn't help himself: suddenly he found Thomas Harms very sensible. Then he looked at his watch and said casually, "Time for chow, young man. How about lunch?"

"*Famos!*" said young Harms, who like everybody else had adopted the favorite expression of his senior boss in Bangkok. "I know a little place, Mr. Petersen, behind the banks...a narrow Chinese alley. First-rate tea house. How about it?"

"Sure," said Petersen, feeling more cheerful than he had in a long time.

"You can have all sorts of delicacies there," said

Tommy. "Breaded chopped meat, sweet and sour pork, shrimp, Peking dumplings, the works! But we'd better hurry. The place fills up. I'll go change."

He disappeared into a cement block room and reappeared a few minutes later in a neat white suit, his hair still wet from a shower. "*My* treat, Mr. Petersen," said Baby Face, formerly of Petersen and Company, as they drove to a narrow alley that rose up steeply behind the bank houses on the waterfront. Silently they walked step by step up into the teeming Chinese world. And as they ate Peking dumplings and breaded chopped meat and drank Chinese tea out of tiny cups with no handles, Hannes Petersen found out something about the various stops young Harms from Flottbeck had made on his way here. As old Mr. Wong had indicated, he had really learned Chinese life from the bottom up.

At first Tommy had spent his money carelessly in the capital, Victoria, as he had been accustomed to do in Bangkok. Then he had left some of his cash locked up in a cupboard in his hotel room, and it had been stolen. It was a small hotel but much too expensive now for Thomas Harms. It was swarming with Chinese, Japanese, and Philippine businessmen to whom Tommy couldn't make himself understood. During the day he lounged around the harbor. It calmed him in some strange way— a foreign yet homelike atmosphere. There was an extraordinary air of activity and toughness. During the Japanese occupation, the greater part of the harbor equipment had been removed. The rest the Japanese had let go to ruin. Since the end of the war, the authorities in Hong Kong had rebuilt the port to an extent that astonished everybody. Hong Kong was again one of the busiest harbors in the world, but Thomas Harms, gazing at the junks, motorboats, and ships from all over the world, didn't know what he could find to do here. All he knew was that he never wanted to see Karin Holm again, and that he couldn't go home to his parents in the shape he was in. He still had his camera and took pictures of the harbor which he sold for a few dollars in the little Chinese shops that wound up the hill behind the waterfront.

One day, in a dimly lit sailors' dance hall, he saw a girl with blond Swedish hair and slanting, dreamy Asiatic eyes. He stood there, rooted to the spot. He wanted to flee but his long legs wouldn't carry him. There was a dreadful emptiness in his head. After her dance was finished, Karin Holm walked up to him. "Quick! Dance with me!" And then everything had been even worse than it had been in Bangkok, before Madame Boulgakoff had enlightened him about Karin's past. She loved him and wanted him. For the moment she had him, in a dirty Chinese boardinghouse in Hong Kong. She couldn't take him to the luxurious apartment Mr. Yu was paying for. It was a very simple story, the kind that repeats itself a thousand times. She had him, and lost him because she had him.

He couldn't make enough to live on with his photographs, although photography was a highly popular art and industry in Hong Kong. But one had to have a name. For a short while the grandson of old banker Harms lived on his mistress's money. That broke him completely. One had to be born to that sort of thing. With what money he had left and the sale of his silver signet ring, Thomas Harms fled, without saying goodbye, to Kowloon, the settlement of the refugees from Red China. There, as Mr. Ketaki had surmised, there was room for him.

Tommy didn't mention the episode with Karin Holm. He ate his pork with white chestnuts and said, "Victoria became too expensive for me, so I took the ferry to Kowloon."

"Very sensible," said Petersen. He waited until Tommy had drunk a cup of tea. There were two red spots now on his pale face. Poor devil...Petersen wondered what had really happened. He didn't say a word about young Harms's former fiancée.

Kowloon. The gentlemen from the crown colony took the funicular up to Kowloon to get some fresh air and to socialize. From the Height of the Nine Dragons you looked at a barren hill where the border to China began. The refugees were housed in huts, side by side. The border smugglers had given them a good going over in every sense of the word before they had even reached Kowloon. Thomas Harms, with his few Hong Kong dollars, was a Croesus compared with the Chinese teachers, engineers, newspapermen and businessmen who had found refuge here: a place to sleep, a kitchen, a workroom, all separated by canvas curtains. In Kowloon Tommy had met a Dr. Liu, a Chinese scholar from Shanghai, a university professor who had become a Christian. One morning he was sitting with the old scholar on the stone steps when Father Mollman spoke to him. The Shanghai teacher's wife and daughters were in their hut. There they were germinating beans in containers filled with water, which they sold to hotels and restaurants. Tommy and the old scholar were making brooms, that is to say, Tommy was. The old man was trying to help. Tommy had been in Kowloon a week when Father Mollman spoke to him, after a conversation with Dr. Liu.

"Of course he's Roman Catholic," Tommy told Petersen in a tone as if the father's faith was a serious flaw, "but he's extremely sensible. You have no idea, Mr. Petersen, how wonderfully Father Mollman explained things to me." Tommy didn't go into what the father had explained to him, probably things concerned with the way to approach suffering and master it. Tommy was obsessed with Father Mollman, whom he had seen to his ship a few days ago. "What he went through in Tsingtau! I can tell you, Mr. Petersen, insane! Absolutely insane!"

"He was in the prison?"

"Sure. Eighteen months!" In a few sentences Tommy described the fate of the German missionary in China. The missions were plundered, the missionaries kidnapped. More and more of Father Mollman's fellow brothers had been dragged to Tsingtau. Then it had been his turn: three times a day interrogations that lasted for hours. The father's memory was helped along with beatings. He had been presented with a long list of sins, almost all of which demanded the death penalty. The German father had always managed to get by. He was well schooled in logic and argumentation. Then he was sent back to his cell, always handcuffed. The heavier his handcuffs became, the lighter was his spirit. His breviary and rosary were taken from him, so he prayed without them. At last he had been dismissed, under threats, and then his courage and Rhenish blitheness had helped so many refugees in Kowloon.

"He was *famos!*" said Tommy. "He is going to look up my father and mother in Hamburg and explain everything to them. He thought too that I should stay here, at least for a while." Baby Face paused, then he said, "I'm going to get married, Mr. Petersen."

"Again! My dear Harms..."

"This time it's the right one," Tommy said firmly. "I think you know the girl. You met her at old Mr. Wong's party."

Phoenix Yu was the right one. Petersen thought so too as he enjoyed a cocktail in Mr. Yu's magnificent home after two days of doing business, mainly with the Wongs in Hong Kong. Phoenix made a less ornamental impression in her own surroundings than she had at the Moon Festival in Mr. Wong's house. In an English sport skirt and a silk blouse, she was simply a young, modern Chinese girl. She had no desire to live up to her father's ideal of her. Mr. Yu, with his workworn hands and soft heart would have liked to transform his daughter into a luxury doll, a mixture of Chinese court lady and Hollywood film star. It was the wish of many middle-aged Chinese fathers. Yu was rich enough to have made this dream come true, but his daughter wanted to work. Her efficient, not-so-small hands and her training in an English missionary school demanded something to do.

The young couple hadn't confided their secret to powerful Mr. Yu. Tommy had the feeling that Phoenix's father had more ambitious plans for his daughter. He was right. A young Chinese banker was invited for this evening. It was his intention to marry Phoenix. The daughter of a former coolie could expect a glorious future with a man who came from an old Hong Kong Chinese family. This was new China too. "Well, we'll see..." Petersen was skeptical. The submissive way Mr. Yu listened to the wise words of the arrogant young banker didn't escape him.

Tommy and Phoenix were sitting on a little bench on the lovely terrace with its view of the lights of Hong Kong and the bay. It was a beautiful, cool evening. Petersen drank in the priceless air of Peak Hill. Phoenix Yu was energetic; the girl had her feet on the ground, all right, and she seemed to be compassionate. Classical Chinese virtues. He hoped Tommy would get her. She was quite willing to wait until he was doing better. For a Chinese bride waiting was nothing out of the ordinary. Chinese brides waited five, ten years without getting in the least hysterical about it. And she was in love with Tommy. Petersen could tell by the way she looked at him surreptitiously and the private little smile she proffered him occasionally like a gift.

Mr. Yu was in great spirits, and in the course of the evening invited Hannes to visit the island of Macao with him. "That you've got to see!" he said, smiling shyly. "I have something rather special to show you in Macao."

"Tommy," Petersen asked. "What would you do if Mr. Yu simply married his daughter off to the young banker? Things like that happen."

292

Thomas Harms reddened, then paled. "I don't know," he said slowly. "Phoenix and I know what we want. Both of us can work, and we want to work. Besides, her father adores her."

"As long as she does what he wants. The Chinese have an unexpected core of toughness. Haven't you noticed that?"

"Yes, I have. But we have time. And my future father-in-law needs me in his business. And how!"

"Needs you right now, Harms. Don't show him too much."

Tommy grinned. "Don't worry," he said. "I've let a fresh wind blow through my hair by now, wouldn't you say? How did your business go?"

Petersen hesitated: in Bangkok he had never confided in Baby Face, but now a quite different young man was sitting opposite him, not only slimmer, but quicker and far more alert. "You know," he said, after a pause, "I'm not satisfied with our negotiations, but then we can't compete yet with the other western countries. What we need in Hong Kong is a *comprador*, a middleman between the Chinese and western firms."

"How about me?" said Tommy, his face more expressionless than ever. "I'm not Chinese, but some people call me 'Hong Kong Tommy.' I do a lot of snooping around the harbor, and I meet quite a few influential people through Mr. Yu. He seems to like me—so far."

"What would your percentage be?"

Young Harms named a sum that startled Petersen. He couldn't possibly mean it! But the young man who had had his brief encounter with the upper crust of the Chinese world and had more than a nodding acquaintance with its nether regions also possessed his share of Hanseatic obstinacy, and knew only too well that he was the answer to what the firm of Petersen and Company needed.

Hannes coughed. It was a small, tactful transition.

The Chinese used a spittoon on such occasions. Although Harms's price didn't suit him at all, he couldn't help but regard the "beanpole," as he had sometimes called Harms, with a certain amount of respect. His instinct told him that Thomas Harms had decided to offer his services as soon as they'd eaten breaded chopped meat and Peking dumplings so harmoniously together; he had just waited for the right opportunity, as was customary in Chinese and Hamburg business circles. He would wait for the right moment with Phoenix too.

"How about a whiskey and soda in my hotel?" Petersen suggested. "We can discuss all possibilities there."

"Very good, Mr. Petersen." Tommy was obviously reserved. He had no intention of giving away anything for free, however charming his former junior boss might be.

"Principally I agree," Petersen said quickly. "Of course I've got to talk it over with my boss. But I think it will work out all right. Are you coming along to Macao tomorrow?"

"Sorry, Mr. Petersen, but at the risk of sounding stuffy, as far as night life is concerned, I've had it!"

There was silence for a moment. Tommy's face was a mask. He was probably seeing in a mirror a piece of his past that didn't please him. A hundred years ago he had met Karin Holm in a nightclub and seen her as a creature of light. Even when he closed his eyes and tried to conjure up Phoenix's face, the mirror still showed shameful reflections.

"Goodnight, Mr. Petersen." He sounded far away.

"Shall I see you before I leave?"

"But of course, Mr. Petersen. I'll be taking you to the airport. I want to give you a little present for Chubb."

"You mean Albert. 'Chubb' is out. The young man's orders."

"When is your family leaving?"

"In January." Suddenly Petersen felt deflated.

"Well then...much fun in Macao," said Thomas Harms, his voice husky.

"Thanks, my dear Harms," said Petersen. "I'll do my best."

19

A Night in Macao

They took the night ferry to Macao. Mr. Yu had procured a visa for Petersen at the Portuguese consulate in no time. Mr. Yu did everything in no time. The crossing took about four hours. Hannes stood with his host at the railing, looking down at the dark water. Mr. Yu explained in a loud whisper that this Portuguese foothold on the South China coast was a very good thing for the Chinese. There were no headaches in Macao. Hannes understood. Macao was a sort of Switzerland in the Far East, a neutral sphere between the western world and China. It delivered all sorts of wares to Mr. Yu and many other influential Chinese, and vice versa. To be exact, Mr. Yu, beside his innumerable other transactions, was selling Red China the material for the little war of misunderstanding in Korea. But not entirely for financial gain. By performing little business favors like this, Mr. Yu was assuring himself that one day he might be buried peacefully and with dignity near Canton, where he had been born. But this the former harbor coolie didn't talk about, certainly not with his German guest.

"Would you like to go straight to a gambling salon, Mr. Petersen? Or shall we do a round trip of the colony first? We can do that with a taxi in a couple of hours."

Petersen knew the Chinese too well not to realize that the second suggestion was mere politeness. Mr. Yu wanted to gamble, like everyone on the island renowned in China and Europe as offering the most exciting games of chance. The Portuguese authorities sanctioned the countless gambling dens on this colorful rocky island, and they were open around the clock.

Strange colony, dangerous night!

Petersen asked himself later why he hadn't noticed that the air on this rock island was rife with dire premonitions. It all began nicely. Petersen and Mr. Yu took a taxi from the harbor to the main street, the Avenida Almeida da Riberior. Then Mr. Yu had paid the driver and they had sauntered in the shadows of a forgotten section of Europe, past the Senate Palace—two pilgrims from another world.

They walked through big and small streets. A faint smell of opium hung over the Chinese quarter. The poppy of forgetfulness was produced for local consumption by the Portuguese government. Behind doors ornamented with dragons in the Street of Many Pleasures unlucky gamblers rested from fickle reality. They provided dreams for themselves and a lot of money for the Portuguese government. At last Mr. Yu and Petersen entered a small gambling house where a malicious fate was waiting.

They entered the gaming room through a curtain. The place was filled three-quarters by gamblers; the rest were bar girls. It was a big, bare room so fetid with smoke one choked. In the center stood the gaming tables. Mr. Yu headed straight for the fan-tan table. A mask fell from his face, his little slit eyes glittered feverishly, his rough hands trembled with excitement. He didn't care whether he lost or won. Gambling intoxicated him as it did all his compatriots. Still, he played with a certain caution, as if by calculation he could force luck to be with him. A Chinese gambling clearly betrays certain traits just as a Chinese doing business or making love. An indestructible, enigmatic, and thoroughly sensible people, even when intoxicated.

The bar at the end of the room seemed to waver in clouds of smoke. Two girls were behind it and the bartender stood between them, a little man with a high forehead, Mongolian eyes, and a chin that threatened to flow away any moment. Senhor Pinto, called "Pin." During the day he worked for Mr. Yu as a spy. Mr. Yu found him useful. Pin trembled when faced with members of the Fifth Column, yet he was good friends with them. Every day new representatives arrived from the realm of Mao Tse-tung. Senhor Pinto played a dangerous game. On his right stood a blond girl with Asiatic eyes, on his left a young Chinese girl whom Mr. Yu had transported to Macao a week ago. Her name was Chaoyi. She was talkative, curious and still fairly innocent. The name of the blond was Karin Holm.

Mr. Yu had settled her in this furthest corner of the East after she had become a nuisance to him in Hong Kong. She was finished. She stood like a prisoner behind the dirty bar, beside a Eurasian whom she despised. From here on the only way for her was down. This was just what Senhor Pinto wanted, because then she would be his equal. Mr. Yu had nothing to say against it. He was no longer interested in Karin Holm. Only his Chinese mania not to throw anything away, however damaged, was why this girl could still buy clothes and rice. And Miss Karin was damaged. She drank like a fish and was just as silent.

She was changed in a frightful way. A large red scar ran from the corner of her left eye in a semicircle down to her mouth and divided her face into three unequal parts. This scar made a caricature of what had once been a beautiful face. But, Mr. Yu thought, gamblers didn't look at bar girls. They tossed a drink down absentmindedly and went straight back to the gaming table.

Senhor Pinto had met Karin during Mr. Yu's first weekend in Macao. At the time she had been undamaged and healthy. It was shortly after Tommy's flight to Kowloon. Senhor Pinto had been enchanted, as every man had been who had seen Karin Holm in those days. Then a jealous Australian sailor in a dance bar in Hong Kong—which Karin frequented occasionally, naturally without the knowledge of Mr. Yu—had drawn his knife and thrown it at Miss Karin. He wanted to show the coquettish little beast whom she was supposed to smile at. Karin had hoped she would bleed to death. When she saw herself in the mirror at the hospital, she fainted. Later Mr. Yu had taken her to Macao, out of pity, as he assured her several times.

Senhor Pinto had stepped back in horror when he had seen her again, but then he told himself that now she would be thankful to have him. But she hated him more than ever. He was and remained short, ugly, dangerous, and stubborn. Sometimes he stood behind her like a demon and stared at her beautiful naked back. There was nothing wrong with Miss Karin's back...

Karin loved life now with the love-hatred of the disfigured. She treated Senhor Pinto with ridicule and arrogance. He would never have her. The thought that she could still make a man suffer cheered her. Didn't she know how dangerous the bartender was?

"Hello," she said, staring at Petersen without smiling. Perhaps then she would look less repulsive. "Hello," said Petersen, who had found his way to the bar through clouds of blue smoke after two games. He had never been so horrified in his life. This...this was unreal!

He ordered expensive drinks that smelled of decay. Karin watched him, her eyes narrowed. A thought was taking shape in her besotted brain. She sat down gracefully at Petersen's table and said, "It would help me a lot here if you'd take me with you to your hotel tonight."

"I'm sorry. That's impossible," said Petersen.

"*Ah so*," said Karin, and distorted her ruined face with a smile.

"How did it happen?"

"I've forgotten. Isn't the scar fading?"

"Yes...of course."

"How are you, Johnny?"

"All right, thanks."

"Have you lost your tongue? Has your wife left yet?"

"Not yet."

"How would you like it if your daughter had to kowtow to dirty Chinese?" Karin asked gently.

"Don't talk nonsense, Karin!" Petersen tossed his drink down and got up. This was too much.

Senhor Pinto came rushing over and forced Petersen to order more expensive drinks. He couldn't take his glittering eyes, filled now with Portuguese passion and Chinese business acumen, off the elegant foreigner who seemed to know Karin very well. She had turned the undamaged side of her face to him. That way there was still the illusion...

"I want to pay," said Petersen.

"Just a minute, sir," said Pin in his broken English, and brought another round of drinks. Petersen felt too resigned to object and the bartender put the drinks down fast on the marble-topped table. Through clouds of smoke Petersen could see that Mr. Yu was still gambling and showed no signs of wanting to leave. Petersen's indifference—or was it perhaps scorn?—annoyed Pin, and it showed in his narrowed eyes. He could become violent quite unexpectedly and right now he was in a foul mood. This was too bad for the other bar girl. She ducked as if she had expected him to hit her. In her nervousness she knocked over a glass. Senhor Pinto picked up the shards and cut the girl's arm so that a few drops of blood fell on the counter. Chaoyi stared at Pin with her big round child's eyes. She was so startled, she forgot to scream. She wouldn't stay here. She would beg Mr. Yu to take her back to Hong Kong to her parents. "Forget it!" said Mr. Pin, who could read minds. "You stay here!"

Karin had watched the incident, amused. Chaoyi was very young and very pretty. Karin hoped she would have a miserable life.

"I want to go back to Bangkok, to the Russian Restaurant," she said, looking at Petersen sideways. "At least there a European is treated right. Please, Johnny, pay my fare. I've lost all my money gambling."

An old melody was humming in Petersen's ears. That was what Karin had said on the pier when Martha had arrived. When she had come to destroy their marriage.

"Are you deaf? I'll fly back with you."

"Good night!" Petersen got up abruptly. All he could think of was *out!*

"It's all your fault, Johnny."

Petersen shrugged. If he hadn't come along, it would have been somebody else. "It's no use, Karin. All that's over and done with. Goodbye."

He started to thread his way through to Mr. Yu. It was 5:00 A.M. "Goodbye, Johnny," whispered Karin Holm, and turned her hideously disfigured face to him. Her wonderful hair was a golden crown above it. "All the best, my friend. Is the only thing you love now your beautiful daughter? Wouldn't it be amusing if one day your beautiful daughter were a waitress like me in a filthy Chinese dive?" She began to giggle drunkenly.

She's gone crazy, thought Petersen. He had a wretched feeling in the pit of his stomach. "Idiot!" he said furiously, meaning himself. How could he get so upset over the ravings of a drunken whore? But his common sense was one thing, his nerves and his heart something else again. He was filled with a strange fear. Tiny! She was so innocent, so sheltered, so much more childish than her eleven years. A good thing Martha was leaving with the children in January.

Petersen had reached the gamblers through clouds of smoke. "Good night, Mr. Yu," he said hoarsely. "Thanks a lot."

"I'll be with you shortly. Here's the reservation for our hotel. A room with bath is reserved for you, sir."

Petersen walked slowly through the hilly city. Mr. Yu was at the hotel ahead of him. His eyes narrowed as he watched Petersen enter the lobby. "Did you enjoy your-self?" he asked.

"Thanks. It was...very different."

Mr. Yu coughed, the dry cough of the harbor coolies, and gave Petersen a strange look. "You look exhausted, my friend. Didn't our visit to the Mustard-seed Garden agree with you? I would be inconsolable."

So the hellish place was called Mustard-seed Garden. "It's nothing, Mr. Yu. I'm just a little tired."

"One shouldn't take long walks when one is tired. Sleep well, sir."

Mr. Yu walked off in the direction of his room. And it was suddenly perfectly clear to Petersen that he knew everything. Karin Holm had never been discreet, and a European lover would have given her face, as far as Mr. Yu was concerned. Mr. Yu had had his bit of fun, very cruel, very Chinese fun. By tomorrow he would have forgotten everything.

Two days later young Harms brought Petersen to the airport. He took a small package out of his pocket, the present for Chubb who was now irrevocably called Albert. "What is it?" asked Petersen.

"A little Chinese junk," said the new *comprador* from Flottbeck. "I carved it myself and Phoenix sewed the sails. I want Chubb...I mean, Albert, to think of the Far East sometimes when he's back in Hamburg."

"How very nice of you, my dear Harms. So...all the best. I'll get an invitation to the wedding, won't I?"

"You certainly will, Mr. Petersen. But it'll take a while."

Petersen shook Tommy's hand. "Well...again, do your best. I...I was really very pleased, Tommy...I mean...hm...yes, you're really managing very well... *famos!*"

Tommy nodded solemnly, like a Chinese mandarin on stage. "Actually," he said, "one is an ass when one

302

comes straight from Flottbeck to the Far East. But one lives and learns."

Petersen nodded. And some remain asses. He, for instance. He was still furious about what Karin had said in the Mustard-seed Garden.

The plane rose into the tropical sky. The long-legged young man got smaller and smaller. Finally he was a tiny dot. Another bit of Hamburg was crumbling away...

20

The Fair on the Golden Mount

Martha fetched Hannes from the airport and said at once, "You don't look well, Hannes. Did you exert yourself too much in Hong Kong?"

"It's nothing, my darling. I just can't fly."

While they were having tea on the veranda, Petersen closed his eyes. "What *is* wrong with you?" Martha asked.

Petersen handed her his cup. "Some more tea, please, Mem," he said, evading Martha's scrutiny. He had years of practice in that. Then he opened his small suitcase and took the little carved junk for Chubb out of it. "Look, Martha. Tommy made it."

"Since when can he carve? Why, that's a work of art! I never knew..."

"None of us knew." Petersen lit one of the cigarettes he was allowed to smoke and told Martha the astonishing story of Thomas Harms. He told everything he had experienced in Hong Kong and Macao, except for his meeting with Karin Holm. In the middle of his story, Tiny came tearing in and embraced him passionately. Cheng was with her, Youngest Grandson in her arms, and a creature Petersen greeted with "And what is *that*?"

"That's Tia, my puppy," Tiny said proudly, stroking the dog. "Cheng and I found him in the *klong*. Tia is sweet, Papa!"

Martha shook her head but said nothing. Petersen was still staring at the puppy, who was running around

Tiny and cleverly avoiding Cheng's kicks. Cheng couldn't abide hungry mongrels. They were an insult to her sense of respectability. She hadn't felt a spark of pity for Tia but hadn't been able to gainsay the golden-haired child's plea. Since then Cheng waged a silent, relentless and sometimes successful war against Tiny's beloved pet.

Tia was a ghastly mixture of all Asiatic dogs, a creature from no-man's-land. In his eyes were mirrored fear, mischief, and blind devotion to anyone who didn't kick him and realized that even street mongrels had to eat water-rice occasionally. Tia had the longest tail of any dog in Bangkok, and although Cheng, grumbling, had washed him, his fur was an indefinite color that looked like dirt. His body was a cross between a sausage and a broken giraffe on matchstick legs. No surrealist could have done better.

"Listen, Tiny," said Petersen. "That animal's a monster!"

Tiny's pretty blue eyes filled with tears. How could Papa hurt Tia's feelings like that? She knelt down and held her hands over the dog's ears. "*Mai pen arai, Tia,*" she whispered. "Don't mind him. *Khun paw mai khao tjai*...Papa doesn't understand." No Siamese child could have expressed herself better. Tiny's tears and her passionate attachment to Tia annoyed Martha. It was high time the child got out of these esoteric surroundings.

"Stop it, Charlotte," she said quietly. "A big girl like you doesn't cry. Papa was joking."

Petersen was crushed. Tiny could twist him around her little finger. Quickly he gave her the bolt of light blue silk he had bought for her in Hong Kong. In a flash all grief was forgotten. "Cheng must embroider the silk with little white birds...please, please, Cheng!" she cried, her eyes bright, and she ran off into Martha's bedroom.

"Where is she going?" asked Petersen. He had received only a very fleeting kiss from his pretty daughter.

"To look at herself in the mirror," Martha said drily.

"That silk is much too fine for Hamburg, Hannes. When is the child to wear it?"

"She's still in Bangkok," Petersen replied, irritated. His pleasure had evaporated. He looked at Cheng, Youngest Grandson and Tia with distaste, especially the monstrous dog who ran after Tiny on its matchstick legs. "Horrible animal!" he said so furiously that Martha had to smile. Hannes was obviously jealous of Tia.

At last the day of the big temple fair had come. It was held every year in November at the Temple of the Golden Mount in Bangkok. Unfortunately, on the morning of the great day there was vexation in Bangkapi. Cheng, who as Tiny's *amah*, had of course wanted to go along, declared she had to stay home. She held Youngest Grandson outstretched like a package for mailing. "He very sick," she said in her broken Siamese. "Cheng must take care of him."

Martha found this perfectly all right. She shared Chubb's dislike of the domineering woman. But since she had always been nice to Cheng, the woman thought that the Mem couldn't do without her. Martha appreciated Cheng's loyalty, but in the last months her devotion to Tiny had taken on a tyrannical aspect. Cheng now had a great deal of influence over Tiny, and with Chinese tenacity and caution took advantage of it behind Martha's back. Tiny was standing beside Cheng and Youngest Grandson, who as far as Martha could see looked perfectly healthy, and never took her eyes off her *amah*. Her delicate little features were already puckered for weeping.

"What's wrong with Youngest Grandson?" asked Martha.

"Bad wind blow on him. Cough like little ghost. Cheng buy very very good medicine. *Very* expensive."

Martha ignored this commercial side of Cheng's mother love. In Siam "bad wind" was held accountable for everything from galloping consumption to a light cold. "Has he got a fever?"

Cheng proudly pronounced a temperature that no living person could have survived. Like many Chinese, she was vague about figures.

Martha gave Cheng a pill and a bottle of cough medicine. Cheng accepted both without enthusiasm. Bad medicine. Expensive and helpful medicine was either bright red or a poisonous green.

"Cheng stay home today."

At this point Tiny got into the act. "Then I'll stay with Cheng and Tia," she said weepily. "If Cheng doesn't come with us to the Golden Mount, I won't go!"

"That's absolutely silly, child," said Martha, astonished. "What would Papa say?"

Instead of answering, Tiny, sobbing now, threw her arms around Cheng. "I'm staying with you, Cheng...always, always!" she stammered in her faulty Chinese.

"Little Missie no say that," Cheng murmured. Her eyes downcast, she peered at Martha surreptitiously, triumphantly. Missie was angry, even if she didn't show it. The foreign devil-woman didn't love her child with the golden hair the way Cheng did. Cheng bowed as low and humbly as she had done after her arrival, when she had engineered the dismissal of the Malayan *amah* in order to be Tiny's *amah* herself.

"Stop crying, Charlotte!" Martha said when Cheng had finally left. "I don't want any more nonsense from you, do you understand?"

Tiny was beside herself. "I won't go!" she screamed and stamped her foot. Her face was purple. Was this a fit of tropical rage?

"Cheng is my Chinese mother! She told me so herself!" Tiny's sobs were heartrending.

Martha was suddenly alert. What had the child said? Cheng was going too far. Martha gave Tiny a handkerchief and said amiably, "Well, if that's what you want, Lottie, if you'd rather stay with Cheng, it's all right with me. Only be careful with Youngest Grandson. I don't think he's ill, but he might develop a fever."

Tiny stared at her mother, her eyes open wide. Then she said, still crying but definitely calmer, "I thought you said Papa wanted me to go with you."

"All of us want you to come with us, darling. But nobody's going to force you to have fun. Now be a good girl and have a nap."

"Yes, Mama." She sounded very unsure.

"You can think it over, dear. We won't be leaving before nine. The marionettes go on so late. You wanted to see them, didn't you?"

"Yes, Mama." A big pause. Tiny had stopped crying. She was looking at her mother shyly, sideways. "Are you angry, Mama? Would you prefer it if I stayed home?"

"Of course not, silly girl! We're all going together to the Golden Mount. You've never been out so late, have you?"

"Only in Hamburg, in the bombings. Chubb has told me all about it. I can't remember it too well. Was it very bad, Mama?"

"That's all over and done with now. Go have a good sleep, dear."

"May I wear my blue dress? Cheng must press it for me."

"Well, as an exception. I was saving it for Hamburg. For your birthday this summer."

"You're *sweet*, Mama. Do...do you think Cheng will be angry if I go out tonight?"

"Cheng will be happy that you are going to see something so exceptional," said Martha, knowing better. She didn't like the whole business.

"I like Cheng so much. Why did she say she was my Chinese mother?"

"She doesn't know how to express herself very well, dear."

Martha let down the blinds. Cheng was in the kitchen house, eating her noon rice. It was the only time she ever left the child with the golden hair out of her sight.

Tiny yawned. "Cheng can't read or write, Mama, but she can embroider beautifully, can't she?"

"Yes," said Martha. "She's very clever with her hands."

She left the room thinking that Cheng was definitely not a good influence for her excitable daughter. But they were leaving in January...

Martha wasn't the only one who was annoyed that day. Madame Boulgakoff had her minor irritations. On the day before the three-day festival, Ah Bue had walked out on her without a word of explanation. The substitute for Ah Bue had already broken five teacups. Where on earth was Ah Bue? She could at least have presented herself with the usual excuse that great-grandmother was dying. This sort of thing made Madame furious.

Before leaving for the Golden Mount, she read two things, the importance of which became clear to her only later. The first was a notice in the *Bangkok Gazette*. Madame Boulgakoff was interested in the column that dealt with criminals, kidnappers, drug smugglers and similar enterprising characters. The Siamese police were arresting opium smugglers daily. Madame trembled at the thought that one day Mr. Lu, her opium source off the Yarawat Road, would be among those arrested. She read about the kidnapping of children because of the high rewards promised. She might be lucky and one day find one of the poor little things. And besides, she liked to read about the misfortunes of others. It made one realize that there was such a thing as compensatory justice.

Madame skimmed through the column detailing crimes. A Chinese woman called Chung, the leader of a dangerous gang of burglars, had been arrested while breaking into the Oriental Hotel. She had crept into the room of a certain lady and had sprayed her with some anesthetizing fluid. But the lady hadn't been asleep, and her sensitive nose had noticed a strange smell. She had

309

opened her eyes, and just as Chung was reaching for the jewel box on her dressing table, the woman had leaped out of bed and caught her. This Chinese woman, who had in the meantime betrayed several of her accomplices, was to be deported, "a thing that was usually done with unpopular foreigners in Bangkok," said the paper.

Madame Boulgakoff screwed up her eyes and let the paper drop onto the coconut mat that served as a carpet in her office. She didn't know that Chung was Ah Bue's mother. She had seen her once at the market when she had hired Ah Bue. The slightly blurred newspaper picture showed a middle-aged Chinese wearing the wide bamboo hat of the market woman. She had sly eyes and greedy hands. They're all like that, thought Madame Boulgakoff, who found the woman repulsive. Then she looked at the clock. In ten minutes she would leave for the fair. At a certain stall Mr. Lu would be waiting for her with a small package. Madame Boulgakoff took a deep breath in anticipation. She was overwhelmed by a feeling of the infinite possibilities of life with the same intensity as the melancholy and hate that so often overwhelmed her. Russian emotions...glorious emotions with a trace of bitterness ...because of the deterioration of all beauty and elegance in a place like the Russian Restaurant on Suriwongse Road.

But before Madame Boulgakoff took off on her pilgrimage to the Golden Mount, she read the letter that had come that afternoon from Macao. She read it with sadistic pleasure. Miss Karin suddenly wanted to come back to Bangkok as quickly as possible. She had been much happier in the Russian Restaurant than she was in the Mustard-seed Garden in Macao. Someone was trying to kill her.

"Please help me, Tatiana," she wrote in conclusion. "You know that all your guests come to the Russian Restaurant only because of me. By the way, when I got here young Harms wanted to marry me, but he's too

310

green for me. You are always right, darling! Everybody tells me I am more beautiful than ever. Please send me money for the fare right away. I'll work it off. Your loving and obedient *Karin*."

Madame Boulgakoff hadn't come down with the last rain either. If this shameless Eurasian who had run away from her so treacherously suddenly and so humbly wanted to come crawling back, something was wrong. When Karin got back to Bangkok—and somehow she always managed to leave and come back—there'd be time enough for negotiations. She was a beauty, no doubt about it, but she made everybody's life miserable with her moods. Madame Boulgakoff tore up the letter and dropped the scraps on the mat. Of course she wouldn't answer it. A waste of stamps. Beautiful Karin was probably clinging to a frail branch.

Madame Boulgakoff rose and shrugged. It was consoling to think that beauty faded but the Russian Restaurant endured. The first people she met at the Golden Mount were Mr. Petersen and his wife and their two children. Tatiana stared wide-eyed for a moment at Tiny. What a beauty! She would have her share of misfortune, no doubt about that. Then she hurried, her eyes halfclosed, past the lit-up stalls to the place where bamboo articles were sold. She had already forgotten the German family.

The children were thrilled. The were walking hand in hand as in the good old days, and Tiny's little finger was pointing at the thousand lights, the toys, and the Asiatic sweets piled high at the foot of the Sraket Temple. It was a wonderful night, not too hot. On top of the artificially constructed mountain called Pu Khao Tong the great stupa glowed. In it were stored sacred relics of the Buddha brought from India. Crowds of pilgrims and foreigners wandered constantly up and down the many steps of the stupa, to meditate when they got there or just to look around. The walk up to the stupa alone was a Buddhist pilgrimage. All along the way there were little caverns, reliquary shrines, statues and *salas* that reminded the children of their great-uncle's *sala* in Rong Muang. Only once a year, in November, were the religious and the sightseers allowed to visit the relics of the stupa; only in November was a garnet-colored cloth wound like a fire cloud around the socle of the shrine. And only in November, in the profound silence of the stupa, was there the noisy magic of the fair at the foot of the Golden Mount: stalls, booths, mobile kitchens, dancers, clowns, marionette theatres, displays of freaks, and the yearly meeting of princes and beggars, pilgrims and pickpockets, natives and foreigners. Tiny received a parasol for herself and for Youngest Grandson.

At the base of the stupa two young Siamese in bro-cade costumes were dancing while marionettes on long sticks played scenes from a legend on a miniature stage and Siamese clowns did their excrutiatingly funny acts in pantomime. There was an aroma of roasted peanuts and sacred pilgrimage. Old Siamese women with short hair and patched white jackets chewed betel and asked Chubb and Tiny, *"Pai nai?*...where are you going?" and Chubb always answered politely, *"Pai tio*...just walking." One of the old ladies wanted to know what the material of Tiny's dress had cost, and Petersen's answer pleased her. Peter-sen had whispered an amount three times the actual price so that his daughter would be respected. Martha shook her head, smiling. One couldn't be angry with these naïve old women who looked up at one admiringly and not a little slyly.

The noble Siamese families were in high spirits and their mood was shared by all Bangkok beggars and pick-pockets. Petersen clung to his wallet. He'd had his expe-riences. Suddenly he grasped Tiny by the hand and said hastily, "Come away, darling." Because in front of one of the stalls sat a middle-aged Siamese exhibiting a freak

312

with no feet and a head as big as a pumpkin on its mis-shapen body. Many people were standing around laughing. The woman exhibiting the freak was laughing too. Tiny began to cry and hid her face in Petersen's sleeve. "Well, there you are," said Martha, sounding resigned.

The Petersens were still watching the marionettes when a familiar voice addressed Chubb. "Well, my boy, how do you like it?"

It was Charles Krüger. He and Doris came to the temple fair every year. Charles Krüger was slightly annoyed. He had driven to Wilhelm Christian's house to take him along to the Golden Mount but Petersen senior was staying home. He went to the Golden Mount only with Pauline.

"We've had a letter from Lisa Petersen," said Doris Krüger. "She is furious that Hinrich's got to stay in Hamburg."

"Lisa can't begin to judge conditions in Bangkok," said Martha, with the patience she used to use on pupils who had been left back. "I'll explain it all to her."

Charles Krüger took Tiny by the hand and led her to the booth with the bamboo wares, where Madame Boulgakoff was talking to two Chinese. One was Mr. Lu from the side street off Yawarat Road, who supplied Madame Boulgakoff with the poppy of forgetfulness. There was something infinitely sly yet bored in Mr. Lu's face with the high forehead, the opium hollows in his cheeks and his dark little eyes, almost covered by their heavy lids. It was the demonic face of an insignificant civil servant—alert, dignified and corrupt—that would have fitted very well into a lost China. Mr. Lu came to the fair mainly to buy little girls to make beards for the theatre for him and be misused for other dark purposes. Beside him stood a middle-aged Chinese woman whose face under many bandages was totally unrecognizable. Perhaps Mr. Lu, who when he smiled revealed cruel little rodent-like teeth, had thrown something in the woman's face?

313

Nobody could say later how the surging, perilous crush in front of the marionette theatre and the stall with the bamboo wares came about. There was always a certain amount of crowding at the temple fair, but it was rarely as chaotic as on this evening. The Petersen family were suddenly separated. All around them was a sea of brown faces, arms, and legs. The heat and the incredible crush made it almost impossible to breathe. An irresistible wave drove Martha and Petersen in the direction of the temple steps, away from the marionettes, the stall, and the children.

"Tiny is with Albert," said Hannes, to calm Martha, who was crying, "Lottie! Where are you? Tiny! Chubb!" The only echo was the sound of a thousand Asiatic voices. Around the small world of the Golden Mount there was indescribable pandemonium. Once Martha thought she saw the parasol Tiny had been given, but it turned out to have under it a naked little Siamese. A very fat Siamese beside Martha shoved his way forward. He seemd to find the crush just so much more *sanuk*. He smiled at Petersen and said cheerfully that a fair like this was "hard work." Martha stared at him as if he were mad. An ominous presentiment of what she didn't know threatened to choke her, and she could only whisper, "Lottie...Lottie..." Petersen held her firmly by the arm. "But dearest, don't get so excited! It'll soon clear off and we'll find the children."

"Yes, Hannes," said Martha, still in a whisper. She tried to smile. Suddenly Madame Boulgakoff was standing beside her. She was staring at Petersen. In her overwrought condition, Martha found the sight of her more than she could bear.

"Have you seen our children, by any chance?" Petersen asked her. "My wife is very upset."

"I don't know your children, sir," said Madame Boulgakoff, and moved away.

And then, just as suddenly as it had begun, the crowd

314

dispersed. A wailing, white-haired Siamese woman, nothing but skin and bone, was carrying a lifeless child to a booth that sold sweets. The child had been crushed to death in the crowd. The booths shone once more in the reflection of the oil lamps and lanterns. Everywhere people began to laugh again, to eat and drink, and to renew their pilgrimages to the top of the mountain. Petersen and Martha hurried back to the marionette theatre to find Chubb and Tiny. Martha had calmed down somewhat just as soon as the crowd had melted away, but she wanted to drive home with Tiny. Petersen and Chubb could stay on with the Krügers. Martha looked at her watch as she walked past a huge Chinese family to the booth with the bamboo wares. It was all exactly as it had been before, only the children weren't there.

"They'll be here any minute," said Petersen. Martha jumped as someone accidentally bumped into her. "Don't be so terribly nervous," said Petersen. He sounded annoyed. "After all, Albert is fifteen years old and he always looks after Tiny. See, there they are!"

You really could see Chubb's red face bobbing up for a moment among the many dark faces. He couldn't run. Martha had to be patient. More and more people had come driving up to the Golden Mount in rickshaws and cars. Ulla Knudsen appeared suddenly, arm in arm with her mother, and greeted her junior boss and his wife in her shrill voice. "Isn't it wonderful, sir? What do you think of our fair, Mem? Please be careful, Mami, that nobody steps on your feet or Ulla will have to carry you home!"

Mami Knudsen giggled happily and pulled at Ulla's sleeve like a spoiled child. She wanted to see the clowns and the booth with hot rice cakes and banana pancakes. "Such a crowd!" Ulla still had time to say. "All Bangkok is at the fair again. I always tell Mami..."

"Have you seen our children?" Petersen interrupted her. "I thought I just saw our boy."

"No," said Ulla Knudsen. "I haven't seen anybody. I have to look after *my* child here," and she laughed shrilly. "Yes, Mami, I'm coming. No, you may *not* go alone!" With which words Miss Knudsen had caught up with her mother who looked as fragile as a Siamese doll in her starched white blouse and her red *phanung*. Martha hadn't said a word. She hadn't taken her eyes off the glittering mass of people, constantly weaving back and forth, making it difficult to focus.

They were standing now in front of the booth with the bamboo articles. Mr. Lu and the other Chinese men were still there; only the woman with the bandaged face was gone. Probably she had been a customer who had been chatting with Mr. Lu and the owner of the booth, but in spite of the stupor she was in, Martha noticed that the woman wasn't there. It didn't concern her in the slightest; in the state of tension she was in, her powers of observation must be playing tricks on her.

"Papa, Mama!" Chubb came running up to them, breathless. "Tiny is with you, isn't she?"

He stopped dead when he saw his mother's face. Petersen supported Martha because she was swaying slightly. "For God's sake, Martha! We'll soon find out..."

Chubb stammered helplessly, "I thought...I thought Tiny was with you. I...I kept calling..."

He looked at his father and was silent. All the blood had drained from his face. "Where is she?" he asked with difficulty because there was a hard ball in his throat. He looked around wildly. Nothing but alien brown faces. "Tiny!" he screamed so loudly that Petersen covered the boy's mouth with his hand. A crowd had gathered and were watching the stunned Europeans curiously. They were chatting and laughing, not heartlessly, because they knew nothing about the state of shock the three Europeans were in; they only heard the big blond boy screaming at the top of his lungs and that was irresistibly funny. Especially since they didn't know what the word *Tiny* meant. An evil spirit must have taken possession of the boy, an evil spirit who was very funny, because the young *farang* had turned red as a turkey and big tears were running down his cheeks from under his glasses so that he couldn't see.

Just then Ulla Knudsen came back with Mami. Never had Petersen felt so relieved at the sight of his private secretary. He explained to her that he was going to look for his daughter who he was sure was waiting for him in front of one of the booths. "Please stay with my wife, Ulla. Don't move. I'll be right back!"

Good-natured Ulla, who truly admired Martha, could scarcely conceal her delight at suddenly being called upon to protect the Petersen family. At the same time she was horrified. Her junior boss was taking the thing too lightly. Who could tell what had happened to the child in the crush? "They found a dead child in the crowd a while ago," she whispered to her mother in Siamese, forgetting that Chubb could understand every word and Martha every second word.

"Be quiet, Ulla," said Mami Knudsen with unaccustomed firmness. Suddenly their roles were changed. "Talk...talk...talk..." she muttered angrily. Shyly she stroked Martha's hand and looked up at her with gentle eyes. "Everything will be all right, Mem," she whispered in Siamese.

Martha came to and looked at Mami Knudsen as if from far away. Slowly she walked up to the booth with the bamboo wares. "Do you speak Chinese, Miss Ulla?" she asked.

"Of course, Mem. I speak Chinese, Siamese, Malayan, English, and French *very* well," Miss Knudsen explained. She had added the bit about the French because it sounded good with all the rest.

"Please ask the man if...if he has seen a child in a light blue dress...a blond child..." Martha's voice broke. All her strength was gone. She, the support of her family, now sought support from Miss Knudsen. Ulla was a show-off, unbalanced and loud as a brass band, but she was also a daughter. She would understand...But Mr. Lu shook his head indifferently.

"Who else was here?" Ulla asked the wife of her junior boss.

"A Russian woman. She was staring at Tiny. I noticed it," said Martha in a voice that was strangely dead.

"That must have been Madame Boulgakoff," Ulla said quickly. "I saw her a while ago. Perhaps she's looking after the child."

Anyone looking after Tiny would have been all right with Martha, even the Russian woman with the cruelly amused smile.

At that moment Charles and Doris Krüger came back and were stunned to see their friend and Chubb in such a state. While Ulla explained the situation, Chubb was sobbing unabashedly and wiping away his tears clumsily with his dirty fist. Fifteen years were no protection against shock and fear. Doris meanwhile was attending to Martha. She walked into the bamboo booth and got a small stool and made Martha sit down on it. "Hannes will be right back," she kept saying. "Tomorrow all of you will stay in bed, and then everything will be in order," as if everything were already in order.

Martha nodded. Doris Krüger was so normal, any thought of tragedy in her presence was absurd. "I don't know why I got so frightened," she whispered. "Ridiculous of me," and she pressed Doris Krüger's hand gratefully.

"Yes...of course," Doris Krüger said softly. She could see Hannes coming.

He was alone.

Everything Martha experienced after that was a nightmare.

Charles Krüger took over. He drove to the nearest

318

police station and sent Hannes to Prince Pattani. One of the prince's nephews was the most important official in the Criminal Investigation Department. Ten minutes later Charles Krüger came back with three policemen who had been given a complete description of Tiny. A large reward would be announced in the papers next morning. The investigation would be started at once. Martha was to go home with Doris, who would stay overnight with her in Bangkapi. Martha didn't want to leave the booth. On legs that would barely support her, she was still looking for her child. This was where she had lost her, this was where she would find her again. But in the end reason won out and she drove home with Doris Krüger and her desperate, sobbing son. She didn't shed a tear. All sorts of thoughts crowded through her mind: If only she had left the child with Cheng, Youngest Grandson, and Tia!

When they arrived, Doris Krüger cut Cheng's wailing short with a wave of her hand. "Go straight to Dr. Johannsen," she said, and gave Cheng too much rickshaw money. "Mem isn't well. I'm sleeping here tonight."

Dr. Johannsen came at once and gave Martha an injection to make her sleep. She was going to need all her strength. Then he sat down in the big hall with Doris and waited with her for the men. "Do go home, Doctor," Doris Krüger told him every five minutes. "You'll have forty Chinese waiting for you again in your waiting room tomorrow." But the big man from Bremen, who was so close to the Petersen family, silently shook his head.

Charles Krüger was the first to arrive. He could barely stand upright. They had searched the entire area, all the way up to the stupa, and asked everyone they met. Loudspeakers had asked the same questions and announced the reward. The same announcement would be broadcast over the radio first thing in the morning and be featured in every Siamese, Chinese, Indian, and Malayan newspaper and in the two or three English-language papers.

319

At 2:00 A.M. Hannes appeared with His Royal Highness, Prince Pattani. Ah Chang served drinks and sandwiches. He looked gray with sorrow. Petersen didn't say a word. He went up to see Martha, then looked in on Chubb who had wept himself to sleep, and was holding a damp corner of the sheet in his fist as he had done as a child. Petersen, stooped like an old man, crept out of the room.

At 3:00 A.M. a police car drove up. Petersen remained rooted in his chair. The Prince had gone home after promising all his help and influence. He would get in touch with his nephew first thing in the morning.

Charles Krüger and Dr. Johannsen could see a screeching Siamese woman and a child in a light blue dress. Dr. Johannsen rushed to the car but recoiled when he saw the child close up. It hadn't been trampled on, as he had feared. In a light blue dress, with blond hair, the little girl was lively enough, but she was the child of the Siamese woman and a Swede, hence the blond hair. The light blue dress had intrigued the policemen, so they had dragged mother and child with them.

Charles Krüger gave the Siamese woman some money as compensation. She nodded and yelled at the policemen to drive her home. With the money she and her daughter would celebrate the third and final day of the festival on the Golden Mount.

Doris Krüger had finally fallen asleep. Petersen sat in the hall with his friends until five o'clock in the morning. He had told Ah Chang to go to bed. The friends had little to say to each other, but their presence comforted Petersen. Eventually they all fell asleep in their chairs. Tomorrow was another day.

21

A Child Is Lost

"I'm sorry, sir, but we can't find a trace of your daughter."

Major Karawek Nayadharn's round, usually jolly face expressed his sympathy. He was a stocky, sturdy Siamese with short hair, snow-white teeth and lively black eyes, which in spite of his youth were ringed by wrinkles. The important connection of this police officer was his relationship to Prince Pattani, who had obtained this influential position on the Bangkok police force for him. Not that the major would have been a poor civil servant in his own right, but he was slightly lacking in diplomacy. Yet he had a goodly portion of innate slyness and he was adroit. He loved boxing. In his youth he had competed successfully, and occasionally it came in handy when he was on a case.

The Petersen case was a big *lambag*, thought the thirty-five-year-old major. A week had passed since the festival on the Golden Mount. The child seemed to have disappeared from the face of the earth. Even after tripling the amount of the reward, on old Mr. Wong's advice, no one had come forward to claim it.

"Have you questioned and watched all the people my wife and I have mentioned?" asked Petersen. He sounded exhausted. His eyes were dim. The same hammering was pounding at the back of his head as it had on the day Martha and the children had arrived.

"We've kept an eye on the Russian Restaurant especially, sir. None of the personnel know anything about a child that Madame Boulgakoff might have brought with her. And no suspicious people were seen there. Our best man is continuing to watch the place."

Petersen said nothing. Martha's idea that Madame Boulgakoff had looked at the child strangely and might have kidnapped Tiny for a high reward had to be written off as a figment of her imagination. "And the Chinese woman with the bandaged face?" Martha stuck to her feeling that this strange creature, who had been standing beside the booth, had something to do with the kidnapping. She had nothing but her instinct to go by; she could be right or wrong.

"Nobody knows the woman," said the major, suppressing a yawn. It was the time of day when one liked to relax with iced lemonade or a strong mocha. Just then Oldest Grandson appeared with both refreshments.

The household continued to function, and life in Bangkok, with its constant rounds of parties, political intrigues, and Buddhist ceremonies, went on as if nothing had happened. Only Tiny was missing. Sometimes Petersen wondered how the tropical sun still dared to rise and set in such splendor. For him and Martha life had been brought to a standstill. Chubb was with Nang Siri in Sukhothai, visiting Count Sri. Martha had gratefully accepted her suggestion to take the heartbroken boy to different surroundings.

"There may of course be an innocent explanation," said the major, breaking the silence. "A lot of farmers come as pilgrims to the Golden Mount. They don't read papers or listen to radio. They are good but very simple people. One of them may have your daughter. Does she speak Siamese?"

"She can make herself understood. She can certainly say who she is and where we live," said Petersen.

"Perhaps the little girl is in a state of shock and can't speak."

If she is still alive, thought Petersen, staring dully, straight ahead. Unlike Martha, who after the first paralyzing shock had developed a restless activity, Petersen was comatose. Everything glided past him like a Siamese shadow play. His world had become colorless.

"Could I please have another glass of lemonade?" said the major. In the course of pouring it for him, Oldest Grandson dropped the crystal jug. Nothing so clumsy had ever happened. Petersen sprang to his feet, cursing; Oldest Grandson jumped back. But the custom of many years triumphed. Petersen sounded kind as he said, "It doesn't matter. Get some more lemonade."

The major's black eyes narrowed to slits. Suddenly he looked like a good-natured but slightly dangerous fox. "Your servants," he murmured. "I shall question them today. May I have your permission?"

"If you feel it is necessary. But our servants are true-blue. You should see the way our Chinese *amah* runs around all over the place, looking for the child all day. I won't have a thing said against our servants. They've been with us for years."

"I mistrust *everyone*, sir. The more you trust them, the more certain I am that a clue to the crime may be in your own house. At least that's been my experience. For instance, have any of your servants run away since this happened?"

"Not one. They can't do enough to please us."

This was true. For their faithful servants the saddest part was that neither Martha nor Petersen noticed what Ah Chang was cooking for them, nor did they ever praise the girl who took care of the flowers in the morning for her artistry and the loving care she took with her beautiful arrangements, which she distributed all over the house in vases and bowls. They scarcely took note of what was going on around them. Hannes preferred to be in his office. Uncle Winn was all sympathy. The tragedy was mentioned only briefly, but Petersen senior had many meetings with his friend, old Mr. Wong. If anyone had a trace of the ingenious perspicacity which the good major lacked, then it was the senior boss of Wong and Sons.

"If any of your servants should run away, please let me know at once. It's important."

"Naturally, Major. What does His Royal Highness think about the case?"

"Prince Pattani is not of the opinion that your daughter is with the rice peasants," the major replied hesitantly. "He thinks such itinerants, who are not city-wise, wouldn't have the initiative to take a foreign child with them. And what for? They don't want to blackmail anybody. Our Thai farmers are free men and good Buddhists."

The major spoke suddenly with suppressed passion. There was a hard expression on his otherwise good-natured face. Only one of those money-hungry Chinese could have done such a thing! They would sell Thailand and themselves for a ransom. At least that was the opinion of Major Karawek Nayadharn. "During the last months, have you fired any servants?" he asked.

"No. That is to say...yes. I fired a little Chinese girl who had been insolent. But that was months ago."

"What was her name?"

Petersen had to concentrate. His brain was functioning very slowly these days. Finally he said the impudent little girl's name had been Ah Bue.

"Does she have any relatives in your house?"

Petersen jumped up excitedly. "We may have a clue there!" he said, so loudly that the major almost slammed the door in Oldest Grandson's face. He made a gesture of apology. The iced lemonade was suddenly unimportant.

"Ah Bue is the daughter of Chung," Petersen went on, "who was arrested with her gang shortly before the festival on the Golden Mount. You remember, Major?"

"Of course I do. We're still looking for a few accomplices. Where is the girl Ah Bue now? Do you happen to know?"

"Working in the Russian Restaurant," said Petersen, getting more excited all the time.

"I'll go at once with my men," said the major, getting up with the agility of a classical dancer in spite of his corpulence.

"I'll go with you. If Ah Bue wanted to take her revenge on me and has the child hidden somewhere..."

"I'm sorry, sir," said Major Nayadharn, with unusual sharpness. "You can't come with us. You would endanger everything if you were recognized. Besides, we won't be going in uniform. May I change quickly here?"

Without waiting for an answer he whistled to a young Siamese fruit seller in front of the entrance gate and told this officer of his to wait for him at the Russian Restaurant. "It may be a clue," he said softly. "As soon as I find out anything, I'll let you know."

When Major Nayadharn left in civilian clothes, carrying his uniform in a suitcase, Cheng was watching from the servant's quarters. She waddled over to her father, all excited. "The policeman has gone. He has changed his clothes. Perhaps they will find my daughter with the golden hair," she murmured, suppressing a sob.

"Go and get beans from the market," said Ah Chang. He coughed and stabbed sullenly around in his bowl of rice. Nothing tasted right since the child had disappeared. The many rumors being spread constantly by the servants in his house and those of the neighbors, embellished with the lush fantasy of the Asiatics, upset him. He had forbidden his daughter and his grandsons to dish up these horror stories at every meal, but only Youngest Grandson obeyed him, since he couldn't speak well enough yet. He had recovered miraculously from his serious illness on the eve of the temple fair. Ah Chang got up to fetch the soy sauce. Of course...the bottle was empty. He threw it at Cheng's head. She ducked, and without a word gathered up the shards so that honorable father wouldn't cut his bare feet in their torn sandals.

"Why no soy sauce, you lazy toad?" screamed the old man. "Next time I'll wring your neck! *You'll* never find the child! Gone all day, gossiping at the market and eating your father's rice!" The old man spat on the floor. In his rage he had forgotten that Cheng was eating Petersen's rice. "Get going!" he growled, calmer now, "And bring peanuts. The master likes them roasted with his cocktail!"

"Master doesn't drink, doesn't eat, doesn't say very fine food tonight..."

"Shut up!" said Cheng's honorable father. "Why didn't I throw you in the river when you were born?"

Ah Chang sat down on a small stool and looked at his daughter with disgust. Cheng had just touched his sorest point. The fact that Master hadn't even praised his duck Peking-style last night—Ah Chang's particular specialty— had caused him great sorrow. His grief over Little Missie paled in comparison. Actually he didn't really care a hoot about Little Missie, but he shared the anxiety of Master and Mem, of whom he was truly fond. He couldn't really understand why they were making such a fuss about the little female fish. What were daughters anyway but life-long disappointments because they hadn't been sons? Ah Chang could only shake his head over the princely ransom to which Nang Siri had also contributed generously. At best one sold one's daughters; but to shell out money for them? Never! "Bring me a watermelon," he called out to Cheng. Watermelon was a small consolation in a house where happiness had crept away on felt soles.

It was a sad house, the house in Bangkapi.

Phom, the chauffeur, and Meh Chan, the girl who arranged the flowers in the morning, felt the same way about it. At the moment they were attending a cheerful Siamese party with Phom's sons, Rat and Pig, and were enjoying a fish fight in a corner of a neighboring estate. Phom had called in sick. He simply had to have some fun for a change and fish fights, with betting, were *sanuk*.

Meh Chan looked up at Phom adoringly, although there was little about Phom to adore. He was looking with satisfaction at his unwashed, unkempt sons. Not only were their names repulsive, they were so ugly that no evil spirits would dream of attacking them as they had attacked the girl with the golden hair. Phom considered the repulsiveness of his sons an asset. "They won't make any *lambag* for me," he muttered.

Meh Chan nodded dreamily. She hoped the mother of the two little boys would never come back to Phom. Meh Chan was expecting Phom's child and wanted to go back to her rice village in South Siam with him.

"My father has very few debts," she whispered.

Phom didn't respond to Meh Chan's wooing. Meh Chan spoke almost as much as his wife who had disappeared. He watched the fish fighting, a life or death struggle. Next time he wanted to bring along his own fish. If it won that meant many *satangs*. Phom had a lot of debts. He had smoked too many cigarettes and drunk too much rice schnapps.

"The reward for the blond child is very high," he said suddenly, staring at Meh Chan with his round black eyes.

She nodded shyly. There was such a funny expression on Phom's face. She wondered if he had the blond child hidden somewhere. He talked about the reward day and night, his eyes sparkling like hard, fine gems.

Meh Chan got up with the grace of a young Siamese. Suddenly she was afraid of Phom. She was a country girl and was often afraid of the big city on the Menam River. She wanted to go back to her hut in the canal garden. There the bananas grew into one's mouth. There it was peaceful and quiet. Tomorrow she would fix a bowl of orchids for the big tall Mem. She would steal them from the gardener. "I'm going home, Phom," she said.

He didn't hear her. He was staring transfixed at the

glass tank with the two new fishes. Or was he seeing the enormous sum of money that Nai Petersen had put up for the return of his daughter?

Two days later Martha and Doris Krüger drove into the Chinese district of Bangkok. Doris wanted to buy some herbs at the shop of a grocer in Sampeng whom she had known for years. She often picked Martha up these days to go shopping with her in her big, old-fashioned car. "Has anything come of the search for Ah Bue?" Doris asked.

Martha shook her head. "She had disappeared without leaving a trace. Madame Boulgakoff told the police that she left the Russian Restuarant before the festival began. Dear Mrs. Krüger—how is one ever to find a little Chinese girl here?"

The crowd on Yawarat Road was frightening. Hundreds of young Chinese girls were slipping in and out of the streets and alleyways. All of them looked like Ah Bue to Martha.

"What did Ah Bue's mother have to say?" asked Doris.

"Chung says she doesn't know where her daughter is. She sits in prison and shrugs her shoulders. Later..." Martha paused. Her gray eyes widened. She grasped Doris Krüger's arm and gasped, "Chauffeur! Drive straight ahead! Fast!"

"But Martha! What on earth..." Doris Krüger was startled.

"The Chinese woman with the bandaged face!" whispered Martha. Again words failed her. She pointed into the crowd. "She was standing beside Lottie. She...she must know..."

"Lert!" Doris called out to her chauffeur. "Stop the car! Get out and run after a Chinese woman with a bandaged face and a big bamboo hat! Did you see her?"

Lert stretched his long brown neck out of the stiff

snow-white collar of his uniform. "Lert not see anything!"

"Quick!" Martha cried. "Look Lert! Over there!"

The chauffeur looked in the direction Martha was pointing. He saw the Chinese woman. She had put quite a distance between herself and them in the meantime. Lert got out and began to run. But the woman must have noticed something. Had she seen the car with the two foreign women? Anyway, she began to run too, crying loudly, evidently something to the effect that the foreigners were after her. "Help me! Quick! Strange devils want to catch me!"

Suddenly there was a chase. All the Chinese were against the three foreigners: Martha, Doris Krüger, and the Siamese chauffeur, Lert. No sign of a policeman. The Chinese encircled the woman with the bandaged face, forming a wall. Then suddenly, like a ghost, she had disappeared! Into a side street? Down a cellar? Into one of the dark back rooms of the Chinese shops filled with thousands of colorful items?

Martha was white as a sheet as they drove away from Yawarat Road. "You're not going to faint, are you?" asked Doris Krüger.

"Don't worry, dear Mrs. Krüger," Martha said grimly. "You see, I wasn't imagining things. Or why did the woman run away from us? We must drive to Major Nayadharn right away."

For the first time since Tiny's disappearance, a fighting light gleamed in Martha's gray eyes.

Hannes too began to hope, although the woman with the bandaged face would probably be just as hard to find as Ah Bue. They were sitting that evening on the veranda with the blue blossoms. A letter from Chubb had just been delivered, and they read it by the light of the hurricane lamp. "I wrote to him the other day," said Martha. "He must go back to Hamburg alone in January, with Dr. Johannsen. I'll stay in Bangkok until. . ."

There was a pause. Petersen understood that Martha would stay until she held Tiny in her arms, dead or alive. "I thought you would," he said, and stroked her hair. As in the old days there were some stray hairs behind her left ear. She had no time to look in the mirror. Strangely, the stray hairs that had always irritated him now reminded him of happier days.

"Old Mr. Wong came to see me at the office." Petersen sounded weary. "He is dead set against Uncle Winn's idea of raising the reward again. He sees the case as far more complicated. He doesn't think it is blackmail. He thinks it may be an act of revenge or something obscure like that. He keeps asking if we have enemies."

"Either I trust everyone now or no one, Hannes."

"We've got to think," Petersen murmured. "My head is bursting."

Martha got up and poured him a glass of pineapple juice. He didn't touch it. Just then Oldest Grandson came toward them. "Master," he said softly, looking despondent. "Chauffeur Phom run away with his two sons. He send best greetings. To Mem too. He say he not happy any more in Bangkapi. No more *sanuk*. Master cruel to Rat and Pig. Mem not smile any more. *Mai di*...very bad... no good."

It wasn't clear from what he had to say whether he agreed with his enemy, Phom, and shared his views. A house in which no one smiled was really "no good" for an Asiatic.

"Aren't they just like children?" Martha asked when Oldest Grandson was gone.

Petersen didn't reply. He had to report Phom's disappearance to the major at once. He didn't believe that Phom had anything to do with the kidnapping, but the major might be right. One couldn't trust anybody any more. Petersen closed his eyes and brooded: what enemies did he have in this paradise east of Suez? The time machine moved into the more recent past. A night in

330

Macao. A bar obscured by clouds of smoke! A sinister bartender...a disfigured girl... *Karin*. Chrysanthemums and silver birds on her brocade dress, death in her voice ..."*Wouldn't it be amusing if one day your beautiful daughter was a waitress like me in a filthy Chinese dive?*"

That was it! He had been deaf and blind! Karin's words still weighed like lead in his stomach, but he had been too indifferent.

"Martha!" He sounded excited. "I must go to the Russian Restaurant at once! Something has occurred to me...perhaps Madame Boulgakoff knows..."

"Can't it wait until tomorrow, dearest? You look exhausted."

"Speak of the devil and..." Petersen said.

A rickshaw had driven in at the gate. A Russian woman in a wrinkled suit, with badly dyed hair, got out and walked slowly up to the veranda with the blue blossoms. Madame Boulgakoff had chosen ten o'clock in the evening for her first visit to the Petersen house.

"Excuse the late hour, Madame," she said politely to Martha. "My name is Boulgakoff. I am the owner of the famous Russian Restaurant on Suriwongse Road."

It was the first Petersen had heard about the restaurant's fame, but he said nothing. It was evident that Madame Boulgakoff was going to make her entrance into this foreign house in style.

"The fate of your unfortunate daughter breaks my heart," she intoned dramatically. "The Far East is a moloch who swallows everything...bank accounts... noble emotions...and children."

"A whiskey or lemonade?" asked Petersen. With a gesture of her hand Martha had meanwhile asked their strange guest to be seated.

"A strong whiskey, if I may," said Madame Boulgakoff in her normal voice. "I have such weighty news for you that all of us are going to need a drink."

Petersen mixed the drinks. His hands were shaking.

If he showed signs of impatience, Madame Boulgakoff would spin out her prologue *ad infinitum*. She had learned something from the Chinese.

At last she decided the time had come. She had downed two double whiskeys fast, as if she were afraid somebody would snatch them from her. She took a letter out of the shabby handbag that held her money and a few photos of a Russia that was ancient history. "Does the name Karin Holm mean anything to you?" she asked casually, and looked at Petersen with cruel amusement.

Petersen and Martha nodded. Something in Martha's throat was choking her. The girl Karin had begun her underground work of destruction of Martha's family the moment she had arrived. What was she up to now?

"People are cruel and stupid," Madame Boulgakoff explained. "Karin Holm—God have mercy upon her—had more than her share of these attributes."

"Wouldn't you like to tell us..." Martha began, but Madame Boulgakoff interrupted her. "That is the reason why I undertook the irksome rickshaw drive to your house," she explained. "You have no idea how shameless the Thai rickshaw coolies are. During the Japanese occupation, the Chinese weren't allowed to drive their rickshaws any more. Not that I care anything for the Chinese...on the contrary. But..."

Madame Boulgakoff interrupted herself. Her hosts didn't seem interested in Thai sociopolitical problems. She handed Martha a letter creased and marred by grease spots. "I received it three days ago," she said casually.

"Why didn't you notify us at once?" Petersen managed to say, with great effort to keep calm. He leaned over Martha's shoulder to read the letter.

"I read Miss Holm's letters when I have nothing better to do, which happened to be this evening. I set out at once to enlighten you."

"Thank you very much, Madame," Martha said tonelessly.

332

They read Karin Holm's letter twice, as if they suddenly couldn't read English. Madame Boulgakoff meanwhile helped herself to a third whiskey and soda. The amount of soda was infinitesimal. "No," Martha whispered. "It can't be true!"

Madame Boulgakoff ignored the remark. These rich women had no idea what all could be true in this world. Driving around Bangkok in their cars, giving cocktail parties, and keeping their husbands away from certain restaurants...that was all they could do. But they got what was coming to them. Life was no fun, even if Madame Petersen had always thought it was. An arrogant woman, Madame Boulgakoff decided, watching Martha with the impersonal interest of a doctor in a mental institution. Would she scream? Would she faint? Strange...Madame Petersen remained calm. Hypocrite! thought Madame Boulgakoff.

But Martha was calm only because she was stupefied. Karin Holm called the plan for a crime "a joke," a prank to punish Mr. Johnny for taking Tommy Harms away from her by wickedly defaming her character. On the evening of the Moon Festival she had planned this "practical joke" with Ah Bue. It had been Ah Bue's idea, and Karin had agreed to it. She had given Ah Bue a necklace of red beads to keep her silent and cautious. The two women had decided in the Russian Restaurant to kidnap Petersen's little daughter as soon as there was an opportunity. Seventy-five percent of the ransom money was to go to Ah Bue, since Karin was too timid to commit the crime herself. She was satisfied with having punished Petersen in a way he wouldn't forget for the rest of his life. With such a high ransom—the girls had decided on a sum that had been surpassed long ago—a small fortune would be left over for Karin anyway. Ah Bue, who was on very bad terms with her mother, wanted to buy herself a shop in Sampeng with the money, and sell her Chinese embroidery. She had confided in Karin that she wanted to

333

get out of the life her mother had planned for her—prostitution and thievery. Ah Bue couldn't see any other way to free herself. It was also pleasant to know that she would be avenging herself on cruel Nai Petersen at the same time. But Karin didn't know that it was Madame Boulgakoff, not Petersen, who had enlightened young Harms as to Karin's past. As so frequently happens, in this case a criminal act was based in part on a false premise, but that hadn't prevented the kidnapping.

But why was Karin confessing all this to the owner of the Russian Restaurant now? Because she had suddenly become conscience stricken. In the waiting room of a hospital she had thought everything over. Karin had consumption. The doctor had told her so after the examination. Consumption was one of the most frequent scourges in the Far East. The letter had been written in the Mustard-seed Garden. Karin had evidently gone back there to get her clothes and jewelry. She had expressly agreed with Ah Bue that nothing was to happen to Tiny. It was, as already mentioned, to be solely a punishment for an arrogant foreigner.

At the Moon Festival Ah Bue had discussed with Karin where one could take the child for a week or longer. Finally she had thought of a house in Klong Toi. Nobody was living in the house because the Siamese declared it was haunted by an evil spirit. But a Malayan gardener and his family lived in one of the servants' houses. The landlord had left them there to prevent the electric appliances and water pipes from being stolen. Ah Bue and her mother, Chung, had had jobs in the villa next door before Ah Bue, through Cheng, had come to the Petersens' in Bangkapi. Chung had stolen in Klong Toi too. She had met Cheng at the market and promised her half her salary for three months if she would find her daughter a job at Nai Petersen's house. Cheng, who had known nothing of Chung's thievery, had of course agreed. The money was put aside for Oldest Grandson who wanted

334

nothing but to learn and read. He went two evenings a week now, with Petersen's permission, to a Chinese school on Silom Road.

Unfortunately Miss Karin had failed to describe the house or name the Malayan gardener who lived there with his family. They might have moved away in the meantime, Madame Boulgakoff suggested; or the house could have been rented. Of course one should send a wire at once to Karin Holm in Macao and promise her she wouldn't get arrested and would get a large reward if the child was found. Karin Holm was their only hope. Her conscience-stricken heart could be the solution to everything. Characteristically she had written in a postscript that Madame Boulgakoff should please look into the matter and find the Malayan family and the child if Ah Bue should happen to leave the Russian Restaurant or turn her back on Bangkok. One never knew with these worthless Chinese and heathens, Karin wrote virtuously. She didn't write that after years she had gone to confession and that the priest had insisted that she tell Madame Boulgakoff the whole story right away. Miss Karin was dreadfully afraid of dying. Petersen would of course also reward Madame Boulgakoff.

Petersen rose and said that he was going to send Miss Karin a wire right away.

"That's no use, sir," Madame Boulgakoff said slowly. "You can save yourself the money." Her expression was inscrutable. She took a newspaper clipping out of her pocket. It showed a young girl whose face was split in three unequal parts by a dreadful injury.

"The Portuguese police sent me Karin's letter. It was lying on the bar, addressed to me," she murmured. "What a frightful end...but everyone gets his punishment."

Petersen read the article. Martha closed her eyes as if refusing to participate any longer in this melodrama of the Far East. But it was no use. Miss Karin had been murdered with her mother's Javanese dagger by a man

335

named Senhor Pinto. The newspaper article promised details just as soon as the police had all the facts. The most important fact was already established: Senhor Pinto, a former Japanese spy in Hong Kong, had disappeared. According to the papers, a little Chinese girl, Chaoyi, who had recently found employment in the Mustard-seed Garden, had informed the police, sobbing, that Miss Karin was lying "quite, quite dead" in the bar, that was to say, in the room behind the bar where she had just written a letter to Madame Boulgakoff two hours before her mysterious death.

"It may be for the best," said Madame Boulgakoff, who had meanwhile found out about Karin's gruesome disfigurement. "For a girl with no means in Asia, her face is her only capital. Rich women don't have to be beautiful."

If the remark was aimed at Martha, it failed in its purpose because the latter paid no attention to the reference. Instead she suggested driving right away to Klong Toi to look for the house. What a blessing if Lottie had spent a few days with a decent Malayan family, even if she was weeping all the time. Martha refused to think of all the tears Lottie must have shed since the fair on the Golden Mount. The child had to be brought home right away.

Petersen couldn't think of Karin Holm's fate. That night the dead girl existed for him only in one respect—her connection with the kidnapping. "Thank you, Madame," Martha said warmly. "You have done us a great service."

Madame looked at the tall pale woman thoughtfully. "The fate of my neighbors wrings my heart," she said complacently. With her dyed hair and her rumpled, mended white suit she looked like a character from a Chekhov play.

"Do you speak Malayan?" Petersen asked suddenly. One couldn't ignore practical necessities, not for a moment. They couldn't just drive there. The Malayans were a foreign body in Thailand. They had their own language, their own traditions, and lived in their own gardens.

"Malayan is one of the few languages I have been spared in the Far East," Madame Boulgakoff said. "So at least I don't have to listen to their lies. Good night, sir. Best wishes, Madame."

But the Russian woman hesitated. She had done a lot for these people. She could just as easily have torn up the letter. Mr. Johnny had never treated her in a very friendly fashion. In the past her misfortunes had not exactly broken his heart.

Petersen interpreted her hesitation correctly. "Tomorrow you'll get a check for your efforts on our behalf, Madame," he said amiably, but cautiously. Without Uncle Winn and Nang Siri's generous help his savings would soon be used up by Ah Bue and Miss Karin's "prank." But he was ready to give his last *satang* for Tiny.

"Who do we know who speaks Malayan?" Martha asked after Madame Boulgakoff had got into her rickshaw, satisfied.

"Ulla Knudsen!" Petersen answered, after thinking feverishly. He rushed to the veranda door. "*Khon rot*," he yelled. "*Reu, reu!*"

"Phom has run away, remember? He was unhappy here," Martha said drily. "I'll drive." She was already on her way to the garage. "Do you think it's all right to disturb Ulla at this time of night?"

"Of course," Petersen replied. "She plays cards with Mami until midnight." And then, "Ulla is a decent girl."

"That she is," Martha replied with conviction.

They drove in silence to Klong Toi with Ulla Knudsen. Martha looked straight ahead at the road they were taking. Petersen had had nothing to say against Martha driving. He couldn't have driven. He was trembling all over. There was a revolver in his trouser pocket.

"We must be very careful, Mrs. Petersen," Ulla said

in a conspiratorial voice that irritated Petersen, but she was right. Poor Ulla couldn't help it if she got on everybody's nerves, but the way she had come tearing home from a party and had offered her help with every resource at her command had touched Martha deeply. Petersen, too, was impressed. Ulla Knudsen had done a lot of business with Malayans. Of course it wasn't going to be easy to find the house of the Malayan gardener in Klong Toi, but it was by no means impossible. She told Martha to stop at the corner of a narrow road, actually a dirt road. The houses along the road, the small open shops, the herd of water buffalo driven by a tall Indian—everything was rural and had been passed over by time.

Ulla disappeared in a Chinese coffee shop. She knew the owner. Martha parked on the opposite side of the road. It would be better if the people living in Klong Toi didn't see that there were other people in the car. They might warn the Malayan family. In Bangkok foreigners attracted attention for miles.

Ulla came back to the car looking triumphant. "We have to drive on a little farther. The haunted house is on a road parallel to this one. The Malayan gardener is still living there!" She was breathless, and there were red spots of excitement on her cheeks.

"I'll go in with Miss Ulla," said Petersen. "Please stay in the car, Martha. We can't leave it alone and we've got to creep into the property carefully, where it's dark. I hope there are no dogs."

In spite of his experience with the rabid animal, Petersen wasn't afraid of dogs. He only meant—and he was right—that dogs could bark and warn the people inside the house. He was determined to bring Tiny back with him. "It won't take long, Martha," he whispered.

"I hope not," she said.

Mohammed Ali lived with his wife Saleha and five sons, who helped him with his work in the garden house of the huge property. There was a Siamese pavilion, and a covered passage running around the main house. The washhouse stood on the right, beside the canal, a jungle of banana bushes and marsh plants around it; to the far left, beyond a stretch of lawn and beside a hedge stood the gardener's house, surrounded by tall pines. Like a cemetery, thought Petersen.

Miss Knudsen had hurriedly formulated a plan to introduce Petersen. They could see a light in the house. Except for the chirping of the crickets and the screech of an occasional lizard, there wasn't a sound.

The gardener came out of his house at once when he saw the *farangs*. Ulla was wearing a European dress and white straw hat, and with her rather heavyset body looked very Danish in the dim moonlit night. "The gentleman wants to rent the house," she said.

If their arrival at such a late hour surprised Mohammed Ali, who was wearing a dark fez and a garish plaid sarong, he didn't say so. His wife, Saleha, a slender middle-aged woman in a shiny sarong, with a tight-fitting, torn cotton jacket over it, appeared carrying her youngest son. Her big animallike eyes appraised their visitors as she whispered something to her husband. "What did she say?" Petersen asked nervously.

"She asked if we were English," Ulla explained softly. "She doesn't like the English."

Mohammed Ali decided to tell his visitors that the house was empty because it was haunted. The electricity wasn't functioning. He couldn't show it to strangers. Saleha had meanwhile wandered over to a pond in the garden and was tickling her screaming son with a water lily. Apparently it was her intention to calm the infant but the method with the lily was obviously wrong.

While Ulla engaged the gardener in a conversation and gave him some money so that he would let them in, Petersen took a few steps backward in the direction of the garden house door, which Saleha had left ajar. With one leap Mohammed Ali was at Petersen's side. "No infidel enters my house!" he cried.

Petersen simply pushed him aside. "Careful!" cried Ulla. She had grabbed Mohammed Ali's arm. A dagger fell to the ground. Mohammed Ali was small and weak, and Ulla was tall and strong.

"Nothing's going to happen to you," she told him in Malayan. "But you must tell us the truth. Where is the blond child?"

By now Petersen had searched the three rooms and the kitchen with his flashlight. An ancient woman was sitting in the second room, singing to two half-asleep children. They had smooth black hair and Malayan faces. Not a sign of Tiny!

Mohammed Ali had calmed down. He led them to the pavilion and gestured politely to a rickety bench. On the way there he yelled at Saleha: she should get back into the house fast with the child and the lily, and where was her veil? Saleha drew a silvery piece of gauze out of her sarong and obediently covered her hair and part of her face. She had been brought up in the old, traditional style and she obeyed her husband.

"Ask him if he knows anything about my daughter." Petersen was wiping his forehead with hands that trembled. A great big shimmering soap bubble of hope bobbed in front of his eyes, about to burst.

"Nothing," answered the gardener. "Know nothing."

But Ulla didn't give up so quickly. She promised Mohammed Ali a sum of money that made his eyes shine. A stream of Malayan words burst forth from his bluish lips that had been so firmly closed before. Yes, a little Chinese girl had turned up one day after the Moon Festival. She had said she worked for a rich English family. She wanted to vex these English people a little. Mohammed Ali had probably smiled one of his rare smiles and had said, "All right. Very good. A nice idea!" The English had frequently vexed the Mohammedans in the Far East a little. In short, the girl wanted to bring a blond child to

340

him, to stay for a week. She had stressed the fact that the child was to be fed and treated well. She repeated the fact that the whole thing was a prank. The English family would pay a large sum of money, of which Mohammed Ali, after doing his duty by the little girl, would get a share. The little Chinese girl had said this would take place around the time of the festival on the Golden Mount. But then she hadn't been seen or heard of again. The gardener swore by the beard of the prophet that she had never come back. Anyway, if she had brought the child, he would have sent them away. After thinking it over he had decided that he didn't want to look after an infidel child in his house. His old mother had forbidden it.

"Does he know where Ah Bue is now?"

Ulla translated. The tears were coursing down her faded face. She couldn't bear to look at her junior boss.

"No," she said as softly as her shrill voice permitted. "He never saw Ah Bue again." Mohammed Ali had a little something to add. "He thinks it is possible that Ah Bue gave up the whole plan. She made a very childlike impression on him," Ulla explained.

"Come on, Ulla," said Petersen in a voice that was dead. "We don't want to keep my wife waiting any longer."

As he left the grounds he looked again at the shabby little garden house where he had hoped to find his daughter. The Malayan family had a quiet night ahead of them; their children were at home. Perhaps they had enemies, but not enemies as deadly as Petersen's. Martha and he had often been envied for their money and their luxurious home and the many parties they went to; yet tonight they were the poorest of the poor in the city on the Menam River.

On December 15, old Mr. Wong visited his friends in Bangkapi. Petersen was not at home. He had another meeting with Mr. Ketaki, who so far had found out nothing. The Indian private detective was indignant over how cleverly Ah Bue was managing to elude him. Because both Petersen and Mr. Ketaki were positive that Ah Bue had kidnapped the child and for some reason or other had not hidden her with the Malayans.

Old Mr. Wong brought two visitors with him: a tall Italian in the white robes of a priest, and a young Chinese. Old Mr. Wong had decided, after his last conversation with Petersen senior in the *sala*, to open up unofficial channels. Father Aldano was in charge of the Mission for Destitute Asiatic Boys which the brothers of the Order of the Salesians had founded in Bangkok and in several rural areas of Siam. "This is my friend, Father Aldano," old Mr. Wong said, "and this is Chia Yu-sen Joseph." He pointed to the young Chinese with the bright, intelligent eyes. This meant that the young man came from the Chia family, was called Yu-sen by them, and had been baptized Joseph. Joseph was Father Aldano's personal factotum. The father had found him as a child in a dive in Sampeng and had brought him up. Joseph knew every nook and cranny of Bangkok's Chinatown by experience. He would find Ah Bue and the child, he said, smiling broadly.

Martha rang for drinks. She looked ghastly. It was two days after the vain outing to Klong Toi. She hadn't told Uncle Winn anything about it. Dr. Johannsen had advised that the old man shouldn't have too much excitement. It was two weeks now since Tiny had vanished. Martha was trying desperately to hang onto a last shred of hope. In nine days it would be Christmas. Chubb was coming back from Sukhothai with Nang Siri for the occasion. He was to spend Christmas Eve with Charles and Doris Krüger, Dr. Johannsen, and Dr. Tyler at Great-uncle Winn's.

Father Aldano contemplated Martha thoughtfully. He was accustomed to repressed suffering in the faces of East and West. She should cry once, he thought.

Old Mr. Wong had risen. Martha accompanied him to his new American car. "Thank you, Mr. Wong," she murmured. "You are such a comfort to me."

Old Mr. Wong looked at Martha out of his weary, knowing, experienced eyes. "My best wishes are with you, Madame," he said softly. "You know we have a wise old saying which sometimes has helped me." Martha waited silently. "We cannot prevent the cranes of misfortune from flying over our heads, but we can prevent them from building nests in our hair."

"I don't like it," said Chia Joseph, as they waited on the veranda for Martha to return.

"What don't you like about it?" asked Father Aldano. Joseph often expressed himself generally so that it was difficult to know what he really meant.

"The servants of this house," said Chia Joseph. "They come creeping up from all sides when visitors come for "Master" or "Missie." What is Oldest Sister doing here, so near the veranda?" Joseph's sharp eyes had discovered Cheng hiding behind some bushes, obviously listening to what was going on on the veranda with the blue blossoms.

"That must be little Charlotte's *amah*," said father Aldano. "Old Mr. Wong told me that she adores the child. She may be wanting to hear if they have found any clues."

"No good," said Chia Joseph. It was his favorite expression and he used it indiscriminately.

"Signora," Father Aldano addressed Martha, who had just come back. "Could you give my young friend here a photograph of your daughter?"

Martha opened her bag and reluctantly took out one of her last pictures of Tiny. Chubb had taken it in the garden. It showed Tiny in a bathing suit, with her long light curls; Cheng, with Youngest Grandson at her feet, and the miniature dog, Tia, who had bounded into the picture at the last minute.

"The little dog was poisoned yesterday," said Martha, without giving it much thought. "We don't know by whom. My daughter loved Tia." She shook herself. How could she have spoken of Tiny in the past tense like that?

"That's strange," said Father Aldano, in his faultless English. "Have you any idea who might have done it?"

"No," said Martha. "We don't have any idea about anything, Reverend Father."

She couldn't look at the priest. At that moment the horror of what had happened overwhelmed her to such an extent that the tears rushed to her burning eyes. Joseph had risen tactfully and was dickering with his bicycle. Then suddenly he was standing in front of Cheng, who stepped back in surprise.

"Everybody in this house very sad. No good," was how he opened the conversation.

Cheng looked at him angrily. What did all these visitors want in Bangkapi? She picked up Youngest Grandson, who was rolling in the grass in front of her, and disappeared without a word into the kitchen house.

Chia Joseph looked intently at the picture of the child with the golden hair sitting so happily on the grass beside her Chinese mother. A very beautiful child, according to the picture, even without color. Joseph tried to imagine Tiny with black hair, short and smooth, like the Chinese children wore it. She would be as beautiful as the morning star, he thought. Chia Joseph was seventeen years old and very conscious of the importance of his position of honor in the mission. He looked up at the veranda. Martha Petersen was still talking to the "Christian Mandarin," as Chia Joseph liked to call his religious protector.

Father Aldano spoke and Martha listened. The isolation into which a human being is driven by unexpected misfortune, and that separates him from his best friends, was eased in the presence of this calm Italian with the lively dark eyes and the soothing voice. Suddenly the priest wasn't a stranger, although she had never come in contact with a Roman Catholic before. He was so simple and sensible. He came straight to the point—but the point was neither simple nor sensible. Martha was tortured by something she hadn't even told Hannes. In sleepless nights she now often wondered if she had given Tiny enough love. She had always found so much fault with the little girl. From the start Chubb had been the child of her heart. And now cool, reasonable Martha was in a state of dreadful doubt that made her sometimes reproach herself for sins of omission, at other times look upon that doubt as merely the result of shattered nerves. And before she knew how it had happened, she had told Father Aldano, hesitantly but firmly and logically, all about it. There was a pause. Martha wiped the sweat off her forehead with ice-cold hands. It was a terribly hot day, although it was the fifteenth of December. The tropics weren't governed by a northern calendar.

Father Aldano had grasped at once that the tall pale woman with the fine serious features was tortured by something that, like all burdens of the soul, was real yet unfounded. Under normal circumstances he felt she must be an excellent educator of the young. Martha's conclusion, which she found very hard to express, was that God was punishing her for not having loved her daughter enough.

"You are torturing yourself unnecessarily, Signora," said Father Aldano. He was smiling, a smile of great spiritual charm and experience. "When you tried to curb the vanity and exaggerated sensitivity of your little daughter, you were doing what every good educator and mother should do. What are 'sins of omission'?" He made a wide, very Italian gesture that seemed to include human frailty and God's mercy. "Do you seriously believe that God takes revenge and punishes in such a manner? You are much too sensible for that, Signora! You have just told me that you pray to God every night and beg for strength and patience. Beg Him tonight that you should not show less sense and understanding in misfortune than you have always exhibited in happier days."

Martha looked gratefully at the Italian priest in his white robes. He really had helped her.

"Love our Lord, Signora; don't fear Him," he said gently, and made a ceremonial little bow of farewell. "Life is wretched when one puts fear in the place of love. Fear is *ersatz*. Isn't that what you say in German—*ersatz*?"

Martha smiled. "I have always looked upon an *ersatz* life as something dreadful."

"I can believe that," said Father Aldano.

He drew a small book out of a pocket of his wide robe. "For a quiet hour, Signora," he said, softly. "A compatriot of yours wrote this little book in the fifteenth century. It is very practical when...hm...when one needs advice."

Martha opened the thin book. It was in English. On the yellowed title page were the words, *The Imitation of Christ*.

"How can I ever thank you enough?" Martha said. "I know Thomas à Kempis. He was my father's favorite."

Father Aldano smiled suddenly like a boy. "Then I would have liked to converse with the Signore. Oh Signora!" Again the wide all-embracing Italian gesture. "If we bookworms were ever to get together somewhere in this world, then we would forget place, time, and duty, wouldn't we? Unfortunately I must trouble you further, but not much." He walked to the edge of the veranda and gestured to his faithful and curious Joseph. "Please, I want you to tell Joseph everything that you know about this girl Ah Bue and her mother. Describe them as best you can, and don't forget their relatives, Signora! With the Chinese, family plays a decisive role."

Martha told everything she knew. Joseph asked respectfully in his pidgin English who had brought Chung and Ah Bue to the house. It occurred to Martha for the first time that Ah Chang, or his daughter, Cheng, had done that. But of course you couldn't hold them responsible for their relatives, she added hastily.

"Of course not," Father Aldano agreed.

"No good," Chia Joseph said, shaking his head. You

couldn't tell whether he was referring to Ah Chang's family or Martha's final remark.

After the priest and Chia Joseph had left, Martha felt a little hopeful for the first time.

That evening, while Martha was reading in the little book that her new Italian friend had given her, her daughter was sitting in a room with no echo. "When do I go home?" asked Tiny, in Siamese.

A woman whose face was completely obscured by bandages murmured that Tiny would still have to wait. "But don't cry! That would be no good. Then somebody would be *very* angry."

"I want to go back to my mother," the child said in a feeble voice, pushing away her bowl of rice and fish.

No echo. It was as if the child hadn't spoken. Tiny said again that she wanted to go home to her mother, this time a little louder.

"Your mother has gone away," murmured the woman with the bandaged face.

Charlotte Christiane Petersen got up from the mat on which she sat all day. "That isn't true!" she said in her Siamese jargon. "My mother wouldn't go away without me. You're lying!" She tried to run to the door.

What happened then wasn't nice. It hurt. And she wasn't allowed to cry. That made everything worse.

"I want to go home," she whispered stubbornly. "Mama, Papa, Chubb...Cheng...Tia..." She mumbled the names of all those she loved as if she wanted to cling to her identity in that way. It was very clever of the child. The woman with the bandaged face said nothing. The names were lost in the room with no echo.

"Chubb!" the child said again.

"What is your name?" asked the woman with the bandaged face.

"Charlotte Christi—"

It hurt a lot. This time she sobbed.

"What is your name?"

"Hsi-Jen," whispered the child. It meant Penetrating Scent.

"Will you remember that? Or things will go badly with you. You want to go back to your father soon, don't you?"

"Yes," Hsi-Jen said quickly. "When?"

But the woman with the bandaged face was gone.

"When?" the child asked of someone who had come into the room. "Tell me, *chieh-chieh!*"

But *chieh-chieh*, Older Sister, laughed. "You're very stupid," she said.

The child wept silently. "Don't cry, Hsi-Jen," said Older Sister. "Don't you love me?"

"Yes," said Tiny, "I love you very much. You dress me and cover me at night. You are very very good."

"And you are very, very beautiful," said Older Sister. "Don't you like yourself with your black hair?"

"I don't know. There's no mirror here. What will Mama say when I come home with black hair?"

"She is in Europe, Little Sister. Your father will like it. Will you tell him that Older Sister was good to you?"

"Of course. When do I go home?"

Older Sister laughed again. It wasn't a nice laugh. The child was too tired to notice it. "Mama...Papa ...Chubb..." she murmured.

The house with the room with no echo was half an hour by car from Bangkapi.

22

Spider and Silkworm

On December 18, three days after the visit of old Mr. Wong and his friends, Martha Petersen took a rickshaw to the Chinese quarter of Bangkok at 10:00 A.M. She had to search for her daughter. Instinct led her again and again to Yawarat Road, where the unknown woman with the bandaged face had fled from them. Cheng was waiting with Martha's parasol beside the rickshaw which she had fetched on Martha's orders. She was shaking her head and her eyes were red from crying or smoking.

"May I come with you, Mem?" she asked shyly. "Master say Mem not go alone. Bad, bad people looking for Mem."

"That's all right, Cheng, I'll go alone." Martha tried to be friendly and patient. Tiny's *amah* bowed and walked away slowly to the kitchen house. Martha watched her go. Cheng's whispered words and eternal warnings wearied her. Nobody was looking for her in Sampeng. Nonsense! she thought nervously.

The rickshaw coolie had asked twice where he should take the *Mem farang*. Martha shook herself. "Stop on the corner of New Road," she told him. She wanted to walk to Yawarat Road.

She tried to avoid attracting attention in any way, although she wasn't exactly unobtrusive, in her white dress and dark glasses and her parasol of Chinese parchment. But in the crowded Chinese quarter everybody seemed concerned only with himself. Of course if anyone wanted to follow Martha or run away from her, the city on the Menam River was a huge spider web in which the Petersen family had been trapped at the fair on the Golden Mount.

Martha let the rickshaw coolie go on the corner of Yawarat and put an end to his yelling for more money by simply turning her back on him and walking away. In her bag, which she pressed close, there was a letter from Chubb. His letters always gave her pleasure. He didn't plague her with questions. He knew he would receive a telegram the moment his sister was found. In six days he was returning to Bangkok with Nang Siri. Chubb was a little afraid of his parents since they were so unhappy. Misery changes family relationships unpredictably. There had been something forced about the conversations at home before he had left with Nang Siri. It was as if one were just making noise to drown out the tortuous stillness at meals. He had kept out of his father's way. In the months since his arrival, he hadn't really been able to establish close ties to Petersen, and now they might be separated again for years. Still, Martha was longing for Chubb's departure. He had to live a normal life again, insofar as one could call life with Hinrich and Lisa Petersen normal. But she had no choice. It consoled her that the boy would be with Dr. Johannsen until they reached Hamburg.

Lost in thought, Martha reached Yawarat Road. A few steps away from her a Chinese reader and writer of letters had set up his little table on the pavement. There were plenty of mothers in Sampeng who wanted to write letters to their sons or grandsons in far-off China or have them read to them. Besides, Mr. Lin sold all sorts of secrets and information. Nowadays one couldn't rely in business matters on family connections alone.

Mr. Lin set up his little table under his parchment sunshade in front of a coolie dive; a ragged young Chinese was just coming out of it. He walked up to Mr. Lin and whispered something to him. Martha was about to walk away when suddenly the tattered Chinese laughed. Martha thought she knew that laugh. She took off her dark glasses so as to see better in the bright sunlight, and uttered a soft cry. It was Chia Joseph, who three days before had visited her with Father Aldano and taken a picture of Tiny with him. But he turned his back on her so resolutely that she understood. At the same time he gave her a sign with his right hand. Was she to wait? Or disappear? At any rate she had the strong feeling that she was not to betray the fact that she knew Chia Joseph. She stepped in front of a shop with mirrors, like dozens of others on Yawarat Road. The Chinese passion for mirrors was especially noticeable here. In a wall mirror she watched the course of the conversation. It lasted a long time, like any Chinese transaction. Finally Chia Joseph took an envelope out of his pocket which surely contained money, because Mr. Lin stretched his neck, spread his hands complacently across his naked chest as if pleased, and wrote something down for Chia Joseph, which the latter stuck in his ragged trouser pocket. Then Chia Joseph put on a pith helmet, tilting it low over his face, and sauntered slowly into a side street opposite. There he got into a rickshaw and didn't turn around to look at Martha again.

She got into a rickshaw and told the coolie, "Follow that rickshaw! Don't lose it!"

They drove one behind the other through narrow streets and alleyways Martha had never seen. Like other foreigners she knew Yawarat Road with its Chinese theatres and restaurants and little open shops. But the secret life of the Chinese only began behind Yawarat. At last they landed at Rayawongse Road, which led from New Road down to the river.

Chia Joseph got out of his rickshaw and strolled to a warehouse by the river. Martha followed him. She felt dizzy. The heat was unbearable. Or was it the feeling that she was closer to her goal? She looked around to see if anyone was following her.

In the warehouse Chia Joseph told her that Ah Bue was hiding from the police somewhere near here, probably with the child, in Mr. Lin's opinion.

"Where?" whispered Martha. Again she could feel the strange paralysis of her vocal cords that had attacked her first that night on the Golden Mount.

"In Sapan Han," whispered Chia Joseph. "Does Mem know?" Martha shook her head helplessly at the young Chinese who was looking at her sharply. "Not far from Rayawongse Road. I go first, Mem follow slowly."

Martha nodded. "Can Mem still go?" Chia Joseph asked, looking worried.

"Certainly," Martha replied.

"Will Mem recognize Ah Bue?"

Martha nodded again.

The strange pair moved off. Luckily Chia Joseph found two rickshaws that would take them to Sapan Han at a proper distance from each other. Martha didn't look around as they drove off and therefore didn't see that a third rickshaw was following them. In it sat a woman dressed in black, wearing a conical bamboo hat. Her face was bandaged. It was the spider that had woven its deadly web around the Petersen family. The spider itself was not in the net. The spider was outside, drawing the web tight. Cheng had been right: Martha was in danger. Only Martha? With every step Tiny was in far greater danger.

Sapan Han was an old, colorful bridge street with a roof over it. Underneath it flowed the canal Klong Ongang in the water of which fleeting shadows were mirrored. On this strangest of all Bangkok streets there were innumerable tiny shops filled to overflowing with curios and produce. Chia Joseph stopped in front of a stall with fresh fruit and baked Chinese fruitcakes. Martha stopped in front of the shop next to it where Chinese brocade pillow cases with dragon and bird patterns were sold. "*Tau rai?...*How much?" she asked. A foreigner in Sapan Han was nothing exceptional.

Meanwhile Chia Joseph was talking to the baker, a dried-up old Chinese woman who every now and then walked into the back of her store, scolding Ah Bue and another young Chinese girl who were preparing fruit tarts. So this was where she had hidden from the police! Sapan Han hid the secret that had brought the Petersen family to the verge of despair. "Hmm," mumbled the old Chinese woman, and hid Chia Joseph's money in a carved box with a shaky lock. "I'll send the girl out. None of this is my fault, young brother. I didn't know the police were looking for her. Lies...nothing but lies ...that's what they dish up nowadays! But like the fish in the pot, the lie jumps to the surface!" The old woman paused for a moment and stared at Chia Joseph. She looked frightened. "Is she really the daughter of the thief Chung?"

"The stranger knows her," said Chia Joseph, pointing Martha out discreetly. "We have to be very careful because of the child."

"Because of what child?" asked the old woman.

"Never mind," said Chia Joseph, who had been watching her with his observant eyes. "Just wait a minute. I'm going to get somebody."

Two minutes later a sturdy young Chinese stood with Chia Joseph in front of the shop with the fruit-cakes. He was perfectly willing, for a certain sum, to grab anybody and take him or her to the nearest police station with Chia Joseph.

"Bue, Bue!" cried the old woman. "Come help me sell. Many customers!"

Ah Bue appeared obediently and looked around shyly. Martha had withdrawn into the shadow of a flower stall so that Ah Bue wouldn't notice her. Chia Joseph let Ah Bue wrap up two cakes in a clean plane tree leaf. He laughed. It was a sign for Martha who promptly appeared and said in English, "That's her! Quick! Quick!"

At once Ah Bue was caught between Chia Joseph and his helper. She screamed like a captured animal, and with her free right arm threw a big knife from the table at Martha. Insane hatred flashed in her slanting dark eyes.

Martha felt a stabbing pain in her right arm and saw that drops of blood were soiling her white dress. She walked up to the screaming girl and whispered to Chia Joseph, "Ask her where my child is."

"I don't know," Ah Bue replied.

Chia Joseph struck her in the face, hard. "You'll know when you get to the police, you toad!" he yelled. He ran into the shop, knocking over the table with the cakes, and looked for the child with the golden hair. She wasn't there!

"Mem is hurt! Mem go home quick!" he said, waving to a rickshaw standing at the end of the bridge street. A huge crowd had assembled by the time Martha and Chia Joseph got into the rickshaw. In a second rickshaw Chia Joseph's helper held Ah Bue on his lap like a doll. He had meanwhile bound her hands and feet. "Then we go to nearest police station." Chia Joseph told the coolie.

With her last ounce of strength Martha managed to sit up straight. She said, and it sounded far away to her, "She'll confess. We must go straight to the police station."

A little later Martha drove back to Bangkapi with Chia Joseph. Petersen was at home and had waited lunch. "Cheng!" he cried, as he lifted his almost fainting, bleeding wife out of the rickshaw. "Where are you? Mem is hurt!"

Oldest Grandson came running, trembling. "Mother is at market. Grandfather send her for duck," he stammered.

"Chia Joseph, drive at once to Major Nayadharn! Tell him that you have found Ah Bue! Hurry! Hurry!" Petersen said in Chinese. "Our child is in danger!"

While Chia Joseph tore off in the rickshaw, Petersen carried Martha to the veranda with the help of Ah Chang and Oldest Grandson. Martha had opened her eyes. She looked at Petersen, her eyes wide and unblinking. "I...I haven't...found her," she murmured. "I... I think she is..." but she couldn't say the word.

Just then Cheng came running and Ah Chang scolded her. "No duck!" she cried. "Cheng run all the way to Talat Noi..." then she was silent. Oldest Grandson must have told her that Missie was lying on the veranda, bleeding. Cheng rushed to the veranda, wailing.

"Cheng," said Petersen, strangely calm. "Take a rickshaw and drive to Dr. Johannsen. If he isn't home, ask where he is and go there. Mem is ill. Hurry!"

"Yes sir," Cheng whispered. "Cheng is quickest in house."

The rickshaw coolies had a big day on that December eighteenth.

When Ah Bue was finally brought before Major Karawek Nayadharn two hours later in his private office at police headquarters, she had cried so much that her eyes were virtually swollen shut. "Sit down, Ah Bue," said the major, surprisingly gently. "We don't want to punish you. Nai Petersen will pay you a big reward if you tell us where you've taken the child."

"I don't know, sir," Ah Bue groaned. She was trembling from head to toe.

"How would you like to be locked up in a cellar with a lot of rats?" asked the major, even more gently.

Ah Bue jumped up from the floor, her eyes wide with fright. "No!" she screamed. "No rats!"

Major Nayadharn smiled, satisfied. Ah Bue was still a child. One could intimidate her by simple means. The major had other methods at his disposal but he didn't like to use them where they didn't seem necessary. He loved flowers and young things...

"So, Ah Bue," he said amiably, "now confess. We are all alone, nobody can disturb us. Has your mother had anything to do with the kidnapping?"

"My...mother?" Ah Bue's heart was beating like a hammer.

"I'm sure you know she escaped from prison, don't you?" said Major Nayadharn, adopting a chatty, familiar tone. "Is she hiding in Sapan Han? Are all of you baking fruitcakes now and throwing knives around?"

"My mother isn't in Sapan Han," whispered Ah Bue. "I haven't heard about her running away."

She was so excited that she kept mixing Chinese words with her Siamese.

"So let's begin," said Major Nayadharn, in a completely different tone now. His eyes had narrowed to slits. He sat enthroned in the bare room like a calm but inexorable god. Under the wooden floor you could hear scraping noises. "Rats," said the god, and called over a young man in khaki uniform.

"Write down everything," he told the young officer. "The truth and the lies." Major Nayadharn was of the opinion that a prisoner's lies also revealed the truth.

Two hours later the major took off for the Petersen's house in Bangkapi. After interrogating Ah Bue, he had gone to Sapan Han again with two police officers and had had a talk with the fruitcake woman. She had given him the long cake knife. Ah Bue's finger prints were on it but there were no traces of blood.

"Ah Bue did not throw the knife that wounded your wife in the arm," the major told Petersen. "We have determined that without any doubt. Chia Joseph and his helper had just grabbed Ah Bue firmly by her left arm. Of course she wanted to throw the knife at Madame, but actually someone else threw the knife that wounded Madame, and that knife had disappeared. We have searched the whole area."

"And what about my daughter?" asked Petersen.

He was wearing dark glasses, yet the last rays of the setting sun streaming across the veranda into the reception room hurt him. Martha was lying upstairs, her wound bandaged. Father Aldano was with her. He hadn't been able to speak to Chia Joseph yet. He was shattered by the latest turn of events, but with Martha displayed only serenity and a patience born of resignation.

"Your daughter?" Major Nayadharn said darkly. "We must go on looking for her. We are of the opinion that Ah Bue did not kidnap her. There was the intention, sir," he said quickly, raising his delicate Siamese hand in affirmation, "but it was evidently not carried out. We just confronted her with the gardener, Mohammed Ali, from Klong Toi. We had told him to say that she *had* brought the child to him. Her indignation was violent and sincere. I can tell things like that. Of course Ah Bue remains under arrest until your daughter is...found."

Petersen didn't seem to be listening any more. *Who* had thrown the knife at Martha? The old woman in the cake shop, who had been so self-righteous about it all? Someone else? Perhaps the woman with the bandaged face whom Martha hadn't seen again? "Have you found any trace at all of her, Major?" asked Petersen. He was dead tired. But one dared not fall asleep...

"Unfortunately not. We have stationed an officer near Yawarat Road. By the way, why does everyone believe so implicitly that the person in question is a woman? As a foreigner, your wife may not have an eye for whether a man or a woman is hidden under a smock or wide trousers. There are so many thin Chinese women who are built almost like men, and fat men who in a woman's smock and wide trousers can't be told apart from a fat Chinese woman...at least not at first sight, and certainly not in the state of excitement Madame Petersen was in at the Golden Mount, and that morning at Yawarat Road. Unfortunately our man hasn't yet been able to find this person with the bandaged face."

Major Nayadharn couldn't know that the police officer had stopped for an iced lemonade in a coffee house and therefore hadn't seen a person with a bandaged face and a conical bamboo hat that hid the shape of the head get into a rickshaw and follow Martha and Chia Joseph to Sapan Han.

"We asked in the leper colony if perhaps one of the lepers had run away. That might explain the bandages. *If* this person had anything to do with the case at all."

What on earth could a leper want with Tiny? The thought made Petersen shudder. But he controlled himself. Major Nayadharn was doing his best.

"Have you questioned Ah Bue's mother again?"

"Of course, sir. We told Ah Bue at first that Chung had escaped. I thought we might find out something more that way. No, we've got to try something quite different. I want to question your servants again. They seem terribly excited over Ah Bue's arrest. How is Madame Petersen?"

"Fortunately it's only a flesh wound. Dr. Johannsen is satisfied."

"Madame must not go out alone again, sir. You must make it clear to her that she is being followed the minute she leaves the house. That knife wasn't meant for Madame's arm. If she hadn't happened to move just at that moment..." The major paused. The great Buddha had preserved the foreign lady from the worst.

"I've spoken to my wife about it, Major. She understands, naturally. But..."

"I know, sir," the major said softly. His otherwise cheerful face was serious and filled with compassion. "By the way," he said after a pause, "we are keeping your chauffeur and his sons under observation. Right now he is in Dhonburi."

"So far away?" Petersen was astonished.

"Yes," said the major. "So far away. Wouldn't you say that it was high time somebody turned up to claim the reward?"

At about the same time old Petersen was sitting in his *sala*. He was expecting a visitor. Since the catastrophe he had become more silent than ever. What could he talk to Hannes about? The poor man was so distraught he had practically given away an order of typewriters the other day, not that it mattered. But the old man had little to say to Martha too. He visited her faithfully every day and sat silently on the veranda with her. He knew what she was going through. If anything like this had happened to his Linchen...

As usual when he wanted to be alone, Mae Wat came waddling up to the *sala*. She was supposed to be baking a rice cake for old Mr. Wong who was to arrive in half an hour. Old Mr. Wong had "so many ticals and gold bowls" at home, you could tell he was Chinese. She always did her very best when she saw him getting out of his big American car, modestly and unobtrusively. Now she knelt before her master and declared that she had very good news for him. Good news? thought old Petersen. Was there any such thing anymore in Rong Muang and Bangkapi?

It turned out that Mae Wat had discovered a bees' nest in the garden. According to Siamese folk superstition, the visit of bees brought good fortune. That was what she wanted to tell the master.

If the master was disappointed, he didn't show it. The old Siamese woman had remained faithful to him without once asking for a raise for staying on, although no one was "happy" in the big empty palace. "Here are five ticals for the good news," the old man said. "But now we don't run off to gamble. Big Mr. Wong is coming to tea."

"Mae Wat never run away when master expect guests," Mae Wat replied, looking virtuous. This wasn't true, but Mae Wat seemed to believe it. "Mae Wat is not *khon rot* Bangkapi!"

Khon rot Bangkapi was Hannes Petersen's chauffeur Phom, who at the moment was in Dhonburi with his sons, Rat and Pig. Petersen had refused to engage a new chauffeur at this time. The police were against it too. The family's unkown enemies could all too easily smuggle in one of their accomplices.

"Phom here, Master," said Mae Wat. It seemed to have just occurred to her. "Rat and Pig with him."

Old Mr. Petersen leapt out of his chair. "And you only tell me that *now?*" he cried. "Have you gone crazy? That's important, you old fool!"

Mae Wat stepped back, frightened. Master Pe-ter-senn didn't mean to be angry but he was roaring worse than the tiger who had broken into Mae Wat's village one night when she had been a child.

"Phom is afraid," she whispered. "He has brought fruit and coconut cake for Mem Bangkapi. On big lacquer tray."

"Send him to me at once!" Petersen ordered. He found it strange that Phom should suddenly turn up again. Did he know something? Had his gambling debts grown over his head? Or had he come for the reward?

Old Petersen forced himself to calm down. He was already sorry that he had yelled at Mae Wat. Vehemence got you nowhere with the Siamese. It caused them to collapse like a house of cards, and there was nothing more to be got out of them if they were sullen or frightened. So Petersen senior told Phom that he wished him happiness and health and was very pleased to see him in Rong Muang. If he hadn't known Hannes' chauffeur so well he would never have recognized this miserable, tattered figure dressed in ragged pants, a dirty plaid bath towel around his hips, as Hannes' neat chauffeur in his white uniform and cap.

"Haven't things been going well for you?" asked old Petersen.

Phom shook his head and looked around him fearfully. "Phom must go again right away," he mumbled. "Only ask if blond child is found."

The old gentleman took ten ticals out of his pocket and laid them on the wicker table in front of him. "These are for Phom," he said, in a friendly voice, "if he tells me everything he knows."

Phom was silent. Greed flared up in his dark eyes. "Rat and Pig very hungry," he said somberly. "No rice, no fish."

"Rat and Pig will get rice from Mae Wat," old Petersen said patiently. "Don't be afraid, Phom. Everybody knows how good and honest you are. Master Bangkapi is *very* sad that you don't want to drive him and Mem."

"Bad house...very bad house in Bangkapi," mumbled Phom. "Phom very afraid. Robbers and murderers...woman with bandaged face creep around..."

Old Mr. Petersen jumped up and grabbed the stocky little Siamese. "What are you talking about? Woman with bandaged face? Who? Where? Do you know her?"

Phom let out a high-pitched scream. "Phom know nothing," he whispered, his face grey. "Phom afraid ...Phom go back to Dhonburi...quick...quick..."

Just then a big American car drove up. Old Mr. Wong, who had brought his friend a small ceramic bowl of great value, put it down carefully. "Run to the *sala*," he told his chauffeur. "Hurry! Old Master can't hold off the Siamese!"

An unbelievable scene was taking place in the *sala*. In his deadly fear Phom had begun pummeling the old gentleman with his fists and feet according to the Siamese art of boxing. Old Petersen had slipped out of his hands like a fish and was about to kick him, when old Mr. Wong's chauffeur grabbed Phom. He was a big, strong North Chinese and nobody could get easily out of his iron grip.

Nothing came of the tea. They drove Phom to Major Nayadharn, Phom whimpering the whole time and apologizing to old Petersen for his rudeness, and howling that he didn't want to be murdered like the blond child from Bangkapi. An hour-long interrogation followed.

Next day, at the same afternoon hour, old Mr. Wong had his tea with Petersen senior in the *sala*. Chia Joseph had come with him and after a long talk had gone back to Yawarat Road. One couldn't give up the search for the person with the bandaged face, who was evidently not merely a figment of Martha's imagination. Calmed down by Major Nayadharn's friendly encouragement, Phom had told all he knew. It was plenty, but not enough for taking action. Yes, he had twice seen a person in black Chinese trousers and a loose black jacket in Bangkapi. *Not* on the Petersens' grounds—Phom stuck to that—but near them. The person had a bandaged face and was carrying a basket of food on her arm. She had jumped into a rickshaw when she had seen Phom. He had run out on the street by chance because Rat and Pig, in spite of instructions forbidding them to do so, had run out to see a Chinese funeral nearby. This was a few days after the festival on the Golden Mount.

Then Phom had seen the person once more, and this time something had happened that had made him flee to his married sister in Dhonburi. Phom had gone in his best *phanung* with his sons to a temple not far from the Petersen property. The three were carrying baskets of sacrificial gifts. They intended to give them to the Brothers of the Yellow Robe for the altar, so that the Enlightened One might return the child with the golden hair to its parents.

When Phom and his sons had reached the corner and were about to get into a rickshaw, the person with the bandaged face had appeared and also got into a rickshaw. Again she was carrying a basket with food on her arm. Phom had of course heard long ago about the bandaged woman whom his Mem in Bangkapi had seen in Sampeng. He had whispered something to his rickshaw coolie in Siamese, but at that moment the person had grabbed him from behind with an iron grip and thrown him face down on the ground. And before the slow-witted Siamese had recovered from the shock, the person had got into a rickshaw and driven off. A wild chase had followed. Phom had screamed and pointed with his finger in three different directions, but the person—the grip was a man's, Phom maintained, looking fearfully around him—the person was gone.

"Why didn't you inform us of this at once? Or at least tell Nai Petersen?" asked the major, hardly able to conceal his despair. Everything was going wrong in this case!

"I didn't want the person with the bandages to cut my throat next time," said Phom, not without justification.

He was detained at first, but he was lucky. There was no reason to doubt his story. All Petersen's servants corroborated the fact that he and his sons had left the house with sacrificial gifts. Cheng testified that Phom had come back with a bruised face—he had apparently fallen—and his screaming children, without having visited the temple. Phom was in a state of shock. Next day he had disappeared. His sister in Dhonburi, who was interrogated separately, confirmed, without evidencing any fear, the fact that her brother had fled to her because he feared for his life and that of his children. The person who had kidnapped the child knew him and was pursuing him.

"I have wired my wife that she should stay in Sukhothai with my grand-nephew," Petersen senior told old Mr. Wong. "After these recent developments it is better if our boy doesn't turn up in Bangkapi right now."

"That is very wise of you, dear friend," replied old

Mr. Wong. He was sitting in the *sala* in a white tropical suit of the finest silk, spreading an atmosphere of calm and spiritual well-being. His friendship was priceless to Petersen senior. Old Mr. Wong asked for nothing and expected nothing. He stood on his Tao mountain top and looked down with mildly ironic compassion at the foolish and sinful world. He helped Petersen simply by being there.

"We don't know what to do next," mumbled Wilhelm Christian Petersen, "and it looks as if the Siamese police feel the same way."

"Major Nayadharn is very efficient," said old Mr. Wong. "But a police officer has his limitations. To be sure, he must see with his eyes and hear with his ears, but for this crime that is not enough. One must concentrate, as our Chinese mystics did—hear and see with the *spirit*. Only then will we know who has stolen the child, and why."

"Do you know?" old Petersen asked straight out.

Old Mr. Wong looked at his honorable friend with compassionate irony. "I am trying," he said. "I am training Chia Joseph, with the permission of my good friend Father Aldano. The good major has done nothing but catch silkworms until now. They have spun themselves into their own cocoons of fear or greed and are prisoners. The spider, as one says in my country, spins her web and stays outside. She is therefore free to do good or evil." Old Mr. Wong laid his fine ivory hand on his old German friend's big strong hand with the blue veins. "I know what you are thinking," he said, smiling. "Old Wong is a chatterbox and a bookworm. But let me think. Enough people are acting."

Wilhelm Christian Petersen was disarmed. "We don't have a better friend in the world," he said simply, his high forehead beaded with sweat. "But dear Mr. Wong, it is very hard to sit here and think when quite possibly our child..." he hesitated, then he went on more calmly.

"Everything we have tried has failed. What's to happen next?"

"Right now, nothing. The spider must be sure that we have given up. I advised Major . . . but that is beside the point. You know, dear friend, what victory consists of?"

Wilhelm Christian Petersen stared at his friend silently.

"Out of many little defeats," said old Mr. Wong.

He rose, bowed with exquisite politeness, and went home to think in absolute silence about this complicated case.

23

Christmas In The Tropics

On December 21, Tiny's *amah* came back from the market screaming. Cheng's face was bleeding, and in her fright she had dropped her basket with the chickens and beans. She staggered to where Martha was sitting on the veranda with old Mrs. Wong, who was visiting Martha with her little servant. Martha was still wearing a light bandage on her arm. Otherwise she was well again, and she had promised Hannes not to look for her child alone anymore.

Cheng reported, whimpering, that a person with a bandaged face had been standing beside her at the market. When Cheng had tried to grab the person, he or she had stabbed her in the face and fled. Cheng had no chickens and beans. This seemed to upset her more than the assault.

"Don't cry, Cheng," Martha said gently. "We'll eat in the city. Please call the chauffeur."

After refusing to do so for a long time, Petersen had finally gratefully accepted old Mr. Wong's offer to use his private chauffeur during this period of crisis. Martha still couldn't drive because of the injury to her arm, and Petersen's eyes were still painful, a nervous disorder, he was sure, which made him feel insecure when driving. And they needed a chauffeur now more than ever, not only because of the intense tropical heat which made walking impossible but because as soon as anything new happened, time was of the essence.

"Ping-erh," Mrs. Wong told her little servant. "Mrs. Petersen and I are going to the police with Cheng. Stay here until we come back."

The pretty young Chinese girl, half-servant, half-daughter, nodded.

During the ride Martha and Mrs. Wong spoke English. "I can't understand," Martha said, "why Ah Bue hid from the police when she had nothing to do with the kidnapping."

"She wanted to escape from her mother." Mrs. Wong gave Martha a warning look. "Don't mention any names, please, Madame. Your servant is listening to us."

"She is faithful," said Martha, "and adores our daughter." She felt very sorry for Cheng although actually she didn't like her.

"The major wants to let the little one go," said Mrs. Wong.

Martha was surprised. Ah Bue, who had planned the kidnapping, was now to be let go? The old lady explained that Ah Bue had certainly formulated the plan but hadn't carried it out because her mother's arrest had frightened her. Her only thought after Chung's arrest had been to disappear. She had made a comprehensive confession. The Wong family, who knew only too well the Chinese peculiarity of giving up carefully thought out plans at the last minute, felt that Ah Bue's justification for her behavior was plausible. Major Nayadharn had been to see Mr. Wong and had discussed the case with him. Mr. Wong had taken the opportunity to give the major some advice, which he had not discussed with old Mr. Petersen. He suspected someone whom nobody in their wildest dreams had thought of until now. He had admitted his suspicion only to the major and begged him, for the sake of the child, to be as cautious as possible. In his opinion the child was alive and the kidnapper was interested above all else in her safety. Major Nayadharn had never been as surprised in his life as he was that day in the private office of old Mr. Wong. "Are you sure this is not a figment of your imagination?" he had asked.

"I have thought about it for a long time," Mr. Wong had replied. "The case is concerned only secondarily with money. Otherwise the child would have been returned long ago. Something quite different must be involved."

Major Nayadharn had nothing to say to that. He couldn't imagine what Mr. Wong, whom he had known and respected for years, could possibly be driving at. At last the old man explained that this had to be a case of an *idée fixe*, an aberration of the emotions, and in this connection he had told the major whom he suspected, and why. Only Major Nayadharn, Father Aldano, Chia Joseph, and old Mr. Wong himself were now on the trail of this fantastic clue.

At police headquarters, Cheng was as stubborn as a mule. Not until Major Nayadharn threatened to hold her for her own protection, would she repeat her story with typical dramatic embellishments. In the end one got the impression that a nine-headed dragon had attacked Cheng with a mighty sword. Cheng pointed to the plaster with which Martha had covered the wound after disinfecting it, much to Cheng's disgust.

The major left Cheng in the charge of a young police officer and went to Martha and old Mrs. Wong, who were sitting out in the hall on a wooden bench, watching the little pickpockets who were chatting, smoking, and playing cards behind bars. It seemed to be a very cheerful jail. Phom and Ah Bue were not among the prisoners.

"Your *amah* shouldn't go out alone any more either," said Major Nayadharn. "Because of her loyalty to your family, she is in serious danger. It would be a good thing if some little Chinese girl went with her to the market. Has she any daughters or nieces?"

"Only Ah Bue," said Martha. "But she has three sons. Couldn't one of them go with her?"

"A very good idea, Madame," said Major Nayadharn, frowning so sharply that one got the feeling he was looking for an even better solution. "I have spoken to her sons," he said. "They are so frightened and confused, they would only make their mother more nervous. How can one expect three mosquitoes to protect a hen?" He seemed to be addressing the opposite wall.

There was a pause. Everybody was thinking whom to suggest as a possible companion for Cheng. It had to be someone not yet infected by the general atmosphere of uncertainty and fear.

"How about our Ping-erh?" asked old Mrs. Wong. In a few words she explained to the major that Ping-erh was one of their most trusted servants. She would know exactly what to do if Cheng was attacked again. "Excellent! We thank you, Madame," said Major Najadharn, sounding relieved. "Would you be so good as to send the girl to me as soon as possible without it attracting any attention?" He hesitated, then he said slowly, "I don't want Cheng to know that she is being protected. She makes a very obstinate impression. Besides, she would feel she was losing face if a little girl was hired to watch her. It would be better therefore if Ping-erh continued to stay with you and followed Cheng to the market every morning, inconspicuously. Do you think she could do that?"

"Certainly," said old Mrs. Wong. "I shall send her to you immediately, Major."

On the way back to Bangkapi, Cheng didn't utter a word. She was still trembling with excitement and her face was very red. She had never been to a police station in her life and seemed to recall her encounter with the nine-headed dragon as much more pleasant.

"Lie down right away when we get home, Cheng,"

said Martha in her faulty Siamese. "Or you may get a fever."

"Cheng *not* lie down!" Cheng replied obstinately. "Cheng go look for blond child." Cheng's Siamese was on a par with Martha's.

"You are *not* going to look for blond child," Martha told her, her voice raised angrily. "I forbid you to leave the house, Cheng! Do you hear?"

Mrs. Wong laid a pacifying hand on Martha's arm. "I'll explain it to her, Mrs. Petersen. She is overwrought. Leave Cheng to me."

"Isn't it strange," Martha said in English, "that loyalty so often goes together with a tyrannical nature? An uncle of ours had a housekeeper from the country just like Cheng. Nobody could handle her, yet she would have gone through hell and high water for my uncle and his two daughters."

"It would be nice in this world," said old Mrs. Wong, "if virtuous people were also always agreeable."

Between December 23 and 24, when all the Europeans in Bangkok were preparing for Christmas Eve, little Charlotte Christiane Petersen's fate was decided. An underground activity took place in various houses and living quarters of the city at that time which led to the solution of the case. The child might not have been discovered, although Chia Joseph finally stood facing her. The picture in his pocket showed a child with *blond* hair. As a result, he, like all the others, was looking for a blond girl. Only at the last minute did it occur to him that for a few moments some time ago he had visualized the blond child with black hair, and had found her as beautiful as the morning star. That had been during his first visit to Martha, with Father Aldano. Only thus, through a fleeting flashback, did Chia Joseph discover the kidnapped child.

On December 23, Cheng went to the market as usual. She had hoped that Master and Mem would order a proper Christmas dinner in spite of everything, or at least spend Christmas with old Mr. Petersen. All Europeans in Bangkok celebrated Christmas with a big dinner in jolly company. But Master and Mem were staying home. They didn't care what Ah Chang cooked.

Little Ping-erh followed Cheng inconspicuously until, quite suddenly, she lost sight of her. This happened so fast that she never noticed that Cheng was no longer standing in front of the fish stall until it was too late. Before the Christmas festivities there were always so many servants around the fish stalls that dainty little Ping-erh, squashed between Chinese and Siamese cooks, couldn't stretch her little neck high enough. Her market basket had meanwhile been torn out of her hands. As she looked desperately around her for the woman she was supposed to watch—the major had told her to scream for the police in any emergency—she suddenly saw the mysterious figure that had evaded the Petersen family for weeks: the person with the bandaged face and the conical bamboo hat. Ping-erh's heart began to beat fast. Poor Cheng was in danger! What should she do?

While Ping-erh was trying to think, she felt a slight pressure on her left arm. A tall, very slender young Chinese woman, heavily rouged, was standing beside her. Her lacquer-black hair, with a fire flower stuck in it, looked like a wig; the traditional bangs on the forehead framed her face so shinily and smoothly. Ping-erh was about to say something when the Chinese woman put a note into her sweating little hand, and for a second put a forefinger as a warning against Ping-erh's mouth. How strange! Surreptitiously Ping-erh read what the young Chinese woman had written on the note:

"Follow me inconspicuously in a rickshaw at once. Pay no attention to the woman with the bandaged face.

I'll do that. Tear up this note and swallow it. Don't be afraid. I work for M.N."

That had to be Major Nayadharn. It was the sign the major had impressed upon her. His agents used only the letters M.N.

Again three rickshaws drove one behind the other, but this time the spider sat in the front one and two young Chinese women were following. Nobody thought of Cheng any more. Ping-erh thought she saw her chatting with a fisherwoman, but there were so many Chinese women who looked like Cheng, and anyway it didn't matter now.

The rickshaw with the bandaged unknown stopped in Yawarat Road where Martha had first noticed her. It had been no figment of Martha's imagination. She had been right from the start, but her half-knowledge had only done harm.

The rickshaw with the young, rouged Chinese woman stopped too. She had the slim slender hips of a boy, tiny breasts, long legs—an enchanting prostitute, or so it seemed. Ping-erh got out of her rickshaw and started to look in a shop window that displayed black teeth and little gold caps decorated with tiny colored stones. The slim Chinese woman came and stood beside her and said softly, "If I am not back in...let's say an hour, tell M.N."

Ping-erh nodded. Her throat felt tight, as if she were being throttled. Her childlike little forehead was beaded with big drops of sweat, but she remained standing obediently where she was and saw the tall, rouged agent disappear slowly behind the person with the bandaged face. The street life of Yawarat was teeming all around her. Ten minutes passed, thirty...no sign of the agent.

There! The figure with the bandaged face came out of an alley and looked all around cautiously. Just to be safe, Ping-erh took out her handkerchief and began to wipe her face; but the spider wasn't looking in her direction at all. She didn't even know that little Ping-erh existed. She got into a rickshaw. Her bamboo basket, which had been filled with food, was empty. Ping-erh, with her sharp eyes, could see that. Her first instinct was to follow the bandaged woman in a rickshaw; then she remembered that she had to wait for the young Chinese girl. Five minutes later a European woman came out of the narrow street that led to the obscure alleys of the Chinese quarter. Ping-erh was very astonished, because this European woman, who was wearing a shabby suit and a faded straw hat over her badly dyed hair, was being followed by the young agent, who whispered to Ping-erh, "Go home! Quickly! It's all settled." Then she jumped into a rickshaw and drove behind the European woman across New Road to Suriwongse Road.

The rickshaw with the European woman stopped in front of a house that badly needed a coat of paint. A big colorful sign hung between two trees with flaming hibiscus blossoms. A pair of dancing European peasants was painted on it. The Siamese rain had smeared the colors. Under the picture was printed: *Russian Restaurant. Russian Specialites around the clock. Bar. Dancing on Saturday Night.*

The agent stared at the words, or rather at the blurred picture. Strange costumes, she thought. Then she drove as quickly as possible to Major Nayadharn who was waiting for her impatiently. "Did you follow her?" he asked.

"Follow whom?" asked the Chinese woman, wiping the sweat off her face.

"The person with the bandaged face!"

The agent nodded. It was unbearably hot. "If you don't mind," she said, and with a quick motion took off her wig with the symmetrical bangs. "I followed her," said Chia Joseph. "I think it's the child you're looking for. Her hair is black now."

The major whistled. "Smart!" he murmured. "Very smart! Notice anything else?"

Chia Joseph, who had meanwhile removed his smock, nodded.

"She walked into the Russian Restaurant, you say?" the major asked, when Chia Joseph had finished. "Not young? Shabby? Face pitted by opium? But that's unbelievable! That's Madame Boulgakoff! She's been on our list for a long time. Illegal gambling—forbidden in Thailand," he added virtuously, probably meaning the games he didn't play. And then, "I thank you, Chia Joseph. You are a jewel!"

"Shall I tell Mr. Petersen in Bangkapi?" asked Chia Joseph as he was leaving.

"No!" cried the major. "Don't mention a word of any of this to anybody or we'll deliver a dead child into her mother's arms. If they panic, the child's lost! We don't want our foreigners to think that in Thailand children are kidnapped and murdered," he concluded solemnly. "It's not so much a question of the Petersen family now but of the reputation of our country!"

Chia Joseph nodded. He noticed that under certain circumstances the Siamese could be just as afraid of losing face as the Chinese.

"Drive to old Mr. Wong," said the major, "and ask him to go to Father Aldano just as soon as he can. I'll give you a police car."

"And the Russian woman?" asked Chia Joseph, the insatiable curiosity of the Chinese shining in his eyes.

"I'll take care of her this evening," said the major. "She won't escape us. Sleep well tonight, Chia Joseph. We'll need you again tomorrow."

In the afternoon of December 24, Martha, Petersen, and Uncle Winn were sitting on the veranda with the blue blossoms. Uncle Winn had given them his bit of news. He had received a telegram from Nang Siri. In two hours she would be arriving in Bangkok with Chubb. She wanted to be there to receive her guests for the Christmas festivities, and Chubb had been begging to go home for such a long time that his great-aunt had given in. "Tomorrow morning we'll go to see Chubb," said Petersen, and Martha nodded.

"Don't you want to come over this evening?" Uncle Winn begged for the last time. "All our old friends will be there."

"Dear Uncle Winn," Martha said softly, stroking his hand. Then, with effort, she went on. "You know how it is. Hannes and I would rather stay home."

She sighed. She thought again about the person with the bandaged face, this frightful, ruinous spirit. Petersen was looking at the blossoming wilderness of his garden. The bushes and flowers bloomed the year round. Never did Europeans miss their seasons so intensively as at Christmas time. I am tired, thought Petersen. It was grim beyond belief that one couldn't bring one's son home for Christmas without fearing for his life.

It was six o'clock in the afternoon when Uncle Winn left them. "Well, my loved ones . . ." He wanted to say that against all hope one had to hope on Christmas Eve, but he couldn't bring himself to say it. He bowed to Martha and said, "Do your best, lass," and stroked her hair. Martha fought back the tears and said, "Give my love to our boy and Nang Siri, and all the very best for you, Uncle Winn."

When he was gone, Martha went to the kitchen house. Ah Chang and daughter Cheng were busy preparing an unwanted meal, namely quantities of European and Chinese feast-day dishes. Martha and Hannes would have to bow to the loving tyranny of their faithful Chinese servants.

"I told you you could go out and celebrate with your friends, Ah Chang," Martha said gently.

The old cook looked at her, his eyes wide with astonishment. "Celebrate no good, Mem," he said, in his slow Siamese. "Ah Chang cook fine fine Christmas dinner. Mem eat. Master eat. Everybody happy."

"Thank you, Ah Chang," Martha's voice was a whisper. The faithful old cook was trying in his way to spread "happiness." One couldn't let him down.

7:00 P.M.

In the houses of the Europeans there was already a secret rustling of packages gift wrapped in fancy paper. In the German homes there were little palm trees decked out like Christmas trees. Doris Krüger had decorated a small tree at the last minute, when she had heard that Chubb was going to spend the evening at Uncle Winn's. "The boy's *got* to have a Christmas tree," she said. "Don't interfere! I know better about such things."

"Can you understand Hannes and Martha?" Charles Krüger said peevishly. "I don't think it's at all nice of them not to go to Christian's. We could cheer them up."

"Oh, for heaven's sake, Papa!" said Doris Krüger. "One just can't put oneself in their place!" Her usually cheery red face was distorted with unshed tears. Then she ran out, saying, "I must see to the dogs, and then we must dress. Mrs. Tyler and I want to help Nang Siri."

Charles Krüger was about to call after his wife that he would come later with the champagne from Saigon, but he didn't get around to it. He was staring at his big white gate where at that moment an old rattletrap of a Ford was driving in. A tall Italian, dressed in the white robes of a priest, sat in it beside a slim, rouged, Chinese girl. A very strange sight! Since when did Father Aldano go driving with flower girls? Charles Krüger knew Father Aldano very well. He had three of the Salesian's former pupils in his paper factory; the young men were good workers and went to mass at the mission house every Sunday.

What Father Aldano, who left his companion in the car, had to say to the Petersens' oldest friend was so unbelievable that Charles Krüger thought he must be dreaming. Father Aldano stayed for a quarter of an hour, during which time he instructed Charles Krüger in everything he had to do.

"Unfortunately I've given my chauffeur the night off," he said, "but never mind. I'll drive myself."

"God will reward you, Signore," said Father Aldano, and drove off.

"What's the matter, Charles? Has something happened? What did Father Aldano want?" Doris asked as she came back from the kennels.

"Listen, Mama. I'll be coming a little later. The boy can bring over the champagne."

"That won't do, Papa. Late for dinner? What on earth is the matter?"

"Nothing's the matter, Mama. It's just that Father Aldano has asked me to come over to the mission. Just for a minute. Lert is singing solo. I simply couldn't turn Father Aldano down."

"But you've given Lert the night off!"

"Good heavens, Mama! Don't act as if I'd never driven a car!"

"Well, be *very* careful, and don't drive too fast!" But Charles was already on his way to the garage.

Charles Krüger drove to the Russian Restaurant at a speed that would quite justifiably have horrified his wife. Madame Boulgakoff, Chia Joseph in his fancy dress, and a ragged rickshaw coolie were waiting for him. "Please ride behind us, sir," said the rickshaw coolie, and gestured to two uniformed policemen.

"You get into the car with Mr. Krüger and wait with him on the corner of Yawarat," Major Karawek Nayadharn ordered. In his ragged outfit you couldn't have told him apart from any Bangkok rickshaw coolie.

"Have you understood everything, Madame?" he asked the Russian woman. "One slip can cost the child's life. The establishment is up two flights of stairs, as you know. If there is any panic, they'll throw the child out of the window. I've seen it happen more than once."

"What do we do if Mr. Lu isn't home?" Madame Boulgakoff asked excitedly.

"Please, Madame, keep calm! I am with you. Six of my men are already in front of the house, dressed as Chinese. If Mr. Lu isn't home, we wait until he comes. We'll look for him first in the restaurant. You know him well, don't you?"

Madame Boulgakoff nodded. She knew her opium dealer better than anyone else in Bangkok. "You promised me not to use what I know against me later," she reminded the major.

"If you help us to save the child, I will never mention the word opium," Major Nayadharn assured her. He had smoked opium occasionally himself until crime in the big city had spoiled his appetite for it. Anyway, the smuggling of opium wasn't under his jurisdiction in the Criminal Investigation Department of Bangkok.

And while the rescue column slowly penetrated the Chinese quarter of Bangkok, while Chia Joseph trembled with fear for the first time in his life and Father Aldano prayed to the Almighty for help, while boys' voices singing the first Christmas hymns in the Salesian Mission could be heard on the still, hot tropical streets, old Mr. Wong sat in his private room and asked Ping-erh: "Did you see the woman with the bandaged face in Yawarat this morning?"

Ping-erh said no.

"Did you watch Cheng to see that nothing happened to her?"

"She was only at the market for a short while," said Ping-erh.

"That's good, little daughter," said old Mr. Wong, and closed his eyes.

Ping-erh left the room on tiptoe. Big Old Father seemed to be very very tired.

When Madame Boulgakoff had gone to Mr. Lu's house on December 20, he had not been at home. Only his daughter Brocade, the little girls, and the blind old woman had been in the sparsely furnished room. Madame Boulgakoff had not noticed that one of the little girls in Chinese trousers and a flowered smock had light skin and blue eyes. Madame Boulgakoff had come to the house with no echo to buy opium, not to look at little girls who were busy making beards for the theatre. Only later, when Major Nayadharn and Father Aldano had explained to her that the girl in question had to be the daughter of the Petersens, did she recall that something strange had happened: The black-haired child, whom Brocade in her shrill voice called Hsi-Jen, had tried to come up to her to say something. She had thought the child wanted to beg and had pushed her aside, but Brocade had dragged the little girl quickly into another room. Madame Boulgakoff had left the place without giving it another thought—a half-caste child, a nuisance like all the rest of them. The incident had sunk deep down into her opium-befogged consciousness until suddenly, in a flash, it had surfaced out of the dark of forgetfulness.

Madame Boulgakoff had at once declared herself willing to play her part in saving the child. Since Karin's death, something was nagging at her—one might call it conscience or remorse. It was too hot in Bangkok, Tatiana Boulgakoff had decided long ago, to put up with mosquito bites, let alone a guilty conscience. But Karin's ghastly end had torn her out of her lethargy. She had been the one who had started the intrigue with young Harms to keep Karin in Bangkok. Of course she couldn't have had any idea that the beautiful Eurasian would follow young Harms to Hong Kong instead of drowning her sorrow in vodka at the Russian Restaurant. We never know where our little jokes and games with fate will lead us. But then it had happened: Karin had written to her that her life was in danger; she had been murdered by Senhor Pinto, and with the pathos of the Russians, Madame Boulgakoff told herself that although she had certainly not thrown the knife, she *had* sharpened it. Now there was an opportunity—contrary to her customary inclinations—to do a good deed that would bring its reward, and she was *not* thinking, on this night of December 24, of Petersen's reward. Unexpectedly she had fallen from a paralysis of feeling into the Russian ecstasy of brotherly love. Father Aldano had played his part in keeping her in this mood.

Madame Boulgakoff walked slowly up the rickety stairs that led to the rooms occupied by Mr. Lu. Everything was just as it had been yesterday morning and on the afternoon of the Chinese Moon Festival. The blind old woman was cooking something that smelled of vinegar and decay on her little coal stove. The oil lantern, with its classical hill landscape, burned dimly. By its light, the little girls crouched, pasting beards according to Brocade's directions, for a big theatre on Yawarat Road that seemed light years away from the crooked alley in which Hsi-Jen was locked up "as a joke," and was waiting to be brought back to her parents. Why didn't Mama put an end to this joke?

Hsi-Jen ate very little of the delicacies that were brought to her by a person wearing a conical bamboo hat and many bandages on her face. She was so thin that you could count her ribs, but she was well. The vital self-preservation of the Petersens was keeping this fragile, spoiled, weepy child alive in strange but not sinister surroundings. Tiny was too inexperienced to sense anything sinister in Mr. Lu or Brocade, with her secretive smile, or even in the person with the bandaged face who sometimes took her in her arms and fed her. At moments like that Tiny cried with longing for Cheng and Youngest

Grandson and the dog, Tia. She didn't know that the little dog had been poisoned and that Second Grandson had buried him in a tropical grave.

All day long Hsi-Jen made theatre beards; in the evening Brocade took her for walks in dark alleys. Never did they go as far as Yawarat Road with all its lights. Hsi-Jen had no idea how close they were to Yawarat Road.

Brocade was very rarely nasty to her; only when she tried to talk to strangers who came to see Mr. Lu or to the blind grandmother. Brocade was often very affectionate; a strong motherly feeling was just as alive in this corrupt child as in Cheng or old Mrs. Wong. The bandaged person needn't have warned that not a hair of the child's head should be harmed. They had only dyed it. Mr. Lu, who had agreed to hide the child for an indefinite time, paid no attention to the little stray bird. It was a part of his agreement with the masked person that he would never try to rent the beautiful little girl for dark purposes. If he did it would mean exposure, deportation, or jail for Mr. Lu for opium smuggling. The unknown person who had suggested the kidnapping to him shortly before the festival on the Golden Mount had made that perfectly clear to him. Mr. Lu didn't know who the person was; nor had he known the child's name until the papers publicized it. He was far too indifferent and greedy for money to let a third of the reward elude him. The money had been promised to him on the day the child was to be picked up. The masked person couldn't say when that would be. She was doing this under instructions, she had explained. And so four weeks or a little longer had passed until old Mr. Wong had had the salutary idea to mistrust the obvious and to seek the motive for this act in the darkest recesses of the human soul. It was thanks to him that the spider was finally trapped.

"Where is your father?" Madame Boulgakoff asked

the thin little girl, Brocade, who when Madame Boulgakoff entered the room at once shoved the child with the
blue eyes through a wobbly door and locked it. Hsi-Jen
tried to talk to everybody. She was sly, Brocade thought
often. One didn't notice it at first because she cried such
a lot. Brocade had always been told that the strangers
with the pink skin were very stupid.

"What do you want from Mr. Lu?" Brocade asked
cautiously. Her father had impressed upon her a long
time ago to answer anyone who wanted to know where
he was with a question of her own.

Madame Boulgakoff called down the stairs, "Ch'ing-
chao! Come up!"

A young Chinese girl who bore the name of Fleeting Light swept into Mr. Lu's establishment. Chia
Joseph had put on even more rouge this time, and not
without artistic pleasure had woven strings of pearls
into his wig. He bowed without saying a word and
looked around him surreptitiously. Where was the child
with the blue eyes whom he had seen here yesterday,
when he had followed the person with the bandaged
face, and had entered this room after she had gone? He
saw the door Brocade was standing in front of and
moved a little closer to it. Brocade saw his move and
pressed closer to the door. It would have been simple for
Chia Joseph to push the child aside and open the rotten
door with one kick, but if the spider was with the child
behind that door, she was in danger of being killed in rage
or panic, or dragged even farther away, somewhere
where one couldn't follow. It had taken them three
weeks to discover *this* place.

He stared at Brocade without saying a word and
wondered what to do next. They had expected that the
kidnapped child would be squatting in a corner with the
other children, making theatre beards, as she had been
doing yesterday. If only he had taken her with him then!

But he hadn't known if somebody wouldn't have recognized him in his disguise, and above all he had seen the Russian woman, who today was helping them to rescue the child. Even in her shabby European clothes she was such a singular sight in this obscure Chinese alley that Chia Joseph had decided she must have kidnapped the child and was keeping it hidden here until the amount of the reward went even higher. What should they do now? Major Nayadharn was waiting downstairs. He was to come up if they called out: *Phon tra'wen...Police!* The major downstairs had to be very careful too, but ragged rickshaw coolies were lounging around all over the house and its entrance.

Madame Boulgakoff took the initiative. "Ch'ing-chao is a big attraction at the Black Star," she said in Chinese.

Brocade nodded and seemed relieved. The Black Star was a nightclub that occasionally borrowed little people from Mr. Lu and paid well. Besides, there was a room in the Black Star where they sold Big Smoke. Mr. Lu delivered opium regularly to this charming nightclub in darkest Sampeng.

"My father is downstairs in the restaurant. He has to go to the theatre after that." Brocade gave her information breathlessly. "Ask the waiter who limps where he is."

"It would be better if you went downstairs and got him," said Madame Boulgakoff. "One never knows who is listening in the restaurant."

Brocade had to think. The Russian woman was right, but her father had told her never, under any circumstances, to leave the room without taking the blue-eyed child. She had locked the child up, to be sure; still, she was much too afraid of Mr. Lu to disobey him. A Chinese daughter in a poor family is very much more obedient than a Chinese daughter in a rich family.

"I can't do that," said Brocade. She didn't know that with this she had destroyed her visitors' plans. They had wanted to get the child out of the next room while Brocade was away.

The blind old woman was crouched apathetically in front of her pots and pans, and the other children knew nothing. Besides, they would have preserved their Chinese indifference to anything that didn't concern them personally, even if they knew that the Russian woman and the rouged Chinese girl had abducted the child.

"Shall we come another time?" Chia Joseph asked in a high-pitched, unnatural voice, which however didn't attract Brocade's attention. "I don't have much time. In an hour things get going at the Black Star. There must be other children we can hire. And I know another place where we can get the Big Smoke. At—" he whispered. Actually he said to Madame Boulgakoff in pidgin English, "Keep absolutely quiet!"

Brocade hesitated. She had inherited her father's greed for money and it was stronger than her scruples. Papa Lu always gave his daughter and accomplices a percentage for clever business mediations.

"All right," she said. "I'll get my father."

But at that moment Mr. Lu walked into the room and with that overthrew Major Nayadharn's plans completely. Madame Boulgakoff suppressed a scream. She couldn't explain to herself *why* Mr. Lu wasn't in the restaurant at this early hour. He always was! And the Chinese were creatures of habit. But by a mysterious stroke of fate he was standing in the room, and a different rescue effort had to be thought out in moments. Chia Joseph was sweating under his wig. In spite of the infernal heat in the dimly lighted room, his hands were ice cold. It's all over, thought Madame Boulgakoff with her Russian fatalism. Her features relaxed. They always did when the dreadful thing finally happened.

Downstairs, on the corner of Yawarat Road, Charles

Krüger's big car was standing, and the old man was waiting, his heart beating fast. The poor little girl! In what condition would he bring her back to her parents? He stared at brilliantly lighted Yawarat Road. Here they went on selling, dancing, and working until dawn.

In the meantime Tiny's fate was being sealed. She was standing in the dark little room into which Brocade always shoved her when visitors came. She was used to it, and it didn't make her cry anymore. In this house she had learned for the first time in her life that tears made no impression on those around her. Tiny was going through something akin to the imprisonment thousands of Dutch children had experienced at the beginning of Japanese rule in Java: years and years behind barbed wire in filthy camps, eating dry rice, their fathers lost. Even so, in most cases their mothers were with them. But Tiny's mother, as Brocade had explained over and over again, had gone away. She still couldn't believe it. Mama had been the personification of safety and protection ever since the bombings in Hamburg.

"Mama," Tiny whispered behind the locked door. "Papa...Chubb...Cheng...Tia..."

Meanwhile Mr. Lu asked what the ladies wanted. In Madame Boulgakoff's case he knew, and asked her if she had money with her. At that moment there was a noise behind the locked door. A child's voice crying weakly, "Help! Rats! Help!"

The Russian woman leapt for the door; Chia Joseph yelled as loudly as he could, "Police! Police!" and what happened then happened so fast that none of those present could later remember the sequence of events. Chia Joseph recalled flinging himself on Mr. Lu, while Brocade, trembling, quickly joined the other children and picked up one of the beards. She had the feeling that one child among the other children would be less conspicuous. Chia Joseph had grabbed Mr. Lu, but not before he could prevent the latter from drawing a revolver out of his pocket and shooting in the direction of Madame Boulgakoff. The bullet grazed her and went through the door into the room where Tiny had suddenly discovered rats. The Russian woman, only half conscious, was pounding the door when Major Nayadharn smashed it open with his fist. Mr. Lu had meanwhile been handcuffed by two policemen. He gave his daughter an imploring look not to betray him. The blind old woman screamed shrilly: "Who is shooting here?" and began to whimper. "Save yourself, son. Save yourself and Brocade."

"Shut your mouth!" screamed Mr. Lu, with none of the respect of a son toward the matriarch of the Lu family.

Major Nayadharn and the Russian woman tore into the room to get the child. The room was empty. Only two rats were scampering around and disappeared lightning-fast under the big wardrobe in which Mr. Lu kept his beards and some of the costumes in which he dressed his little "daughters" for evenings at the Black Star.

"Where is the child?" asked Madame Boulgakoff, her voice failing her.

The Major meanwhile had opened the wardrobe and looked at everything in it fleetingly. Costumes and beards. Police officers, dressed in Chinese pants and sleeveless cotton shirts, were searching the workroom with the children. Mr. Lu was smiling, in spite of his handcuffs. Actually he wanted to cut his throat for having come up just then. They had been serving roast duck skin, which his mother loved, and he had brought a few small pieces, dripping with fat, up to her in a saucer. The saucer had dropped out of his hand when the rouged young Chinese woman had leapt on him, and her tight blouse had split. For a few seconds Mr. Lu had found himself staring at the chest of a young man. Then he had tried to shoot the Russian woman who was at the bottom of all this. So a paid police agent had done him in!

He'd find ways and means to render him harmless. First of all Brocade would visit him in jail. The important thing was that Brocade shouldn't be arrested. A smart girl, the way she sat there with the children, all fear erased from her face.

Meanwhile Major Nayadharn knocked on the walls of the small room. No secret exit! And if there had been a secret exit, the person with the bandaged face would have used it long ago to take the child somewhere else. The major's face was gray. His full lips were pressed tight. The senseless failure of a plan that had had every promise of success left his spirit drained and a cramplike pain in his stomach. He was very sensitive. Everything went to his stomach. "Let's go," he said dully. They were taking the blind old woman with them too. Madame Boulgakoff nodded. She had felt this was the end.

Mr. Lu and his mother were on the stairs already, with their police escort, when Brocade rose and left the silent children. Like a sleepwalker she approached Chia Joseph. Her black slanting eyes were open wide. "Hsi-Jen," she whispered. "Foreign little sister dying."

Chia Joseph bent down to the trembling child like an older brother. "Brocade doesn't want to go to prison. Brocade always very very good to Hsi-Jen. Love Hsi-Jen." She sobbed. Without her father and grandmother she was simply a frightened, abandoned child. She hid her face in Chia Joseph's hand.

"Where is foreign little sister?" asked Chia Joseph. "Everybody will give you presents. Quick... show older brother the hiding place."

Brocade stretched out an indescribably dirty hand in the direction of the empty room. "Secret door in hall," she whispered.

Chia Joseph said something to Major Nayadharn, who was still standing motionless beside the unconscious Russian woman. "Stay," Chia Joseph whispered in Siamese, which Brocade couldn't understand. She had never penetrated the Siamese world in Bangkok. "Secret door..."

Major Nayadharn came to life. Experience and instinct told him that the child would only trust a Chinese. Chia Joseph knew how to treat lost children. He came from a milieu much like Brocade's.

Brocade drew Chia Joseph silently to the wardrobe the major had searched so cursorily. She opened it and pushed the costumes and materials aside. Chia Joseph threw them on the worm-eaten floor. Then Brocade got into the wardrobe and pushed the back panel to one side a little. It moved easily because it had been set in loosely. Through this opening, Chia Joseph and Brocade entered a long dark passage that led to the stairwell of the house next door. In the middle of the crooked passage lay a little figure in black Chinese trousers and a dirty, high-necked, flower-embroidered smock. Soft silky black hair fell across the child's white forehead.

With a cry Brocade fell on the child's motionless body. "Hsi-Jen," she wailed. "Little Sister! You must live or woman with bandaged face kill Brocade!"

"Come, Little Sister," said Chia Joseph in a choked voice, and crossed himself. "We mustn't disturb foreign little sister in her sleep."

And so it came about that in the end it was Chia Joseph who carried little Charlotte Christiane Petersen through brightly lit Yawarat Road to old Mr. Krüger's car. It was 11:00 P.M. Two police officers were supporting the bleeding Russian woman, Major Nayadharn behind her. His police car was waiting.

"I think she's still alive," he told Charles Krüger, who was staring, beside himself, with wide open eyes, at the unconscious black-haired child in Chinese dress. "Quick! To the nearest pharmacy, sir!" And to the two police officers, "Take Madame to St. Louis Hospital!" At that moment Brocade pushed forward, close to Chia

Joseph, weeping piteously. "Take me with you, Older Brother!"

Major Nayadharn shoved the child into the police car and told his driver, "We'll take her to Father Aldano first."

It seemed ages until Tiny opened her eyes in the Chinese pharmacy. Dr. Ho, the apothecary, had given her an injection, and Charles Krüger had wiped her forehead with a stimulating liquid. At the same time he had prayed wildly to heaven: it couldn't be God's will to have him bring Martha a dead child! At last Tiny opened her eyes, but she closed them again right away. "Rats!" she whimpered. She seemed to be reliving how in her fright she had fled into the wardrobe she knew only too well, and with great presence of mind had pushed aside the back panel so that she could slip into the passage. Then, in her fear of the rats, she had shoved the back panel closed as tightly as she could. She had already fled from the apartment twice like this with Brocade, when the police had been on their way to pay a call on Mr. Lu. Brocade, with her sharp eyes, had always seen them coming and had at once disappeared with Hsi-Jen in the wardrobe. From the neighboring house they had been able to warn her father.

When Tiny opened her eyes again, a familiar face was bending over her. "Uncle Charles," she stammered. "I...I want to...go to...Mama in..." She wanted to say "Hamburg," but Charles Krüger had already lifted her into his car. "We're going to your Mama, lass," he murmured, so shaken he could scarcely speak. And so they drove to Bangkapi on Christmas Eve: Charles Krüger, Chia Joseph, and a delicate, but incredibly tough little girl.

After leaving Brocade with Father Aldano, Major Nayadharn drove to old Mr. Wong.

Petersen and Martha were still sitting on the dimly

lit veranda when Charles Krüger's car drove through the gate. "Hannes!" cried Martha. "Isn't that Krüger's car?"

But the car had already stopped and Charles Krüger was opening the door. A young Chinese in a torn smock got out of the back and came slowly up the steps with a child in his arms. "Hannes!" Martha cried again, but Chia Joseph had already laid the child in her arms. Charles Krüger had turned away and was busying himself with something on his car. "Mama," murmured Tiny, "Mama...Papa...Chubb..."

Suddenly there was life and feverish activity in the quiet house that for weeks had stood under the shadow of death. Petersen yelled for Ah Chang and Cheng. Martha was trying to take off Tiny's smock. Her tears fell on Tiny's face, her painfully thin body and her silken black hair.

"It was only a joke, Mama," Tiny whispered. "I am so—oo tired..."

She flung her emaciated arms around Martha's neck as if she never wanted to let her go. Petersen stood with his back turned; then he pulled himself together and pressed Charles Krüger's hand. He wanted to thank him and the others, but when he looked around for Chia Joseph, he had disappeared. "Charles," murmured Petersen, "we..." He couldn't go on.

Charles Krüger said softly, "Let it be, Hannes. I'll go get Chubb. And...so...a Merry Christmas, my dear ones."

When Petersen senior and Nang Siri drove up to deposit Chubb with his parents, things had quieted down in Bangkapi. Ah Chang had finally grasped the fact that right now Little Missie couldn't eat a Christmas dinner, and had stowed his goodies away carefully in the refrigerator. Tomorrow Little Missie would make up for it, Petersen had assured him. Cheng had finally stopped her earsplitting wails, and with Martha, had bathed Tiny. They had sent Oldest Grandson at once to the Chinese grocer opposite the *klong*. He had come back with a liquid that smelled horribly but had really removed the black dye from Tiny's hair. Now she was lying in bed in a pink nightie, like a freshly washed Christmas angel; only her head, with its short, fuzzy blond hair reminded one of a plucked chicken. Her beautiful blond curls had been sacrificed to the scissors as soon as Mr. Lu had abducted the child. He had received payment for her daily room and board from the person with the bandaged face, and therefore had not been interested in seeing the child leave earlier.

Oldest Grandson had pushed Tiny's bed into Martha's bedroom at her request. She wouldn't part from her daughter for a minute. She sat and watched her sleeping child under the mosquito net and sent one prayer of thanks after the other up to God in heaven. Cheng was still nodding in front of the child's bed when Major Nayadharn came into the room with Petersen. Cheng rose at once and started to leave the room. The major nodded at her and said in a friendly voice, "Now are you happy, Cheng? Is everybody happy again?" Cheng nodded and smiled, showing all her gold teeth. "Tomorrow big Christmas dinner for Little Missie," she said, and disappeared in the direction of the kitchen house.

Major Nayadharn stared, lost in thought, at the blond child under the mosquito net and waved away Petersen's and Martha's thanks. "Thank old Mr. Wong," he said. "He was the one who thought of the way to rescue the child."

They were sitting on the veranda, looking at the *lampu* tree. "He'll tell you everything himself," he said. "He is coming to see you tomorrow. A great man...a very great man, old Mr. Wong."

Then he told them how the child had been rescued and how heroically the Russian woman had taken part in it. "By the way, the child, Brocade, who showed us the secret passage because she was so worried about your daughter...something should be done for her. She saved the child's life."

Major Nayadharn stood up. He looked silently at the *lampu* tree that had witnessed Martha's happiness and her despair. What he had to say now, when in just a few minutes the church bells would be ringing in Christmas in the city on the Menam River, wasn't easy. Madame Petersen was glowing with happiness, a happiness that flowed from the soul and made her wonderfully beautiful.

"Madame," said Major Nayadharn, "unfortunately I must inject a note of sadness into your great joy. I...I have to make an arrest."

"An arrest? Here in the house?" asked Martha, her heart beating fast. "Our servants...no...that is impossible! They have all been so loyal to us. Are you sure you are not making a mistake, Major?"

Martha knew at once that it was a foolish question. She turned very pale.

"I'll send the gentlemen up to you," said the major. "I think it would be best if all of you stayed with the child."

He bowed with the urbane politeness of the high-ranking Siamese, and grasping the revolver in his trouser pocket with his right hand, moved in the direction of the servants' quarters.

It was already dark. Old Mr. Wong's chauffeur slept in the first room, the washerwoman with her children next door. The girl who arranged the flowers in the morning had the room next to hers because she didn't want to walk the long way from her house to the Petersens' every day. Then came the new floor coolie a little way away from that, and the kitchen house with the quarters of the Chinese family. There, too, all lay in darkness. Ah Chang, the master of the house, had a room of his own. His two oldest grandsons slept next door. And in the third room of the spacious house Cheng slept with Youngest Grandson. The Indian watchman was housed with his wife next to the garage at the end of the garden.

But Major Nayadharn didn't walk toward the garage. He crept quietly up to where the other servants were living. Two police officers came walking noiselessly from the canal. "Stay here behind the palm trees," whispered the major. "If I need you, I'll whistle. I don't want any excitement now. I must surprise her."

Cheng sat on the threshold of her bedroom and waited. Youngest Grandson was sleeping peacefully under his netting. He looked like a sausage wrapped in tulle and was breathing noisily through his open mouth. His little round head was half-covered by his smooth black hair.

Cheng's room was very clean and bare. A picture of her native village hung on the wall. In a corner lay the conical bamboo hat she wore to protect her from the sun when she went shopping at the Bangrak market for her honorable father. A solid wooden chest stood against the wall, locked. It held Cheng's clothes and underwear and everything that belonged to her personally. Youngest Grandson didn't have much to wear. At night he wore a shirt that reached down to his navel, and over that a little woolen jacket for the cold season.

Cheng had just put her work clothes—wide, black, heavily darned pants, a blue and white striped, high-necked jacket—into the chest and had put on her silk trousers and a black silk jacket. A jade arrow, her only piece of jewelry, was stuck in her smoothly combed hair, into which she had rubbed a scented oil. That was how Cheng sat, still and finely dressed, on the threshold of her room, and waited for death.

It was evident to Cheng that she could not bring shame upon her family. As soon as old Mr. Krüger had arrived with the golden-haired child, Cheng had taken poison. It was already taking effect in the strong, resilient body that should have gone on serving her sons for many years. Cheng wouldn't let herself be arrested. The police major's friendliness hadn't deceived her for a moment. He had found out that Cheng was the woman with the bandaged face. How he had found out, Cheng couldn't say. And it didn't matter anyway. She had played her game to possess the golden-haired child and had lost. There was nothing left for her but death and a short wait before the wandering started. In the next world they would credit her for having seen to it that her honorable father and her three sons did not lose face.

Cheng looked out into the big garden that lay, silent and magical, in the moonlight. In the main house the lights were still on on the Mem's veranda. The child with the golden hair, who had been called Hsi-Jen for a few weeks, was fast asleep. Cheng thought dully of how her love for the foreign child had changed everything around and inside her. At first the love had been a sweet pomegranate, then a bitter fruit. Later, when the departure of the stern Mem had been definitely decided, Cheng had felt a nagging pain that had gradually risen from her heart to her head. Her head had ached all the time. In the end the pain had become a dragon that had driven Cheng on in a game full of error, danger, and crime. Yes, in the end she had thrown the knife at the Mem. The love for the foreign child had shaken Cheng's existence to the core and had torn the firmly woven texture of her days and nights. Without realizing it, she had been hurled out of the cycle of Chinese feasts and traditions, out of the proper times for work and rest. Since the festival on the Golden Mount when she had shown Mr. Lu the beautiful child in the blue silk dress so that he might hide the little girl for her, she had been an outcast under the disguise of a devoted daughter and dutiful mother, a destroyer of other people's happiness who calmly went on cutting chili and beans and roasting duck in a kitchen house in Bangkapi. Until—the bandages hidden under her bamboo hat—she had slipped off to the market, and in a hut that belonged to a fisherwoman, had put on the bandages in order to bring the child delicacies and see that no evil befell her at Mr. Lu's. She had thought it would all be so easy. Mem and her son were to leave in January. A few days later she would return the child to its father and receive the big reward which would enable Oldest Grandson to go to a school in Hong Kong. Cheng hadn't wanted to keep any of the money for herself. She would have gone on living with Master Petersen and the beautiful child in Bangkapi, now and forevermore. It had all been so simply conceived. And all of them would have been happy...

Cheng rose. Her limbs felt heavy. She walked over to the kitchen house. Beside the big red *ong*, the barrel to catch rain water, a fire was still burning. With her foot Cheng pushed the rest of the bandages that were still smoldering into the fire. Nobody must see them, especially not Honorable Father, who had always been so patient with Cheng. He had let her keep a third of her salary and had even kept aside some duck and young bamboo vegetables for her, although she could just as well have eaten rice with soy sauce.

Cheng looked into the kitchen at the pot filled to the brim with rice. She had cooked the rice for tomorrow this evening; the family should not be disturbed by her death at breakfast. Everything was there—the cooked rice, every kernel a transparent pearl, the smoked fish, the ducks' eggs, the fruit. Ah Chang's chickens were asleep beside the rain barrel. Down by the canal was Tia's grave. Cheng had had to kill the dog because he kept running to the market after her. Served it right that he didn't get to see the child with the golden hair again. Tia had stolen a part of the love that the golden-haired child had formerly given to her Chinese mother.

Cheng looked around once more at her familiar world—the kitchen house, the chickens, the rooms of the two oldest sons, the canal, the garden laden with fruit, the crickets, the fireflies, the swaying palm trees that added an element of motion and uncertainty to the scene. Then she walked slowly to her room and closed the wooden door behind her. The dark shadow of death had already almost reached her simple, confused heart. She stretched out beside Youngest Grandson with a sigh. He was sleeping peacefully. He was strong and merry. Soon he would be able to help in the kitchen.

Cheng sank deeper and deeper into a good and necessary sleep. She had committed a great sin and was fully aware of it. But she had hurried to pay for it. Every honorable Chinese paid his debts before the New Year Festival; Cheng had paid hers a little earlier. She closed her eyes. Her small, clearly defined world in Bangkapi was already beginning to dissolve into the night. The peace of death was spreading over her coarse, rough-hewn face. Her hand was growing cold. In it she held a little piece of the corner of the mosquito net under which Youngest Grandson was sleeping. The little corner of netting was a frail but insoluble bond that still united her with her family as she lay dying. She had erred and brought shame upon herself. But all her life she had been an obedient daughter. She had worked for her honorable father and given him three healthy grandsons.

When Major Nayadharn walked into Cheng's room, she was lying still and cold beside her youngest son. The Major looked at her silently, then he went back to his two officers. "Get Mr. Petersen. I must speak to him." When they left, he knocked on Ah Chang's door. The old cook opened at once. He slept lightly and only for a few hours.

"Ah Chang," the major said gently. "Your daughter has fallen asleep. The joy caused her heart to stop beating."

At that moment the bells began to ring for midday

mass in the nearby Ursuline convent. They rang out a message of peace and the promise of a redeeming love.

Old Ah Chang swayed for a moment when he walked into Cheng's room. She had been a good daughter, even if she had chattered incessantly like a duck. He knelt down beside her and looked at her with tired, disbelieving eyes. She had always been so strong! And diligent, and clean! There she lay in her fine clothes, mute, silent, untouchable. I will give her an expensive funeral, thought Ah Chang, and went back to his room, bowing low and shaking his head.

At two o'clock in the morning, Petersen walked softly into Martha's bedroom. He hadn't slept yet. Major Nayadharn had explained everything to him as briefly as possible. Petersen and Martha had listened silently. It was too much. They were beyond grasping anything more. All they could think of was that Tiny was home. The thought erased all others.

Petersen stood in the middle of Martha's room and looked at the little group under the mosquito netting. Tiny, with her shorn angel's head, lay on Martha's arm. That was how she had fallen asleep. On Martha's left, Chubb was asleep in his clean pajamas. His head, with its unruly blond hair, had slipped off the pillow. His right hand was stretched out as if he still wanted to cling to a curl of Tiny's hair in his sleep. Martha lay peacefully between her two children. They looked like a painting of fulfillment. A simple and eternal happening: a mother's happiness.

At that moment a transformation took place in Petersen for which the shock and suffering of the past weeks had set the stage. It was less an emotional reaction, but rather a break with the habits of intellect, namely that life in the tropics was the only possible form of existence for Johannes Petersen. With the picture of his sleeping family in his mind's eye he went back to his room.

He looked for a pen and airmail paper, and finally

found both between two sport shirts that Cheng had washed and ironed beautifully. He sat down at the open window and wrote for over an hour. Finally he rose and yawned, but before he lay down under his mosquito net, he addressed the airmail envelope. The letter was for Hinrich Petersen in Hamburg. Petersen explained why he had so suddenly decided to return to Hamburg with his family. Did Hinrich still feel inclined to come to Bangkok for a few years? Uncle Wilhelm Christian would be very pleased.

Then Petersen got into bed and began to count to three hundred to fall asleep. He was half-dreaming when it occurred to him that he hadn't given Martha a Christmas present. He got up, half-asleep, and picked up the letter to Hinrich Petersen. He hadn't sealed it yet. With his flashlight he crept into Martha's room and laid the letter on the thin linen sheet covering her. Martha would get her Christmas present with the morning sun. Petersen couldn't say that this present had cost him nothing. He walked out onto the veranda of his bedroom and gazed at the garden he loved. In the moonlight the orderly wilderness looked like a landscape from another world, detached from reality, and with an ephemeral charm.

24

Rice in Silver Bowls

Between Christmas and New Year Nang Siri invited Johannes Petersen and their friends to a rice buffet. It was the first of many farewell dinners that would involve the Petersen family in a social whirl until the day of their departure on January 25. Martha was very much against these festivities that were exciting and tiring, but she realized that the many friends Hannes had made in his twelve years here would not accept a refusal.

Chubb and Tiny had already moved to Uncle Winn's house. Tiny, except for a few attacks of fear at night, seemed none the worse for her experience. She cried much less, on the other hand, this eleven-year-old girl, to whom such an extraordinary thing had happened, had become strangely patient and resigned. Martha watched her daughter, astonished and not a little apprehensive. How would she adjust to life in Hamburg? She had decided to tutor her for a year herself. Tiny needed a long period of separation from the shocks and beauties of tropical life. Chubb, on the other hand, should be fitted into the life of a schoolboy as quickly as possible. How Hannes Petersen was going to adjust was a book with seven seals for him and Martha.

Right now they were sitting, after Nang Siri's lavish and ceremonial rice buffet, in one of the various pavilions in the garden, sipping iced drinks and talking about the miraculous dispensation in their family life. Martha was still deeply disturbed and moved by Cheng's suicide.

"It was the best thing she could have done," old Mr. Wong said. "You would like to know how I got the idea that the *amah* had committed the crime? That was very simple, Madame. And yet again, on the other hand, very involved. Misfortune is always very simple and very involved. At first I noticed that the high reward remained unclaimed. This gave me the idea that the kidnapping was not simply an effort to blackmail. Something more profound, more complicated, had to lie behind it. An *idée fixe*...a confusion of the soul."

"But...how did you ever think of Cheng? Her loyalty and her grief were...seemed so sincere!"

"They *were* sincere, Madame. But Cheng's loyalty had become fanatic, and grief confused her simple mind. But I would not have thought of her if two newspaper articles hadn't attracted my attention."

"Newspaper articles?"

"We find out almost everything from the newspapers," said old Mr. Wong. "I deplore this source of information but, like everybody else, I use it. Believe me, there are crimes that are triggered by a specific time element even if the instincts that led to them are as old as the Himalayas. One evening, as I was thinking about your daughter's case, I read the article that led to the solution in a Chinese newspaper. It was about a Chinese washerwoman, who during and after the Indo-chinese War had reared a European child as her daughter. The father of the girl had been an officer on a British warship. Nothing was known about the mother. The Chinese mother insisted over and over again that Mary—that was the child's name—was her daughter, and was going to be a washerwoman too. An American general, whose shirts this woman laundered, found the child after the war and placed her in a European school in Hong Kong. The article did not tell what the Chinese mother had to say to that. She had taken care of the girl for fourteen years and adored her."

Old Mr. Wong drank a glass of iced coffee, then he went on.

"This article reminded me of a sensational case fought by Dutch parents after the Indo-chinese War against a Malayan *amah* in Batavia, who didn't want to give back the child that had been left behind during the war. The *amah* declared the girl was her daughter, and she was to marry a Mohammedan Malayan instead of going to school in Holland."

"And what about the child?" asked Martha.

"The Dutch child? By then she was almost grown-up. She wanted to stay with the *amah* and do whatever she wanted."

Suddenly Martha felt cold. Tiny, after the few weeks spent at Mr. Lu's, exhibited an eastern resignation, although during her captivity she had stubbornly and bravely clung to her identity. But the East Asian influence was strong. Hadn't Cheng's influence over Tiny given Martha pause weeks before the festival on the Golden Mount? Martha recalled many little disagreements in which Cheng had nearly always managed to get her way, subtly, slyly. Cheng—a respectable, tragic mother figure.

"Cheng overdid it," old Mr. Wong went on. "That increased my suspicion. When she came running home bleeding and declared that the person with the bandaged face had attacked her at the market, it was too much, and it betrayed her."

A week later Petersen and Martha moved into Uncle Winn's house. Their house stood empty. They had sold the furniture at auction. Hinrich and Lisa Petersen were to live the first six months with Uncle Winn in Rong Muang. It wasn't advisable to let them move into a big house with a horde of Asiatic servants before they could speak Siamese and had become accustomed to some extent to life in the tropics. Hinrich had agreed to every-thing at once. He wanted to greet Hannes and his family in Hamburg and hand over his house and office to them. Then he would fly to Bangkok with Lisa.

Uncle Winn was genuinely looking forward to his oldest nephew's arrival. He thought well of him, thanks to his letters, which revealed a quiet energy and respectability. If Petersen senior was slightly appalled at the thought of Lisa, he didn't say so. Through conversations with Hannes he had concluded that Lisa was silly, *etepetete*, and no substitute for Martha, who had really won his heart. And Martha loved Uncle Winn.

Martha had thought about a lot of things during these last weeks. After Tiny's return, their lives rested on something akin to a calm sea. Ah Chang had declared he didn't want to go into service again. He had saved enough money to buy a small restaurant in Sampeng, which he would run with his sons and Ah Bue. Ah Bue had been released and had at once offered her services. She didn't know where to go, and besides, there was Youngest Grandson to look after. Family remained family, Ah Chang had to admit grudgingly. Of course she couldn't be compared to Cheng. The old man often entertained Ah Bue with tales of Cheng's exemplary qualities which grew more impressive all the time. This he felt he owed to his dead daughter.

Martha had a lot of helpers as she packed up the Bangkok period of her life, above all Doris Krüger, now a close friend, and of course Ulla Knudsen who, in tears most of the time, spent many hours with Mem Petersen and couldn't be budged from Tiny's side when Martha and Hannes had to go to another farewell party. To her indescribable delight, Ulla was staying at Uncle Winn's house until the Petersens left. She ordered Mae Wat around, who of course obeyed none of her orders. "The half-woman is crazy!" Mae Wat told Sangvien. But Ulla could do as she pleased. Martha would never come across so much devotion and humble helpfulness, even if coupled with the most absurd presumption. And it was a comfort to Petersen that Ulla would be watching over Hinrich's first business efforts in the Bangkok offices of Petersen and Company.

It was what he was thinking of when he got into a rickshaw at half past five in the morning, a week before their departure, to say farewell to Bangkok alone. He didn't really know why he was driving to Wat Arun all by himself; he simply had the feeling that he must say good-bye privately to the Cambodian towers of this temple that had overthrown all his former conceptions of beauty and had witnessed his happinesses and defeats. When he arrived at the porcelain temple, the sun was already up. Its rays transformed the colorful, glazed tile facade of the towers into jewels of fairy-tale splendor. Petersen turned to the big staircase that led up to the terraces and the top of the highest reliquary shrine. He reached the balcony and looked down for the last time at the Siamese capital. The Menam River glittered in the sunshine. In the east he could see the Royal Palace with its snow-white walls and shimmering towers. Petersen trained his binoculars on the temples, the native huts, and the lush greenery. It was all so familiar. Bangkok was still a small paradise in a chaotic continent.

In the south, far from the orchards of Dhonburi, Petersen saw once again the smoking chimneys of the rice and sawmills of Bangkolem and Bukalo. Here Bangkok's importance in world trade was anchored. Here was the harbor that Petersen had loved from the start. Through his binoculars he could see the quays, the rice boats and the ships from all over the world, arriving and departing. Yes, the highest tower of Wat Arun was the right place to say farewell to Bangkok.

He turned to leave. This phase of his existence was over. Suddenly he saw that he wasn't alone any more on the terrace. A tall young man in a white tropical suit was standing beside him, looking at him so strangely that it could have been considered rude if the young man's gaze hadn't been so humble. Now Petersen looked at the man more intently. Of whom did he remind him? The stranger was a mixture of Europe and the Far East: a huge figure with an Asiatic face, gold-brown skin, and black, dreamy, Mongolian slanting eyes. His forehead was high and somehow European, and his shiny black hair grew from both sides of his forehead like a dark halo. In the middle there was no hair at all. Like Uncle Winn's, thought Petersen, and knew at once—the strange man had to be Justus Petersen, his uncle's mysterious son who had lived hidden away somewhere but who had recently stayed with Chubb and Nang Siri in Sukhothai with her brother, Count Sri. Petersen had seen him for a moment at Pauline's wedding.

Justus Petersen stared at his relative from Hamburg, whom he had watched curiously at the wedding. Still he said nothing. He had the talent of the Siamese to be able to conduct a conversation with his eyes.

"I think we are related," Hannes said finally. "I am Johannes Petersen from Hamburg. We met some time ago at Pauline's wedding."

Justus-Prasert placed his slender, aristocratic hands together in the Siamese greeting, and bowed. He was taller than Petersen but more lithe.

"I had the privilege to know your son in Sukhothai," he said slowly. "An intelligent and admirable boy."

Only years spent in the Far East and innate tact prevented Petersen from laughing out loud. He had never discovered anything admirable in Chubb! He'd have to tell Martha that!

After having said this, Justus-Prasert reverted to that pleasant and uncompromising silence which was an important aspect of every conversation with a Siamese. One didn't dash in an uncivilized fashion from one topic to the next.

"Are you staying in Bangkok for any length of time?" Petersen asked, feeling embarrassed as it occurred to him suddenly that he hadn't seen Justus in Rong Muang, and that Nang Siri hadn't mentioned that her son was in Bangkok. How tactless of him to ask this young man what his plans were! He was behaving like a newcomer!

Justus punished the foreigner's curiosity by simply ignoring Petersen's question with a friendly smile. "My mother has told me that it is your intention to return to your native land in a few days," he said. "Permit me to express my sincere wish for a happy passage."

"Thank you," murmured Petersen. There was a long pause. Justus Petersen moved his huge body closer to the terrace railing. "It is a satisfaction to look down upon the city from this height," he said finally. "One is joined with her yet has the necessary distance. The wind of wisdom blows more purely up here."

Again Justus was silent, and Petersen too said nothing. The Siamese passion for metaphor had always defeated him. Justus Petersen seemed obsessed by this passion because he mentioned that custom was a bird whose plumage had a different color in every land. Didn't Petersen feel that the plumage of the bird of custom in the tropics was exceptionally brilliant?

Petersen agreed that it was. He had made up his mind to say farewell in the next pause. But things didn't turn out that way. Justus Petersen drew himself up to his full height and said, without looking at his German relative, "Would you be so good as not to mention our friendly conversation in the presence of my father. I...I shall visit him when the time comes."

"Your father is very worried about you, dear Justus," Petersen said energetically.

"A bad habit of the West. I deplore it deeply that my father worries about me so unnecessarily. Everything happens on the orders of the Higher Wisdom."

In spite of the calm, conversational tone, the young man's eyes had narrowed. A slight aura of mistrust and deeply rooted mortification hung over the terrace. And something else formed a part of what Justus Petersen had just said: the grandiose and incomprehensible indifference of the Asiatic to things related to his own future.

"May I say farewell?" Justus said. "It would have been my inestimable pleasure to get to know your family better, but it was not to be."

Petersen thought in vain of what could possibly have prevented Justus from visiting him and Martha. It couldn't have been urgent business!

"I am living right now near Wat Kalaya, the Temple of the Magnificent Friend," Justus said with a slight indication of apology. "You can see the temple. It lies south of Wat Arun. One rests there as in a green cradle."

"How nice!" Petersen said, more embarrassed than ever. Green cradle! He had swallowed enough metaphors. "Farewell, Justus!" he said hastily. "I wish you all the very best for your future." He bowed, and without any further formalities left the descendant of Hamburg patricians and Siamese aristocrats in the timeless Buddhist world of Wat Arun.

Justus Petersen watched his impatient relative go, his face expressionless. He found it in order that the *farang* at last returned to his native land.

Petersen had told Madame Boulgakoff that he was coming, and she was waiting for him in the bar. She had recovered from her accident on Yawarat Road and was in an unusually good mood, thanks to the generous check Peterson and Company had sent her. She greeted Petersen with the words, "I would never have thought that the sunshine of good fortune would one day shine on me," and poured herself a double brandy.

Petersen nodded. It was evidently going to be a morning of metaphors. He was hungry, and anyway he had never liked picturesque language before breakfast. "May I have something to eat?" he asked.

"Siamese or ducks' eggs with canned bacon?" asked Madame Boulgakoff, who could switch from the sunshine of good fortune to the more mundane delights of this earth without any difficulty whatsoever.

"I'd like to eat *kao pat* once more, with chili, fish sauce, two fried eggs, and green onions. *Kao pat* is a dream, don't you think so, Madame?" Petersen too had gradually been drawn into a poetic mood.

"If there's enough chili in it and the eggs are not too old, it's edible," Madame Boulgakoff said with little enthusiasm. "By the way, they found Karin's murderer as he was crossing the border from Macao into the Communist sector. Not even the Communists wanted Senhor Pinto for a comrade," she added contemptuously.

Petersen's appetite was gone. He could feel the Russian woman watching him with cruel amusement. Everyday life had her in its clutches again. She had behaved admirably in Mr. Lu's establishment, but such moments of sacrificial uplift were not the rule, not with Madame Boulgakoff.

Instead of answering, Petersen looked around the shabby bar. "You were going to renovate, weren't you?" he asked, his tone snide.

"After your departure, sir," replied Madame Boulgakoff without batting an eyelash.

Petersen nodded. Both of them knew that the place would never be improved, nor the habits of its owner. Madame was certainly looking for a new opium dealer, since Mr. Lu had got stuck in the web of the police with her help.

"Poor Karin," she whispered, her face crumpling up before Petersen's eyes. Big tears rolled down her painted cheeks from which the old makeup was never properly removed. "All of us are at fault," she moaned. "We will all end up in hell."

Just then a young Chinese girl brought Petersen's

rice dish. "You've forgotten the chili, stupid girl!" screamed Madame Boulgakoff. "Back in Russia I'd have horse-whipped you until the blood ran on the floor!"

"I'll get the chili, Mem," said the Chinese girl, unimpressed.

Petersen had risen. "You must excuse me," he murmured. "I can't eat."

"Sentimental nonsense!" said Madame Boulgakoff. "One can always eat when someone else pays!"

Petersen couldn't resist this attractive invitation, and fortified himself with a double brandy. Actually it wasn't Madame Boulgakoff who had spoiled his appetite. A phantom was sitting at the table with him, a beautiful, very young girl with gold-blond hair and dreamy Asiatic eyes, who had been denied the gift of innocence until Thomas Harms had come and awakened a longing in her.

"She should be standing there today," Madame Boulgakoff gestured in the direction of the bar. She had read his thoughts with Russian precision.

"Do you mean there where the wood is splintered?" Petersen asked maliciously. He took out his checkbook and wrote a check. "For a new bar for your pretty girls," he said. He would have liked to redecorate the whole place if in doing so he could erase the past.

"After your departure...after your departure," Madame Boulgakoff said dreamily.

Petersen drove straight back to Rong Muang from the Russian Restaurant. "Where have you been?" Martha asked, as she went to meet him. "I was worried. You must have left very early in the morning."

"Exactly, Fräulein Doktor," said Petersen. "I took it upon myself to drive around Bangkok once more at dawn. He poured himself a whiskey and soda without looking at Martha. "Hannes," she said, her tone changed, "are you sorry that..."

"You must be suffering from sunstroke," Petersen said, his voice rough, but then he went up to Martha and flung an arm across her shoulder. "You'll have to be a little patient with me," he whispered as he turned toward the stairs that led to Pauline's room. "Any news from Pauline?"

"Uncle Winn had a letter this morning. The baby is expected any moment. He's as excited as if he were having the child." Martha smiled. "You know, Hannes..." She hesitated. Petersen looked at her absentmindedly. He hadn't been listening.

She wasn't going to have an easy time with him in Hamburg, this inveterate resident of the tropics who was used to a palatial house, servants, and the luxuries of a secure private life. Only a sea trip of six to eight weeks lay between two completely different worlds and ways of life. Petersen had lived for years in the only country east of Suez that still served rice in silver bowls. In the midst of starving and rebellious neighbors, Siam, smiling and cautious, had preserved the fullness and decorum of another life. And its silver bowls were still filled to the brim with the best rice in East Asia. At this table, decorated with lotus blossoms, Johannes Petersen had almost forgotten Europe's bitter struggle for survival. And now Martha had snatched the full silver bowl from under his nose. Not for a moment did it occur to her that he would ever have given up the rice table without her arrival on the scene. No...she would not have an easy time with Hannes in Hamburg. But then, one wasn't married to have an easy time, thought Martha, and walked resolutely back into the house.

The Petersens were not the only ones leaving Bangkok. Mr. Lu and his blind mother would no longer live in the city on the Menam River. Mr. Lu's departure was not as voluntary as that of the Petersen family.

Major Nayadharn had the date of Mr. Lu's deportation in his notebook, and on the same morning that saw Hannes Petersen saying farewell to Bangkok, Major Nayadharn went to see old Mrs. Wong. The old lady received him at once in her wing of the house and listened silently to what he had to say.

"I would appreciate your opinion," he said, almost shyly. "Brocade may of course remain in Bangkok. Not only was her assistance decisive in the rescuing of the child, but Sister Mary tells me that she is being very helpful in the school for the blind. She is used to dealing with blind people because of her grandmother. And then, Madame, Brocade is still a child. Good influences would give the wheel of her fate a favorable turn." Major Nayadharn liked to use picturesque language when he wasn't conducting an interrogation.

Old Mrs. Wong nodded. In her opinion the major was extremely intelligent for a Siamese. "Brocade is going to eat her noonday rice with me today," she said. "Sister Mary was kind enough to give her the day off." Sister Mary was the British principal of the Bangkok school for the blind. Her report on Brocade praised the girl highly. She knew how to treat the children gently but firmly.

"I'll have the girl called," said old Mrs. Wong. "She has to decide."

Brocade was so changed that Major Nayadharn scarcely recognized her. Sister Mary had plaited her hair into two neat braids with red ribbons. She was wearing long black satin trousers and a clean smock. Her sly little face was clean too. She greeted the major with a polite bow.

When the major told her that her family was going to be deported there was silence in old Mrs. Wong's big airy private pavilion. Brocade stared straight ahead. Nothing in her face betrayed any emotions. Only her thin little hand twisted the buttons of her smock.

"You can think it over, Brocade," said the major. "The children in the school love you. You are making them very happy."

Brocade remained silent. Suddenly she knelt in front of old Mrs. Wong and spoke to her in rapid Chinese. "Madame must explain," she begged.

And so old Mrs. Wong explained to the Siamese police officer that Brocade wanted to be deported with her father. In the eyes of the world Mr. Lu might be a corrupt opium smuggler who trafficked in children and who would turn everything, even his own daughter, to money if the opportunity arose. For Brocade though, Mr. Lu was Honorable Father and she would serve him until she could serve a husband and sons, if Mr. Lu allowed her to marry honorably.

"That's all right, little daughter," said old Madame Wong. "I have explained everything to Major Nayadharn."

Long after the major had left and Brocade had been driven back to the school for the blind, old Madame Wong sat in her pavilion thinking about the events of the day. Many departures hung in the air. The pleasant and the uninvited guests were leaving this rich, hospitable land. But to the old Chinese lady it seemed as if she were stranded in paradise, and as if Brocade, even if under unpleasant circumstances, had attained a goal that she, Mrs. Wong, would reach only after death.

Brocade was going back to China.

The day of their departure had arrived. The last week had passed unbelievably quickly. And now Johannes Petersen, Martha, and the children were standing on the pier surrounded by their many friends. In five minutes they would board the ferry that would take them to the Danish ship *Koh Si Chang*. All of them were wearing the jasmine garlands around their necks that Nang Siri had woven for them. Martha had taken off her glasses because her tears made it impossible to see through them. Uncle Winn still had his arms slung around her shoulder as if against all reason he wanted to keep her in Bangkok. Chubb and Tiny were standing hand in hand, just as on their arrival over a year ago. But this time they were surrounded by big and little friends. Father Aldano, three of his pupils, and Chia Joseph were trying to cheer up both children. Ulla Knudsen was crying so hard that Madame Boulgakoff, who had turned up with a Russian icon for Tiny, gave her a vicious shove.

"Don't try to attract so much attention!" she hissed, and wasn't so far wrong. Ulla was savoring her grief so that the Siamese princes, Chinese bankers, and many Europeans might see how close she was to the Petersens. His Royal Highness, Prince Pattani, stood apart from the group, waiting to say goodbye to his friends once more, his face impassive. Charles and Doris Krüger and the entire German colony surrounded Hannes Petersen and the doctor from Bremen. Dr. Johannsen, unchanged, was calm and cheerful. Johannes Petersen was white under his tan. Yes...of course...one would meet again...in Hamburg or Bangkok or on the moon...

At the last moment old Mr. Wong appeared with his wife, all his daughters, including little Ping-erh, and a gilded basket of fruit. "One cannot prolong such exquisitely painful seconds long enough," he whispered.

Martha looked at him silently. He had given her a piece of white jade. He had helped Hannes take his first steps in Bangkok. He had thought his way through to who had abducted Tiny. "We can never thank you enough," she whispered, fumbling for a fresh handkerchief. She, always so composed, was overwhelmed by the pain of parting.

"We are separated only by several seas," old Mr. Wong said quietly. "In spirit we remain united."

At the last minute Nang Siri surreptitiously pressed a small sealed package into Martha's hand. "A little present from my oldest son, for Chubb," she whispered. But he was not to open it until they got to Hamburg. Martha pressed Nang Siri's fine slim hand. She didn't know that the package contained an old ring with the name *Justus Petersen* engraved on it. Uncle Winn had given this heirloom to his oldest son, but now Prasert had passed the ring on tactfully to young Albert Petersen, who one day would perhaps bring it back to the Far East. For Uncle Winn it was settled that "our boy" would come back to Bangkok after completing his studies.

They embraced once more, and then, as through a veil, Martha saw her friends and relatives, behind them the servants: Phom with Rat and Pig, the girl who arranged the flowers in the morning, the washerwoman with her twins, the gardener, the old cook surrounded by his family. And of course Mae Wat and Sangvien. Only Cheng was missing. As the ferry began to move away from the pier and Tiny, held aloft by Petersen, let her jasmine garland flutter in the wind, Martha, with Chubb at her side, had her eyes fixed on the tall old man leaning on his dainty Siamese wife. "Uncle Winn!" she cried, above the sound of the engine. "*Lebe wohl!*"

On the quay the crowd that had stayed to wave had dispersed. Only old Petersen still stood motionless at the water's edge, leaning heavily on Nang Siri. Charles Krüger came running back to the pier from his car, shaking his head. He took his old friend gently by the arm. "Come, Krischan," he said softly, using the old nickname. "It can't be helped."

25

The Old Man In The *Sala*

Three days after the departure of his family, Wilhelm Christian Petersen was lying in his *sala* in the dawn, growing accustomed to being alone. Nang Siri was away again on a business trip. She couldn't help Winn in his sorrow. He had grown ever more silent. He hadn't thought it possible that he would miss Johannes Petersen, with whom he had so many differences of opinion, so much, and not only in business matters. He had behaved most generously to his departing junior partner. He didn't want Martha to find herself suddenly "short."

With Martha's departure a source of warmth was gone. The old man didn't even want to think of the two children. A feeling of loss enveloped him as he stared out at his lotus ponds in the early dawn, sticking his chin out and trying to ignore his dilemma. It didn't help. There was this dreadful emptiness. Not even his old friend Charles Krüger, with whom he was going to have lunch today, could talk him out of it. But Charles knew that.

The old man was so lost in thought that he didn't notice the strange figure approaching the *sala*: a tall monk in a yellow robe whom the servants in the kitchen house had greeted kneeling. Eyes lowered, he walked up to the *sala*. The head and eyebrows of the *Bhikku*, or Buddhist monks in Thailand were close shaven, the eyes—deep set and dreamy, with a Mongolian slant—were still lowered as the figure with the flowing robe entered the *sala* and greeted the old man ceremoniously.

Wilhelm Christian Petersen jumped to his feet, his sharp blue eyes widened. It wasn't possible... "Justus," he murmured.

"Joy and peace be with you all," said Bhikku Prasert.

Silently old Petersen listened to his oldest son as he slowly described the way that had brought him out of error and delusion to the *sangha*, the Brotherhood of the Yellow Robe. Justus had not walked the eightfold way alone. The prayers and sacrifices of his Siamese mother, the powerful influence of Count Sri in Sukhothai, and his own deep desire had brought him to where there were no differences between race or caste, where one mastered life by self-denial and meditation.

Justus spoke German with his father. It was a final courtesy, and it touched the old man. He looked broodingly at his son whom, in spite of all disappointments, he had still looked upon as the heir to his enterprise in Bangkok. But in this early morning hour he no longer fought against a knowledge he had always realized instinctively but had chosen to banish from his consciousness: "Justus Petersen" had been an idealized image, born of northern fog and dispelled in the tropical sun. This young monk, who with quiet dignity explained that the sphere of meditation was only another aspect of activity, was a son of the land in which Wilhelm Christian Petersen had been a guest for forty years, a popular and honored guest—but a guest. And now, after years of mistakes and confusion, his son had found peace in a world that in the Far East decided the life and death of millions of people. A crystalline coolness, gentle determination, and the ambience of Pali wisdom emanated from Bhikku Prasert.

The old European realized suddenly, with a visionary power that was foreign to his practical nature, that Buddhism was the powerful and timeless background of this land, before which the events of the present rolled away meaninglessly. The only important things were Buddha, his teachings, and the Brotherhood of the Yellow Robe, the three jewels of Thailand. In the future, the Siamese of all social circles and grades of intelligence would put on the Yellow Robe and beg for their food with the beggar's bowl, and be the spiritual masters of the land.

And as old Petersen looked at his son, he saw that the features of the young man were illuminated by a peace that could not be communicated. A homeless human, who for years had lived in a vacuum between East and West, was now at home in the vastness of East Asia. The wishes and the lust that had afflicted Justus Petersen in the twilight of his worldly existence were flowing like dead leaves down the Menam River, together with his irrational hatred of his father. No one had forced Bhikku Prasert to visit the old man in the *sala*. His heart and his indestructible Siamese courtesy had made him undertake the pilgrimage to Rong Muang in the dawn.

After Bhikku Prasert had taken leave ceremoniously and received the blessings of his father, Wilhelm Christian Petersen remained seated in the *sala*, lost in thought. His resignation was void of all bitterness and evanesced with the rising sun. He experienced a curious feeling of pride. He had reciprocated the hospitality of this country. He had given Siam his oldest son.

The old man had fallen asleep again when Mae Wat came in on tiptoe and looked at her master in a great state of indecision. Nobody was allowed to waken Master Peter-senn in the morning. That was a rule that even the mistress obeyed. The mistress was away again, but she had been present at Prasert's very private consecration in the *sangha* in Bangkok. Mae Wat was still overcome by the honor Bhikku Prasert had bestowed upon his family.

"Nai!" whispered Mae Wat. "A hurry news!"

Wilhelm Christian Petersen didn't move. Mae Wat had never forgotten her place to the extent of touching the master's arm to awaken him. One never touched —that was annoying and insulting.

416

Mae Wat looked at the paper that had flown through the air, then she walked over to a table with books and newspapers lying on it and knocked it over. It fell with a loud noise.

The master jumped to his feet. "What in hell!" he cried in German, then he saw his grinning cook and in her workworn brown hand the telegram she now handed to him, bowing low. She then crouched on the floor and waited calmly for further developments. She had awakened the master cleverly and now was enjoying the clumsy haste with which he opened the telegram from Manila. *Farangs* remained *farangs*!

Petersen senior had to read the message from his son-in-law twice because the print swam before his eyes: *Just arrived Wilhelm Petersen Desmond STOP Mother and son okay STOP expect you as soon as possible STOP Lawrence.*

"Mae Wat!" yelled Petersen. "Little Master has arrived in Manila! *Nangsao Pauline sabei maak!*" Yes, his Linchen was very healthy!

"Mae Wat cook big feast dinner tonight!" She was still grinning from ear to ear. "Master give Mae Wat many ticals. Chickens very very expensive now!"

Old Petersen obediently put his hand in his pocket and incautiously gave Mae Wat twenty ticals whereupon she was gone like a flash before Master could think better of it. But Master had other things on his mind. He had to send Siri a wire at once and find out when the next plane left for Manila. His little Linchen! And she had really named her son Petersen!

The old man sat down on his bed in the *sala* and took a deep breath. Everything that had oppressed him had dissolved in this joy. Gone were the years of anxiety because of Pauline and Prasert; the pain over the departure of his Hamburg family was eased. An intelligent conservative in exotic surroundings gave himself an accounting of his actions and decisions and was satisfied with them. Life went on—it robbed and fulfilled according to unfathomable laws. His nearest and dearest relatives were at this moment approaching his gray native city on the Elbe, and in Manila a new Petersen had seen the light of East Asia.

Old Petersen stretched to his full height and looked with satisfaction at his little piece of paradise. He had lived the full life of a man, with its early ecstasies, its endless rebuffs, and final fulfillment. In an era of vanishing individual strength and a growing collective enslavement, he had stood his ground with inherited doggedness in the unfathomable world of the Far East. He had lived as it pleased him, had preserved his personality intact, and had given his name to an heir.